The Ghosts' Trial

Volume I

Into the Shadows

a three-volume novel by

Martyn Bellamy

First novel in the

Emily Blackwood series

Copyright © 2025 Martyn Bellamy, all rights reserved.

Martyn Bellamy

Copyright Notice

© 2025 Martyn Bellamy

All rights reserved. No part of this book may be reproduced, stored in a retrieval system, or transmitted in any form or by any means - electronic, mechanical, photocopying, recording, or otherwise - without prior written permission from the publisher, except for brief quotations used in reviews or critical articles.

This is a work of fiction. Names, characters, places, and incidents are either the product of the author's imagination or are used fictitiously. Any resemblance to actual persons, living or dead, events, or locales is entirely coincidental.

For permissions inquiries, please contact:
novels@bellamys.biz

First Edition: March 2025

The Ghosts' Trial – Volume One

Table of Contents...

Volume I Into the Shadows 1
Table of Contents… 3
Chapter 1: A Fresh Start 4
Chapter 2: An Old Ally 32
Chapter 3: An Unexpected Visitor 69
Chapter 4: Glimpse of GenTech 104
Chapter 5: Mark Hastings Returns 139
Chapter 6: The Initial Disclosure 170
Chapter 7: Memories of the Firm 210
Chapter 8: In Doubt 249
Chapter 9: The Confidential Meeting 288
Chapter 10: Legal Quagmire 332
Chapter 11: Threatening Shadows 373
Chapter 12: Looking Back to Africa 405
Chapter 13: Whistleblower's Fear 439
Chapter 14: Mark's Warning 481
Chapter 15: A Leap of Faith 519

Martyn Bellamy

Volume One

Chapter 1: A Fresh Start

Emily Blackwood let out a soft breath as she unlocked the door to her new office for the very first time. The polished brass plaque on the door read "Emily Blackwood, Attorney-at-Law," a formality she had indulged in solely to make herself feel more secure. The phrase reminded her that she was still worthy of the professional title she had worked so hard to earn, even though she had left behind the marble-floored corridors of Hastings & Cole, the prestigious law firm that had shaped her career for nearly a decade. She stepped into the reception area, a modest space with off-white walls and a faint smell of fresh paint. There was a single desk against the wall to her left, currently holding a neat pile of boxes filled with files, law texts, and the basic stationery she had salvaged from her old life. The floor was a simple grey carpet - no more expensive hardwood or imported rugs as she had grown accustomed to at Hastings & Cole. This was a no-frills zone, yet it was utterly hers.

The Ghosts' Trial – Volume One

At half-past seven in the morning, the building felt deserted. The landlord had told her that most of her neighbors were small businesses - accountants, therapists, and marketing consultancies - and they tended to arrive closer to nine. She reveled in the hush, hoping that the stillness of this early hour would calm her sense of impending panic. During her last week at Hastings & Cole, Emily suffered nights of restless half-sleep, worrying about money and whether clients would be willing to trust a solo practitioner who had quit an enviable partnership track. The quiet corridor made those fears momentarily subside, leaving a gentle hum of excitement in their place.

She set her purse on the desk and unzipped her coat. The morning chill remained in her bones, but she told herself that this chill was the crisp edge of a new start rather than the cold hand of dread. She slid open the shutters on the main window to let in some light, revealing a view of a parking lot and, beyond that, the faint outline of the city's skyline. High-rises shimmered in the morning sun, a reminder that, less than a month ago, she had an office on the twenty-third floor of one of those very buildings. That vantage point had made the city look small and manageable, whereas her new perspective placed her on ground level, eye to eye with the reality that going it alone was going to be tough.

Footsteps in the corridor made her ears perk. She looked up to see Tessa Moretti in the doorway, balancing two cups of coffee and a bulging purse. Tessa was Emily's former paralegal at Hastings & Cole, though the term "assistant" barely captured what she had done. Tessa was the one who had gently reminded her to eat lunch during marathon legal research sessions, proofread endless filings for any typos, and kept Emily's calendar from collapsing into chaos. Tessa, upon hearing of Emily's departure, had stunned her by offering to come along without any guarantee of job security. The gesture had moved Emily profoundly, though she had initially resisted. She had worried about Tessa's livelihood, but Tessa had insisted that she wanted a challenge, to help build something new. That loyalty was one of the few things keeping Emily's confidence from vanishing altogether.

"Morning, boss," Tessa said with a grin, handing Emily one of the steaming coffees. She wore a bright purple scarf over her blazer, with her hair pinned back in an elegant twist. "The lift was acting up. I took the stairs and nearly broke my neck on a loose tile. We may need to add 'building repairs' to the complaint list."

Emily gave a light laugh. "Thank you for risking life and limb for me. And for the coffee."

Tessa waved a dismissive hand. "You can pay me back by actually letting me decorate this place. A plant here and a rug there - maybe a splash of artwork. We want clients to feel they've stepped into a professional environment, not a clinic waiting room."

Emily sipped her coffee, nodding. "Agreed. Everything about this office needs to suggest competence." She surveyed the bare walls, mentally placing a framed diploma or two, along with a few paintings she had in storage. "We could aim for sleek minimalism, but perhaps not so minimal that we look like we're scrimping."

Tessa raised an eyebrow. "Speaking of scrimping, are we certain we can afford a second desk? Because I don't fancy sitting on the floor with my laptop."

Emily gave a weary smile. "Yes, we have money for a second desk, courtesy of my cautious severance from

Martyn Bellamy

Hastings & Cole. That will keep us afloat for a bit, so we just need to make sure we pick up clients quickly."

The words rang in the air like a call to arms. Securing clients was the make-or-break challenge that every solo practitioner faced. Emily had left Hastings & Cole with a small financial cushion but without any real pipeline of her own. Ethically, she could not poach the firm's clients, so she had to build something fresh. Tessa took another sip of her coffee, looking pensive. "We do have that lead," she said, placing emphasis on the indefinite article. "A friend-of-a-friend scenario. I mentioned it last week."

Emily nodded. "Yes, your sister's co-worker with an employment dispute? That's a small claims matter. Possibly not the big fish we need, but it is a start."

Tessa stepped over to the window, peering out at the parking lot. "Big fish or not, it is a paying client. He left a voicemail last night, said he'd call again in a day or so." She looked back at Emily. "And remember, some of Grisham's best legal stories started with small beginnings."

A small, amused chuckle escaped Emily's lips. The mention of John Grisham reminded her of how many nights she had spent devouring legal thrillers, believing she had glimpsed a nobler side to law. Reality proved more complicated, though. Big firms had real-world tactics that rarely reflected the crusading heroism of a fictional lawyer. Yet she had left that well-oiled machine exactly because she wanted to make a genuine difference and to set her own ethical boundaries. Maybe Tessa was right: every big case started with a single phone call. The story that launched an empire might reveal itself in the unlikeliest scenario.

She set down her coffee cup and opened the top box on her desk. Inside were case files from her old pro bono efforts - low-level criminal defense and family law matters that Hastings & Cole had allowed her to handle in small doses, mainly to burnish the firm's philanthropic image. She had grown attached to those clients, though they were never a priority for the senior partners. As she lifted the bundle of manila folders, an envelope slipped free and fell to the floor. She picked it up, recognizing the name of one of her favorite clients from a few years ago. He had written to her after his case was resolved, thanking her for treating him with dignity. It reminded her that the law was more than a profitable enterprise - it was a tool to protect those in need. The memory steadied her breath. Despite her anxieties, she knew she was on the right path.

As she was lost in thought, Tessa placed a hand gently on Emily's arm. "We're going to be fine," she said in a low, supportive voice. "There's always risk, but you have your principles. Your network might be smaller than that of a corporate giant, but you have enough grit for an army. People will see that."

Emily felt gratitude welling inside. "Thank you. Let's unpack and get ourselves set up," she said, trying to harness her fleeting wave of optimism. "I want to be ready when that phone rings."

They spent the next hour unboxing files and supplies. Tessa used a microfiber cloth to clean the glass of a second-hand bookshelf they had bought, while Emily wrestled a battered office chair out of its packaging. The phone on Emily's desk was brand new, but it still felt archaic compared to the sleek, multi-line system she had used at Hastings & Cole. This phone had one line, which might never ring, or so she feared. Nonetheless, it sat there like a promise, a direct connection to whoever might need her help.

The Ghosts' Trial – Volume One

Once the space began to resemble an office rather than a cardboard storage room, Tessa started rummaging in her bag. "Here," she said, handing Emily a small potted cactus. "From my grandmother's succulent collection. She told me it symbolizes resilience and adaptability. I thought it was apt for you - and for me, actually."

Emily took the cactus with a laugh, cradling it in her hands. The tiny spines glinted in the sunlight. "I love it," she said. "Better a cactus than flowers that wilt. We're going to endure, you and I."

They found a suitable spot on the windowsill for the cactus, a proud sentinel overlooking the parking lot. Emily stepped back to admire the cosy view: Tessa's partly organized desk, the battered second-hand bookshelf, and the boxes stacked neatly in a corner. It was all meagre in comparison to her old office, yet a strange sense of warmth filled her chest. This was real and honest, and she felt oddly liberated by it.

By mid-morning, the corridor outside filled with the mild bustle of neighbors arriving for work. A few stuck their heads in to greet the new occupant. Emily exchanged polite introductions with a tax accountant, then a psychotherapist who specialized in family counselling. The therapist suggested that they might occasionally refer clients to each other if any child custody matters arose, which gave Emily an unexpected dash of hope. Building local connections, even in small ways, was vital to her survival.

Just after eleven, Tessa's phone chimed with a text, which she read with a faint frown. "This is from Luca - my sister's co-worker," she said, glancing up. "He wants to see if you're free to talk at noon. He says it involves a wrongful termination claim. Possibly discrimination. Could be interesting."

Emily considered it. "Absolutely, let's talk to him. It might be straightforward, but it could also turn out to be a more involved matter. We cannot afford to dismiss any leads right now. Let's schedule it."

Tessa typed a quick reply, and Emily returned to unpacking the final box. The idea of meeting a new client within these plain walls thrilled her, as if it signaled that the job had truly begun. During her last days at Hastings & Cole, she had felt overshadowed by the massive corporate clients and the never-ending pipeline of high-stakes deals that came with huge price tags. The personal angle of a wrongful termination case seemed refreshing. Though it might not pay extravagantly, at least it spoke directly to someone's dignity rather than an impersonal merger.

Shortly before noon, Emily and Tessa settled at her desk with notepads. They had no reception area staff, so Tessa would have to manage phone calls and scheduling on top of paralegal work. The solitary phone rang with a loud, almost startling trill. Emily took a breath, lifted the receiver, and introduced herself.

A male voice greeted her, subdued and a little shaky. "Ms. Blackwood, thanks for taking my call," he began. "My name is Luca Colombo. I've been working for an electronics retailer for the past six years. I've never had a write-up or anything negative on my record. Then last week, out of nowhere, I was fired. They said it was due to cutbacks, but I have a strong suspicion it's because I took medical leave. I have some health issues. The timing seems too convenient."

Emily glanced at Tessa, who was jotting details on her notepad. "I'm very sorry to hear that," Emily said, keeping her voice calm. "I understand how difficult this must be. Can you walk me through the situation? Start at the beginning of your concerns."

He launched into an explanation of how he had been dealing with a chronic condition that sometimes required brief periods of rest. His boss had originally been sympathetic but, when Luca requested leave, the company abruptly changed its tune. They insisted that staff reductions forced them to let him go. Emily listened carefully, occasionally asking clarifying questions. She noticed an underlying tension in Luca's voice, a sense that he was not merely worried about lost income but also about his reputation. The company had implied that he was somehow a poor performer, which contradicted his track record.

When the call ended, Emily gave him an appointment for the following week to discuss further. She set down the receiver and exhaled, looking at Tessa. "Definitely something there. I'll need to look at the employment law details in depth. It might be complicated if the company claims an across-the-board reduction, but if we can show that Luca was singled out because of his medical needs, then we have a case."

Tessa smiled, tapping her notes. "It is a small start, but it is a start."

The Ghosts' Trial – Volume One

Before Emily could respond, there was a knock on the open door. She looked up to see a man in a crisp grey suit standing in the threshold. He was tall, perhaps in his late thirties, with closely cropped dark hair. Emily's breath caught for an instant, because she recognized Mark Hastings - her old colleague, now turned rival. He had an easy smile that never quite reached his eyes, in Emily's experience, and the sight of him here felt like a rude intrusion into her newly claimed space.

"Emily," he said, leaning against the door frame with a practiced casualness that reminded her of the old days. "I heard you moved in here. Thought I would drop by, say hello, and see how you are settling. May I come in?"

Emily exchanged a quick look with Tessa, then gestured for him to step inside. "Mark, that is quite a surprise." She tried to keep her tone neutral, but she suspected that her voice carried traces of suspicion. "What brings you downtown?"

Mark shrugged, removing his gloves and tucking them into his pocket. "We have a client meeting in the building next door. One of our associates forgot some forms, so I popped over to see you. How is everything?"

Emily forced a cordial smile. "Just getting organized," she said, not wanting to reveal too much. The memory of the moment she resigned from Hastings & Cole hovered in her mind. She had given the standard two weeks' notice, but the managing partner had practically escorted her to the door the next morning, determined to prevent her from copying or retaining any firm documents. Mark had not intervened, and that had left a sour taste in her mouth.

Tessa stood quietly by her desk, arms crossed in a defensive posture. "We are doing fine here," she said, her tone polite but tinged with protectiveness.

Mark gave a slight nod and appeared to notice Tessa for the first time. "Ah, Tessa, always the real lynchpin of Emily's work." He flashed a grin that was meant to be charming, though Tessa's face remained impassive. "It is good to see you too."

Tessa simply nodded in response, allowing Mark's empty flattery to float away. Emily wondered if Mark was sincerely trying to be friendly or if he had ulterior motives. There was no reason for him to be threatened by her small practice, yet she knew Hastings & Cole tended to keep track of departing attorneys, especially those who had parted on less than perfect terms.

"Well," Mark said, glancing around the office as though appraising its modest furnishings, "I must confess, I admired your gumption in leaving. I always knew you had a strong moral compass. I just want to be sure you are aware that it can be brutal out here as a solo practitioner."

Emily felt her jaw tighten slightly. "I appreciate the concern," she replied. "Though I believe I have a reasonable grasp of what I am doing."

Mark opened his mouth as if to say something further, but then he paused. The moment hung awkwardly, broken only by the distant hum of conversation in the corridor. Emily found herself wanting him gone, away from her newly established territory. He seemed to sense her discomfort, for he cleared his throat and took a step back.

"I just wanted to say good luck," Mark said. "And, if I hear of anything that might help you get your feet on the ground, I will give you a call." He paused, seeming to weigh his words. "There is a case on the horizon, a big one. A pharmaceutical matter, from what I gather. We are positioning ourselves to take on the representation, though it is still hush-hush. If you are looking to do a bit of research or get in on a piece of it - "

"Thank you, Mark," Emily interjected, holding up a hand. She managed a polite but firm tone. "I think I will manage. Congratulations on whatever big matter you are about to secure."

For a moment, she could have sworn she saw a flicker of regret in his eyes. Then he grinned, nodded once more, and made an exit as smoothly as he had entered. Tessa let out a breath once he was gone, as though she had been holding it in a coil of tension.

"I do not trust that man," Tessa said, turning to Emily. "He has a habit of showing up uninvited. He always seemed to have a hidden angle, even when you two were colleagues."

Emily could only nod. "He has grown more cunning over the years. I doubt he wandered over just for a friendly hello. Perhaps he wanted to gauge how desperate I am for clients. Or maybe he wanted to measure the threat I pose."

Tessa's eyebrows rose. "Threat? His firm is massive. They handle million-dollar deals and top-tier litigation. I doubt we threaten them yet."

Emily exhaled, pushing a hand through her dark hair. "Precisely. We do not threaten them now. He might be checking to see if we could be used in some side role or roped into a conflict check. I remember the day I left - he said he respected me but that I was making a mistake." She frowned. "I suspect he wanted me to stay so I could do the less glamorous but morally questionable tasks that the senior partners requested. That was my future there."

Tessa gave a sympathetic nod. "We can only guess. Shall we get back to the joys of setting up your computer and scanning system?"

Emily laughed softly, relieved to shift her focus to something tangible. "Yes, let's. I will not let Mark Hastings sabotage my day. We have real things to accomplish."

They turned their attention to the administrative tasks that needed to be done - configuring a basic docketing system, hooking up a small scanner, and verifying that their modest Wi-Fi plan could handle any remote court filings. Tessa handled much of the technology side, while Emily created a skeleton framework for how they would store digital files to remain fully compliant with data protection regulations. The time slipped by quickly as they worked, and soon Tessa announced she would fetch a quick lunch from the café down the street.

Left alone in the office, Emily stood at the window, sipping a glass of water. She gazed upon the rows of cars, the grey tarmac, and the rooftops glinting under midday sun. She found herself thinking of the mention Mark had dropped: a pharmaceutical matter. Big Pharma typically contracted with the largest firms in the city, so it was hardly surprising that Hastings & Cole had found such a client. Yet the mention of it scratched at her curiosity. She had handled a pharmaceutical sub-case once, a pro bono matter involving a woman who claimed that her husband had died after using an unsafe medication. That case never reached trial due to settlement and non-disclosure agreements. Emily had felt uneasy about how swiftly it had concluded, as though a hush had settled over everything. Now she wondered if Mark's cryptic comment was a subtle hint that the same scenario might be repeating.

The Ghosts' Trial – Volume One

She thought about her principles, about the reasons she had left. She wanted to champion honest, earnest clients - not the morally ambiguous or wholly unethical corporations she had once represented. She reminded herself of that vow, even as she allowed a flicker of curiosity to remain. The phone rang again, snapping her out of her reverie. She approached the desk, heart fluttering with a mixture of eagerness and tension. Another new client, she hoped. Perhaps the start of something big.

"Emily Blackwood," she answered, forcing her voice to project calm confidence. There was a brief crackle of static, then a voice, low and cautious.

"Ms Blackwood, my name is Alan Priest," said the caller. "I - I was referred to you by someone who said you are trustworthy. Is this an okay time to speak?"

Emily paused, slightly puzzled. She could not place the name Alan Priest. "I can talk briefly, yes," she replied, "but I am not entirely sure who recommended me. May I ask what this is concerning?"

Alan's breath caught on the line. He spoke in short bursts, as though worried about being overheard. "I would prefer to discuss in person. It is sensitive information about a company… a pharmaceutical company, in fact. I am not certain I can safely share details over the phone. Could we arrange a meeting? I promise I am not wasting your time."

The mention of pharmaceuticals sent a tiny jolt through her. The memory of Mark's casual revelation flared, and a peculiar sense that forces were converging made her stomach tense. She tried to keep her voice measured. "I understand. I can make time to meet tomorrow morning, if that suits."

Alan hesitated. "Thank you. Yes, that is good. I would prefer to meet at a safe location - perhaps, near your office in a couple of days? I can be there at eight. If that is too early, I can wait."

Emily pressed her lips together. "Eight is fine," she said, writing down an appointment reminder. "Just so I know whom to look for, can you describe yourself, or would you prefer something more discreet?"

He swallowed audibly. "My hair is light brown, medium build, early forties. I will wear a dark jacket and a red tie. We can meet at… let us say, Brew & Bean on the corner of Ellis and Main. I appreciate your willingness to help. This is - this is very serious, Ms. Blackwood."

The line went dead before she could utter another word. Emily hung up slowly, her skin tingling. She had no idea who Alan Priest might be, or what issue he was bringing to her doorstep, but the anxiety in his voice had felt genuine. The mention of pharmaceutical wrongdoing matched perfectly with Mark's cryptic reference to his new client. She found herself caught between caution and an odd sense of anticipation. She had left Hastings & Cole to take on cases where justice mattered. Perhaps this was that opportunity. However, if it involved crossing swords with a massive corporation, she could find herself dangerously outmatched.

Tessa returned a few minutes later with paper bags of sandwiches. Emily relayed the details of the phone call, and Tessa reacted with her usual level-headedness. She pointed out that plenty of individuals had grievances with pharmaceutical companies, many of which lacked the resources to fight. She also reminded Emily that if this was indeed a matter that Hastings & Cole intended to defend, it could place Emily in direct opposition to her old colleagues, Mark included.

"Are you ready for that kind of standoff?" Tessa asked quietly as she unwrapped a sandwich. "You know they play rough. The last time you saw them in action, you were on their side, under the shield of a big firm's resources. Now, it is just us."

Emily absently picked at the corner of her own sandwich. "I understand the risk," she said slowly. "There is a lot I do not know yet. Alan might turn out to have incomplete documents or an emotional vendetta. Or his evidence could be explosive. I want to do the right thing. If there is something truly unethical going on, I cannot turn a blind eye."

Tessa nodded, chewing thoughtfully. "We can hear him out. Then we can decide. Just remember we are short on finances if this becomes a protracted war."

Emily smiled, appreciating her friend's candor. Tessa never sugar-coated reality, which was precisely the grounded perspective Emily needed. "Well, if this war does come, perhaps it will turn us into the David that topples Goliath. Goodness knows we could use a victory."

They ate their sandwiches in contemplative silence. Outside the window, a few grey clouds drifted across the sun, creating shifting patterns of light on the parking lot. Emily tried to imagine how the meeting with Alan Priest might unfold. A man with knowledge of wrongdoing, perhaps a whistleblower, or perhaps simply a disgruntled former employee. If it was whistleblowing, it could be a huge legal risk for him, potentially placing him in harm's way if the company was truly nefarious. She felt the surge of adrenaline that accompanied the possibility of championing someone powerless against a corporate behemoth.

The rest of the day progressed quietly. Emily spent her afternoon on the phone with a utilities company regarding an incorrect bill for the office, then tackled some administrative tasks, finalized the arrangement of her desk drawers, and drew up a preliminary list of local business owners who might need legal advice at some point. Tessa fiddled with an online scheduling app that might help them keep track of client appointments without requiring a dedicated receptionist. Occasionally, Emily's thoughts drifted back to the phone call from Alan Priest, playing over the tension in his voice like a loop. She reminded herself that she had to keep an open mind. Not every frantic caller had a valid claim, and not every claim was worth risking everything. However, something about the tremor in his tone told her that, if this turned out to be legitimate, it would be far from simple.

The day wound to a close around six. A few overhead lights in the corridor had flickered on as dusk fell outside. Emily and Tessa locked up the office, feeling an odd blend of achievement and worry. They had officially established the beginnings of Emily Blackwood's practice. Tessa handed Emily a small ring of keys, newly cut for their side entrance, along with a note to remind her to call the sign company about adding the practice's name to the building directory.

Walking to the parking lot, Emily noticed that her feet ached from standing on the office's thin carpet all day. At Hastings & Cole, she had often spent long hours behind a desk, or perched on the corner of a polished conference table. She took solace in the fact that physical discomfort indicated she was actually doing hands-on work, building something new from the ground up. As she and Tessa parted ways, Tessa gave a quick wave and a brave smile, promising to be in early the next day to continue the set-up.

Emily climbed into her own car, a dependable but ageing sedan, and sat for a moment before starting the engine. The streetlights were just flickering on against the deepening sky. She felt that the day had signified a new chapter in her life, brimming with uncertainty and potential. Memories of Mark Hastings' unexpected visit brushed against her thoughts, but she pushed them aside. She had made her decision to break free from that world. The future, however challenging, was now hers to shape. If Alan Priest's matter placed her on a collision course with the glistening towers of corporate might, so be it. She was determined to stand by her convictions.

When she finally turned the key, the engine roared to life with a comforting hum. She pulled out of the parking lot and merged into the steady flow of traffic. Neon signs and bustling pavements reminded her that this city, for all its glamour and grit, was filled with people who needed protection from those who saw them merely as cogs in a profit-making machine. Perhaps she would be the lawyer who made a difference for a few of them. Perhaps that difference would ripple outward, bigger and broader than anything she could imagine. There was a sense of quiet resolve in her now, fueling her as she navigated the labyrinthine side streets.

By the time she reached her modest apartment, the sun had fully set, and the faint drizzle that had begun during her drive now fell more heavily, drumming on her windscreen. She parked and dashed inside, grateful for the warmth and the familiar scent of lavender she kept in a diffuser. Her apartment was small but comfortable, a rented space in a residential area where the streetlights flickered. She shrugged off her coat, draping it across the arm of a chair, and kicked off her shoes, relishing the relief.

After a quick reheated dinner, she settled with her laptop at the kitchen table. She opened her notes from the day, reviewing the bullet points from Luca Colombo's phone call, then typed up a basic summary so she would be prepared for the in-person meeting. After that, she started a new file titled "Alan Priest," a placeholder for tomorrow's potentially mysterious conversation. She found herself adding a question mark next to his name, as though the unknown nature of his story warranted punctuation.

Her phone buzzed, startling her in the quiet apartment. She glanced at the screen and saw Tessa's name. It was a text that read, *I did some quick online searching for "Alan Priest." Not much info. Possibly an ex-lab tech or researcher. We'll see tomorrow. Get some rest.*

Emily typed a quick reply of gratitude, then closed her laptop. Tessa was relentless in her thoroughness, and Emily smiled at the knowledge that she had such a dedicated ally. Tomorrow's meeting would be the first real test of her new practice, if only because it had the potential to draw her into a realm of high-stakes corporate conflict. She could feel the flutter of nerves in her stomach, tempered by a resolute calm in her mind. She had chosen this path, and she would see it through.

A rumble of thunder echoed outside, prompting Emily to switch off the lights and peer out the window. The rain was heavier now, turning the street shiny under the lampposts. She felt the hush of the moment like a fragile bubble around her. The day's events replayed in her mind: the hopeful phone call from Luca, Mark's brief and unsettling visit, Tessa's unwavering support, and that cryptic conversation with Alan Priest. The swirl of it all made her heart beat faster, even as the quiet of her apartment coaxed her toward rest.

Despite the wave of exhaustion, Emily found herself pacing across the living room, thinking about the abrupt pivot her life had taken. Only a few weeks ago, she had an office with a sweeping view and an assistant who answered phone lines that never stopped ringing. Now she had a single-line phone that might or might not ring tomorrow, a modest office with an enthusiastic paralegal, and a million question marks about her financial stability. Yet there was a purity in this new life, a sense that every client she took on would be one she genuinely believed in. That conviction soothed her.

She retreated to her bedroom, changed into her pajamas, and slipped under the covers. The rain cascaded against the window, the sound reminiscent of a lullaby. She tried to clear her thoughts, but they raced from one worry to another: the next month's rent, the overhead costs she had not fully calculated, the marketing she needed to do, and the possibility that Alan Priest was about to bring her a case that might either bankrupt her or become the signature story that launched her new practice. As her eyes grew heavy, she reminded herself that no victory was ever achieved without risk. She had sworn an oath to uphold the law and to seek justice, and she had chosen this lonely road because it felt honest.

Eventually, she let the quiet melody of the rain lull her to sleep, her final coherent thought being a whisper of self-reassurance: *I have chosen my path, and I will stand by it.* When morning arrived, she would awaken to meet a man whose plea for help might reshape her entire future. If that were true, then she would face it with all the courage she could muster. For better or worse, this was Emily Blackwood's fresh start. And nothing, not even an entire skyscraper of lawyers from her old world, would deter her from giving it her utmost.

Chapter 2: An Old Ally

Emily Blackwood stood on the threshold of her tiny law office, arms crossed, surveying the nicks and scratches on the baseboards. The space felt both intimately hers and alarmingly vulnerable. For three days, she had stared at a blank appointment calendar, willing it to fill with calls and walk-ins. The rent was paid through the end of the month, but she still didn't have enough in the bank to rest easy about her next obligations. To make matters worse, she'd used up the last of her professional stationery printing so many "Grand Opening" flyers that she was certain the local copy shop's owner knew her by first name, middle name, and possibly high-school alma mater. She craved a big break - something, anything - that would jump-start the practice and reassure her she hadn't made a colossal mistake in leaving Hastings & Cole.

The ring of the front door's old-fashioned bell startled her. Immediately, her posture stiffened. Clients? She tried not to dash toward the reception area like a starved cat eyeing a mouse. Drawing a controlled breath, she walked out of her small corner office and into the modest reception room.

Tessa Moretti, her paralegal and longest-serving ally - albeit "longest" only meant the past few months - entered, hair wind-tousled, cheeks flushed from the autumn chill. She was balancing a plastic cup of coffee and a bag from a bakery down the street.

"Morning," Tessa said, spotting Emily halfway to the door. She gave a half-teasing grin. "Were you waiting by the door for me, or is there a client I'm missing?"

Emily forced a rueful smile. "In my dreams. No clients so far. How's the coffee line? Did you have to push people out of the way? Because you know, I'd represent you in court if you did."

Tessa laughed, which lifted Emily's mood. "No violence. Although the barista was once again mystified that anyone would pay for a triple espresso with an extra shot of caramel. I told them it's for a hard-working lawyer who just set up shop. I figured you needed the jolt."

Emily accepted the coffee, letting the warmth of the cup wash over her hands. "Bless you. If I don't land a client soon, I'll need that triple espresso just to keep from losing my mind."

Tessa set the pastry bag on the small reception desk. "Well, this might help." She reached inside her worn leather satchel and withdrew a slim folder. "I got a call last night from an old friend. She hinted we might be getting a new case. Could be sensitive, though. The prospective client insists on full confidentiality."

At the word "confidentiality," Emily's legal mind kicked into gear. The word rolled around in her head, stirring memories from her time at Hastings & Cole, where hush-hush settlements and sealed depositions were the daily currency. "What's the gist?" she asked, taking a sip of the piping hot espresso.

Tessa flipped open the folder. "Her name is Gina Morales. She works at a nonprofit. Officially, she's just a liaison for someone else - a whistleblower, from what I gather. They might need representation for a case that could, if it goes to litigation, have enormous ramifications. She didn't provide details over the phone - only said that you'd come highly recommended."

Emily's heart pounded a little faster. The word "whistleblower" was catnip for an ambitious plaintiff's lawyer - especially one who wanted to build a reputation for fighting injustice. "Ramifications for whom? A major corporation? The government?"

"Not sure yet," Tessa admitted. "But Gina Morales wants to set up a meeting. She sounded earnest and urgent. She's apparently heard you left Hastings & Cole to strike out on your own, and that you'd be the perfect person to handle this."

Emily felt a rush of unexpected pride to hear that someone out there had taken notice. Then came the inevitable caution, the internal voice that had once served her well in the high-stakes corporate trenches. "We should be careful, Tessa," she said, scanning the single-page summary in the folder. "Whistleblower cases can be extremely tricky. We need to confirm we're not stepping into something bigger than we can manage."

Tessa leaned against the edge of the reception desk, crossing her arms. "Let's face it: we could use something big, Em. If we don't land at least one paying client soon, we might be scrounging for rent money from my mother's couch cushions."

Emily's lips curved into the faintest smile. "Don't worry, we won't be rummaging through your mom's furniture quite yet. But let's not rush in blind. I'll speak with Gina Morales, find out what's really going on."

"Already done," Tessa replied brightly, tapping the folder. "She's coming at noon."

Emily raised an eyebrow. "Today?"

"You said you wanted movement. I'm making movement happen."

Emily couldn't help but laugh - nerves and excitement all dancing in her gut. "Well, okay then. Let's hustle. We need to look professional, put on our best face."

"All right," Tessa said, eyeing the dusty corners of the reception area. "I'll do a quick tidy. Maybe rearrange those ancient law periodicals - some are from last spring, and that hardly screams 'cutting-edge practice.'"

Emily gave Tessa a good-natured nod. "Yes, let's pretend we've been too busy with high-level cases to read them."

Together, they launched into a flurry of activity - wiping surfaces, organizing battered law books on the single shelf behind the reception desk, even attempting to hide the cracks in the wall with strategic placement of framed diplomas. Emily glanced at the clock on her phone: 9:45 AM. Two hours and change until the potential client arrived.

A swirl of adrenaline came and went as she busied herself with preparations. Beneath that swirl, a gnawing doubt lingered: Was she truly ready to jump into a big case after barely hanging a shingle?

By 10:30 AM, Emily had retreated to her office. The space, though small, had a crisp brightness thanks to a single tall window that faced the street. She could see the occasional pedestrian pass by, and each time, part of her hoped they might notice the newly stenciled letters on the door:

Emily Blackwood, Attorney at Law.
Specializing in Civil Litigation and Whistleblower Protections.

That last phrase had been Tessa's suggestion - an attempt to speak to the kind of cases Emily hoped to attract. It was a subtle advertisement that Emily had parted ways with Hastings & Cole because she favored justice over corporate paychecks. So far, it had netted them exactly zero new clients. Yet the phone call from Gina Morales was a shimmering beacon in the gloom.

Emily sat behind her secondhand mahogany desk, the battered surface polished as best as she could manage, reviewing her finances. She had enough for this month's rent, some leftover to pay Tessa a token salary, plus the bare minimum for her personal bills. If the practice didn't pick up soon, the next months would be a precarious balancing act.

Her desk phone rang - only the third time it had rung since she'd plugged it in. Heart pounding, she grabbed the receiver. "Emily Blackwood's office."

A pause, then a man's voice: "Hi, I'm looking for an attorney. Are you taking new clients?"

"Yes - definitely," she replied, glancing around for a notepad. "Could I ask your name?"

"Jacob. Jacob Smith." The voice was clipped, almost formal, but with an undercurrent of desperation. "I need help with an eviction. My landlord is kicking me out for complaining about mold."

Emily's chest deflated like a balloon. She believed wholeheartedly that tenants' rights were important, but an eviction case wouldn't even pay enough to keep the lights on, especially if Smith had no funds for retainer. "Sure," she said carefully. "Would you like to come in for a consultation?"

"Yeah, I guess. But, uh... I don't really have much money."

Emily tried not to let her disappointment bleed into her voice. "We can discuss costs after I learn more details. Would tomorrow afternoon work?"

He hesitated. "Tomorrow's okay. Three o'clock?"

She jotted the appointment into her calendar, feeling that old mixture of duty and frustration that had dogged her occasionally at Hastings & Cole, when she'd felt compelled to do some pro bono work on top of her insane corporate caseload. She wanted to help, but she also knew she had to keep her practice afloat. After she hung up, she sank back in her seat.

One more day, one more inch forward. She reminded herself that the big, groundbreaking cases never appear at a lawyer's door every morning. But if Gina Morales was serious, maybe - just maybe - Emily could catch a break.

At exactly 11:59 AM, Tessa poked her head in the office. "She's here. I offered her coffee, but she said she doesn't have time to indulge. She seems... anxious."

Emily took a deep breath, slipped on her tailored blazer, and rose from her chair. "Let's make a good impression."

Gina Morales was a slender woman in her mid-thirties, dressed simply in pressed slacks and a button-down blouse. Her dark hair was pulled back in a tight ponytail, giving her a no-nonsense air. She stood near the reception area, gaze sweeping over the modest surroundings, as though cataloging every detail.

Emily extended her hand. "Ms. Morales? I'm Emily Blackwood."

Gina's handshake was firm. "Thank you for seeing me, Ms. Blackwood. I know this is short notice."

"Call me Emily," she said, guiding Gina into her office. Tessa followed and quietly took a seat by the door, notepad at the ready.

"I appreciate the familiarity, Emily," Gina replied, taking in the small office. She sat down in one of the two chairs facing Emily's desk, then placed a slim black folder on her lap. "I suppose I should get right to the point. You come highly recommended by someone who values your discretion."

Emily nodded, trying not to show how starved she was for details. "We're definitely discreet. And we handle a variety of matters, including whistleblower cases, if that's what this is about."

Gina's eyes flicked to Tessa, then back to Emily. "You mentioned on the phone that your paralegal is fully trustworthy?"

"She is. Tessa helps me with everything. She's also bound by attorney-client privilege, the same as I am."

With that, Gina seemed to relax slightly. She opened the black folder, revealing a single page of typed notes and a small flash drive clipped to it. "I work with a nonprofit that deals with corporate accountability. We've had... well, let's say we've had an individual approach us with evidence of wrongdoing at a very high level. He's frightened and doesn't trust big law firms. My name is out there because I help guide potential whistleblowers to counsel who might actually fight for their cause instead of burying it."

Emily leaned forward. "And you believe this wrongdoing is serious?"

"Very much so. From what I understand, it involves a major pharmaceutical company. I won't name them yet. Let's call them 'Company X.' The whistleblower claims Company X has hidden evidence of lethal side effects in certain clinical drug trials in Africa and South America."

Emily's heart thudded. That statement echoed so many cautionary tales she'd heard as a junior associate at Hastings & Cole. Big Pharma. Hidden side effects. People harmed. This was no run-of-the-mill complaint. "Does he have proof?"

Gina tapped the flash drive. "He claims to have documents, emails, internal memos. Data that was never meant to see the light of day. He shared only a small portion with me, enough for me to confirm it's not a hoax. Names, internal codes, references to test subjects. It's grim."

Tessa was scribbling notes, but Emily saw her paralegal's eyes dart up in alarm. Emily turned back to Gina. "And he specifically asked for me, or...?"

Gina gave a small smile. "He asked for someone who left a major firm over ethical concerns. He sought out an attorney who wouldn't be spooked by a powerful corporation. A contact of ours heard about your departure from Hastings & Cole and suggested you."

A short silence fell. Emily recalled, with painful clarity, the day she handed in her resignation at Hastings & Cole. She couldn't pinpoint a single cataclysmic event that triggered it. It was more the sum of everything: her growing disillusionment at the firm's willingness to defend corporations at all costs, the sense that justice was merely an afterthought. In the end, she'd chosen a more challenging road. She'd told herself she wanted to stand up for the little guy. Now, here was the little guy's champion, practically begging for her representation.

"Ms. Morales, I appreciate your confidence, but I need to ask: what does the whistleblower want? To go public? To file suit? Or does he want to approach the authorities, like the Department of Justice?"

Gina pressed her lips together, considering. "He's undecided. He's terrified - he's seen colleagues lose their jobs, their reputations, even their sense of safety after coming forward. He wants to protect himself, but also do the right thing. If he can find counsel willing to take his evidence seriously, he's prepared to support a lawsuit or an investigation. Without that, though, he's at risk of being labeled a disgruntled ex-employee, or worse."

Emily sensed the gravity of Gina's request. Her mind raced with the enormous scope: lawsuits involving multinational pharmaceutical corporations typically demanded huge resources. They entailed armies of expert witnesses, complex discovery, and the potential for countersuits or intimidation strategies. Going up against "Company X" would be a David-and-Goliath scenario, except David might not even have a sling or a decent stone.

And yet, the moral imperative gnawed at her. "Have you or the whistleblower approached any other attorneys?"

"We approached a couple of well-known large firms that advertise themselves as whistleblower-friendly. But once we hinted at the target, they quietly declined. Conflict of interest, they said. Or they sent us links to other attorneys, who also refused. It's a pattern - this pharma giant is so deeply entwined with major firms that they can simply block us by default."

Emily nodded, not surprised. "What do you need from me right now?"

"We need an attorney who will meet with the whistleblower in a secure location, review his documents, and advise him on next steps. Possibly represent him in a legal action. Could be a wrongful death suit, a class action, or a whistleblower claim under the federal False Claims Act. We need clarity, and we need it soon."

"Understood." Emily took a breath, feeling the weight of the decision. "I'd like to see any preliminary materials, to get a sense of the scope. That might also help me gauge if I have the resources to do this."

Gina slid the flash drive across the desk, expression grim. "On here you'll find sample emails, data reports, and references to the drug trials in question. Before you look at it, though, I want to clarify something: If you decide to help, you may put a target on your own back. This corporation - 'Company X' - doesn't mess around. They have extensive legal and security divisions."

Emily's stomach fluttered. She glanced at Tessa, who gave her a small nod of support, though her expression was subdued. Then Emily looked back at Gina. "I appreciate the warning. But as long as what's here is legitimate, I'll do what I can to ensure this whistleblower is heard."

Gina relaxed slightly. "Thank you. That's all we can ask. If you decide not to proceed, please wipe the files and forget we ever had this conversation."

Emily took the flash drive, turning it over in her fingers. "I'll review it tonight. If I see evidence that a real crime has been committed... or if I see that real people are suffering as a result of this drug trial... I'll reach out. We can schedule a meeting with the whistleblower if we're proceeding."

Gina closed the folder. "That's all I ask. And please, for his sake, keep this quiet for now. I'd like to give you his name, but he's very insistent on complete discretion until he's certain you'll take the case."

"I understand," Emily said softly. "Client confidentiality, even at this stage, is paramount."

Gina stood, smoothing the wrinkles from her blouse. She extended her hand again. "Thank you, Emily. I feel better already."

After Gina left, the echoes of her footsteps receding down the hallway, Emily let out a long exhale. Tessa closed the office door and sat back down, notebook in hand.

"That sounded massive," Tessa said, her eyes gleaming with equal parts excitement and dread. "A major pharmaceutical company? Possible hidden lethal side effects?"

"It is massive." Emily slid the flash drive into her desk drawer, as if stashing away a dangerous artifact. "And if we're not careful, we could find ourselves in big trouble."

Tessa arched an eyebrow. "You worried about Mark Hastings?"

Emily froze. Mark Hastings - her old colleague at Hastings & Cole - had contacts everywhere. In her gut, she knew that if "Company X" turned out to be a current or former client of Hastings & Cole, Mark would be front and center in the fight against her. She

47

forced a shrug. "Let's not jump to conclusions. But I won't pretend it's not a possibility. Hastings & Cole represents a lot of major pharma clients."

Tessa bit her lip. "You think you can handle it? Or do we need to partner with someone bigger?"

Emily recalled the snickering voices at Hastings & Cole when she announced her departure. *She'll never last on her own,* they'd said. *No top-tier clients will follow her.* The memory still stung, but also fueled her determination. "First, let's confirm that these claims are real. Tonight, I'll dig into that flash drive, see what's there. If it's legitimate, we can weigh our options. Maybe we can find a specialized co-counsel. Or maybe we'll jump in ourselves."

Tessa nodded, scribbling furiously in her notebook. "We'll do what we always do - our homework."

Emily smiled. "Exactly."

Despite the surge of adrenaline from Gina's visit, the rest of the day proved anticlimactic. Emily took two more calls, both from people seeking free legal advice regarding minor contractual disputes - neighbors quarreling over property lines and a roofing contractor who hadn't been paid. She booked consultations, though she doubted either would yield more than a pittance in fees.

By early afternoon, the phone calls had trickled off to nothing. Tessa had done an admirable job rearranging the dated law journals and tidying up, giving the place a fresh, if modest, vibe. Outside, the sun dipped behind a cluster of office buildings, and shadows stretched across the street.

Emily glanced at the folder Gina had left on her desk. Every so often, her eyes would drift there, as though magnetically drawn to the promise - and peril - it held. If the whistleblower's evidence was as compelling as Gina claimed, then Emily stood on the brink of a sensational case that could both define her career and threaten her livelihood. She found herself fantasizing about the media coverage: *Small-Firm Attorney Takes On Pharma Giant.* With any luck, the story might become a rallying cry for other people harmed by the drug trials. But fantasies aside, she knew the real world was more complicated. Large corporations had entire floors full of lawyers. Emily had Tessa and a phone barely rung in.

"Should I grab us something for lunch?" Tessa asked from the reception desk, where she was re-checking scheduling software. "There's a decent sandwich place across the street."

Emily glanced at her watch - 2:15 PM. "Sure," she said, eyes shifting to the folder again. "I'll review some documents while you're out." She flashed a small smile, trying to sound more confident than she felt.

"Got it. Turkey on wheat, extra mustard?"

"You know me too well."

Tessa grabbed her purse and stepped into the autumn chill. The moment the door swung shut, Emily turned the lock - just for peace of mind - and walked back into her office. She closed the door softly, then sank into her chair and pulled the flash drive from the drawer. The small red LED flickered once when she slid it into the port on her laptop.

She opened the root folder and found a handful of subfolders labeled "Correspondences," "Trial Data," and "Summaries." She clicked on "Correspondences" first. Inside were half a dozen PDF files, each with emails purportedly from employees of what was presumably GenTech or a similarly large pharmaceutical outfit (the names in the email addresses were partially redacted). The tone of the emails was chilling: references to "patient mortalities," "unreported complications," and "need for secrecy." One exchange mentioned a test site in Ghana, citing an unusual spike in negative outcomes that had somehow not made it into official reports.

Heart thumping, Emily skimmed a PDF containing a chain of messages discussing "Protocol 42S," which apparently included dosing experiments on volunteers. One manager wrote: *We can't let these numbers reach the FDA in this form. We have to reevaluate how we're recording fatalities.* Another responded: *We'll handle it internally. Secure all raw data files. Only revised stats move forward.*

Emily's hand flew to her mouth. The language was damning - unmistakably so. If these emails were genuine, they signaled a catastrophic cover-up of lethal side effects that should have halted any clinical trial. *People could be dying because of this drug,* she thought, goosebumps prickling her arms.

Caution warred with anger in her mind. Emails could be forged, though these looked convincingly genuine, including professional disclaimers and internal company signatures. She noticed partial headers, time stamps, disclaimers typical of large corporate email systems. The attention to detail was too extensive for an amateur forging job.

She set aside the PDF to open another folder labeled "Trial Data." Inside, there were references to "XK-77," presumably the name of the experimental drug. A spreadsheet indicated patient IDs, test sites, dosage levels, and outcomes. Many cells read "Deceased" or "Withdrawn - negative reaction." Another column listed reasons, including "respiratory failure," "neurological complications," or other dire conditions. She noticed that the official trial summary for these "unfortunate outcomes" was drastically minimized - reporting only a fraction of what the raw data spreadsheet indicated. That mismatch alone could spark a flurry of regulatory and criminal inquiries.

Emily's pulse raced. This was bigger - and more horrifying - than she'd imagined. Should she partner up with a more established firm? Did she have the bandwidth or financial resources to wage war against a company that, based on these documents, was not only manipulative but outright dangerous?

She opened a final folder marked "Summaries" and found a single, short Word document. It was an outline of the allegations, presumably compiled by the whistleblower or Gina's nonprofit. The bullet points summarized the alleged wrongdoing:

1. **Concealment of adverse effects**: Intentional underreporting of lethal or near-lethal complications in multiple trial sites.

2. **Falsification of regulatory reports**: Official summaries to the FDA and other health agencies omitted key data, painting a deceptively safe profile for the drug XK-77.

3. **Targeting vulnerable populations**: The trials appear to have been conducted in regions with limited oversight or legal recourse, likely to minimize potential blowback.

When Emily finished reading, she let out a slow exhale. The moral stakes were crystal-clear. If GenTech (or whichever pharma giant was behind XK-77) managed to get this drug approved and widely marketed, countless more lives could be in danger. And the whistleblower was risking everything to prevent that.

She closed her laptop, her hands shaking slightly. *This is the real deal,* she thought. *People's lives, corporate greed, potential criminal conduct.*

Before she could gather herself further, the door rattled as Tessa returned, balancing a tray with two sandwiches and bottled water.

"Lunch is served," Tessa announced. Then she caught sight of Emily's face and froze. "You all right, Em? You look like you've seen a ghost."

Emily stood, crossing to shut her laptop. "I saw enough. This is definitely no joke."

Tessa set the tray on the desk, curiosity radiating from her posture. "So it's legit?"

"All signs point to yes. If these documents are authentic, someone systematically concealed lethal outcomes in a drug trial. A lot of them."

Tessa stared, stunned. "If this is real... what does that mean for us?"

Emily pressed her fingers to her temples. "It means we might be the only lawyers willing to help the whistleblower bring the truth to light. But it also means we'll be going up against an opponent who won't just roll over."

Tessa put a hand on Emily's shoulder. "I've got your back. And so does your reputation. People at Hastings & Cole talked about your tenacity, even if they didn't always agree with you. That's why they gave you a seat at the table so quickly, remember?"

Emily offered a small, grateful smile. She recalled the late nights combing through discovery documents, how she'd actually found a certain thrill in piecing together a case from reams of corporate data. "We'll need that tenacity in spades. If this corporation is as powerful as it sounds, they'll try every legal tactic in the book - and maybe a few that aren't in the book."

Tessa nodded. "So, do we tell Ms. Morales we're in?"

Emily weighed the question. Her sense of responsibility said yes, they should at least meet the whistleblower, confirm the authenticity of these files, and figure out next steps. But she also felt a pang of fear at the idea of standing alone in front of a massive legal onslaught.

"Let's do it," she said, resolving to remain calm. "I'll call Gina tomorrow and schedule a meeting with the whistleblower. There's too much at stake to walk away."

Tessa's eyes brightened with resolve. "In that case, you need a decent meal." She handed Emily one of the sandwiches and uncapped a bottle of water, as though fueling her for the battle ahead.

They ate mostly in silence. Between bites, Emily's mind reeled with scenarios: She'd file a complaint in federal court, probably under the False Claims Act if the company had sought government funds or approvals. She'd face a powerhouse defense that could bury her in motions. She'd need experts on pharmacology, clinical trials, and epidemiology. She'd need investigators who could track down data in Africa and South America. Her modest budget barely covered a short flight to the next state - how would she handle international research?

Despite the wave of questions, a flicker of excitement pulsed through her. She'd left Hastings & Cole to *do the right thing*. She'd wanted to defend the voiceless, not line the pockets of corporate defendants. This was the chance she'd dreamed of, albeit in a more daunting form than she'd ever expected.

By the time she'd finished half her sandwich and Tessa had polished off hers, Emily realized she hadn't heard the doorbell ring at all for nearly an hour. The building's hallway seemed eerily quiet. The quiet unsettled her. Absurdly, she found herself walking to the front entrance and tugging on the lock just to confirm it was secure. When she gazed out through the glass, she saw no one lingering, no suspicious parked cars. Yet her sense of foreboding wouldn't lift.

Tessa joined her. "You've got that paranoid look, Emily."

Emily shrugged. "Gina said 'Company X' has extensive security. If they can bury an entire data set about lethal side effects, I'm sure they can figure out which small law office just got hold of that data."

Tessa's eyebrows knitted. "You think they'd spy on us?"

"I wouldn't put it past them. Corporate espionage, intimidation - these things happen."

Tessa placed a hand on Emily's shoulder. "We'll keep the doors locked, be mindful of what we say over the phone. If it gets hairy, we'll take extra precautions."

Emily nodded, forcing herself to breathe. "Right. No reason to panic. We'll stay vigilant."

Around four o'clock, as Emily and Tessa were prepping to finalize the day's notes, the doorbell tinkled again. Startled, Emily exchanged glances with Tessa; they hadn't scheduled any late-afternoon appointments except for a possible walk-in or the random eviction consultation tomorrow. Could it be Gina returning unannounced?

Emily rose to greet the visitor. As she entered the reception area, she froze. Standing in the doorway was a man wearing an impeccable gray suit, glossy shoes, and a practiced half-smile. His hair was meticulously styled, his jaw clean-shaven - familiar in a way that made her heart twist.

"Emily," he said, that half-smile flickering into something warmer. "You look... well. It's been a while."

She forced a polite nod, hoping her face masked the swirl of emotions. "Mark Hastings. To what do I owe the pleasure?"

He stepped in, glancing around at the austere reception furniture and half-empty filing cabinets. "I wanted to see your new operation. Congratulations on going solo." He said it with a hint of genuine respect, though Emily caught the slight raise of his eyebrows as he took in her obviously modest surroundings.

"I appreciate the courtesy visit," she said flatly, stepping behind the reception desk so she wouldn't have to stand too close. Tessa lingered in the corner, posture taut. She had heard enough about Mark Hastings - Emily's former colleague - during late-night venting sessions.

Mark turned, noticing Tessa. He nodded politely but didn't introduce himself. Instead, he looked back to Emily. "I was in the neighborhood for a client meeting. I thought I'd drop by, see how you're settling in."

"A phone call would've sufficed," Emily replied, crossing her arms. "We're busy."

Martyn Bellamy

Mark's eyes flickered with amusement. "Yes, well, I won't stay long. Just making sure you're... comfortable." His gaze landed on the single plaque of Emily's admission to the federal bar. "I hear you might be looking to take on some bigger cases. Congratulations, again, on your ambitions."

The way he said "ambitions" set Emily's teeth on edge, as if it were a warning. She decided to call his bluff. "Let's cut to the chase, Mark. Did you come by to gather intel? Fishing for what cases I might be considering?"

His jaw tightened, but he kept his voice even. "Intel? No. That would imply I'm up to something." He glanced at Tessa, then back at Emily. "I was just curious if you've heard any interesting rumors - like, for instance, about a whistleblower going after a certain pharma client."

Tessa's eyes narrowed, but she said nothing. Emily felt her pulse pound. She managed a small scoff. "I don't deal in rumors."

Mark nodded slowly, raising his hands in a gesture of surrender. "Of course not. I simply heard through the grapevine that an ex-employee from a big pharma might be sniffing around for representation. Our firm had a conversation about it the other day. Thought maybe you'd want a friendly heads-up: it's a dangerous case, if it exists at all."

Emily glared. "What makes it dangerous, Mark?"

"Big companies don't like trouble," he said quietly. "Whistleblower suits can be... complicated. Sometimes the people who jump in end up regretting it."

Her temper flared. "Is that a warning or a threat?"

Mark's mouth twitched. "A reminder, let's say. You left Hastings & Cole because you didn't like how we handled corporate defense. I get it. But you know how ruthless the other side can be. I don't want to see you get in over your head."

Tessa took a step forward, her voice cool. "Emily's perfectly capable of handling herself. Now, is there something concrete you wanted to say, Mr. Hastings?"

He dipped his head in a gesture that could be construed as respectful or dismissive. "Just that if you do run into this 'whistleblower' - be sure you understand the stakes. This client might not be able to pay your fees.

And the defendant, if it's who we think, won't hesitate to crush you."

Emily felt her palms clammy. She wasn't sure if Mark's warning came from genuine concern or if he was an advance scout for the corporation, already trying to intimidate her. Either way, her pride wouldn't let her fold. "I appreciate the heads-up," she said, forcing a level tone. "But I'll run my practice as I see fit. I don't need Hastings & Cole's interference or concern."

Mark offered a thin-lipped smile. "Understood. Good luck, Emily." He gave a curt nod to Tessa before stepping out into the hallway. The door swung shut behind him, the bell's chime fading into sudden silence.

Tessa let out a slow whistle. "That was definitely a fishing expedition."

Emily's chest felt tight. "Yeah. Word travels fast, I guess. If Mark is sniffing around, the corporation might already know about the whistleblower's approach."

"Does that mean we need to hurry up, or hold off?"

Emily thought of the damning evidence she'd just seen. "We do both - move quickly to protect the whistleblower, but also tread carefully. Because if

Mark's involved, that likely means Hastings & Cole could be defending the pharmaceutical company. They can bury us in legal motions if we're not ready."

Tessa nodded, her face resolute. "Then we'll be ready. Right?"

Emily inhaled, letting the last traces of Mark Hastings's presence dissipate from the room. "We have to be. If this is truly about lethal side effects and a massive cover-up, then every day we wait is another day people might be at risk."

As five o'clock approached, Emily's shoulders ached from tension. She sorted through the day's notes - Jacob Smith's eviction matter, a possible property dispute case, and the big question mark that was the whistleblower's case. Tessa tidied up the front desk, turned off the overhead lights, and then joined Emily in the office.

They locked the door behind them, stepping out into the brisk early-evening air. A swirl of leaves scurried across the sidewalk. Emily paused to double-check the office door, verifying the deadbolt was secure. She imagined Mark Hastings's well-shined shoes on that very spot just minutes earlier, delivering his cryptic warnings.

"You heading home?" Tessa asked, hugging her arms to keep warm.

Emily nodded. "Yeah. I'll do a deeper dive into the flash drive from there, maybe cross-reference some of the corporate addresses with publicly available info. I want a sense of how broad this scandal could be."

Tessa gave her a half-smile. "Don't stay up all night. We've got a big day tomorrow."

They parted ways on the sidewalk, Tessa heading toward the subway station, Emily to her battered sedan in the adjacent lot. As Emily drove home, she glanced in the rearview mirror more often than usual, alert to any headlights that lingered too long behind her. Paranoia? Perhaps. But Mark's sudden appearance, plus Gina's caution, made her realize she wasn't operating in a safe, predictable environment anymore. The stakes were real, and she had just staked her claim in a battle she might not be prepared to fight.

When she arrived at her tiny apartment, she parked and walked inside, flicking on the lights in her living room.

The Ghosts' Trial – Volume One

Stacks of law books and trial guides were scattered on every flat surface; her furniture was a patchwork of used store bargains. It wasn't glamorous, but it was her sanctuary. She tossed her purse onto the couch, feeling the weight of the day press down on her.

Grabbing her laptop from the bag, she settled at the small dining table and plugged it in. In the quiet stillness, she methodically reopened the files from Gina's flash drive. She told herself she was just double-checking. But as she read each email chain more carefully, wading through the spreadsheets and notations, the dread and anger inside her grew. There were references to early trial participants in Ghana, Sierra Leone, parts of Brazil, and others in remote clinics that lacked robust oversight. The phrase "Minimize local visibility" popped up more than once.

Emily's jaw clenched. This wasn't just about a few unfortunate outcomes. The data indicated systemic deception - collusion among higher-ups to push a drug through trials at breakneck speed while covering up casualties. In her time at Hastings & Cole, Emily had seen corporate defense strategies that aimed to sanitize a product's image. But burying lethal side effects? That was criminal.

She eventually closed her laptop, massaging her temples. *Tomorrow, I call Gina Morales and set up a meeting with the whistleblower.* She'd ask a thousand questions, confirm every detail. And if everything checked out, she'd find a way to handle the case - alone if she had to, or with a co-counsel if necessary.

Before trying to get some sleep, Emily made one last phone call - this time to a friend from law school, Raquel Kim, who worked at a medium-sized litigation firm across town. Raquel had always been more sympathetic to David-vs.-Goliath cases. If Emily needed backup, Raquel might be the perfect ally.

The call rang through to voicemail. Emily left a short, cryptic message: "Hey, Raquel, it's Emily Blackwood. Got something big cooking. Let's grab coffee soon - maybe tomorrow if you're free. I could really use your insight."

She ended the call and stared at her phone's dark screen. Would Raquel be able to help? Would she even want to, considering the target might be a behemoth pharma corporation? Emily pushed the doubt away. She couldn't go into this unprepared. Whistleblower cases were no joke, especially when the potential defendants had unlimited resources.

Shutting off the living room light, Emily found her way to the bedroom. She changed into sweats and sank onto the bed, her mind swirling with every possible scenario. Lawsuits could drag on for years. She might see her own practice bankrupted by the legal costs alone, never mind the mental toll. But how could she sleep at night if she turned away? The images of those test subjects from the spreadsheets - those "unreported fatalities" - haunted her. In her gut, she knew she didn't have a real choice. Her conscience, the same conscience that had urged her to quit Hastings & Cole, wouldn't let her walk away.

She lay back on the pillow, eyes on the dim ceiling, and remembered Tessa's unwavering voice: *We'll do what we always do - our homework.* That sounded so simple, so matter-of-fact. As if going up against a giant was just another case, one they would take on with thoroughness and dedication. But Emily knew better. In truth, they might be stepping into the ring with a heavyweight champion who would use every dirty trick in the book to ensure they never heard the final bell.

Yet a flicker of hope persisted - hope for justice. Hope for the possibility that, by shining a light on these atrocities, they could prevent more deaths. Tomorrow she'd take the next step. And the day after that, the next. She told herself she'd navigate each hurdle as it came, trusting in her skills, her conscience, and the small but mighty team she had.

Eventually, exhaustion overwhelmed her swirling thoughts, and she drifted into a fitful sleep, the final image in her mind that of the data spreadsheet with a single word repeating across the last column: "Deceased." She vowed to remember those names, or at least those ID numbers, if it meant giving their suffering a voice. She might not be a crusading hero in the grand sense of the word, but she was determined to make sure someone was held accountable.

Chapter 3:
An Unexpected Visitor

The morning began in a hush rather than a flurry. Emily Blackwood stood by the secondhand coffee maker in her cramped office kitchenette, waiting for it to brew the day's first pot. The machine hissed and spat in that inconsistent way typical of something bought on sale - like her battered desk, her mismatched chairs, and nearly everything else in the modest space she could barely afford. Outside, downtown traffic clattered over potholes, and the sunlight struggled through the single window, illuminating boxes of legal files she hadn't found time - or reason - to organize.

She glanced at her phone. No new voicemail from prospective clients. No last-minute texts from old acquaintances at Hastings & Cole, the glimmering white-shoe firm she'd abandoned. It was 8:17 a.m. The emptiness of her message feed reminded her that although she was free from the corporate treadmill, she was also on her own. If no one walked in for help, Emily's fledgling practice would struggle to last beyond a single year.

"Anything happen overnight?" Tessa Moretti's voice preceded her footsteps. Emily's paralegal and all-around confidante had arrived early, balancing a cardboard tray with two paper cups - one a latte for Tessa, the other black coffee for Emily, who consistently forgot how bitter their shared brew tasted when she was the one making it.

"No calls, no messages," Emily said, sighing. "I was up for an hour last night thinking about whether I should call my old clients, see if they need a small-practice attorney for something. Anything."

Tessa clucked her tongue in sympathy. She carefully set down the tray on the far corner of Emily's battered desk, near the half-open laptop that displayed an empty Monday calendar. Then she swung off her jacket and hung it on a hook behind the door. With her business-casual clothes and the methodical way she approached everything - down to her note-taking - Tessa radiated a kind of organized determination that Emily admired.

"Give it time," Tessa said with a confidence Emily didn't quite share. "We only opened doors a few weeks ago. Our sign still has that 'wet paint' look. Clients will show up."

Emily forced a smile. If Tessa believed it, she could muster the faith to at least pretend. In truth, the rent for the office suite weighed on her mind, not to mention student loans, monthly bills, and the cost of the legal research services she needed to stay competitive.

She carried her fresh coffee back to her desk, leaving the kitchenette's percolator behind. The little device hissed in annoyance as if unhappy at being abandoned. Through the window, she glimpsed a swirl of passing pedestrians who looked like they had somewhere pressing to be, while she had nowhere pressing to go.

She booted up her laptop, scanning local legal news websites for anything that might hint at a case or a prospective client in her practice area. She used to handle corporate litigation at Hastings & Cole, an elite environment where she wore expensive suits and recited memorized codes in high-stakes negotiations. Now, she was rummaging among local bulletins hoping for anything from a personal injury claim to a small business dispute.

Tessa approached with a piece of mail. "Bills," she muttered. "A lot of them."

"Great," Emily said drily. "At least the mailman's consistent."

They fell into a comfortable routine: Tessa sorting the daily influx of envelopes while Emily scrolled through headlines. There was a short news piece about an investigative reporter named Prisha Shah who had once uncovered malfeasance in the city council. Emily hovered over the link, half-hoping there was some new scandal that might yield a case she could take. But nothing. Just a summary of past achievements.

Barely an hour later, the front door to the suite rattled open. Emily heard the muffled chime they had installed - a small bell that Tessa had taped to the doorframe because they couldn't afford a more sophisticated alert system. Usually, the sound heralded a delivery driver, sometimes the occasional visitor scoping out the viability of hiring an attorney.

Emily leaned forward, straining her ears. Tessa popped her head into the corridor. "That's not the usual FedEx guy," she muttered, and gestured for Emily to come see.

He looked out of place in an unremarkable way - brown hair slicked back unevenly, wearing an ill-fitting navy windbreaker over a wrinkled dress shirt and black slacks that ended half an inch too short at his ankles. His eyes darted around as though worried someone might follow him inside.

"Hi," Emily said, plastering on her best welcoming smile. "I'm Emily Blackwood. How can I help you?"

The man's eyes flicked in Tessa's direction before returning to Emily. "Are you - alone?" His voice was raspy, like he hadn't spoken or slept in a day or two.

Tessa and Emily exchanged a glance. Emily noticed the man was clutching a plain manila envelope. Maybe he was a prospective client, or maybe the envelope was a subpoena.

"It's just the two of us," Emily said carefully. "Why don't you step into my office, Mr. - ?"

"Priest," he offered. "Alan Priest."

He stared back at the door as if he expected it to fling open any second. Tessa gave him a reassuring nod, stepping out of the way to let him pass.

When the three of them made it into Emily's small corner office, he seemed to relax just slightly - though his eyes still carried a haunted tension. He gripped the manila envelope with both hands, the edges of it bowed from the pressure of his palms.

"Mr. Priest, can I get you a cup of coffee?" Emily asked. She didn't want to push too hard too soon, but something about him radiated fear.

Priest opened his mouth, closed it again, and finally shook his head. "No, thanks," he said. "I - I have no idea where to start. I think you might be able to help me, but…" He glanced around the modest office - two wooden chairs, a filing cabinet, a half-functional printer. "You're not with Hastings & Cole anymore, right?"

Emily felt her stomach flip. "No, I'm not," she said, trying to mask her surprise. "I left a few months ago to start my own firm."

Priest swallowed. "Right, that's what I heard," he murmured, mostly to himself. "Look, you might regret speaking to me, Ms. Blackwood. But I've got no one else to turn to."

He lowered himself into the chair, looking suddenly exhausted. Tessa lingered in the doorway, her presence calm and steady. Emily motioned for her to stay; there was no sense in leaving them alone if this was going to be a serious consultation.

"All right," Emily said gently. She eased into her own seat, leaning across the desk, hands folded. "Why don't you tell me a bit about what's going on?"

Priest began haltingly, as if each sentence might land him in danger. "I work - I worked - for a pharmaceutical giant called GenTech. In their research and development sector."

He hesitated, took a breath. "They're...not what they seem," he said. "They're big, wealthy, and extremely powerful. They handle a variety of drug trials all over the world. But there's - things they don't want the public knowing."

Emily's brow furrowed. She had heard of GenTech in passing. A few years ago, her old firm had done some work for them, though she'd never directly handled that portfolio. Mark Hastings, a rising star at Hastings & Cole, had occasionally boasted about them as a major client.

Priest continued, "I'm basically a nobody there - a mid-level project manager. But I had access to certain databases, certain documents." He tapped the envelope. "I noticed inconsistencies in records from trials in Africa, specifically in Zimbabwe and Uganda. Then in Peru. Unexpected deaths labeled as 'adverse events' or 'natural causes,' but there were patterns."

He spoke faster, almost breathless. "I reported it to my immediate boss. She told me to keep it to myself. Next, I find out my job is under threat, I'm being cut out of projects I used to oversee. I had friends in the labs who told me to watch my back, so I started collecting evidence. If I ever ended up fired or worse, I wanted a record."

Emily and Tessa listened intently. She could sense Tessa's quickening breath from across the small space. This wasn't the typical slip-and-fall or a messy divorce. Priest was describing serious wrongdoing at a major corporation.

"How…serious are we talking here?" Emily managed.

Priest's nervous energy was palpable. "Serious enough that I'm scared for my life." He met her eyes. "You must think I'm paranoid, but I've been followed. I've seen men outside my building who don't look like average passersby. My email at work was suddenly locked. Someone at GenTech knows I've been snooping. And I think they want me silent."

"Why come to me?" she asked, keeping her voice even. A sliver of anxiety coiled in her stomach. If Mark Hastings or any other big-time lawyer caught wind that she was even looking at GenTech the wrong way, there might be professional hell to pay.

He pushed the envelope forward on the desk. She noticed small dark circles under his eyes - signs of a man who hadn't slept properly in days, maybe weeks. "Because you used to be part of a big firm that does - did - business with GenTech. You know how these guys operate, legally and otherwise. But you're not tied to them anymore. You're the only one who might actually do something with this."

Emily felt the weight of the words settle on her. Tessa leaned in, glancing from Priest to her. In Tessa's expression, Emily read a mix of curiosity and concern - this was the kind of case that could catapult their practice into the headlines but also bury them financially and psychologically if they weren't prepared.

"What is in there?" Tessa asked gently, nodding to the envelope.

"Copies of emails, internal memos, trial results that were never published. Enough, I think, to open an investigation." Priest paused. "But it's not everything. I still have more stored in a secure location."

Emily slid the envelope closer to her side of the desk. Her mind flashed with the memory of Mark Hastings' voice telling stories of how unstoppable GenTech's legal team was. If half of what Priest claimed was true, she was sitting on an explosive claim that might overshadow anything else in her career.

She drew in a deep breath. "This…this is big," she said quietly. "You understand the risk that comes with going after a company like GenTech. They have endless resources. They can file motion after motion, bury a small firm - like mine - in paperwork."

Priest offered a grim nod. "I know. But they can't buy everyone. You might be new on the scene, but you have a reputation. People I trust told me to find you specifically. They said you care more about doing the right thing than winning. But you'll still fight to win if you believe in something."

Emily wasn't sure whether to be flattered or terrified by that statement. She glanced at Tessa, who swallowed, her gaze fixed on the envelope.

"I...have to look at the documents first," Emily began. "Do some due diligence. We're just a small office, so we don't have an army of associates."

"I'm not asking for a guarantee," Priest said. "Just promise you'll read them. If you decide this is worth pursuing, then I'll tell you more, and we can figure out how to proceed."

Emily nodded. "All right. Let me see what's here." She almost added that she'd keep everything confidential, but it was implied. Priest was effectively a whistleblower - privileged communications would protect him in some capacity, but not from physical threats or corporate intimidation.

Priest took a shaky breath, then forced a tight smile. "You're already doing more than most." His voice went quieter. "Ms. Blackwood, they'll come after you if they find out you have this information. Please be cautious."

He rose to his feet, stuffed his hands in his jacket pockets, then paused as if uncertain whether to retrieve the envelope again. After a moment, he left it where it sat on the desk.

"I - I can't stay," he said. "I've probably lingered too long as it is."

Tessa straightened. "Alan, wait - shouldn't we…?"

But he was already turning to the door. "I'll be in touch," he said, voice clipped. "Just keep that somewhere safe, all right?"

Emily followed him to the front door, half-worried he might faint or collapse from nerves. But he managed to open it swiftly, stepping onto the street. She peered through the glass as he hurried away, glancing over his shoulder every few seconds.

She locked the door behind him and turned to find Tessa at her elbow. "Well," Tessa said softly, "that's one way to start a Monday."

Emily exhaled shakily. She lifted the envelope in one hand. "Let's see if this is real," she said. She tried to steady her voice, but she could already feel the pulse of adrenaline in her veins.

Back in her office, Emily carefully opened the manila envelope. Inside were printed copies of emails, each bearing GenTech's corporate header. Some were short missives from mid-level managers discussing "increased mortality" or "unexpected side effects" in certain test groups. Others were lengthy threads with entire chains of recipients, referencing "urgent priority" or "strategic redirection of data."

She set them aside, revealing what looked like spreadsheets and tables detailing patient outcomes from a series of clinical trials. Emily's prior experience at Hastings & Cole had taught her to read between the lines. The columns of data showed casualty rates higher than any drug trial would normally tolerate. At the bottom of some pages were disclaimers about "statistically insignificant anomalies," but a quick glance suggested these anomalies occurred more often than chance would allow.

Tessa hovered behind her, flipping through the pages when Emily paused. "This is horrifying," Tessa whispered, reading a summary about a patient who died three days after taking an experimental drug. The cause of death was vaguely attributed to "chronic pre-existing condition," yet the disclaimers typed in the margins stated no prior knowledge of that condition existed.

"There's definitely something off here," Emily admitted. "But we need the bigger picture. If these are real, it implies GenTech was aware of major health risks in some of their foreign trials and tried to bury them."

Tessa took a breath. "Buried them how?"

Emily's lips pressed into a thin line. "By attributing deaths to random chance, or other pre-existing conditions. If these patients were poor, from remote communities, the results might not attract the attention they would in the U.S. or Europe. Regulatory bodies, if they were even informed, might not read beyond the official summaries."

"This could be a class-action lawsuit, or worse. Criminal negligence if someone can prove it," Tessa said, sounding both excited and alarmed.

Emily nodded. "But you heard Priest. He's terrified. If these documents are genuine, people may have died because of corporate cost-cutting or hush-ups. This is the kind of case that big firms salivate over - but that's only because big firms can crush it on both sides. GenTech will bury us if they want."

Tessa turned to look at the closed office door. "We're going to need to be careful, Em."

Emily appreciated Tessa's steadfast loyalty. They had met during Emily's time at Hastings & Cole, forging a professional bond over countless late nights preparing motions for the firm's senior partners. Tessa had taken the leap with her to start this practice, accepting a lower salary because of her faith in Emily's vision.

Still, Emily wondered if Tessa might end up regretting that choice if GenTech set their sights on them.

They spent over an hour reading everything line by line. Emily spotted repeated references to "Project Faraday," a code name for something that wasn't fully explained in the documents. The spreadsheets and memos indicated trial phases for a new medication intended to treat certain autoimmune conditions. But the side effects listed sounded devastating: organ failure, neurological complications, even uncharacteristic violent outbursts.

Martyn Bellamy

By the time Tessa and Emily finished their initial review, a heavy silence filled the room. They'd only begun to scratch the surface. The documents Priest left were a snapshot, but not nearly the complete story.

"There must be more," Tessa said softly. "He said he had the rest stashed somewhere."

Emily steepled her fingers, resting her chin against her thumbs. "If we decide to move forward - and I mean if - we'll need the whole trove. Enough to establish a pattern of negligence or cover-ups that can stand up in court." She laughed bitterly. "I can't believe I'm talking about taking on a multi-billion-dollar pharmaceutical behemoth from this dingy office."

Tessa gave a faint smile. "Maybe it's the big break we need. The reason we stepped away from the cushy corporate side, remember?"

Emily remembered, all right. She left Hastings & Cole because she had grown tired of a system where she was told to do "whatever it takes to keep the client safe." That might mean slamming smaller opposition with endless motions, or finding legal loopholes that left no recourse for victims. For a long time, Emily had rationalized that she was simply doing her job. But one day, she realized she was miserable burying herself in corporate defenses, so she walked away.

Yet, ironically, here she was - staring at a case that would pit her against her old world in the most dramatic way possible.

After scanning the final pages, Emily placed them all back in the envelope and locked it in a metal filing cabinet. Then she locked the cabinet itself and pocketed the key. "We need to keep digital copies as well, but carefully," she said. "I'll scan them on my personal laptop, store them on an encrypted drive. No cloud storage. Not yet."

Tessa nodded. "Good idea. I'll also do a quick check on Mr. Priest. Just see if we can verify that he actually worked at GenTech. Maybe there's something online or in the local business registry."

Emily felt a twinge of worry. "Be discreet, though. If GenTech is monitoring him, they might pick up on a sudden interest."

Tessa gave her a reassuring pat on the shoulder. "I'll do what I can without leaving a trail."

Before Tessa left the office to do her search, Emily sank into her chair. Outside, the late-morning sun brightened the glass facade of the building across the street. She could see her reflection faintly on the office window: a woman in her early thirties, wearing a simple blouse and slacks, her dark hair tied back into a hurried ponytail, trying not to look as apprehensive as she felt.

She pulled open a desk drawer and took out a photograph - her parents standing in front of their small house, smiling. It was from several years back, but she always kept it close. They had believed in her, saved for her education, insisted she could rise to the top if she worked hard enough. She had risen, only to realize "the top" wasn't a place she wanted to be.

Holding the photo, she sighed. "Mom, Dad," she whispered. "I hope you don't think I'm crazy for doing this."

The memory drifted back to her last days at the prestigious firm. Mark Hastings - charismatic, brilliant, exuding confidence - had cornered her in the hallway outside a partner's office.

"You're making a mistake," he had said. "Leaving now? Throwing away your seat at the big table? People would kill for what you have."

She had stared back at him. "Maybe that's the problem," she replied. "I don't want to be part of a system that defends the indefensible just because it pays well."

They'd parted with strained civility. He hadn't bothered calling her after that. And she wasn't naive: she knew Mark might have parroted her reasons to the entire partnership, spinning it as a meltdown or a moral high horse.

Now, here she sat, about to challenge a client that Hastings & Cole once proudly served. She couldn't help feeling Mark's presence as a spectral caution: big firms have big resources, Emily. They always win.

Tessa returned, holding a yellow notepad with scribbled references. "So, I did a quick search for Alan Priest," she said, leaning against the edge of Emily's desk. "He's not on GenTech's leadership page, but that doesn't mean much. I found an older employee listing from a trade show two years ago - there's an 'A. Priest' listed under R&D staff."

Emily nodded slowly. "At least that checks out. He's legitimate."

Tessa pursed her lips. "He's also not on any social media I can find. Which might be normal for some folks, but it's unusual these days not to leave a digital trace."

"He could be the private type," Emily said. "Or maybe GenTech strongly discourages employees from posting about anything."

"True." Tessa sighed, flipping the notepad closed. "So, what's the next move?"

"We wait for him to contact us," Emily replied. "And we keep these documents secure in the meantime. I'll do some reading on whistleblower protections, especially in cases involving potential international litigation."

As the two women contemplated the strategy, Emily's phone buzzed for the first time all day. She shot a glance at the screen. A local number she didn't recognize.

"Emily Blackwood," she answered, pressing the phone to her ear.

Silence. Then a muffled click. She tried speaking again, but there was no response. The line disconnected.

She exchanged a look with Tessa. "Probably a robocall." The uneasy feeling curling inside her told her otherwise.

They decided to take a late lunch, though neither had much of an appetite. Emily grabbed a sandwich from the deli across the street, Tessa opted for a salad. They brought their food back to the office and ate quietly, each lost in thought.

Between bites, Tessa said, "You know, we haven't exactly told any prospective clients that we're open to major litigation. Most of our fliers emphasize small business disputes, contract reviews, that kind of thing."

Emily nodded. "This wasn't part of the plan, I know. But we can't just walk away from this, can we?"

Tessa's eyes flicked to the locked filing cabinet. "It feels like we'd be betraying ourselves if we did," she said simply.

It was exactly how Emily felt. She forced down the rest of her sandwich, though it tasted dry and unappealing, overshadowed by the moral weight pressing on her mind.

The rest of the afternoon crawled by. Emily tried to focus on drafting a contract for a small local bakery that had recently consulted her about expanding to a second location. She needed that client to keep the lights on - basic rent and overhead. Yet every time she turned back to her laptop, the images of those medical spreadsheets tugged at the corners of her mind.

Shortly after two o'clock, Tessa poked her head into Emily's office. "Someone's here to see you," she said quietly, eyes wide. "He says his name is Mark Hastings."

Emily's heart stumbled. She closed her laptop and stood. "Mark?"

Tessa nodded. "Yeah. The Mark Hastings from your old firm, I assume."

Emily swallowed. She remembered Mark's polished suits, his impeccable hair, and that unwavering confidence. "All right," she murmured, steadying herself. "Show him in."

The Ghosts' Trial – Volume One

Tessa withdrew. A moment later, Mark Hastings stepped through the door, wearing a tailored navy suit that was in stark contrast to the battered chairs and scuffed floors around him. He took in the office with a slight frown - almost pity, Emily thought. Then he smiled, the sort of measured, superficial grin that never touched his eyes.

"Emily," he greeted, as though they were old friends, cordial from years of collaboration.

"Mark." She gestured to the seat across from her desk, but he hovered, as if uncertain it was clean enough to sit in.

He finally settled, crossing one leg over the other. "I was in the area. Thought I'd drop by, see how you're doing."

Emily snorted softly. "The area, meaning…way across town from Hastings & Cole's skyscraper offices?"

He gave a half-chuckle. "I had a client meeting not too far from here. I recalled your new place, wanted to check in." He let his gaze roam over the cramped office and the half-empty bookshelves. "I like what you've done with the space."

She masked a flush of annoyance. "This place suits me. So, how is the old firm?"

He shrugged. "Business as usual. We're picking up a large roster of clients. Big corporate expansions, new lawsuits. You know how it is."

Emily wondered if he'd mention GenTech, but he didn't. Instead, he gave a pointed look at the locked cabinet behind her desk.

"You still up to your neck in doc reviews?" he teased.

"Something like that," she said carefully. "Anyway, to what do I owe the pleasure of your visit?"

Mark cleared his throat, shifting in the chair. "Let's just say I got wind that you might be looking at some sensitive material. Word gets around, you know. I wanted to make sure you're…not biting off more than you can chew."

The tension in the room became palpable. Emily kept her expression neutral. "I don't know what you're talking about."

He offered a half-smile. "Sure you don't." Then, in a more serious tone, "Look, Em. We have a history. I'm giving you a friendly piece of advice: be cautious. Certain companies are extremely protective of their interests, and if you get in their crosshairs, life can become very complicated."

She felt a flare of anger. "That sounds like a threat."

He held up his hands. "Not from me. I'm not threatening you. But I've seen how these big players operate. They file motions, countersuits. They ruin reputations. They have security teams that investigate and sometimes even intimidate."

She swallowed hard, refusing to let him see how rattled she was. "I appreciate the concern. But if you're here as a messenger for any of your big corporate clients - "

He shook his head, forcing another tight smile. "Just came to see an old friend. Offer a heads-up. Don't let your sense of justice overshadow realism. Sometimes the best choice is to walk away."

Emily glared at him, words escaping her in a rush. "I walked away from Hastings & Cole because I couldn't stomach the moral compromises. If you're telling me to walk away from fighting a real injustice, you're validating that decision."

She expected Mark to retaliate, but he merely stood, adjusting his suit jacket. For the first time, a glimmer of genuine concern crossed his features. "I'm serious. This could destroy you if you're not careful."

Then he left, his final words hanging in the stale air.

Tessa peeked in a few seconds later, her eyebrows raised. "What was that about?"

Emily stared at the space where Mark had stood. "He suspects we have something on GenTech."

Tessa frowned. "You think he'll report back to them?"

"I'm sure of it," Emily said. "He's probably under instructions to gauge what I know and warn me off." She felt a pang in her chest: once upon a time, she considered Mark a friend and possibly something more. But that door was closed.

She reached for the locked filing cabinet key again, verifying it was still in her pocket. "We need to be more careful," she told Tessa. "Priest could be in even more danger than we realized."

The rest of the day drifted by in uneasy quiet, with Emily scanning more of the documents, searching for any mention of "Project Faraday." She found scattered references - some involving chemical trials, others referencing a third-party research firm overseas. The more she pieced together, the more it appeared that GenTech had systematically tested high-risk compounds in regions with minimal regulatory oversight.

By six p.m., the downtown bustle had softened into a muted hum. Tessa ordered takeout, but Emily barely touched her portion. They reread certain lines, highlighting them for follow-up. They cross-referenced the names of individuals who'd apparently died. It was heartbreaking to see how each life was reduced to a line on a spreadsheet.

Nightfall came early, winter approaching. Tessa rose to flip the deadbolt on the office door, pulling the blinds closed over the front windows. "Better safe than sorry," she said softly.

Emily nodded. She was about to suggest they finish for the day and pick this up tomorrow when a faint rattle sounded at the door - like someone testing whether it was locked. Her heart leapt into her throat.

Tessa took a step back, eyes wide.

Emily mustered her nerve, creeping to the door. "Yes?" she called, pressing her ear near the wooden frame.

Silence.

She peered through a corner of the blinds. A figure in a dark coat stood on the sidewalk, turned away. As soon as Emily peeked out, the figure strode off with brisk determination, disappearing around the corner.

She couldn't make out any details - gender, appearance, nothing. She felt a rush of unease. "No clue who that was," she said, turning back to Tessa.

Their eyes met. The message was clear: they were being watched. Whether it was Mark's firm, GenTech's private security, or another unseen party, the overshadowed sense of threat felt suddenly all too real.

Despite the unsettling intrusion, Emily powered on, scanning the last set of documents until her eyes blurred with fatigue. Tessa eventually dozed off on the small couch in the corner. Finally, around nine, Emily decided they had done enough for one day.

She gently shook Tessa awake. "Come on, let's call it a night. We should probably leave together."

Tessa yawned and checked her phone. "All right," she mumbled. "I'll grab my stuff."

They filed the documents away, double-locked the cabinet, and shut down their laptops. Emily walked Tessa out to the curb where she'd parked her car. For a moment, neither of them spoke, scanning the street for anyone suspicious. Only a lone taxi rumbled by, headlights sweeping the empty sidewalks.

"Do you want me to follow you home?" Tessa asked, breaking the quiet.

Emily forced a smile. "I'll be okay. You get home safe. Text me when you arrive."

Tessa nodded, eyes still full of worry, then slid into her sedan and drove off, leaving Emily standing under the flickering glow of a street lamp. She had her own car in the lot behind the building. A short walk, but it felt like miles in the darkness.

Every footstep on the pavement sounded amplified as she made her way around the block. She glanced over her shoulder more than once, but saw no one trailing her. The sense of being watched was more ephemeral than real, but the hair on her arms remained upright.

When she finally reached her car, Emily locked the doors the moment she climbed inside. She rested her head against the steering wheel for a moment, exhaling. Did she really want to go up against a multinational entity that evidently had no qualms about intimidation?

Yet as she pictured the spreadsheets listing the names of test subjects, each with "Deceased" typed next to their ID numbers, her anger stirred anew. If GenTech really had caused those deaths, or even just concealed them without caring for the victims, they had to be held accountable.

Emily's apartment was a modest one-bedroom in a renovated building known more for chipped paint than charm. She hurried up the stairs, her pulse still pounding. Once inside, she triple-checked the locks, then slumped onto her worn sofa in the living room. It was cluttered with boxes she still hadn't unpacked since moving out of her plush high-rise near Hastings & Cole - a sign of how drastically her life had changed.

She clicked on the television for background noise, flipping aimlessly through channels. Her mind wasn't on sitcom reruns or the cooking show marathon playing on some random station. Instead, she wondered if Alan

Priest was safe, if Mark Hastings was already drafting a strategy to undermine her, and if someone else - more dangerous - had tried to break into the office earlier.

Unable to find solace in TV, she turned it off and opened her laptop, scanning the local news sites for any hint that GenTech was in trouble. Nothing overt. But she stumbled on an article referencing a "new wave of advanced drug research" in developing countries, praising the philanthropic benefits of early treatments for underserved populations. Emily stared at the screen, chewing on her lip. Was it possible that GenTech hid behind philanthropic claims to carry out risky or unethical testing?

The question haunted her.

Sleep came in fits. She dreamt of shadowy men in suits rifling through her office cabinets, dreamt of spreadsheets that bled into one another, lines of data mixing with the faces of the dead. She awoke sweaty and disoriented. Outside, dawn was just beginning to paint the horizon.

She checked her phone: no calls, no messages from Alan Priest. A knot of frustration twisted in her chest. She needed to talk to him, to see if there was more to the story. Then she remembered Mark's warning. Maybe Alan was lying, or maybe Mark was just doing his job. One thing was certain: Emily stood at a crossroads.

By 7 a.m., she was dressed and out the door, heading back to the office. The city was just stirring to life - delivery trucks, early commuters, the occasional jogger. She brought a coffee with her from a neighborhood café, paying for it with the last of her small cash stash.

When she arrived, the building was as quiet as she'd left it. The door was still locked, the blinds drawn. No sign of tampering. She let herself in, flipping on the overhead lights. The office air felt stale and cold.

She checked her filing cabinet: still locked. She breathed a sigh of relief. Then, with a renewed sense of purpose, she booted up her computer and began drafting a set of preliminary notes - hypothetical legal arguments, potential angles for a whistleblower case, references to the relevant state and federal statutes.

Around eight-thirty, Tessa arrived, bearing two pastries in a paper bag. "Morning," she said, and offered Emily the extra. "You hungry?"

The Ghosts' Trial – Volume One

Emily took the pastry with thanks, but set it aside for later - her stomach churned with unresolved tension. "We need to find Alan Priest," she said, scanning the documents again. "He said he'd contact us, but if we're going to do anything, we need everything he's got."

Tessa nodded. "I could try to track him down with the minimal info we have. It's not the best scenario, but it might speed things along."

Emily drummed her fingers on the desk. "Let's wait another day. If he doesn't come back, then we'll try to locate him. I don't want to accidentally tip off GenTech if we poke around in the wrong places."

Tessa agreed. They fell into another day of waiting, peppered with bursts of anxious research.

But even as she worked, Emily knew that her life had already changed the moment Alan Priest walked in the door. The envelope sitting in her locked cabinet felt radioactive. She wanted to do the right thing. But was she prepared for the war that would surely follow?

By the day's end, no call came from Alan Priest. No new messages, no unexpected visits. Yet the sense of foreboding hung over the tiny office like a storm cloud.

Emily gathered her notes on whistleblower laws, her scribbled outlines of potential arguments, and placed them in the same locked drawer as the envelope.

She turned off her computer, letting the screen fade to black. Tessa offered a few last words of encouragement before gathering her things to leave.

Left alone in the quiet office, Emily stood by the single window that overlooked the busy street. Night was falling again, neon signs flickering to life in shop windows below. She watched the silhouettes of pedestrians, each with their own destinations and worries. She wondered if any of them had lost friends or relatives in far-off medical trials that never made the headlines.

Finally, she drew the blinds and switched off the lights. She grabbed her coat and locked the door behind her, heart thudding. Tomorrow, she might receive new revelations. Or a warning. Or no sign from Alan Priest at all.

But for better or worse, the documents he left behind had pulled her into a moral battle she could no longer ignore. GenTech was out there, bigger and more powerful than any client she had dared to take on - and they wouldn't hesitate to crush her if she got in their way.

Yet as Emily stepped into the brisk night air, she felt a surge of resolve. She had left Hastings & Cole to protect people like those invisible victims. Doing the right thing rarely came without a cost. And if she decided to fight, she would do so wholeheartedly, no matter the odds.

At the thought, she tightened her grip on her purse - where the filing cabinet key jangled against her cell phone. She looked at the dark sky overhead, the city's glow diffusing the stars. A whisper of determination fluttered through her chest. If Alan Priest had entrusted her with the truth, then she owed it to him - and the countless unnamed victims - to see it through.

Even if it meant facing the wrath of a corporate giant that could very well destroy everything she had built.

That night, the ring of the office bell played on a loop in her mind: an unexpected visitor, a simple envelope, and a truth too dangerous to ignore.

Chapter 4: Glimpse of GenTech

Emily Blackwood sat behind her modest wooden desk - an heirloom piece from her late grandfather's office - studying the flickering screen of her laptop. Outside, an autumn chill settled over the city, painting the windows of her small second-floor corner office with tiny beads of condensation. She had come in early, hoping the quiet morning hours might help her unravel the tangle of questions in her mind about a company named GenTech. The name kept popping up with unsettling rumors attached to it, rumors about unethical drug trials in Africa and South America. Nothing concrete, just murmurs and half-reported stories that rarely made it past obscure online forums or foreign-language newspaper clippings. But now, thanks to Alan Priest - the anxious, half-panicked whistleblower who'd shown up days ago - Emily realized there might be a lawsuit buried in these rumors. She just wasn't sure yet whether she dared to take on a corporate giant all by herself.

She scrolled through an article about a group of villagers in Mozambique who had allegedly participated in a clinical trial that ended abruptly.

Dozens had been left with severe, life-altering symptoms. Another Google hit mentioned a new drug trial in rural Colombia. The results were apparently suppressed after several participants turned up seriously ill or died. Emily rubbed her eyes, feeling the weight of the revelations. She'd been at this for nearly two hours already, diving into the digital underworld of medical malpractice allegations, shaky confessions on internet boards, and press releases from GenTech that tried to spin the narrative in a hundred different ways. The deeper she got, the stronger her sense of dread became. She tried to remain analytical, but it was impossible not to feel outrage welling up in her chest.

That was when Tessa Moretti swept into the office, a paper cup of coffee in each hand. Emily often joked that her paralegal was part machine - she always managed to appear exactly when Emily needed her most. Tessa wore her usual business-casual ensemble: black slacks, a crisp white blouse, and low-heeled pumps that allowed her to dart around the office with ease. A bright, canary-yellow scarf provided a stylish accent, one of Tessa's small ways of pushing back against an otherwise drab legal environment.

"Morning, boss," Tessa said, setting the coffees on Emily's desk. "I grabbed these on my way in. Hazelnut latte for you. I made sure they got your name right this time."

Emily gave her a grateful smile, fingertips already curling around the warm cardboard cup. "You're a lifesaver, Tessa. I was starting to run on fumes here."

"Yeah, I noticed. You were in before me again, which is scary. I prefer to creep in, tidy things up, and pretend I've been here all night." Tessa eyed the open documents on Emily's screen. "More on GenTech?"

Emily nodded. "It's…too much. I'm looking at everything from old rumor posts on conspiracy sites to local African or South American newspaper articles. They all point to disastrous drug trials. Fatalities, hush money, hidden data. But the pieces are scattered - there's no single smoking gun. Alan Priest's documents may be crucial, but I still don't know if they're enough."

"I guess that's the million-dollar question," Tessa murmured. "If he's right, and GenTech really has been conducting lethal drug trials, we have a major case on our hands. But if his evidence doesn't hold up in court...we've just handed them ammo to bury us in a defamation suit."

Emily took a sip of her coffee. The hazelnut aroma steadied her nerves. "I can't shake the feeling that there's truth in what Alan said. He doesn't strike me as a liar. More like a guy who's terrified, half in shock that he's even speaking to a lawyer about it."

"Same read I got from him," Tessa agreed, "when he was pacing in the waiting area. I mean, the man looked haunted. Somebody doesn't fake that level of fear easily."

Emily clicked on another search result - this one a PDF of a local newsletter from a remote region of Peru. She skimmed the snippet, which described a 'medical expedition' that had left three families in mourning and two more waiting for autopsy results. "The alleged drug company isn't named, but the timeline fits with GenTech's expansions. They've been pushing for new markets, chasing faster regulatory approvals overseas."

Tessa leaned over Emily's shoulder to read along. "I can see how they might take advantage of countries with looser medical oversight. Maybe they thought no one would notice or care if things went wrong." She made a face. "It's disgusting."

Emily's jaw tightened. "Still, a feeling or some obscure foreign articles won't win a case in a U.S. court. We need to find a direct link to GenTech. The only reason we're focusing on them now is because Alan says those fatal trials were managed through an internal division that specialized in 'experimental testing protocols.' But if we can't validate it with real data…"

"Which means we need to keep digging," Tessa said firmly. "We might also consider calling in some of your old contacts. Could we ask someone from the FDA or the CDC to shed light on how these overseas trials are typically reported - or hidden?"

The mention of her old contacts reminded Emily of her strained relationship with Hastings & Cole, the powerful law firm she'd left a few months back. She had once been close with a few attorneys in the pharmaceutical litigation department there. Mark Hastings, for instance, had walked her through the basics of medical malpractice suits when she first started. Now, though, Emily wasn't sure if any of them would be willing to help, or if it would even be safe to reach out. She suspected Mark might already be representing GenTech or at least be on the short list to do so. It was a known secret that Hastings & Cole had a stable of big pharma clients.

She closed the PDF with a sigh. "I'll see what I can do, but we're a small practice now, Tessa. We can't exactly pick up the phone and get insider info like I used to. Even if we find someone who's sympathetic, they might not want to risk crossing GenTech."

Tessa's expression turned sympathetic. "I know it's tough. But you didn't walk away from Hastings & Cole because it was easy. You left because you wanted to do something more meaningful than helping big corporations dodge accountability. This is exactly the kind of fight you wanted."

Emily took a moment to breathe. She thought about the day she walked out of Hastings & Cole for the last time. The plush carpets, the glass-walled offices, the lingering smell of expensive coffee and polished ambition. She'd liked the sense of purpose and security it gave her - yet she couldn't stand the ethical concessions she was forced to make. She had done well there, no question, but at some point, she realized the cost to her conscience was too high. Now, standing on her own was liberating but terrifying. Financially precarious, legally complicated, but also somehow more real. And the chance to help underdogs like Alan Priest? That was the spark that had always kept her going.

She forced a determined smile. "Okay, let's do this systematically. I want to cross-reference Alan's documents with whatever news items or local reports we can find. Let's put all the data onto a timeline. See if we can align it with GenTech's known expansions. Maybe we'll spot inconsistencies or hidden overlaps."

Tessa grinned. "Finally, I get to use those color-coded spreadsheets you love so much."

"You mock my spreadsheets, but they're about to become your best friend," Emily shot back playfully.

"Wouldn't dream of mocking them," Tessa said with a laugh. "Let me power up my computer and start pulling the relevant quotes, articles, and anything else I can dig up."

They shared a quick exchange of smiles, a warm recognition of each other's strengths. Tessa stepped out, leaving Emily alone with her thoughts. Emily finished her coffee and glanced at the slim manila folder on her desk labeled "AP - Confidential." Inside were the documents Alan had provided. Most were emails and internal memos, each referencing a drug identified only by a code name. The language was technical. Emily was no scientist, but she recognized the talk of "adverse events" and "possible lethal side effects." One email chain in particular suggested that top executives were aware that these trials had bypassed certain "regulatory best practices," though how and when they did this was still unclear.

Her phone buzzed. The caller ID read "Unknown." Her heartbeat spiked. She'd been getting too many of these lately - hang-ups, dead air, or cryptic messages from blocked numbers. She took a breath and picked up. "Emily Blackwood."

She heard static at first, then the tense voice of Alan Priest. "Emily…is this a bad time?"

Relief mingled with concern. "Alan. It's okay. What's going on?"

"Are you alone? I just… I need to talk." His voice was urgent, barely above a whisper.

"I'm in my private office, yes."

"Look, I'm having second thoughts. I mean, I don't want to back out completely - but I'm scared." The words tumbled out, raw. "I got an anonymous text last night, telling me to 'think carefully about my next move.' It threatened my mother's address. They know where she lives."

Emily's stomach clenched. She tried to modulate her voice, keep it calm. "Have you considered calling the police, Alan?"

"No. Police here won't do anything without proof, and I'm not even sure they can be trusted. If GenTech has the connections I think they do, this could get complicated fast."

Emily understood. "Okay. We need to proceed carefully. I'm in the process of verifying the evidence you gave me. I'll let you know if we find anything that strengthens our position. Just…sit tight. Don't do anything rash."

Silence stretched on the other end, filled with static. Finally, Alan exhaled. "I appreciate it. But the more I think about it, the more I realize I'm the only one who can confirm these documents in court. Without me, you basically have nothing."

"I won't lie. Your testimony is crucial." She paused, lowering her voice. "But your safety is more important. If this escalates, I want you to consider relocating temporarily. We'll figure out the details - maybe find a safe spot, or I can coordinate with a protective service. Let me talk to some people."

Alan let out a shaky breath. "I never thought I'd get mixed up in something like this. I just... I stumbled onto those emails. I always told myself I was a cog in the machine, that I could just go along for the ride. But I can't live with what I've seen, Emily. Those people -"

She closed her eyes, imagining what it must be like for him, an employee or contractor suddenly faced with the choice of condemning a corporate titan or saving his own skin. "It's going to be okay, Alan. Just please be cautious. Don't walk into any traps. And call me if anything else happens."

"Thank you," he whispered. "I'll keep you posted."

Martyn Bellamy

The call ended. Emily stared at her phone, unsettled. The intimidation was already starting. A swirl of worry threatened to derail her, but she forced herself to remain composed. If she was truly going to fight GenTech, she had to be prepared for this level of pushback.

She was still gripping the phone when Tessa returned, a stack of printouts tucked under her arm. "Hey, I just found some leads in Portuguese. My Spanish isn't half bad, but Portuguese might as well be ancient Greek. I'm trying to see if Google Translate can handle it."

"Alan just called," Emily said quietly, setting her phone aside. "He's being threatened. People are targeting his mother."

Tessa's face paled. "That's serious."

"It is," Emily replied. "And it means we're definitely onto something. The question is, how big do we want this fight to become? Because if I file a civil suit, or even a petition for an investigation, GenTech will come at us with everything they've got."

Tessa walked around the desk and placed a reassuring hand on Emily's shoulder. "We can't pretend we didn't see the evidence, Emily. You always said you wanted to use the law to protect the vulnerable. If these victims are real - and I'm pretty sure they are - this is one of those times when we have to stand up. The only question is how we do it without getting flattened."

Emily looked up at her paralegal. "We do it together." She smiled, a glimmer of determination back in her eyes. "Let's get to work."

The office buzzed with subdued intensity. Computers hummed, and the fluorescent lights overhead created a faint flicker that sometimes made Tessa's head ache. Legal pads filled with scribbled notes were piled on every flat surface, organized in Tessa's careful script. Emily had begun to assemble a timeline of key events, pinning them onto a corkboard in the corner. It gave the cramped office an air of a detective's lair: news clippings, lines of yarn, and sticky notes forming a messy tapestry of corporate secrecy.

Emily pinned another note on the board. "Early 2020: GenTech obtains fast-track approval for an experimental antiviral drug. The same quarter, unidentified clinical trials in Mozambique see a spike in adverse reactions." She pressed the pin in place, stepping back to observe the bigger picture.

Tessa scanned a new article. "Then, around mid-2021, a local radio station in Zimbabwe reported sudden unexplained deaths linked to a foreign medical team. They never named a specific company, just said it was an American pharma group. But guess which company launched an African outreach program in that same region that year? GenTech's philanthropic wing."

Emily shook her head. "Philanthropy can be a great cover for clandestine trials, especially in places where infrastructure and oversight are minimal. They swoop in, promise medical aid, and local officials are often too overwhelmed or too happy to get free help to question the details."

Tessa typed rapidly, adding this data to the spreadsheet. "I'm noticing a pattern, though. GenTech's press releases always talk about a new wonder drug that's 'close to final testing,' but never mention the specifics. They throw around terms like 'lifesaving potential' and 'cutting-edge breakthroughs.' Yet no mention of actual peer-reviewed clinical trial results."

Emily nodded grimly. "Exactly. And if the trials never officially happened, they can bury the negative outcomes. Meanwhile, they can tweak the data they do present to regulators. But if Alan's emails match these timelines, we can start forming the skeleton of a case for negligence or even wrongful death - provided any families are willing to testify."

Tessa's eyes gleamed with a mix of excitement and apprehension. "That's going to be a challenge. We might need interpreters, foreign affidavits, maybe depositions taken via video conference. Logistically, that's expensive. And that's before we get into local laws about confidentiality and patient data."

"Financially, it's a nightmare," Emily agreed, stepping aside as Tessa pinned up another article. "We'll need to bring in experts who can translate not just the language, but the local medical and legal contexts. And we have no big firm behind us now. It's just us and a handful of pro bono connections I can beg for help. And you know GenTech will try to lock us out with every procedural barrier imaginable."

Tessa's lips thinned in determination. "We'll find a way. We can start contacting international human rights lawyers, or maybe a few non-profits that monitor medical ethics. Some of them might jump at the chance to expose something this horrifying. If we build a coalition, we might stand a chance."

Emily's phone buzzed again, but this time the ID showed a familiar number: **Elaine from Redwood Bank**. Emily swallowed. Redwood Bank held her business loan. With rent, utilities, and living costs, finances were already stretched thin. She'd postponed that call twice this week, but she couldn't avoid it forever. She picked up.

"Good afternoon, Ms. Blackwood," came Elaine's professional but clipped voice. "I'm calling about the payment extension you requested. We need to discuss next steps."

Emily forced a polite tone. "Yes, of course. Thank you for calling back. I just need a little more time. My practice is in transition, and we have a few new clients that should bring in income soon. We had one major settlement that took longer than expected to finalize."

Elaine was diplomatic but firm. "I understand. However, the bank's policy only allows a short grace period. We'll expect an updated payment schedule by the end of the month. If that doesn't materialize, we may have to explore other options."

Behind Emily, Tessa's eyes flicked in concern as she overheard bits of the conversation. Emily rubbed her temple. "I'll do my best to have that schedule to you next week."

Hanging up, Emily slumped in her chair. Tessa gave her a sympathetic look. "Everything okay?"

"Just the bank reminding me that time and money are not on my side. Standard stuff for a scrappy new law office, but it still gets to me. If we dive headfirst into this GenTech case, we're committing ourselves to a massive, expensive battle. I don't know if we can finance it."

Tessa perched on the edge of Emily's desk, crossing her arms. "You always said you wanted to do the right thing, not just the profitable thing. This case might define your practice's reputation for years. If we play it safe, maybe we'll keep our heads above water. But is that what you left Hastings & Cole for?"

Emily tapped a pen against the desk in agitation, staring at the swirl of coffee dregs in her cup. She felt the old push-pull in her chest again: financial security versus moral responsibility. Tessa was right; part of her had always wanted to stand up to corporations like

GenTech. But would that desire be enough when everything else was stacked against them?

"I'm going to talk to Alan again," she said, rising from her chair. "We need more clarity about his documents. If we can confirm even one link to these rumored fatalities, that might be enough for a preliminary complaint - maybe even a motion for an injunction to stop further trials. Then we could force discovery, and if that happens, we might get the real smoking gun."

Tessa nodded. "I'll keep digging on my end. Also, there's a local freelance translator who might help us with Portuguese documents pro bono if we frame it as a human rights issue."

Emily placed a hand gently on Tessa's shoulder. "You're amazing. Thank you."

Tessa shrugged. "We're in this together."

By early afternoon, the second-floor suite felt stuffy. Emily cracked open a small window, letting in a cool breeze that ruffled the pinned articles and maps. She stared at the board for a moment, letting her eyes trace the lines of cause and effect they'd slowly pieced together. It was horrifying. People in remote places had trusted a powerful company to bring new medical treatments, only to be subjected to dangerous experiments.

A pang of rage made her fists clench. She wasn't naive - she knew that corporate corners were often cut in the pharmaceutical world. But seeing it mapped out like this was different. This was more than a few oversights; it was a systemic pattern of exploitation.

She was pulled out of her thoughts when Tessa coughed politely behind her. "I think you should see this." Tessa handed Emily a freshly printed page. It was an internal memo from GenTech that Alan had emailed over a few days prior. Emily had skimmed it before, but Tessa had highlighted a certain passage:

In light of recent feedback and local complications, we'll consider moving Phase III trials to less regulated environments. Executives remain adamant that the project timeline must not be delayed by additional oversight processes.

Next to it was a footnote referencing a corporate liaison in Peru. Emily had missed that detail before.

She read it slowly, her pulse quickening. "This footnote references a 'Project Redwood.' That's the same code name that appears in two of Alan's other documents. So if we connect the timeline, it looks like GenTech systematically used 'Project Redwood' to bypass regulatory oversight by shifting trials to places with minimal enforcement."

Tessa tapped the page. "Yeah, and look here - a mention of 'data reporting to remain internal until further notice.' That suggests they never filed official results anywhere. So the participants' side effects wouldn't show up in any publicly accessible trial database."

Emily felt a grim satisfaction. "This is exactly the kind of evidence that could start to build a legal argument. We can claim they knowingly conducted trials outside standard regulatory frameworks, leading to unreported adverse outcomes. Even if we can't directly prove each fatality, this is a powerful inference that they were hiding something serious."

Tessa exhaled. "Alan really did us a favor. But so far, these are just memos. GenTech can claim they're out of context or that 'Project Redwood' never moved forward. We'll need witness testimony confirming these trials occurred, and that they were lethal."

"I know," Emily said, turning back to the board. "But it's a start."

She placed the memo in a plastic sleeve and pinned it near the timeline, connecting it to news clippings from Peru. A sense of cautious optimism stirred within her. If they could keep building the chain of evidence, maybe they could force GenTech into a position where they'd have to settle - or at least come to the table and negotiate. And if a settlement wasn't enough, if families wanted a full trial to expose the truth, Emily would do her best to deliver that. It was a heavy burden for such a small practice, but she felt the moral weight pressing her forward.

The office door creaked open. Emily looked up from her desk to see a tall woman with neatly braided hair and a serious expression. She wore a burgundy blazer over a white blouse, her posture upright and confident. Emily recognized her from the byline of several medical investigative pieces: **Prisha Shah**, a freelance journalist who'd reached out via email that morning.

"I hope it's okay I dropped by," Prisha said, scanning the cluttered office. "I emailed Tessa, and she said I could stop in if I was in the neighborhood."

Tessa popped her head out from the tiny kitchenette. "Prisha? Oh, wow, you got here fast. Come on in."

Emily rose, extending a hand. "Prisha Shah. I've read some of your articles on unregulated drug imports. They were impressive."

"Thank you," Prisha said. She looked around, taking in the timeline and pinned articles. "I see you're investigating GenTech. Word travels fast among us freelance journalists, especially when we hear rumors about a whistleblower. I wanted to see if there's any truth to it."

Emily and Tessa exchanged a quick glance. Finally, Emily nodded. "Yes, we have a potential whistleblower, and we're building a case. But that's all I can say until we verify the documents and consider legal action."

Prisha stepped closer to the board. Her eyes flicked from one pinned article to another. "This is more than rumor. You have actual data, don't you? Something GenTech would want to hide."

Emily felt a pang of caution. Journalists could be allies, but they could also complicate matters. "We do, but it's incomplete. We need more."

Prisha chewed her lip. "I might be able to help. I've spent time in Mozambique and Peru investigating questionable clinical trials. Most publications back away from the story - it's hard to prove. But if you have internal memos or emails, that could finally crack it wide open. We could blow this story up, create public pressure, and force GenTech to answer."

Tessa raised a brow. "And what's in it for you, if you don't mind me asking?"

Prisha shrugged. "I'm a journalist. Exposing corporate wrongdoing is my job. If there's evidence of human rights violations, I'm ethically obligated to bring it to light. Beyond that, yes, it's a major story that could help my career. But I'm not here to sensationalize. I want facts, and I want the truth out. We might be able to help each other."

Emily exchanged a look with Tessa, who gave a slight nod of encouragement. "All right," Emily said softly. "Let's consider a collaboration. But we have to protect our whistleblower. If we involve the press prematurely, it could scare him or others off. Or worse, it could put them in danger."

Prisha looked earnest. "Understood. We can keep him anonymous for now. I can sign an NDA if you need me to, though journalists don't typically do that. At least I can promise in good faith not to publish anything before you decide the timing is right - provided you let me break the story once you file the suit."

Emily weighed the risks. A well-timed press exposé could rally public opinion, maybe force GenTech to consider a settlement or at least be more transparent. But if it leaked too soon, GenTech might clamp down, intimidate witnesses, or manipulate the narrative in their favor. Still, having a journalist with experience in these regions could be invaluable. She made a mental note to consult with a colleague about the potential pitfalls. For now, she offered Prisha a seat.

"Tell me everything you know about these foreign trials. The off-the-record stuff."

By early evening, the three women had formed a small war room, exchanging leads and verifying facts. Prisha revealed that she had contacts in rural clinics around Africa and South America, places Western media rarely visited. She believed that GenTech had strategically partnered with local officials who lacked resources to scrutinize the trials properly, or who had been incentivized to look the other way.

Tessa made a frantic list of these contacts, star-rating them by reliability based on Prisha's personal experience. Emily found herself impressed by the reporter's thoroughness. This was exactly the kind of grass-roots information that could bolster a lawsuit's credibility.

As they wrapped up, Prisha leaned against the edge of Emily's desk. "I have an old friend who's a translator for the United Nations. She might help with some of these documents if it means saving lives or exposing wrongdoing. Let me reach out to her."

"That would be wonderful," Tessa said. "We've been relying on Google Translate for half these articles. Some local dialects or bureaucratic terms might not be captured accurately."

Prisha nodded, then shifted her posture. "Just remember, I can't hold off my editor forever if I find something groundbreaking. I'm not looking to sabotage your case, but we'll need to coordinate timelines eventually. A big story can apply pressure, but it can also hamper your legal strategy if it goes public too soon."

Emily exhaled. "I appreciate the candor. And you're right - it's a tightrope. Let's keep the lines of communication open. For now, I'll show you a few of the less sensitive documents so you can start verifying. But nothing identifying Alan Priest or any other whistleblower."

Prisha agreed, packing up her laptop. "Fair enough. I'll be in touch soon. Good luck, Emily. And thank you for letting me in."

After she left, Tessa sank into her chair with a tired grin. "I think we just got ourselves an ally. Maybe we can actually do this."

Emily grabbed her jacket from the back of her chair, noticing how late it had become. Outside, the sky had turned a dusky purple. "We need allies. Even with them, this is going to be an uphill battle. But if we can tie the overseas deaths to actual GenTech decisions, we have a chance to at least get them into court. And if we do that, maybe we can save lives."

Tessa smiled wearily. "So, are you officially taking the case?"

Emily paused. "I still need to talk to Alan in person, make sure he's fully on board. But yes, I think so. My conscience won't let me walk away from this. Not after everything we've seen."

They shared a knowing look. For the first time in weeks, Emily felt a sense of purpose that rose above her financial fears. This was why she'd left the safety of a prestigious firm - to stand up for people with no voice, to challenge the machines of corporate power when they overstepped. She just hoped she could survive the fight.

Later that night, with Tessa gone and the office quiet, Emily found herself alone at her desk. The overhead lights buzzed faintly. She rubbed her temples, willing away the tension headache that had built up over the day. A single small lamp illuminated the manila folder Alan had given her - pages of cryptic emails, organograms, trial sites, and budget proposals labeled with code names.

She reached for her phone, intending to text Alan and schedule a meeting, but hesitated. Maybe it was better to let him have a night of relative calm. She could see from his shaky phone call earlier that he was nearing a breaking point. Instead, she grabbed a legal pad and wrote down the big questions swirling in her mind:

1. **Jurisdiction**: How to file a suit for overseas harm in a U.S. court?

2. **Standing**: Which specific victims or families could we represent?

3. **Financial Logistics**: Where to find resources for translations, expert witnesses, and potential travel?

4. **Alan Priest's Role**: Is his testimony strong enough? Will he hold up under pressure?

The list took up two full pages. Emily's shoulders slumped at the enormity of it all. She'd built a reputation as a meticulous, ethically driven lawyer at Hastings & Cole, but she no longer had their resources or brand name. Now she had Tessa, an office the size of a large closet, and a mounting pile of bills that Redwood Bank wouldn't let her ignore. Yet for all her anxieties, a little voice inside urged her onward: *This is the case you were meant to take. Don't back down.*

She stood and walked to the window. Below, streetlights dotted the avenue, and headlights of passing cars cut lines through the gloom. The night air was crisp, a harbinger of colder days to come. She could see her own reflection in the glass: tired eyes, determined jaw, a single strand of dark hair escaping her usually neat bun. This was not the face of someone who would give up easily. She thought about the lives potentially lost or destroyed because GenTech found a way to sidestep accountability. If she could stop them - if she could force them into the light - maybe she could make a difference that mattered.

A surge of resolve coursed through her. She turned back to her desk, flicking off the overhead light. Pulling on her coat, she grabbed her keys and phone, then shut the door behind her. It was time to go home, get a few hours of sleep, and come back tomorrow ready for another day of digging. The fight against GenTech was only beginning, but Emily had found her purpose again.

And though she was just a small solo practitioner with a devoted paralegal, she was determined to stand up for truth - even if it meant risking everything she had.

Morning light spilled through the office windows as Emily arrived at dawn, coffee in hand. She'd hardly slept, replaying scenarios in her mind - possible legal arguments, ways to protect Alan, how to handle the press. As she unlocked the door and flicked on the lights, she noticed Tessa's desk was already stacked with new files. Tessa must have come in even earlier than she had.

"Morning," Tessa called from behind a precarious tower of printed documents. "I decided to get a head start. A friend of mine from college is now working at a small NGO that investigates unethical medical practices. She sent me more stuff: case studies, NGO reports, testimony from survivors in Brazil. Some of it might help us link GenTech to the same pattern of abuse there."

Emily took off her coat and joined Tessa, scanning the top sheet of paper. "This is perfect. The more dots we connect, the harder it'll be for GenTech to dismiss this as a few isolated incidents."

She set her coffee down, leaning against the desk. Her eyes were bright with conviction. "I made up my mind last night. I'm going to take the lawsuit. We'll file an initial complaint on behalf of 'John Doe' - Alan's pseudonym - alleging corporate misconduct leading to wrongful death overseas. We might need to refine the details once we have more direct contact with victims, but that'll get the ball rolling. Then I'll push for expedited discovery, hoping we can get a protective order in place for Alan."

Tessa broke into a grin. "You sure? This is going to be a war."

"I'm sure," Emily said, a quiet strength in her voice. "I didn't leave Hastings & Cole just to settle parking disputes and minor claims. This is the real deal - an actual chance to do something that matters. I can't let it slip by."

Tessa opened one of the newly arrived case study documents. "Good. Because I already started drafting a complaint template. We can adjust it as new facts roll in. The NGO data might help us narrow down the specific allegations - like where and when the trials happened, who authorized them, and which international or U.S. laws might apply."

Emily felt a surge of affection for Tessa. They had worked together for years, but this was the first time they were standing on the edge of a case so monumental. "Let's finalize a preliminary complaint by the end of the week. I'll coordinate with a couple of local attorneys who might be willing to consult, just to make sure we're not missing any critical angles. Then we find a way to protect Alan and line up additional whistleblowers if possible."

Tessa nodded. "I'll also keep searching for experts who can testify about international clinical trial standards. Maybe we can get an epidemiologist or a medical ethicist to back up our arguments."

Emily reached for the folder labeled "GenTech - Project Redwood." She opened it, flipping through the pages. Every line of text felt like a new step on a treacherous journey. But she found herself strangely calm, the decision made. "We're taking them on," she repeated, as if reminding herself. "We're going to fight for those people who never had a voice."

And with that, they both settled into a long day of drafting, coordinating, and preparing. Emily juggled calls to colleagues, wrote potential arguments, and mulled over the best way to break the news to Alan. Tessa created a bulletproof system for storing and categorizing every scrap of evidence. Their tiny office in an old downtown building had never felt so alive - nor so precariously balanced between triumph and disaster.

By late afternoon, day four of Emily's nascent legal career was drawing to a close, but not without leaving its mark. The boards were now filled to capacity, every inch of cork crowded with printouts, sticky notes, and colored yarn. Emily's desk sported multiple drafts of the initial complaint, each with scribbled notes in the margins. Tessa juggled phone calls from curious reporters, cryptic tipsters, and an NGO liaison who offered guarded support in the event of a full-scale lawsuit.

"Emily," Tessa called from across the room, "I think we've got enough to at least frame a coherent complaint. It's not bulletproof, but it's a start."

Emily looked up from her laptop, where she was typing a quick email to Alan. "Great. Let me see it. We'll refine the language, especially around the wrongful death allegations. We'll want to keep it flexible so we can amend once we have actual family plaintiffs from overseas."

"Absolutely." Tessa set the printed draft on Emily's desk. "I'll keep reaching out to potential medical experts. I heard from one at a teaching hospital who studied unregulated trials in East Africa. She might be willing to talk off the record."

Emily nodded, picking up a pen to mark corrections. "Send me her info. Also, can you schedule a meeting with Alan for tomorrow evening? We need to lay out the plan and see if he's willing to stand as a plaintiff or key witness."

Tessa gave a thumbs-up. "On it."

For a moment, neither spoke. The hum of the computer and the rustle of papers filled the space. Emily glanced around, taking in the controlled chaos that was now her life. She thought of the large, immaculate offices at Hastings & Cole, the heavy glass doors, the plush conference rooms. She had none of that here - just a paralegal, a cramped suite, and a dream of doing the right thing. But it felt right. It felt real.

With the final lines yet unwritten, Emily felt a surge of anticipation. She didn't know where this case would lead her - possibly to court, possibly to settlement, possibly to ruin if GenTech fought back with all its might. But as she glanced at Tessa, saw the unwavering determination in her eyes, Emily knew she wouldn't face the battle alone.

She skimmed the complaint one last time, reading the paragraphs that would soon place her in direct opposition to one of the largest pharmaceutical companies in the world. *"This is it,"* she thought, heart pounding. *"The moment I become the kind of lawyer I've always wanted to be."*

She set the draft aside and met Tessa's gaze. "Let's finalize it. Tomorrow, we become GenTech's biggest problem."

Tessa grinned in agreement. And so they pressed forward, prepared to lift the veil on one of the darkest secrets the pharmaceutical world had tried to hide - unaware that this was only the beginning of a battle that would test their courage, their morals, and their very safety in the weeks and months to come.

Chapter 5:
Mark Hastings Returns

The fluorescent ceiling lights in Emily Blackwood's modest office hummed quietly, a constant reminder of how far she'd come - and how far she might yet have to fall. She lifted her gaze from the stack of case file papers spread across her desk. As the only attorney at Blackwood & Associates, she had no buffer from the sharp edges of her new reality. Her name might have been on the door, but it was her nerves fueling every phone call and email.

She shifted in her creaky office chair. A faint pang of nostalgia for the plush swivel chair at Hastings & Cole, her former big-law perch, skimmed across her mind. She shook it off. She'd promised herself she wouldn't look backward, especially after everything that had transpired in her final months there. Yet old habits died hard - especially when the biggest sign of trouble looming on her horizon was tied directly to the firm she had fled.

Tessa Moretti, her paralegal and de facto office manager, appeared in the doorway. The late-morning sun cast a glow across Tessa's hair, making her look almost ethereal - though Emily knew well that her friend's vibe was less angelic and more razor-sharp.

"Just got off the phone with the court clerk," Tessa said. "They're scheduling next month's docket. Any chance we'll be filing the complaint against GenTech soon?"

Emily pressed her lips together, glancing at the partially open manila folder that contained Alan Priest's cryptic emails and research. Ever since the anxious whistleblower had darkened her doorway, everything else had fallen to the wayside. That GenTech might be involved in unethical trials - possibly leading to deaths - had yanked Emily's moral compass into overdrive. Financial concerns, while still pressing, had briefly receded in her mind.

Yet she had held back from filing. There was something too big, too dangerous about taking on this multinational corporation by herself. She wanted more time to evaluate the documents, to double-check the legal theory. More time to confirm or deny her fears about GenTech's potential for lethal retaliation. Even Tessa didn't know the depth of Emily's worries.

"Don't pencil anything in yet," Emily said, closing the folder. She tapped its cover absently. "I'm still assessing the best angle of attack."

Tessa gave a decisive nod. "I get it. But also, we're going to need an angle, period. Rent is due in two weeks." She placed a gentle hand on the doorframe. "Don't let me push you, but I'd rather see you move than freeze."

Emily managed a small, grateful smile. Tessa had a knack for telling brutal truths gently. "I appreciate it," she said softly. "One way or another, I'll figure it out."

She expected Tessa to leave, but her paralegal lingered. "Any word from - ?"

"Alan hasn't called," Emily replied preemptively, reading Tessa's question from her expression. "I think he's lying low. Not surprising if he's got GenTech's security team on his tail."

Tessa twisted her lips, as if to say, This is serious. Then she pivoted to the matter at hand. "You hungry? I'm stepping out for a quick bite."

"In a bit," Emily said, "but thanks. I want to review the notes on GenTech's African trial allegations."

Tessa nodded, then disappeared into the hallway.

Emily sank back into her chair, her gaze drifting to the half-empty shelves that lined the office walls. When she'd opened Blackwood & Associates, she had dreamed of eventually filling them with volumes of trial transcripts and treatises - tangible proof of her successful practice. Instead, the gaps reminded her how much she had yet to accomplish.

The phone rang, snapping her out of her thoughts. She eyed the display. The number wasn't familiar.

"Blackwood & Associates," she answered, smoothing her voice into professional calm.

"Emily?" The voice on the other end carried a surprising warmth, undercut by an edge she recognized from years of late-night strategy sessions. "It's Mark Hastings."

She nearly dropped the phone. Just the mention of his name was enough to make her heart jolt. Not only was Mark Hastings her former colleague at Hastings & Cole - he was also the one person she had, at times, thought might be an actual friend in that cutthroat environment.

She cleared her throat, her brain scrambling to figure out why he was calling.

"Mark," she said, layering her voice with cool civility. "Didn't expect to hear from you."

He let out a short laugh. "I think that's an understatement. It's been a while."

The unspoken subtext: it had been months since Emily walked away from the hushed hallways of Hastings & Cole, citing irreconcilable ethical concerns over one of the firm's cases. Mark had offered moral support initially, but then parted ways with her under tense circumstances.

"Is this a social call?" Emily asked. She couldn't imagine it was; Mark never really did anything without purpose.

"No," he admitted, dropping the polite veneer. "I'd like to talk about a matter that might soon land on my desk. I believe you might already have some…interest in it."

The line crackled slightly, but the tension between them seemed to fill the silence. Emily thought of Alan's documents, of the menacing puzzle of GenTech's rumored wrongdoing. She had a sickening hunch.

"GenTech?" she ventured.

He paused. "Yes."

Her pulse quickened. So Hastings & Cole might represent GenTech. It was exactly the scenario she had dreaded - battling her old firm in an arena where they held every advantage. She forced her voice to stay steady.

"I'm listening," she said finally.

"Do you have time to meet?" he asked. "I'm free this afternoon. We could grab coffee or lunch. On me."

She weighed the proposition. If she refused, Mark might interpret it as fear. Yet if she agreed, she risked inadvertently revealing too much. In the end, curiosity and a hint of strategic caution won out.

"All right," she said. "There's a café near my office - the Flatiron Bean. Two o'clock?"

"Perfect. Text me the address," Mark replied.

They said their polite goodbyes, and Emily hung up. Blood pounded in her ears as she tried to parse his tone. He hadn't threatened her, but he hadn't needed to. Merely showing up was enough to send a message:

Hastings & Cole was circling around GenTech, and thus around her as well.

Emily barely tasted the sandwich Tessa had left for her on the desk. By one-thirty, she felt more anxious than she cared to admit. As she stood, smoothing wrinkles out of her blazer, she caught a glimpse of herself in the small mirror she kept inside a filing cabinet drawer. Sharp brown eyes, a tight line to her mouth. She'd lost a few pounds over the last few months - stress had a way of killing her appetite. A part of her missed the polished, confident persona she'd worn like armor at Hastings & Cole. She had always worn designer suits, courtesy of her inflated big-law salary. Now she was in a sale-rack blazer that couldn't hide the strain in her posture.

Still, she reminded herself, she'd chosen her new life for a reason. To do the right thing.

She locked up her office - Tessa was still out - and walked a few blocks to the café. The city bustled around her, horns blaring, pedestrians jostling. It was a far cry from the sterile hush of the old firm's high-rise building, but she found the chaos strangely comforting.

Inside the café, she spotted Mark immediately. He stood near the counter, clad in a suit that practically screamed custom tailoring, the lines so crisp they might have been cut by a laser. He still had the wiry build of someone who spent too many hours behind a desk but who maintained an air of athletic readiness. His sandy-brown hair was carefully trimmed, and there was an incisive glint behind his frameless glasses.

The moment he saw her, a faint flicker of emotion - she couldn't quite decipher it - crossed his face. They exchanged stiff pleasantries, then Mark paid for their coffees without asking her preference. Typical, she thought, trying not to bristle at the presumption.

They chose a small table near the window. Emily pressed her palms onto the cool surface of the tabletop, inhaling the rich aroma of espresso.

Mark jumped right in. "I heard a rumor that you met with Alan Priest."

Her pulse leapt. GenTech's people must have ears everywhere. "He came by my office unannounced," she said, voice measured. "I'm not sure I should discuss potential clients."

Mark sipped his coffee and studied her. "Potential. So you haven't officially taken him on?"

"Why?" Emily asked, skirting the question. "Is Hastings & Cole thinking about stepping in for GenTech?"

A subtle twitch of his jaw told her he was treading carefully. "We've had some calls. The higher-ups are deciding whether the case - if it even turns into one - is large enough to require outside counsel. It might."

Her mind whirled. GenTech was massive, with in-house legal staff. If Hastings & Cole was being contacted, that meant GenTech expected a major war - class actions, government inquiries, the kind of litigation that can topple a pharmaceutical empire or, ironically, help them stonewall critics for years.

"What's your involvement?" she pressed.

Mark ran a finger around the rim of his coffee cup, a gesture she recalled from nights spent hashing out briefs in the firm's deserted conference rooms. "I've been placed on a short list to handle the matter. I suspect my experience in corporate defense is the reason. Among other things."

Among other things. She heard the unsaid remainder: Emily's abrupt departure months ago might also factor in. Hastings & Cole's senior partners could be calculating how best to neutralize or intimidate their former rising star.

She crossed her arms. "So you wanted to give me a friendly warning?"

He exhaled. "Emily, I don't want to see you get buried here. GenTech is enormous. If you're…dabbling in this alone, you could do real damage to your practice. And maybe to your personal well-being."

The words made her stiffen, and not just because they carried the faint whiff of a threat. She couldn't tell if Mark was genuinely concerned or simply playing the role assigned to him by the firm.

"There's a human dimension to this," she countered. "Alan Priest claims GenTech knowingly put lives at risk. That they tested experimental drugs on vulnerable populations in Africa and South America. If that's true, and we can prove it - "

Mark shook his head. "He's not the first disgruntled ex-employee to spout conspiracy theories. Besides, these aren't the sort of allegations you can handle easily. You'd need a small army of attorneys, experts, investigators. Even if you filed, you'd be hammered with motions to dismiss, countersuits, an avalanche of discovery. It would be never-ending."

She swallowed. He was stating the obvious: the might of a global pharma corporation could shred her finances and stamina if it wanted to. "Then I guess I'd better do my homework."

He looked at her intently. "I'm telling you this for your own good. I know you left Hastings & Cole because of an ethical line you refused to cross. I respected that. But that was still small potatoes compared to this. If GenTech hires us, we're going to defend them aggressively. They won't pull punches. Nobody in that seat will."

"Is that a threat?" she said, her voice dangerously low.

Mark glanced out the window, perhaps registering that passersby were moving too close for comfort. He leaned in, dropping his voice. "It's a fact. You and I both know how the big firms operate. You throw resources at every angle until the other side collapses or agrees to settle on your terms."

Martyn Bellamy

Her stomach twisted in knots. She wanted to snap back, to accuse him of betraying the ideals they used to talk about in law school - the naive illusions that the legal profession was about truth and justice. She wanted to remind him how he once told her that her unwavering moral streak was exactly what the field needed. But she also recalled how that conversation ended - he had toed the line at Hastings & Cole, taking the path of least resistance for the sake of his career.

"Then why are you telling me all this?" she asked, keeping her tone even.

He set his coffee down. "I'm giving you a chance to walk away. If you do, no one will blame you. This case is bigger than some solo practitioner's crusade. You can find a safer fight."

Fury prickled the back of her neck. "If Alan Priest is telling the truth about GenTech, then it's not just a 'fight' - it's a moral imperative. I'm not some ambulance chaser. I don't pick clients based on who pays best. I care about what's right."

Mark's eyes flickered with…admiration? Regret? Maybe both. It was gone in a second. "I figured you'd say that." He cleared his throat. "Listen, the official conflict check at the firm hasn't fully run yet. I'm sure it will come through soon. When it does, the partners will finalize who's assigned. If it's me, you and I will be on opposite sides of the 'v.' in a high-stakes lawsuit."

"You sound almost resigned," she said, narrowing her eyes.

He lifted one shoulder. "Big-law life isn't always about personal choice. I took the path I did. You took yours. Neither one is free from consequences."

She studied his face. He looked older, tenser than the Mark she remembered, though it had only been months. The man who once teased her for micromanaging a motion's formatting now wore the haunted expression of someone who felt a pang of guilt - but not enough to deviate from his career track.

"You didn't come here just to warn me," she said, a note of accusation creeping in.

His jaw tightened. "No. I came because I…owed you. For old times' sake, I wanted to make it clear that this is going to be huge. It might be unstoppable. Don't let it swallow you."

She exhaled through her nose, forcing herself to remain calm, though every instinct screamed that she was in the crosshairs now. "You're basically telling me to drop it?"

A shadow passed over his features. "I'm telling you to think carefully about the cost - to you, to anyone you care about. Once GenTech's legal department engages, they'll treat this like any other lethal threat to their business model. You cannot imagine the resources they'll pour into burying you."

Outside, the sun was too bright. Inside, the café felt stifling, as though she couldn't get enough air. Emily refused to break his gaze. "Thanks for the coffee," she said finally, pushing her cup away. "And your concern. But you should know something: I don't scare as easily as I used to."

A flicker of a sad smile touched his lips. "I believe you."

They stood, and the awkwardness in the narrow space made every movement more pronounced. Mark started to extend his hand, then seemed unsure, finally jamming it into his pocket instead.

"Take care, Emily," he said.

She nodded, her throat too tight to speak.

She left him there, feeling the weight of the moment chasing her out onto the sidewalk. She paused, inhaling the cool air, trying to calm her racing thoughts. The city's cacophony - delivery trucks, car horns - felt strangely distant.

Mark's warning reverberated in her mind: *They won't pull punches. You can't imagine the resources they'll pour into burying you.*

Yet the alternative - doing nothing - was equally horrifying. Alan Priest had risked his safety to bring her those documents, trusting her with evidence of something monstrous. If Emily backed down now, who else would take the case? Hastings & Cole certainly wouldn't. Other big firms would likely be too cozy with pharma money. Could she live with herself if she just ignored the potential catastrophe GenTech was unleashing on the most vulnerable populations on two continents?

Squaring her shoulders, she started back toward her office, ignoring the disquiet that fluttered inside her. If this was the path she had chosen, so be it. She had never run from a fight worth having.

By the time Emily arrived at her building, Tessa was already back, sorting through a messy stack of mail on the reception counter. She shot Emily a quizzical look. "You look like you've just seen a ghost."

Emily forced a wry smile. "Close. I saw Mark Hastings."

Tessa's eyebrows shot up. She dropped the envelopes in her hand. "Are you serious? He called you?"

"He wanted to meet," Emily explained, stepping behind the counter to pick up the scattered letters. As she did, she noticed a sealed envelope with Hastings & Cole's insignia in the corner. The irony was almost too much. "And apparently, they decided to send me something as well."

She slit open the envelope, Tessa leaning in curiously. Inside, a single sheet of high-quality letterhead read:

Dear Ms. Blackwood,
We would like to confirm that Hastings & Cole is currently undertaking a conflict-of-interest review in anticipation of representing GenTech Pharmaceutical in

forthcoming legal matters. If you have information related to these matters, please be advised that any prior associations or communications you may have had with our firm do not extend to representation on your behalf in this context. We recommend you consult your own counsel. This letter does not constitute a waiver of any rights or privileges, nor does it establish any legal relationship.

Sincerely,

Julia Bell,

Partner,

Hastings & Cole

"Charming," Tessa remarked, tapping her foot anxiously. "They're basically making it official: if you plan to sue GenTech, you'll be going toe-to-toe with your old firm."

Emily's hand clenched around the letter. "Mark gave me a verbal heads-up, but this is more formal - 'be advised we're taking the case, keep your distance.'"

Tessa pursed her lips. "So they're letting you know they're not messing around."

"Exactly." Emily slipped the letter back into its envelope, a swirl of emotions gripping her. "GenTech is big enough that it can bury us in motions. Hastings & Cole is infamous for its scorched-earth litigation tactics. I learned from the best, unfortunately."

Tessa shot her a sympathetic glance. "You going to be okay?"

Emily let out a low breath. "I'd be lying if I said I'm not intimidated. But we expected resistance, right?"

"True," Tessa said softly. She paused, then added, "So how did Mark seem? I mean, personally."

Emily rubbed her forehead, recalling the lines of tension around Mark's eyes. "He seemed…conflicted. But not enough to bail. He's chosen his side."

Tessa grunted. "It's not too late for you to step away, if you want."

Emily met her friend's concerned gaze. "I can't. You know that."

Tessa nodded, admiration shining through her worry. "Then we fight this, step by step." She turned back to the mail pile and snapped her fingers as if recalling something. "By the way, you got a voicemail earlier from a Dr. Marjorie Franklin. Said she might have some knowledge about GenTech's trial protocols, and she'd be interested in speaking with you. I left the message on your desk phone."

Emily's heart quickened. Another lead? Possibly an expert witness or a researcher. Maybe the pieces were slowly falling into place after all. "I'll return her call," she said, "right after I do a bit of background checking."

She grabbed her laptop and settled behind her desk, Tessa following close behind. The letter from Hastings & Cole sat in front of her, an unwelcome reminder that her next move would carry enormous consequences.

As she waited for her laptop to boot, Emily's mind drifted unwillingly to memories of her last day at Hastings & Cole. She recalled standing in the corner office assigned to her after her second promotion, clutching a cardboard box of personal items. The senior partner's voice still rang in her ears, telling her that her refusal to "play ball" on a morally dubious defense strategy had effectively cut her off from any future in the firm.

The sense of betrayal came back in a rush. She had given them her nights, weekends, even the best years of her social life. And in return, they dismissed her concerns about forging questionable evidence in a high-profile commercial litigation case. She couldn't stomach it. So she walked.

But Mark - Mark had remained behind. At first, he'd been quietly supportive, urging her not to burn any bridges. He'd even hinted that eventually, he might join her if she truly started her own shop. But that never happened. Once the senior partners realized she wasn't bluffing, the atmosphere shifted; Mark's name had disappeared from her phone's missed calls, and she'd heard almost nothing from him until today.

She bit her lip, trying to quell the swirl of conflicting emotions. Maybe he had found a comfortable niche in big-law, ignoring inconvenient ethics. She used to think more highly of him. Perhaps she still wanted to - but reality kept biting back.

"Got it," Tessa declared, holding her tablet. "Marjorie Franklin is a pharmacologist with a background in clinical trial oversight. She's done work in Latin America, apparently raising red flags about certain fast-track drug approvals."

Emily's eyes flicked with interest. "Sounds perfect to help me parse Alan Priest's documents. She might be able to confirm if the data in those files is doctored."

Tessa nodded. "Should I try to schedule a meeting?"

"Yes." Emily gave her a quick smile. "And let's see if we can confirm her credentials. If she's legitimate, she could be a crucial asset."

As Tessa walked off, Emily finally played back the voicemail from Dr. Franklin. The woman's voice was cautious but direct:

"Ms. Blackwood, I was given your name by a…mutual acquaintance who suggests you're looking into GenTech's overseas research practices. I have information that might be pertinent to your inquiry. My schedule is tight, but I'm willing to share what I can. Please call me back - discretion is key."

Emily replayed the message twice. *Mutual acquaintance?* Possibly that was Alan Priest, or maybe someone else who was aware she'd started investigating. The noose around GenTech's secrets seemed to be tightening, and if Dr. Franklin's intel panned out, Emily might have the foundation of a case strong enough to survive the first wave of attacks.

But Mark's warning echoed in her ears: *You can't imagine the resources they'll pour into burying you.* She felt a grim determination crystallize within her. She was no stranger to tough odds - she'd grown up in a working-class family, earned scholarships to college and law school, and had learned to stand her ground among the cutthroat ranks at Hastings & Cole. If the fight was truly for innocent lives, for people who had been exploited for medical experimentation, then that fight was hers to undertake.

Tessa popped her head in an hour later, her eyes dancing with curiosity. "So, is Mark's reappearance totally messing with your head?"

Emily let out a short laugh. "Define 'messing.' I'd be lying if I said this was a normal day at the office."

Her paralegal strolled in, perched on a corner of the desk. "I remember how you used to talk about him - like he was some legal genius who still had a soul. You once said he was the best part of Hastings & Cole."

Emily folded her arms. "Maybe I believed in him too much. People change."

"Or he's stuck. Which is another form of change," Tessa said gently. "Anyway, do you think he's giving you a genuine heads-up, or is he playing puppet for the partners?"

Emily shook her head. "It felt…both. He obviously wanted to warn me, but he also stayed loyal to the firm. He's in self-preservation mode."

Tessa fiddled with a pen. "That's what big-law does to people. It's easy to get lost in the illusions of success - and forget why you became a lawyer in the first place."

A pang of empathy for Mark threatened to undermine Emily's indignation. She pushed it down. "He made his choice. Now I've made mine."

Despite the tension in her chest, Emily forced herself to keep working that afternoon, combing through the files Alan Priest had provided. They detailed preliminary findings from GenTech's trials on a new antibiotic that, according to internal memos, was tested on volunteers in remote regions of Africa. The data, if accurate, showed dangerously high rates of adverse events - but the official, sanitized reports revealed only minor side effects.

She stared at the contradictory pages. Something in her sank. If even half of Alan's documents were legitimate, people had almost certainly died or suffered harm without receiving help. *They let them take the fall to speed up a drug pipeline?* She could barely wrap her mind around the callousness.

The deeper she dug, the more the lines between sorrow and outrage blurred. She paused only when Tessa nudged her, brandishing a takeout coffee cup. "You look like you might pass out," her paralegal said, setting the cup down. "Drink this."

Emily murmured thanks, realizing hours had slipped by without her noticing. Her eyes felt gritty from reading endless lines of text.

"You know," Tessa offered, "when we do decide to go public with all this, it's going to rock a lot of boats. Remember that 'Disappearing Witness' story I found about an ex-GenTech employee? It's not just rumor. People vanish or recant all the time when threatened by a corporate giant."

Emily nodded, exhaustion melding with an electric current of determination. "We have to be prepared. And that means bracing for Mark Hastings on the other side."

She swallowed hard, steeling herself. What Mark represented wasn't just an old friend turned adversary; he embodied the entire resource-heavy world she once inhabited and had turned her back on. He brought with him the unstoppable juggernaut that was Hastings & Cole.

Yet if she had learned anything from her time there, it was how the system worked - and how, if used carefully, the law could still protect the underdog. Even if that underdog was herself and a handful of vulnerable whistleblowers.

She took a deep sip of the coffee, feeling the warmth spread through her. "Tessa, let's keep forging ahead. If Mark thinks I'm going to crawl away with my tail between my legs, he's mistaken."

Her friend's face lit with a small but resolute smile. "That's the Emily I signed up to work with."

Late in the evening, the office lay in near silence. Tessa had left for the night. Emily remained, scanning through older emails she'd traded with Mark in the final months at Hastings & Cole - back when their rapport had been cordial, even collaborative. She hoped to glean any small clues as to how Mark might strategize if it came to a legal showdown.

She found one exchange particularly telling: Mark had advised her about a tricky witness in a securities fraud case. He'd hammered home the importance of discrediting the witness as thoroughly as possible before trial, even if it felt "like overkill." *Better to overprepare and never need it,* he had said, *than get blindsided in the courtroom.*

That was Mark in a nutshell: methodical, relentless, and surprisingly cunning when pressed. She scrolled further, finding the half-joking sign-off in which he'd teased her for losing her "rose-colored glasses."

Her phone buzzed, startling her. She expected it to be Tessa, but to her surprise, the screen showed a blocked number. She tensed, thinking of the strange calls she'd started receiving after Alan Priest's visit.

With a deep breath, she answered. "Emily Blackwood."

Static crackled, then a voice, so low she had to strain to hear: "Ms. Blackwood, sorry for the late call."

She recognized it: Alan Priest. He sounded terrified.

"Alan?" she prompted gently.

"Yes. I - I heard GenTech might be hiring a new law firm. I can't talk long."

Her heart thumped. "I don't know the specifics yet, but it's possible."

A shaky exhale. "Listen carefully. You need to watch yourself. I've been followed."

Emily's spine tingled with dread. "By whom?"

"I think it's GenTech's private security. They're sending a message - nobody is untouchable."

Her grip tightened on the phone. "Are you safe right now?"

"Relatively. I'm lying low. But you have to promise me that if something happens, you'll keep pushing forward with the evidence. You can't let them bury it."

Despite the swirl of fear, Emily's resolve sharpened. "I promise, Alan. I need you to stay safe. I can't fight this battle alone."

Silence fell, then his voice dropped to an urgent whisper. "They'll try to kill this case before it starts. That means intimidation, bribes, you name it. If you see Mark Hastings or any big-firm attorney, they'll try to talk you out of it or discredit you. Don't believe them."

She hesitated. Should she mention her conversation with Mark? She decided against it - no need to spook Alan further. "I'll be careful," she said. "You be careful too, okay?"

Another hiss of static, then the line went dead.

Emily stared at her phone, the dial tone droning ominously. *Kill this case before it starts.* That was exactly the approach Mark described in more subtle terms. Hastings & Cole would do what it did best: bury opposition under an avalanche of legal maneuvers, hush money, or targeted fear campaigns.

She swallowed hard, alone in her dimly lit office. The sense of isolation pressed upon her. Yet she wasn't quite alone, was she? She had Tessa - unflinching, ready to stand by her side. Alan, albeit terrified, was still determined to expose the truth. Now Dr. Franklin, who might bring crucial expertise.

And overshadowing them all: Mark Hastings, the old friend turned foe, stepping neatly into place as GenTech's prospective shield.

It was nearly midnight by the time Emily locked the front door of her office building. She paused on the sidewalk, glancing left and right. Her skin prickled with awareness of how easy it would be for someone to lurk in the shadows, tailing her. She told herself she was being paranoid - but was she?

She fished her car keys from her purse, hurried to her car, and locked the doors immediately after sliding into the driver's seat. She navigated the quiet streets toward her small apartment in an aging complex downtown, half expecting headlights to follow her. None did - at least not that she noticed.

All the same, her mind replayed Mark's admonition: *This is bigger than some solo practitioner's crusade.* She scoffed under her breath. Maybe it was big, but that didn't mean she couldn't make a difference.

Martyn Bellamy

At her apartment, she double-locked her front door, checked the windows, and finally allowed herself a moment to breathe. She kicked off her heels and made her way to the cramped living room. In the silence, she paced, adrenaline still pulsing.

Should I walk away? The question flickered briefly in her mind. It would be the simpler choice, the safer choice - especially with Hastings & Cole plus GenTech gunning for her. She could disclaim Alan Priest's case, send him to a non-profit legal clinic or a bigger outfit. She could bury her head in a safer realm of practice, close a few real estate deals, do some small civil suits, keep her overhead manageable.

But every time she entertained that idea, an image intruded: the potential families in Africa or South America who had lost loved ones to a drug GenTech might have known was dangerous. The moral weight overcame the fear.

With a shaky breath, she dropped onto her couch and flicked on a single lamp, letting its soft glow stave off the darkness. *I can't walk away.* That refrain repeated in her head until she drifted into a fitful doze, fully

The Ghosts' Trial – Volume One

dressed, the looming specter of Mark Hastings's return playing across her dreams.

Chapter 6: The Initial Disclosure

Emily Blackwood stared through the rain-streaked window of her modest office, the same simple space she had gingerly stepped into only a few weeks ago. So much had changed in that short time. She had walked away from Hastings & Cole - one of the most prestigious law firms in the city - and now stood at the threshold of possibly the biggest case of her career, if not her life. The early-evening light cast strange shadows on the worn carpet, and the flickering street lamp outside made everything feel vaguely ominous. She checked the clock on her desk: 6:53 p.m. Alan Priest was due any minute.

She couldn't stop running the last few days' events through her mind. Her paralegal and closest ally, Tessa Moretti, had brought Alan to her attention originally, describing him as a jittery man who seemed to be carrying secrets bigger than anyone could imagine. He had arrived unannounced, wearing a threadbare jacket and clutching a folder that hinted at wrongdoing by GenTech, the massive pharmaceutical corporation currently dominating headlines for its next-generation therapies. Emily had done her best to appear calm during their first meeting, but the documents he revealed - spreadsheets, partial emails, cryptic references to drug trials overseas - gave her more questions than answers. She had known even then that she was getting in over her head. And that was before Mark Hastings, her former colleague at Hastings & Cole, called to warn her off.

In the days that followed Alan's first visit, Emily had scoured every resource at her disposal to learn about GenTech. The company's philanthropic efforts in African and South American countries had been widely praised by governments and charities alike. She found puff pieces lauding the charitable donation of vaccines, the construction of rural clinics, and the training of local healthcare workers. Yet for every glowing public relations article, there was a rumor - unsubstantiated stories of patients dying, of trials that had not been properly recorded, or local families being paid hush money. Most of these leads were intangible, second- or third-hand accounts from small regional newspapers.

It didn't help that money was already tight. Emily's "new" office was actually two cramped rooms in a converted townhouse above a locksmith's shop. She had spent every penny of her savings on the deposit, a few pieces of secondhand furniture, and a half-functional coffee machine. Some days, she worried that leaving a cushy corporate job at Hastings & Cole would end in disaster. Tessa, always the optimist, had reminded her that independence - and especially moral independence - was never free.

And then Mark Hastings had gotten in touch, delivering the news that Hastings & Cole was in advanced discussions to represent GenTech. The subtext was clear: Watch where you step. When she hung up the phone, Emily's stomach had twisted like an overwound clock spring. Mark was a formidable attorney, and she knew from experience how his persuasive methods could turn a judge's head. In a sense, he was everything Emily might have become if she had stayed at the firm. He was loyal, talented, ambitious - and increasingly compromised by the demands of high-paying corporate clients.

Despite the pang of regret she felt every time Mark's name surfaced, Emily had discovered a spark of fresh resolve within herself. She had left Hastings & Cole for a reason: to do more than just chase money and defend the privileged. The potential lawsuit against GenTech was enormous, morally and legally. But Alan Priest was the key. If his evidence proved genuine - if it *really* implicated senior executives in covering up fatal side effects from a drug trial - she could be staring down one of the largest pharmaceutical malpractice cases in decades. It was a terrifying prospect.

A knock at the door broke her reverie.

"Emily?" Tessa called. "Alan's here."

Emily closed her laptop, took a steadying breath, and nodded at her reflection in the window. As Tessa let Alan in, Emily moved to her battered desk. Gone were the thick mahogany surfaces and plush leather chairs of her old corporate office; now she had a chipped wooden desk with mismatched drawers. Yet she felt more ownership here - this was *her* space, financed by her own leap of faith.

Alan Priest entered with deliberate care, almost as though he were checking for invisible tripwires. He looked a shade more anxious than before, with dark circles beneath his eyes and perspiration beading at his temples despite the cool weather. A battered black briefcase hung from his left hand. Emily motioned for him to sit in the less wobbly of the two chairs facing her desk.

"Alan," she said softly, trying to sound reassuring. "I'm glad you came."

"Thank you," he replied, voice trembling. "I - uh, I'm sorry to show up so late. I didn't want anyone noticing me come in the middle of the day. I took the bus. Then I walked three blocks in the rain."

Tessa, who hovered near the doorway, shut it and lowered the blinds. "I'll lock up for the night," she explained. "Make sure no one barges in."

Emily appreciated Tessa's diligence. She hoped it was unnecessary - surely GenTech wouldn't send goons to break down her door in downtown Chicago - but the tension in Alan's posture hinted otherwise.

When Tessa returned, Emily gestured for her to take the seat next to Alan. "You're part of this," she said. "No point in you standing guard out there."

Tessa shot Emily a grateful smile before she settled into the seat. Her notepad rested on her lap, pen at the ready.

The Ghosts' Trial – Volume One

Alan swallowed, lifted the battered briefcase onto his lap, and opened the clasps. "I, um... This is everything." He produced a stack of papers, neatly bound in a plain manila folder. Emily could see pages of typewritten text, spreadsheets, and color-coded email printouts.

The sight of the documents made her heart lurch. *This could be the smoking gun,* she thought. *Or it could be the final anvil that crushes me financially if I pick the wrong fight.*

Alan licked his lips nervously. "I don't know what's in each page line by line, but I do know the broad strokes. I was part of a departmental team at GenTech that handled data analysis for drug trials. Some of us discovered unusual mortality rates in a particular test group."

He paused, a haunted look crossing his face. "I was threatened when I tried to raise concerns. Told that if I wanted to keep my job, I had to shred certain reports, delete them from the servers. But I... I couldn't just do that. So, I made copies."

Emily glanced at Tessa, who was scribbling notes furiously. Then, softly, she asked, "Did you keep any digital backups?"

"Yes," Alan answered. "But those are riskier. Digital footprints can be traced, or files can be corrupted or stolen. If I'd tried to store them online, they might have gotten wind of it. Instead, I used an external drive, then I wiped all references from my home computer." He rubbed his temples. "It's all in a locker at the bus station, under a name that's not mine. At least, not yet."

Emily's throat tightened. She'd heard of whistleblowers taking elaborate precautions, but seeing it first-hand - someone so frightened that they used pseudonyms and public lockers - brought it all home. *This is real,* she thought. *He believes his life is in danger.*

"All right," she said carefully. "Let's start with what you have here."

Alan extracted an email printout, passing it across the desk. Emily scanned it:

We need to finalize the redacted docs ASAP. This is no time for moral hand-wringing.

Fatalities overseas can't be pinned on us if the official docs show that the local clinics were responsible for treatment protocols. All references to supply chain oversight, GenTech advisories, or known side effects must be removed.

Let's keep this project on track. The revenue forecast alone is worth the trouble.

Emily's pulse quickened. She scanned the rest of the page. There were instructions further down - bullets indicating how to reorder or delete entire sections of the trial data before packaging it for a regulatory review.

She turned to Tessa, who looked as though she could hardly breathe. Tessa's wide eyes flicked to Alan. "They... they basically admitted to removing any link to the drug's side effects?"

Alan nodded shakily. "This was one of the emails that started my suspicion. I was a data analyst, tasked with double-checking the integrity of final reports. But the spreadsheets didn't match the official narrative we were sending out. I confronted my immediate supervisor, who told me to 'do my job and be quiet.'"

"Did you talk to anyone else?" Emily asked.

"I tried internal routes first," Alan explained. "I submitted an anonymous memo - purely factual, just pointing out discrepancies. But it fell on deaf ears. Then one day a VP from the Risk Management department confronted me in the parking garage, demanding I 'cease malicious rumors.' Said if I stirred up trouble, I'd be putting my entire future at risk."

A flash of empathy coursed through Emily. She had encountered plenty of unscrupulous tactics during her years at Hastings & Cole, but hearing about an actual intimidation encounter in a dark parking garage made it feel more like a gangster movie than corporate America.

"These side effects," Emily pressed. "Were they fatal?"

Alan grimaced, sliding another piece of paper forward. "Yes. This second document outlines a batch of tests run in rural African clinics. Three sites, each with about a hundred participants. The official cause of death for many of them was listed as complications from underlying conditions - like malaria, or pre-existing kidney issues. But the data shows otherwise. Project Redwood's drug triggered severe immune responses in a significant minority of participants, and a number of them died. The teams on the ground tried to raise the alarm, but GenTech senior management stifled it."

Emily read the second document. It was worse than she had imagined. "According to this," she said softly, "at least thirty people died in just one of the clinics."

Tessa's pen scratched frantically across her notepad, but her eyes glistened with sorrow. "That's horrifying."

Alan nodded. "And that was only in Africa. There was another site in South America. That trial was smaller - fewer than thirty participants. But from what I managed to see, one or two people died there, too. The problem is that GenTech's public statements pinned every single death on the local medical facilities. They claimed that the clinical sites 'failed to follow established protocols.' That's how they avoided media scrutiny."

Emily reached for a third printout. It was full of columns and color codes, apparently cross-referencing the real adverse-event data versus the "final" data that GenTech reported to regulators. The real data showed a cluster of bright red warnings about organ failure, anaphylactic shock, and mysterious fevers that turned fatal. The sanitized version replaced many of these references with "clinical mismanagement" and "unrelated comorbidities."

For a minute, no one spoke. The hum of the fluorescent light overhead buzzed in the heavy silence. Emily let out a slow breath. All this time, she had harbored suspicions that GenTech was up to something unethical - Alan's initial hint had been enough to raise alarm bells - but now, staring at these documents, she understood the full gravity.

"These are pretty damning," she finally said, her voice low. "Alan, you realize that if we move forward with this - and if it's proven authentic in court - GenTech will fight back with every resource they have. They'll come after you, after me, after Tessa."

Tessa gave a grim little nod, swallowing hard. "Yes, they will."

Alan's fingers twitched on the edges of the folder. "I know. That's why I'm terrified. But if I don't come forward, I'm no better than the executives who are burying this. People died, Ms. Blackwood. Families were never told the truth. Doctors were scapegoated. It's morally wrong to stay silent."

The Ghosts' Trial – Volume One

Emily's gaze flicked to Tessa, who stared back with fierce determination. Yes, they were both scared. Yes, their new practice was hardly in a position to take on a corporate juggernaut. But the time for half-measures was slipping away.

"All right," Emily said, inhaling slowly. "Let's see what else you have."

They spent the next hour going through the folder page by page. It held dozens of email printouts, sanitized trial reports with the corresponding original versions, and even slides from internal presentations. The slides, emblazoned with GenTech's crisp logo, touted the potential multi-billion-dollar revenue stream for Project Redwood if it passed regulatory hurdles. One bullet point read:

Projected Net Revenue (North American Market): $1.7B – $2.3B (first 24 months)

"What's most incriminating," Alan explained, "is how these same slides mention 'expected strong safety profile' even though, by that point, multiple fatal side effects had been reported. They knew. They *had* to know. Yet they pressed forward."

Each new document made Emily's stomach churn. She remembered those carefully polished corporate slides from her days at Hastings & Cole - always touting the upside, rarely acknowledging risk except in carefully controlled disclaimers. But the scale of GenTech's alleged deception here was horrifying.

"Have you spoken to any regulators?" Tessa asked, chewing the end of her pen.

Alan shook his head. "No. I was too scared. Official whistleblower complaints require me to reveal my identity, and I wasn't sure how deep GenTech's reach might be. It's a multi-national corporation with powerful political and financial connections. I didn't want to vanish, or have a 'break-in' at my apartment that conveniently destroyed all my evidence."

Emily's mind flashed back to the last phone conversation with Mark Hastings. He had sounded guarded, almost remorseful, when he advised her to walk away. *He must have known something*, she thought, *or at least sensed the magnitude of this scandal.*

"Tessa, let's confirm the timeline of these emails," Emily said. "We need to see if all these messages and attachments align in a coherent narrative."

Tessa smoothed out the pages. "Yes, I'll note each date and see if they match up with the official press releases GenTech was putting out at the time."

While Tessa organized the papers, Emily studied Alan. His eyes darted repeatedly toward the darkened windows, as if expecting a GenTech security team to burst in at any moment.

"You're still employed at GenTech, aren't you?" she asked quietly.

"Yes," he admitted. "But I'm technically on unpaid leave now. Some corporate reshuffling. I think they suspect me of something - they just can't prove it yet. It's like they're trying to isolate me, keep me from accessing any more data."

Emily raised an eyebrow. "So you've made your copies. You have them safe. That's good. But if they place you on indefinite leave, or if you lose your job, how will you support yourself?"

Alan swallowed. "I… I haven't thought that far ahead. My main concern is getting the truth out. People have died. If I wait any longer, more people could die, especially if the drug ends up on the global market."

The sincerity in his voice struck Emily. She remembered the idealism she had once felt, fresh out of law school - a belief that the legal system *could* be used to protect the vulnerable. In the last few years, that optimism had withered under the weight of corporate deals and hush-hush settlements. But now, in this cramped office, she felt a glimmer of that conviction again.

"All right," she said, leaning forward. "We'll need to proceed carefully. There's a lot I need to do before we file any suit. For one, I'll need to verify the authenticity of these documents and talk to a forensic expert who can confirm that they weren't doctored. Then we'll want to draft a complaint - if we go the route of a civil lawsuit, it'll likely involve wrongful death claims or personal injury claims on behalf of the victims, as well as potential fraud allegations."

Alan nodded, though he looked like he might throw up from nerves.

"Legally, we have to confirm standing," Emily continued, thinking aloud. "We'd need at least one or two plaintiffs - families of deceased trial participants, or perhaps surviving patients. The bigger the pool, the more credible the class action. But that means we'll need to find them. We'll need sworn affidavits. That's a logistical nightmare when dealing with overseas clinics."

Tessa spoke up. "I've started looking into some local contacts in the African countries where the trials allegedly took place. Maybe we can partner with local counsel or nonprofits. But that'll take time."

"That's all right," Emily said. "This can't be rushed. We can't just dump the documents in a public setting without ensuring we're prepared for GenTech's counterattack."

Alan began gathering the documents back into the folder. "I trust you," he said, voice quivering. "I trust you to know how to handle this. Just… please, don't let them bury it. I can't live with myself if it all gets buried."

Emily heard the raw desperation in his tone. She wanted to reassure him, but she didn't want to make promises she might not be able to keep. Instead, she placed a hand on the folder. "I'll do everything in my power, Alan."

Half an hour later, after they had arranged a schedule of next steps, Emily walked Alan to the door. The rain was still coming down outside, soft and steady against the street lamps. She gave him final instructions on how to contact her securely - using a burner phone number and encrypted email. He stepped out into the night, shoulders hunched, looking like a man perpetually expecting to be chased.

Tessa came up behind Emily as the door clicked shut. "He's absolutely terrified," she murmured.

Emily nodded. "With reason. Once we go public with any of this, GenTech won't hesitate to destroy his reputation." She paused, biting her lip. "And ours."

Tessa locked the door and flipped the sign to *Closed*. "We're not letting that stop us, are we?"

A tingle of anxiety ran through Emily's body. She recalled the menacing tone in Mark Hastings's voice when he warned her that she was "over her head." She remembered how, at Hastings & Cole, she had sometimes worked on behalf of clients who wanted to bury inconvenient truths. She knew how the game was played. A corporation this size would throw teams of lawyers, PR specialists, and private investigators into the fray.

But Tessa's unwavering gaze reminded her why she had opened this small practice in the first place. "No," she said quietly. "We're not. We're going to do what's right."

They returned to her desk, a sense of weight settling over the room. Darkness pressed against the windows. Emily's desk lamp illuminated the copies Alan had left behind. Tessa began re-checking the chronological order of the emails.

"Emily," Tessa ventured, "do we have enough resources to do this? Financially? Even if we postpone paying ourselves for a month or two, just to keep the lights on… is that going to be enough?"

Emily sighed. "I was asking myself the same question earlier. A case of this magnitude could go on for years. We'll need expert witnesses, depositions, travel budgets, maybe even translators. If we do it alone, we're looking at a David-and-Goliath scenario."

Her mind flicked back to the name of a small public interest firm she had once encountered - Montgomery & Shaw. They specialized in lawsuits against large corporations. She had parted ways with them amicably when she joined Hastings & Cole years back. *Could I reach out to them for help?* She mulled the idea. If they collaborated, it might give her more muscle for the fight.

Then again, that meant sharing credit and potentially losing control over how the case was argued. But as Tessa's question hung in the air, Emily realized it wasn't about her pride. It was about justice for the families who had lost loved ones. If the only route to exposing GenTech was a partnership with a bigger firm, she had to at least consider it.

"I might have a contact," she said after a moment, "a smaller public-interest group that's done pro bono work. They're not flush with money, but they know how to handle high-profile corporate malfeasance cases."

Tessa's eyes lit up. "That could be huge. We need every advantage we can get."

Emily nodded, shutting off the desk lamp. "But first, let's go home. Tomorrow, we'll start making calls, verifying documents, setting up preliminary research. There's no point in destroying ourselves with exhaustion on day one of what could be a marathon."

Still, as they packed up, Emily felt the weight of the folder under her arm like a lead brick. Alan's revelations changed everything. The rightful, moral part of her was outraged. Another part of her - the pragmatic ex-corporate lawyer - was deeply apprehensive about the fight she was about to wage.

Emily managed to hail a cab, Tessa sharing the ride for the first few blocks before jumping out at her own apartment. Rain rattled against the windows as the vehicle wound through downtown traffic. The city lights glimmered on wet pavement, giving everything a noirish sheen.

She thought of her old life - driving home in a sleek company car from Hastings & Cole, wearing suits that cost more than a month's rent in her current apartment. Back then, she never worried about how she'd pay for coffee refills or whether her single pro bono client would be overshadowed by bigger, paying corporate clients. Now, though, each drop of rain felt like a reminder of the storm she was walking into.

At last, the cab stopped outside her modest one-bedroom building. She paid the driver, tipping more than she probably should, then hurried inside. In the dim hallway, old linoleum squeaked under her heels. She felt an odd mixture of fear and purpose.

Once inside her apartment, she locked the door, double-checked it, then set the precious folder on her tiny kitchen table. She flicked on the overhead light, illuminating a space that was little more than a kitchenette merging into a living area. Cheap curtains fluttered near the slightly open window, letting in the distant rumble of late-night traffic.

Finally, she collapsed onto the couch. Her mind refused to slow down. She replayed the day's revelations: The damning emails, the fatal side effects, the knowledge that people across the ocean had died, leaving families behind who might never know the full truth. The weight of it pushed her exhaustion into a dull ache behind her eyes.

The Ghosts' Trial – Volume One

What am I getting myself into? she wondered, staring at the cracks in her ceiling. *If I fail, or if this gets buried... can I live with that?*

Yet the alternative - to do nothing - was unthinkable. She reminded herself of Alan's terror, the moral stand he was taking. He risked everything just to get these documents out. Emily knew she had to match his courage.

Despite her swirling thoughts, she forced herself to get ready for bed. She had a powerful tendency to let anxiety keep her awake until the small hours, but she needed rest. The next few weeks would demand everything from her.

The gray light of early morning streamed through the kitchen window as Emily poured herself the first coffee of the day. She glanced at the clock: 6:12 a.m. Sleep had been fitful, peppered with half-remembered nightmares of phantom phone calls and mysterious figures in suits.

She carried her mug to the table and opened her laptop. Before drafting any legal documents, she wanted to double-check the local and federal statutes regarding whistleblower protection. The last thing she wanted was for Alan to end up unprotected.

An hour later, she had typed half a page of notes - references to the *False Claims Act*, which sometimes applied to pharmaceuticals if government funds or programs were involved; possible entanglements with the Food and Drug Administration's regulations; and more. She also made notes on the potential for filing a *qui tam* lawsuit if GenTech had defrauded the government. But that would require a different strategy altogether, and Alan's documents needed thorough vetting before she considered that route.

The phone buzzed, startling her out of her concentration. She glanced at the caller ID. *Private number.*

Her pulse hitched, but she picked up. "Hello?"

"You're up early," said a familiar male voice.

Emily's hand clenched around her coffee mug. "Mark," she said in a flat tone. "Did you call to give me more unsolicited advice?"

A pause. "I called to see if we could talk off the record," he said quietly. "No hostility, I promise."

She shut her eyes. "So talk."

He exhaled. "Not over the phone. In person. Maybe breakfast at Lila's Diner near the courthouse? Thirty minutes from now?"

Her heart hammered. Lila's Diner was a place lawyers frequented when they had early motions at the district courthouse. She had eaten many a quick meal there, exchanging case gossip with Mark back in their Hastings & Cole days.

She checked the time. If she left immediately and caught a cab, she could make it. The question was - should she?

Curiosity and caution warred within her. Finally, she took a breath. "All right. I'll meet you there."

Emily arrived at Lila's Diner a few minutes ahead of schedule. The place still smelled of fresh coffee and sizzling bacon, its laminate floors scuffed from decades of traffic. She slipped into a corner booth. Outside, the morning sun was fighting its way through thick clouds, casting a pale glow on the sidewalk.

Mark Hastings entered moments later, wearing a tailored navy suit that screamed big-law sophistication.

His overcoat dripped with the remnants of last night's rain. He spotted her and managed a thin smile.

As he approached, she tried to read his expression - regret? Concern? Or maybe just corporate calculation. He slid into the booth across from her, setting his phone facedown on the table. "Thank you for meeting me," he said softly, waving off the waitress when she came to ask if he wanted coffee.

Emily didn't bother with pleasantries. "So, what's this about?"

Mark folded his hands on the table. "I know you've had contact with someone inside GenTech. My firm has reason to believe that a data analyst took confidential materials. Let's just say my superiors are anxious to nip this in the bud before it becomes a legal meltdown."

She forced herself to maintain a neutral expression, but her mind raced. *They suspect Alan. That means time is running out.* "I'm not sure what you're implying," she said coolly.

He tapped his fingers against the Formica. "Emily, don't play me. We've known each other too long. Look, I - " He paused, glancing around the mostly empty diner as if worried about eavesdroppers. "I owe you an apology. I never wanted to come off as threatening. You're a good lawyer and a better person. But you have no idea how big this beast is. GenTech... they don't lose. They'll pull every trick in the book."

She sipped her water. "Then why are you warning me again? Shouldn't you be zealously representing your client?"

Mark's jaw tightened. "I am. But I'm not a robot. If you move forward, you'll be discredited, financially drained, maybe sued for defamation. And your client - whoever he is - will be destroyed. I'd hate to see you ruin yourself just to watch them walk away unscathed."

Emily stared at him, her anger simmering. "Maybe they won't walk away unscathed. If there's real evidence, Mark - if people died - there's a moral responsibility here."

His eyes flicked down. For a moment, she sensed genuine conflict in him. "I know," he said softly. "I know. But maybe the best you can do is a quiet settlement. Keep your practice afloat. Force them to cough up hush money. That's how these things go in the real world."

She felt a swell of bitterness. "Right. The real world. Where big corporations buy silence instead of facing justice."

He nodded reluctantly. "I'm just trying to make you see reason. If you push for a major lawsuit, you'll be outgunned. Even if you gather some victims' families, GenTech will bury you in legal motions. They'll have private investigators comb through your personal life, your finances, everything. It's not a fair fight."

Emily's mind flicked to Alan's haunted face, the data proving that real people had lost their lives. "It's never a fair fight. That doesn't mean you surrender."

Mark pressed his lips together. "Look, I did my job telling you how it is. If you keep going, I can't protect you from the fallout." He paused, an unspoken tension in the air. "You left Hastings & Cole because you wanted your freedom, your scruples. I respected that choice, even if I didn't understand it. But this… you're playing with fire, Emily."

She met his gaze head-on. "Maybe it's time someone did."

He exhaled slowly and reached into his pocket, placing a folded sheet of paper on the table. "Look this over. It's an official letter from my firm to you. Let's call it a courtesy: They'll offer a closed-door settlement if you have any evidence and you agree to keep quiet. They'll also vow to keep your client's identity confidential if it helps them track down who leaked the data. It might save him from a jail term for theft of proprietary information."

Emily's temper flared. "So they're threatening criminal charges if we don't comply?"

Mark said nothing, but his silence spoke volumes.

She stood, refusing to pick up the letter. "Thanks for the coffee invite, but I think we're done here."

His voice wavered as he spoke softly, "Just... think about it. For your sake, if nothing else."

She shot him a final look, a confusing mix of resentment and pity, then walked out into the murky gray morning.

By 8:30 a.m., Emily was back in her office, tension coiled in her gut. Tessa arrived soon after, balancing two cups of coffee and a paper bag of pastries.

"You look like you've had a morning," Tessa remarked, handing Emily a latte.

Emily sank into her chair with a sigh. "Mark asked me to meet him for breakfast. He basically confirmed what we suspected: GenTech is gearing up to crush us. They even dangled some hush-money settlement if we produce the whistleblower - Alan - and bury the evidence."

Tessa shook her head. "You're not seriously considering it, are you?"

"Of course not," Emily retorted, though she could hear the quiver in her own voice. "But the fact they're already making these moves means they know about Alan. They may not have proof yet, but it's only a matter of time."

Tessa set down the pastries. "We need to take the next step, Emily. If we wait, they'll tighten the net around us. That settlement angle is their way of testing how serious we are."

Emily nodded grimly. "You're right. Let's do some immediate checks: first, we verify the authenticity of Alan's documents. Then we consult with that public-interest firm I mentioned - Montgomery & Shaw. If we join forces, we might stand a chance."

Tessa flashed a determined grin. "On it."

While Tessa fired off emails to a data-forensics contact, Emily dialed the main office for Montgomery & Shaw. She had no guarantee they'd be interested in co-counseling. This was a long shot, but so was everything else about this case.

A receptionist answered, eventually routing her to one of the firm's senior attorneys, Lucas Shaw. Emily introduced herself and explained, without disclosing key names or details, that she had a whistleblower case involving a major pharmaceutical corporation with possible fatal side effects.

Lucas listened quietly, then said, "We might be interested, but we need to know more. How soon can you drop by with an overview?"

Emily glanced at her watch. "Could I come by this afternoon?"

He hesitated. "Sure. One p.m.? We'll give you thirty minutes to make your pitch. We're in the middle of an environmental class action, so time is tight."

"It'll be enough," she assured him.

After hanging up, Emily filled Tessa in. "One p.m. with Montgomery & Shaw. Let's get some documents in order - something that outlines the biggest points of Alan's evidence, but that doesn't compromise his identity or the entire trove just yet. Enough to intrigue them, not enough to scare them off."

Tessa typed away at her laptop. "We'll need a sanitized timeline. I can work on that. Also, maybe bullet points on potential legal strategies."

Emily nodded. "Yes. And I'll bring the redacted copies of a few crucial emails. Show them enough to demonstrate that we're not imagining this."

They spent the next several hours preparing. Emily felt as if she were back at Hastings & Cole, rushing to compile a pitch for prospective clients - except now, the roles were reversed. *I'm the one seeking help,* she reminded herself. *And it's not about money or prestige. It's about justice.*

Montgomery & Shaw's office was located two metro stops away in a modest brick building, far from the glass high-rises that housed major corporate firms.

Emily arrived promptly at 12:55 p.m. She wore her best suit, which still didn't quite mask the frayed edges on the cuffs, and clutched a leather folder containing redacted documents.

In the small waiting area, a potted plant leaned precariously, as though it had grown too tall for its container. The receptionist gestured for Emily to take a seat, then returned to her phone. A sense of déjà vu swept over Emily - it was reminiscent of her early days as an associate, waiting in the lobbies of potential clients, ready to prove her mettle.

At precisely 1:00 p.m., Lucas Shaw appeared. He was a tall, lean man in his late forties with salt-and-pepper hair and a straightforward, almost brusque manner. "Ms. Blackwood? Right this way."

He led her down a narrow hall to a conference room barely larger than a closet. Another man, Javier Montgomery - presumably the other name partner - sat reviewing a thick set of papers. He didn't look up as Emily entered.

"Have a seat," Lucas said, closing the door. "We have about half an hour before we need to jump into another call."

Emily took a breath. "Thank you both for seeing me. I'll be direct: I'm representing a whistleblower who claims to have solid evidence that GenTech has hidden fatal side effects from overseas drug trials. I'm looking for a co-counsel arrangement to help handle the scale of this litigation."

That got Javier's attention. He set aside his papers. "GenTech, the biotech giant?"

Emily nodded. "Yes, they're expanding aggressively in emerging markets - Africa, South America. We have documents that suggest they knew about multiple deaths during trials, but systematically redacted the data to push the drug forward in regulatory channels."

Lucas exchanged a glance with Javier. "We know of GenTech, at least from news stories. They have a reputation for philanthropic outreach, but we've heard rumors about corners being cut. How strong is your evidence?"

Emily opened her folder, extracting three carefully redacted printouts of emails. "I've removed details that might identify my source, but this is a taste. The whistleblower was involved in data analysis and has reams of unedited trial results, plus communications from senior executives."

She watched the two men scan the pages. They frowned, flipping back and forth. Javier pointed to a line referencing "fatalities overseas" and "local clinics taking the blame." "This is very direct," he murmured. "If authentic, it's damning."

Lucas set his copy down. "How reliable is your whistleblower? Could this be a disgruntled employee forging evidence?"

"I've done a preliminary check," Emily said. "It lines up with press releases and internal GenTech statements over the last year. We're getting it forensically examined, but I have no reason to believe it's fake. My client also has original files, not just printouts, so the chain of custody is intact."

Javier leaned back in his chair. "You're right - this is enormous. But it's also expensive. Taking on GenTech means bracing for a war. Do you have plaintiffs yet?"

Emily exhaled. "Not officially. We'll need families or victims from the affected clinics overseas. My paralegal is starting to research potential leads. But we can't just cold-call families in Africa or South America without local support."

Lucas nodded, his fingers drumming on the table. "Montgomery & Shaw has done cross-border litigation. It's tough, but not impossible. If the wrongdoing can be shown to have direct ties to GenTech's headquarters here, we can bring a suit in U.S. courts. We might also have to coordinate with local counsel."

Javier rubbed his chin. "Then there's the question of whether we file a wrongful death class action, or something else. If the FDA was misled, a *qui tam* under the False Claims Act might apply, especially if federal funds were used in any capacity."

Emily felt a surge of hope. They were talking strategy - not dismissing her. "Yes, I've considered that. But first we need to ensure whistleblower protections for my client. He's terrified of retaliation."

Lucas stared at the redacted printouts again. "He has every right to be. GenTech will come down on him hard. Possibly even threaten criminal charges for unauthorized disclosure of corporate documents."

"I don't want him left out to dry," Emily said firmly. "That's part of why I'm here, seeking resources and expertise. I can't protect him alone, let alone handle an international corporate fight."

Javier exchanged a meaningful look with Lucas, then turned to Emily. "All right, Ms. Blackwood. You've piqued our interest. But we're not going to jump in blind. We'd need to see more details - a thorough case memo, the unredacted evidence, and, ideally, the whistleblower himself. We'd also want a partnership agreement. This is going to be complicated, and we'll need a clear division of labor and fees."

Emily's chest fluttered with cautious optimism. "Understood. How soon can we talk specifics?"

Lucas glanced at his watch. "We have a court filing for another matter tomorrow morning. But we could meet the day after. Bring the whistleblower if he's comfortable, or at least give us enough unredacted material to confirm authenticity. If everything checks out, we might sign on as co-counsel."

Her relief was palpable. "Thank you. I'll schedule a time as soon as I confer with him."

They wrapped up, and Emily left the office feeling lighter, though the path ahead was still perilous. *Montgomery & Shaw might just be the ally I need,* she thought, *if Alan agrees to it - and if we can keep him safe.*

When Emily returned to her own office, Tessa was printing out a revised timeline of the GenTech emails. She looked up eagerly. "How did it go?"

Emily allowed herself a small smile. "They're open to working with us, provided we show them more evidence. We'll likely have a longer meeting in two days."

Tessa pumped a fist in victory. "Yes! That's a huge step. If they sign on, we won't be alone."

Her excitement was contagious, and for a moment, Emily felt the same spark. But the memory of Mark's ominous words lingered. She decided not to dwell on them. They had come too far to let fear paralyze them.

Emily hung her coat, then said, "Let's see if we can reach Alan. I want to set up a meeting. He should decide if he's comfortable revealing himself to Montgomery & Shaw."

Tessa's expression grew serious. "Right. I'll call him now."

But after repeated attempts, Alan's cell phone went straight to voicemail. Tessa tried the burner number Emily had given him as well, with no luck. Emily felt the knot of anxiety tighten in her chest.

"What if he's just laying low?" Tessa offered weakly.

"Maybe," Emily answered, though she couldn't shake the sense of unease. She considered all the ways a frightened whistleblower might decide to disappear.

Over the next few hours, Tessa kept trying, leaving voicemail messages that politely asked Alan to check in. Emily busied herself reviewing the documents again, her mind half-focused on the possibility that GenTech had already traced Alan's location. She kept picturing a black SUV creeping down Alan's street, men in suits stepping out.

By 7 p.m., with no word from Alan, Emily decided she and Tessa should go home. They locked the office carefully, then parted ways on the sidewalk. The streets glistened under the lingering drizzle from the night before.

As Emily walked the few blocks to her bus stop, she kept glancing over her shoulder. She told herself she was just being paranoid - certainly no one was following her. But paranoia came easily after reading the GenTech emails.

She reached the bus shelter, half-soaked and shivering in the damp cold. The flickering overhead bulb cast everything in a surreal, staccato glare. A moment later, headlights appeared down the street. She checked her phone out of habit. Still no message or missed call from Alan Priest.

A subtle dread wormed its way into her thoughts. *What if he's gone? What if they've already gotten to him?*

The bus arrived. Emily boarded, found an empty seat, and tried to calm her racing heart. She needed rest - tomorrow would be another day of attempts to locate Alan, finalize redacted documents for Montgomery & Shaw, and pray that this entire effort wouldn't implode before it even truly began.

Her mind drifted back to the email excerpt she had read that morning: *We need to finalize the redacted docs ASAP. This is no time for moral hand-wringing.*

The Ghosts' Trial – Volume One

In that moment, Emily felt the lines of battle being drawn clearly. GenTech had no intention of letting morality derail their profits. But for the first time in a very long while, Emily believed in the sanctity of her work. She would stand for what was right, even if the cost was steep.

She gazed out the window, watching the city lights blur as the bus rumbled on. Alan Priest's initial disclosure had shattered any illusion she might have clung to about corporate benevolence. Now there was no going back.

Chapter 7: Memories of the Firm

Emily Blackwood pressed her fingertips to her temples, leaning over the single pine desk that dominated her cramped new office. A single lamp cast a dull glow across the clutter of documents sprawled before her. Outside, late-evening traffic hissed through the narrow downtown streets. She should have been reviewing the statements from Alan Priest, the GenTech whistleblower who had stumbled into her life just days earlier, but her thoughts kept dragging her backward in time. She inhaled a slow breath and tried to focus. The intricacies of this burgeoning lawsuit against a pharmaceutical giant were staggering. Yet, no matter how many times she reminded herself of the urgent present, her mind insisted on returning to the tense, unhealed memories of Hastings & Cole, the powerhouse law firm she had left behind.

She was aware she needed to move forward - especially now that GenTech's skeletons might lead to a massive, high-stakes case. But something about Mark Hastings's call earlier in the week had cracked open that locked chest of recollections. With slow deliberation, she dropped her pen and leaned back in her chair, allowing the surge of memories to unfold.

Emily had been fresh out of law school when she first stepped through the stately bronze doors of Hastings & Cole. She remembered the echo of her heels across the gleaming marble lobby, the hushed brilliance of the open-floor library, and the palatable sense of power that seemed to radiate from every partner's office. It was a place full of promise, possibility, and well-guarded secrets. She had felt her pulse race at the prospect of immersing herself in complex litigation alongside the legal titans who inhabited those polished halls.

In her second week there, she had been assigned a routine research task on a commercial real estate dispute. Yet, what should have been a small assignment suddenly caught the attention of Mark Hastings himself. Mark was then a rising junior partner, and though the firm bore his family name - his father had co-founded it - he'd made it clear he intended to succeed or fail on his own terms. Tall, with sandy-blond hair and a calm, level voice, Mark combined an unassuming grace with a formidable legal acumen. When Emily first handed him her research memo, he'd taken the time to read it word-for-word in front of her. After scanning its contents, he'd looked up, given her a tight-lipped but genuine smile, and said, "Impressive. Let's see if you can argue some of these points in front of the partner."

From that moment on, an uneasy synergy had begun between them. Mark recognized Emily's potential. She, in turn, admired his willingness to listen - a rare trait at a firm where junior associates were often treated like disposable cogs. Over the following months, he regularly pulled her onto larger matters: multi-million dollar contract negotiations, complex intellectual property disputes, and the occasional hush-hush corporate meltdown that demanded discretion above all else. He encouraged her to refine her skills, to keep her arguments crisp and her research thorough. The intensity of the environment spurred Emily to prove herself repeatedly.

Yet beneath that drive, she'd always sensed an unspoken tension - something to do with Mark's place in the Hastings & Cole hierarchy. The older partners seemed to carry themselves with a mixture of admiration and guardedness around him. Whispers circulated about Mark's father, Thomas Hastings, who had co-founded the firm with Caroline Cole decades earlier. Some senior associates joked that Mark would eventually become "king of the castle," implying that nepotism would keep him afloat even if his abilities failed. Emily never believed that. In every case she saw, Mark displayed a cool brilliance - an exacting logic combined with a meticulous approach to strategy. She respected his intelligence and had no doubt he earned his place at the table.

As months turned to years, Emily gained a reputation as a prodigious young litigator. She won small but significant victories for firm clients and refined her skills in depositions, negotiations, and extensive discovery battles. Rumors trickled through the associates' grapevine that she was a "fast-track candidate," an attorney who might become a partner in record time. Mark often walked by her tiny cubicle - eventually upgraded to an interior office - and greeted her with a nod or a small grin. They rarely conversed about personal lives, sticking instead to strategy, procedural nuance, or motion practice tips. But an unspoken camaraderie formed in those late-night war-room sessions when they were both tired from reading thousands of pages of documents.

She remembered one particular evening - nearing midnight - when she noticed Mark had come into the associates' lounge, rummaging for a stale cup of coffee. They were alone in that hush of fluorescent-lit stillness, papers stacked around them like ramparts.

"You still here?" he asked, offering her a half-smile that bordered on genuine warmth.

She looked up from her evidence binder, eyes bleary. "Trying to tie up loose ends on the Harmon case. You?"

"Drafting a final argument for the Stavros deposition. This is the last coffee in the pot, if you're wondering."

She chuckled ruefully. "Not surprising. Somebody must have found the pot from last week."

In that moment, there was no pressure of hierarchy, no sense of a partner-figure overshadowing an associate. It felt like two determined attorneys fighting side-by-side in the trenches, albeit with Mark occupying a rung slightly above her in the firm's structure. He'd leaned against the counter, swirling the dregs of coffee in a chipped mug.

"You're good at this, Emily," he said after a moment. She could sense an undercurrent of sincerity that cut through the exhaustion. "Sometimes, I think…if you keep going like this, it won't be long before your name's on the door."

She remembered smiling, feeling an unexpected flush of pride. "Thanks," she'd murmured. A wave of complicated gratitude had washed over her. She admired him, and she also wondered if - just maybe - their friendship and professional rapport might one day become something more. The notion hovered on the periphery of her thoughts, unspoken but tantalizing.

But they'd never crossed that line. Hastings & Cole was not the kind of place that encouraged messy entanglements among its attorneys, and both Emily and Mark were too focused on rising within the ranks. Regardless, there were moments, fleeting though they were, when they traded quick, knowing smiles that felt intimate in ways she didn't fully understand.

As Emily made her way through her second year at Hastings & Cole, she began to notice cracks in the pristine image the firm projected. A real estate development case caught her attention. While officially it seemed straightforward - negotiations over property lines and zoning - she uncovered side documents that hinted at collusion and questionable dealings between a local councilman and one of the firm's high-profile clients. She'd brought her concerns to a senior associate, who promptly brushed her off, warning her to "avoid overthinking and focus on her assigned tasks."

Disturbed by the dismissive response, Emily tried to bring the matter to Mark. At that time, his star was ascendant, and their working relationship, if not personal, was at least built on mutual respect. She scheduled a brief meeting, and, behind the closed door of his corner office, she explained the suspicious documents. The papers suggested bribes to the councilman in exchange for pushing forward a real estate project.

"What should we do?" she'd asked anxiously, holding a file thick with legal disclaimers and coded communications. "I can't just pretend this is normal."

Mark took the folder, flipping through the pages, his brow furrowing. For a moment, she saw conflict behind his calm façade. Then he set the folder down, letting out a tired sigh.

"Emily, I see what you're worried about," he said carefully, "but at best, these are circumstantial. We don't have direct evidence of wrongdoing by the client. If you go public with this, or if you push it up the chain without the firm's blessing, you'll make enemies."

"They might be bribing an elected official," she insisted, heart pounding. "Why is no one else alarmed?"

Mark paused, tapping the folder's edge against the desk. "The reality is, these deals often have 'gray areas.' We'd need more than a few emails and payment records that only imply something suspicious. If you keep going, you'll need to bring in a partner."

"And what if the partners are the ones who've already decided to bury it?"

He looked at her with something akin to pity. "I know it's not easy, but tread carefully."

Emily had left his office that day feeling an unsettling mix of disappointment, anger, and mounting confusion. She'd hoped Mark would champion her concerns, but he seemed, at least in that instance, aligned with the rest of Hastings & Cole: preserve the client's interests, minimize the drama, keep everything contained. She tried to push the matter further, but each time she approached a senior attorney, she hit a wall of stone-faced admonitions: she was told to focus on her own assignments and trust the firm's leadership.

Time rolled on, and Emily's frustrations accumulated. She watched as Hastings & Cole took on increasingly dubious clients - massive corporations with rumored records of environmental violations, unscrupulous lenders accused of predatory practices, pharmaceutical companies that approached the gray boundary of ethical conduct. More and more, she found herself assigned to "defensive" litigation: burying plaintiffs under mountains of paperwork, challenging legitimate claims on technicalities, and using the weight of the firm's resources to outlast smaller opponents.

Her illusions about practicing law "for good" began to crumble. She'd gone into legal work believing in the power of justice, thinking she could protect the vulnerable. Yet, from inside Hastings & Cole, she was seeing firsthand how the wealthy and powerful manipulated the system. And the firm was paid handsomely for enabling them.

She remembered the day she saw the official attorney billing reports for a series of preliminary motions that blocked a critical consumer-protection lawsuit.

Hundreds of hours were devoted to nitpicking the plaintiffs' filing style, contesting small procedural points, and requiring the opposing counsel to produce exhaustive documentation for the slightest claim. All those tactics, while legal, strangled the smaller firm's resources, forcing the suit to settle for pennies on the dollar. Emily had stared at the final invoice, choking on the realization that she was complicit in a strategy that had little to do with right or wrong. It was strictly about winning.

One afternoon, when she could bear it no longer, she confronted Mark again. She remembered it clearly: late spring, the day bright with possibility, and yet the mood in his office was anything but. He'd just finished a phone call with a partner. She could tell from his taut expression that he was under pressure.

"Mark, we can't keep representing people who skate around the law," she blurted as soon as the door closed behind her. "I'm sorry if this sounds naive, but this is tearing at my conscience. I didn't sign up to defend outright corruption."

He looked up from a stack of depositions. "We defend clients within the bounds of the law."

"Is that all we can say anymore? 'We're within the bounds of the law?'" She shook her head, her voice trembling with both anger and sadness. "This place - " She gestured around the office, the symbol of their professional success. "Is it everything we wanted? Or is it making us into something we never intended to be?"

He set down his pen, meeting her gaze. "We can't save the world in every case, Emily."

"Why not try?"

"There are good attorneys who represent large corporations too. Not every big business is a villain, you know."

She pinned him with a fierce stare. "Some are, Mark. Some are, and you know it. We're enabling them."

Silence fell between them, thick as a storm cloud. She saw conflict and war in his eyes. He cared for her, or at least respected her. Perhaps he even shared some of her doubts about certain clients. But the unspoken truth was that Hastings & Cole was the pillar of his career, the seat of his father's legacy, and the gateway to his own ambitions. She sensed that walking away from that -

questioning it on moral grounds - was unthinkable for him.

Finally, he cleared his throat. "We're lawyers. We do our job," he said softly. "Maybe one day, when you have more sway here, you can pick and choose your cases. But for now, we work within the system."

She left the conversation with her convictions rattled. She'd once thought Mark might be a kindred spirit, someone who believed in using the law for good. Now she was less sure.

The final straw arrived in a swirl of events and half-truths. Emily began volunteering pro bono hours at a local legal-aid clinic after hours, wanting to do something that aligned with her conscience. She advised tenants threatened by eviction, victims of wage theft, and refugees confused about their legal status. At first, Hastings & Cole turned a blind eye - it was common for associates to volunteer sporadically in the spirit of public relations. But Emily's involvement grew, and soon the clinic's demands conflicted with the round-the-clock schedule the firm expected from her.

One Friday afternoon, she raced into the office from an emergency hearing at the clinic, her hair windblown and her expression taut. She'd barely dumped her briefcase at her desk when she discovered she had missed an important internal meeting about a high-dollar settlement for a corporate client. The senior partner reamed her out in front of everyone. Though normally poised, Emily felt her frustration bubble over. She shot back with a firm retort, defending her pro bono responsibilities and casting an unflattering light on the firm's priorities.

That was it. The partners called her in for a private conversation, seething. They told her that if she wanted to stay, she had to "focus on real clients" - the ones paying the seven-figure retainers - and lay off the distractions. She remembered glancing at Mark, who was present as a junior partner. He stood by silently, arms crossed, eyes refusing to meet hers.

So Emily turned on her heel and quit - an impulsive move that had been percolating in the back of her mind for months. She walked away that day, ignoring the phone calls from the managing partner's assistant, ignoring Mark's attempts to speak with her in the hallway. She remembered the feeling of her heart pounding, each step of her black pumps echoing in the corridor as she left. She was not sure whether she had made a brave stand or a catastrophic mistake.

Later that evening, as she packed up a few personal items from her desk, Mark finally cornered her near the elevator.

"You can't leave like this," he said, a note of desperation in his voice. "At least talk to me."

She turned, tears threatening to break through her composure. "What's left to say, Mark?"

"You've got too much talent to throw it all away because you're upset about a few moral scrapes. Every large firm has them."

She felt her anger flare. "You call that a 'few moral scrapes'? We defend corporations that might be harming real people, and we shrug it off because the law allows it - or because we can twist the law to let them get away with it."

He exhaled sharply. "Emily, sometimes the bigger picture - "

"The bigger picture is that I'm losing respect for myself," she snapped. "And you - " She paused, wrestling her emotions. "I always thought you believed in me. Instead, you've been standing by while the people upstairs sweep legitimate concerns under the rug."

Mark's jaw tensed. "It's not that simple. I can't just risk everything to chase every moral crusade. This is my family's firm. Our name is on the door."

A tear escaped down her cheek, though her voice remained steady. "That's exactly the problem. You don't want to risk anything at all."

A wave of tension broke between them. She stepped into the elevator, ignoring his last plea to talk further. As the doors slid shut, she watched him lower his head, perhaps as anguished as she was. That was the last real conversation she'd had with him.

The memory made Emily feel cold, even now, in her sparse new office nearly two years later. She'd built a small practice. Finances were perpetually tight. She'd traded glistening marble floors for scuffed linoleum, and the hum of a large support staff for Tessa's loyal partnership and a secondhand office copier. But she hadn't regretted her choice - at least not until GenTech loomed on the horizon, looking like a giant ready to crush her.

Mark's voice on the phone just a few days ago had brought all the conflict surging back. His words had been tinged with caution, almost a warning, as though he wanted to protect her from stepping into quicksand. But Emily had recognized the shift in him; he was clearly on retainer for GenTech, or about to be, meaning they were on opposite sides once again. Where once she dreamed they might share goals, now they would be adversaries in a high-stakes, possibly life-or-death legal showdown.

She was still lost in thought when Tessa Moretti's gentle knock broke the silence. Tessa - her paralegal, confidante, and friend - poked her head through the doorway, brows lifted in concern. "You okay?"

Emily glanced at the clock on her laptop. She had no idea how long she'd been motionless, lost in the labyrinth of her past.

"Yeah," she murmured, forcing a small smile. "Just…remembering things."

Tessa took a few cautious steps into the room. "Things about Hastings & Cole?"

Emily nodded. They both knew how haunted she sometimes felt by that chapter of her life.

"Listen," Tessa continued, voice quiet, "Alan Priest is outside in the hall. He just got here, looks pretty shaken. Something about receiving weird emails again, or maybe someone's following him. I told him to grab a seat in the waiting area, but he's kind of frantic."

Alan Priest, the whistleblower who'd brought them the first wave of evidence against GenTech, had been teetering on a razor's edge of fear and paranoia. If even a fraction of his documents were authentic - and Emily was increasingly convinced they were - GenTech had likely run illegal drug trials overseas, endangering human lives. Possibly worse.

Emily stood, smoothing the creases out of her blouse. "I'll talk to him."

As she followed Tessa down the short hallway that led to their makeshift reception area, her mind lingered on Mark for one more second. She wondered: If Mark ever truly believed people were dying because of GenTech's wrongdoing, would he step in? Or was he now so entrenched in Hastings & Cole's fortress of corporate clients that he'd turn a blind eye, just as he had before?

Alan Priest looked up the instant Emily rounded the corner. He was hunched over in a plastic chair, wearing an ill-fitting jacket and jeans that looked slept-in. His eyes brimmed with anxiety, and he clutched a battered laptop bag as though it contained the sum of his worldly possessions.

"Ms. Blackwood, I - " he began, voice already trembling.

"Alan," she greeted softly, gesturing to him to stand. "Come back to my office. You'll feel safer there."

He nodded, swallowing hard. Tessa gave them space, presumably returning to her own desk. Emily led Alan into her office, closing the door behind them. The whistleblower's hands shook visibly as he shifted the laptop bag into his lap.

"I got another email this morning," he said, voice shaking. "It said…'Stop talking or else.' It came from a throwaway address. And, last night, I thought I saw a car in the parking lot outside my apartment for hours. When I came out to check, it sped away."

Emily's heart sank. She recalled the previous suspicious phone calls that had rattled Alan. Each new incident seemed to confirm that GenTech - or someone affiliated with the company - was onto him. That meant they would eventually come after her too.

She drew a breath, carefully reining in her own apprehension. "Okay, Alan, let's not jump to conclusions. Could it have been someone else's car?"

He let out a frantic laugh. "This isn't the first time I've noticed it. And the emails keep coming. It's not a coincidence."

Emily gestured for him to sit. He sank into the chair across from her desk, looking as though he might bolt at any second. She walked around, taking her own seat behind the desk, trying to exude reassurance.

"You did the right thing coming here," she said, lacing her fingers together on the desktop. "We'll go through your messages. We'll document everything. Tessa and I will see if we can figure out any pattern, maybe get an investigator to see if the email is traceable."

He blew out a shaky breath, setting his laptop bag on his lap. "I'm sorry. I know it's risky for you, me just showing up like this."

Risky was an understatement. If GenTech had a sophisticated security team - and she had every reason to believe they did - Emily's firm could be under surveillance as well. Yet, she felt a burning moral imperative to protect this man and the evidence he held.

"It's fine," she said, "But we have to be smart. Don't volunteer extra information to anyone. If you sense someone following you, call me first. If it escalates, we'll talk to the authorities."

Alan nodded vigorously, gripping the strap of his laptop bag. "These emails aren't just telling me to keep quiet. They mention personal stuff about my family, my old workplace. Someone's digging up my life, threatening to drag me through the mud if I don't back off."

Emily recognized the tactic. She'd seen a subdued version of it during her Hastings & Cole days, when major corporations used private investigators to glean personal details that could discourage a troublesome opponent. Whether it was strictly legal or borderline harassment was a gray zone. But the threat was real.

She forced a calm smile. "We'll handle it," she said, trying to sound as though she had a foolproof plan. Inside, she felt a swirl of dread.

When Alan left, Tessa poked her head back in. "He's a wreck," she observed quietly. "I gave him a glass of water, told him to hang tight until he calms down a bit before going back out. He's in the waiting area. Gave me a new folder too - something about internal compliance reviews from GenTech's labs in Central America."

Emily nodded, worry lines etched across her brow. "Thank you, Tessa."

For a moment, they stood together in the silent room, the weight of the impending case pressing in. Tessa cleared her throat.

"You okay? You look…somewhere else."

Emily sighed. "Just dredging up old memories of Hastings & Cole. Mark, the day I left, all of it. It's got me rattled."

Tessa folded her arms. "You left that place for a reason. Don't forget that. You're building something real here, Emily - something that matters."

A flicker of gratitude rose in Emily's chest. Tessa's unwavering loyalty was a lifeline. "Yeah," she murmured. "I know."

But that knowledge didn't dull the ache of her recollections. The feeling of that final confrontation with Mark clung to her, an echo of regret mingled with righteous anger. Sometimes she wondered if she could have changed his mind, or if she should have stayed just a bit longer to see if the system could be changed from within. But she'd left, and now there was no going back.

As if summoned by her thoughts, Emily's cell phone buzzed. The screen displayed a number with no caller ID. She tensed. Recent calls from blocked numbers had often led to threats, or at the very least, unwelcome surprises. She motioned for Tessa to remain silent, then answered in a low voice.

"Hello?"

A hesitation. Then Mark Hastings's voice, quiet and carefully measured. "Emily."

Her spine stiffened, and Tessa's eyes went wide. Emily mouthed the name *Mark* at Tessa, who immediately nodded and stepped back, allowing Emily a measure of privacy.

"Mark," she said, her throat suddenly dry.

"Look, I…I know it's late. I just wanted to see where things stand. Rumor at the firm is that you've got some inside angle on GenTech."

She almost laughed. It was surreal to be having this conversation with a man who represented part of her past she had tried so hard to seal away. "We both know you don't call me at night just to trade rumors," she said, trying to keep her tone level. "What do you really want?"

A sigh crackled through the line. "Emily, I'm trying to give you a heads-up. GenTech's about to move fast on anything that hints at a lawsuit. If you're holding damaging documents, they'll use every legal - and possibly extralegal - avenue to shut you down."

Her jaw tensed. "Is that a warning, or a threat?"

"It's a warning from me. Off the record," Mark replied softly.

For a moment, she closed her eyes, torn between gratitude and renewed anger. *He's trying to play both sides again.* That was her first thought. But then she recalled how complicated things had been at Hastings & Cole. Mark might genuinely be concerned. Or he might just be trying to glean how strong her case was.

She swallowed. "I appreciate the concern, but I'm not backing down, if that's your angle."

Silence hummed for a moment. She thought she heard him tap a pen or something against a desk. Finally, he spoke again. "Emily, you of all people know that some fights can't be won by pure idealism. GenTech is huge, and it's not just the company. Their board members have connections in government, in finance - maybe in law enforcement."

"I don't need a lecture," she snapped, her patience slipping. "You think I'm not aware this might blow up in my face?"

His tone softened. "Emily…look, I know we left things badly. I never wanted you to walk away from Hastings & Cole under those circumstances. But the truth is, if you push forward now, you'll be taking on more than you can handle."

She felt the old resentment churn. "I can't ignore wrongdoing just because it's risky," she said. "That's the difference between us. Maybe that's always been the difference."

A pained pause. "I tried to protect you back then," he said, voice tight. "I'm trying to protect you now."

"I don't need protection," she replied. "I need the truth. And if your client is burying lethal secrets, the truth will come out."

Mark exhaled heavily. "You're going to do what you have to do. Just keep your eyes open, okay?"

The call ended with a click, leaving Emily staring at her phone. She felt shaken, not so much by what he'd said, but by the swirl of conflicting emotions it conjured. Mark was part adversary, part old friend, part something else entirely. She couldn't shake the sense that he still cared, even if he was tethered to a machine that cared only about profit and power.

She set the phone aside, forcing herself to breathe. Tessa stepped in again, eyebrows raised in a silent question. Emily shrugged. "He wanted to 'warn' me," she explained, bitterness seeping into her voice. "More likely he was testing me."

Tessa frowned. "If he's calling, it means your lawsuit is definitely on their radar. We'd better prepare for anything."

Emily nodded. She recalled the sense of unstoppable might that Hastings & Cole exuded. They had the manpower, the finances, the lobbying connections. She was just one person in a small practice with a single paralegal - and a frightened whistleblower in the waiting room. But her conscience demanded she fight.

By the time Tessa left for the evening and Alan departed, still visibly uneasy, the sky outside Emily's office window had turned an inky black. The streetlights illuminated drifting leaves and passersby hurrying home. Emily gazed at her reflection in the dark glass for a moment, seeing the faint lines of worry at her eyes. She wondered how much of her new life was shaped by that final confrontation at Hastings & Cole.

A memory flashed: Mark's face in the elevator, the raw regret flickering in his eyes when he realized he couldn't stop her from resigning. For better or worse, that was the moment she'd broken from a trajectory that might have led her to wealth, prestige, and moral compromises on a near-daily basis. Instead, she'd pursued a path filled with financial insecurity, overshadowed by the knowledge that her name carried little weight compared to the big firms she used to walk among.

Yet, she felt a certain grim satisfaction in having done what she believed was right. This case against GenTech might be her chance to prove that small voices still mattered - even in a system stacked against them. She straightened, crossing to her desk and powering down the lamp. She was exhausted, physically and emotionally, but tomorrow would bring new battles.

As she locked the office, she made a small vow to herself: she wouldn't allow the painful memories of Hastings & Cole - or the complicated history with Mark - to sway her from doing the right thing. That resolution solidified her determination, lending her a strange sense of calm. If GenTech wanted a fight, they'd get one.

On the drive home, Emily tried to keep her mind on the road, but the recollections kept creeping in. The freeway lights blurred as she recalled the last days at

Hastings & Cole. After she turned in her resignation, a few associates had secretly told her they admired her courage - though none dared to follow her. She'd left behind a half-finished class action defense and a meltdown in the IP division. Her abrupt departure caused waves of gossip. Some pinned her as "too emotional," others claimed "she's never going to make it on her own."

As she merged onto a narrower street, she remembered how Mark had tried calling her multiple times in the aftermath, leaving voicemails that toggled between apologetic and frustrated. She deleted most of them without listening to the end. Only once had she answered. She recalled telling him, "Please don't contact me again unless it's about something real - something that needs changing," before hanging up. His subsequent messages remained short and infrequent, trailing off entirely until this new storm with GenTech broke.

Now, he'd reappeared like an omen, and everything was spinning back into focus. Part of her was oddly gratified - he could have ignored her existence. The fact that he reached out suggested he still wrestled with the moral lines she refused to cross. Another part of her was furious - he might simply be gathering intel for the behemoth she planned to sue.

Her mind circled around one question: *Could Mark ever step away from Hastings & Cole, the way she did?* The deeper question was whether he even wanted to. She decided that at this point, it hardly mattered. She was on a collision course with GenTech, and Mark Hastings would either be a bystander or a roadblock.

She parked outside her small apartment complex - a far cry from the chic high-rise she once inhabited on a Hastings & Cole salary - and trudged upstairs to her unit. After fumbling with the keys, she entered her living room and flicked on a lamp. She dropped her briefcase, kicked off her shoes, and sank onto the couch. The faint hum of the refrigerator in the kitchen reminded her she hadn't eaten since breakfast. Still, the adrenaline in her bloodstream made her appetite vanish.

For a few minutes, she stared at the ceiling, letting the events of the day settle. She tried to separate the present from the past, to ground herself in the reality that she was no longer that uncertain junior associate, powerless against the firm's behemoth structure. She owned her decisions now. Yes, the stakes were enormous, but she had something that transcended corporate might: a moral conviction and a client who truly needed protection.

Memories came unbidden: her last day in the Hastings & Cole library, packing up her law school textbooks and personal notes, feeling stares from paralegals and associates who wondered if she'd lost her mind. She'd left behind a stable career, parted ways with mentors who had pegged her as a rising star. But she also stepped away from the guilt gnawing at her soul each time the firm defended questionable corporations.

With a tired sigh, Emily rose from the couch and headed to the kitchen. She made a half-hearted attempt at dinner - scrambled eggs on stale toast - then poured herself a glass of water. She carried it to her bedroom, flipping on a small lamp. The space was modest, but comfortable enough. A framed certificate from her law school hung crookedly on the wall, next to a black-and-white poster of a classic legal drama. A lonely reading chair sat in the corner.

Pulling off her blazer, she sank into the reading chair. In a different world, maybe she would have joined

Mark and other colleagues for cocktails at some upscale bar after a long day of depositions. She'd be wearing a power suit that cost more than a month's rent here, and they'd toast to another corporate victory, ignoring the cost in human lives. That world now felt both alien and alarmingly enticing in the same breath.

Resting her head against the chair's back, she forced herself to confront a lingering pang of regret: *What if I had done more from the inside?* The question circled like a vulture. But no - she'd tried. She brought concerns to Mark, to senior associates, to partners, only to be dismissed or scolded. Perhaps staying longer would have only eroded her ethics or broken her spirit.

The phone on her nightstand chirped. She glanced at it, half expecting another unknown caller or a threatening text for Alan. Instead, she saw a message from Tessa.

Tessa (9:42 PM): "Just checking in. Did you make it home okay? Alan emailed some more docs. They look intense. We'll go through them in the morning, right?"

Emily typed back a quick response, thanking Tessa for her concern and promising an early start to dissect any new revelations. *Intense.* The word seemed to sum up everything about this case. But at least she had Tessa's partnership. Unlike her time at Hastings & Cole, she now had the freedom to choose how she practiced law, even if that freedom came with constant anxiety about paying the rent.

Setting the phone aside, she turned out the light and let the darkness settle. Tomorrow, she'd have to be sharper, more focused. But tonight, a swirl of memories mingled with foreboding dreams. In those half-waking moments, she saw Mark's face flicker against the backdrop of Hastings & Cole's marble corridors. She heard the echoes of her own footsteps as she left that job for the final time. The recollections were bittersweet, tinged with both sorrow and the fierce pride of having fought for her beliefs.

The next day dawned gray and cool. Emily woke before her alarm, feeling a knot of tension in her stomach. She fixed herself a black coffee and stared through her kitchen window at the dim light creeping over the neighboring buildings. Somewhere in the city, Mark was likely preparing to represent GenTech. Meanwhile, Alan Priest was probably checking over his shoulder for stalkers. Tessa would soon appear at the office, fresh leads in hand.

Emily sipped her coffee, letting its warmth chase away the remnants of sleep. She realized that Mark's call had shaken her more than she cared to admit. A part of her had yearned for him to say, *I'm sorry, I see now that you were right. Let me help you.* But he hadn't. He'd only reminded her how dangerous this fight would be.

She set the empty mug on the counter, squared her shoulders, and steeled herself for the day. If the fight was dangerous, then so be it. She would do what needed to be done, just as she had when she walked out on Hastings & Cole two years ago. Perhaps Mark's warnings were genuine. But genuine or not, they wouldn't deter her.

By eight o'clock, Emily was in her office, scanning the new documents Alan had sent. Tessa arrived not long after, juggling a stack of printouts. The tension in the small workspace was palpable.

"Some of these files go back nearly ten years," Tessa remarked, dropping the papers onto Emily's desk. "Compliance audits, risk assessments…some look like they were doctored or manipulated."

Emily skimmed through one. "GenTech's test results in a clinic in Uganda. The official version that made it to regulators says minimal side effects, but Alan's documents suggest at least three fatalities were swept under the rug."

Tessa shook her head, anger flaring in her eyes. "If Mark Hastings and his firm are aware of this - "

"Maybe they're not," Emily interjected quietly, though she wasn't sure if she believed it. "GenTech could have withheld the most damning evidence, even from their outside counsel. It happens."

"But eventually, Hastings & Cole will learn the full scope, right? They'll have to decide whether to defend it."

"Yes," Emily said, her voice tight. "I just wonder how Mark will react when he sees the evidence. Or if he'll see it at all. Hastings & Cole might keep the dirty details to a small, specialized team until forced otherwise."

Tessa's face hardened. "God, it's so twisted. They claim to be about justice - "

"They're about the law," Emily corrected. "Which isn't always the same thing." She paused, her expression softening. "Look, we can't control Mark or the firm. All we can do is build our case. The question is, how do we proceed without tipping our hand too soon and putting Alan in more danger?"

Tessa nodded, mulling the problem. "We might need a motion to preserve evidence, or we risk GenTech destroying documents. But if we file that, they'll know exactly what we're after."

"Catch-22," Emily murmured.

They both fell silent, the gravity of the situation pressing in. This was precisely the sort of high-stakes puzzle Emily had grappled with at Hastings & Cole - except now, instead of protecting the corporation, she was fighting it. *Ironic,* she thought grimly. *I learned all these tactics to bury the other side, and now I'm using them to bring the truth to light.*

As the day wore on, they mapped out a preliminary strategy: partial disclosures in court, carefully timed press involvement, and a secure method for Alan to share documents without leaving a digital trail. The legal complexities were formidable: international jurisdictions, scattered clinical sites, and corporate shell games. But Emily felt the ember of determination glow brighter with each piece of the puzzle she fit into place.

Her mind kept returning to Hastings & Cole, wondering how quickly they'd retaliate once she began formal legal proceedings. *They'll come at me from every angle*, she thought, recalling the brutal litigation strategies she'd once helped deploy. She would be attacked for being "reckless," for lacking "jurisdiction," for "abusing process." The firm's cavalry would file motions to dismiss, to seal records, to impose sanctions, and anything else to keep the truth from surfacing.

The difference was: Emily now stood on the side of a whistleblower desperate for justice. And for all their resources, Hastings & Cole had one glaring weakness: corporate arrogance sometimes blinded them to the fact that a small, fiercely dedicated team could still pull off miracles.

Night fell again, and Emily sat alone in her office, the hum of the overhead light her only companion. Tessa had left hours earlier. In front of Emily lay two sets of documents: one detailing her existing strategy for the GenTech lawsuit, the other containing personal notes about her final days at Hastings & Cole - reminders of how that world had shaped her.

She picked up the personal notes. A flicker of longing skittered through her. Perhaps if Mark had truly fought for moral principles at the firm, she might have stayed. But he'd been compromised by his own ambitions and loyalties. *Would I have done anything differently if he'd asked me to stay?* That question lingered without a definite answer.

Putting the notes aside, she turned her attention to the lawsuit strategy. A fresh wave of purpose surged within her. Everything that had happened at Hastings & Cole - the cynicism, the moral evasions, the daily reminders that justice was optional - had prepared her for this exact moment. She understood how the formidable walls of big law were built. Now she intended to breach them.

Tomorrow, she would move one step closer to filing a formal complaint against GenTech, bolstered by Alan's evidence. She'd do so with open eyes, knowing that Mark and his firm would unleash every legal weapon at their disposal. But it didn't matter. She was on a mission to uncover the truth, to champion a whistleblower who risked his life to expose corporate wrongdoing. *Perhaps that's why I left Hastings & Cole,* she reflected. *To be free to do what's right.*

In the end, Emily saved her revised notes, turned off her computer, and began the ritual of locking up the office. Standing at the threshold, she flipped the light switch, plunging the workspace into shadows. For a split second, she saw an echo of the old Hastings & Cole corridors in her mind - a reflection of that glossy marble, the hush of power-laden deals, the quiet spaces where ambition sometimes outweighed principle. She blinked, and the vision vanished, leaving only the faint glow of the hallway's exit sign.

She stepped out and locked the door behind her. Yes, the firm still loomed in her memory, and Mark's presence in her life wasn't fully extinguished. But now, with the whistleblower's revelations in hand, a chance at real justice lay ahead. Her departure from Hastings & Cole had been bitter, but it forged the steel in her spine, preparing her for the battles to come.

Soon enough, GenTech would learn what it meant to face an attorney unafraid of crossing swords with a corporate giant - even if her office was small and her resources limited. Her recollections of Hastings & Cole, including Mark Hastings's conflicting loyalties, no longer felt like regrets. They felt like the necessary prologue to the story she was now determined to write.

In the cool night air outside the building, Emily inhaled deeply. Rather than fear, she felt a simmering sense of purpose. She was David stepping onto the field with Goliath. And, in some deeper corner of her mind, she wondered if Mark - caught between his father's firm and a mounting moral crisis - might eventually choose to stand beside her rather than in her way.

But that was a question for another day.

Turning on her heel, she walked toward her car, every step echoing with the resolve she'd gained since the day she strode out of Hastings & Cole. The final fragments of bitterness began to fade, replaced by the urgent call of justice that waited, just around the corner, in the case file labeled *GenTech v. Priest.*

Chapter 8: In Doubt

Morning sunlight filtered through the blinds in Emily Blackwood's modest one-room office, painting stripes across the worn hardwood floor. The day held promise of crisp early autumn air, but all Emily felt was the cold squeeze of mounting dread. Bills were piling up in her small practice - rent, utility costs, even the monthly retainer for her legal database subscription. She found herself perched at the edge of her desk, sifting through a painfully thin stack of client folders. Despite having just launched her solo firm a few months ago, she was already wondering how long she could keep it afloat.

She'd parted ways with Hastings & Cole, one of the most prestigious law firms in the city, determined to follow her conscience. At the time, leaving had felt like a grand act of independence, a step toward forging an identity built on integrity. Now, she felt that identity was threatened. Every invoice reminded her that a lawyer needed paying clients, and right now, she had too few.

Yet, despite all these financial pressures, one case had overshadowed all others: the potential lawsuit against

GenTech. Alan Priest, a nervous whistleblower with trembling hands and watery eyes, had brought her a trove of incriminating documents about GenTech's alleged clinical drug trials in Africa and South America - trials that had left a trail of unexpected deaths. He had come to her door a few days ago carrying nothing but a battered briefcase, a folder of suspicious emails, and a palpable sense of terror.

Tessa Moretti, her paralegal and close friend, had been gung-ho from the start. "You can't ignore this," Tessa had said, eyes blazing with a moral fervor that was as contagious as it was unnerving. "People died. If we don't help Alan Priest, who will?"

At first, Emily had shared that sense of righteous commitment. But the following day, the practicalities of a solo practice slapped her in the face. GenTech was no ordinary opponent. They were a pharmaceutical giant with legal resources that dwarfed her entire enterprise a thousand times over. If Emily took them on, she risked not only her reputation but also the tenuous financial stability she had managed to cobble together since opening her tiny firm.

The Ghosts' Trial – Volume One

That morning, hunched over her battered oak desk, she scrolled through her online banking statements. The red negative sign next to her checking account felt like a personal rebuke. She took off her reading glasses, rubbed her temples, and tried to breathe.

A knock on the door cut through her moment of despair.

"Come in," Emily called, half-hoping it would be a prospective client with a simple legal problem - and a guaranteed retainer.

But the door opened to reveal Tessa Moretti in her standard black blazer and skinny jeans, a spirited mismatch that somehow worked for her. She carried a tray with two takeout coffee cups.

"Brought you something," Tessa said softly.

Emily forced a smile. "You're too good to me."

"I know," Tessa teased. Placing the coffee tray on the desk, she leaned against a file cabinet, arms folded. "How are you holding up?"

Emily laughed humorlessly. "Not great, Tess. The rent is due in two weeks. We have maybe four paying clients right now. None of them will single handedly save this practice."

Tessa took a careful sip of her coffee. "We'll get through it. There are ups and downs when you're starting out solo. You knew that going in."

Emily nodded, but the knot of anxiety in her stomach refused to loosen. She remembered her last paycheck at Hastings & Cole - an absurdly large number for an associate who had been pegged for partner track. Now, she could hardly afford a lunch out. "I just didn't expect the downs to be so extreme, so soon."

Tessa's gaze flicked to the manila folder on Emily's desk labeled "GenTech – Preliminary Research." "I know what you're thinking," she ventured. "You're worried that if you take on GenTech, it could bury us."

"It's not just that," Emily said quietly. "It's also the question of whether I'm even capable of handling something so massive. I left Hastings & Cole partly because I was sick of covering up corporate malfeasance, but also because I believed in my own ability to do better. Now, staring at the possibility of going up against a multi-billion-dollar pharmaceutical titan… I'm starting to doubt everything."

Tessa bit her lip. "Look, we both know it's risky. But come on, Em - this is the reason you became a lawyer in the first place. You have a golden opportunity to expose something horrific, to do the right thing. Isn't that what you always preached to me when I was your paralegal at Hastings & Cole?"

Emily managed a thin smile. She recalled those late nights at Hastings & Cole, sifting through cases that quietly settled for undisclosed sums. She remembered complaining to Tessa how disillusioned she felt whenever shady corporate clients walked away with a shrug and a check that silenced the victims. "I did preach that, didn't I?"

"Constantly," Tessa said, smiling back. "It's what drew me to you in the first place. You had this moral backbone that nobody else in that firm seemed to have. You left that big paycheck behind for a reason. Let's not pretend this is anything else."

Emily sighed. "It's just... if we lose, we lose everything. I mean everything. My practice, my reputation. I'll be lucky if I can afford a studio apartment when this is over. And you? You'd be dragged down with me."

Tessa gave a spirited shrug. "I'll manage. I'm not doing this job for the money. But you, Emily - you're the lawyer. You're the one who can make real change happen. If you back down, that means GenTech goes unchallenged."

They fell silent. Outside, the noise of city traffic drifted through the windows - horns honking, engines humming. Emily's mind replayed the intense conversation she'd had with Alan Priest just the previous afternoon. He was terrified, but committed enough to place the evidence in her hands. He had said, "I have nowhere else to go, Ms. Blackwood. The second I tried to talk to an in-house compliance official, my name ended up on a list. I'm sure of it. I was fired within two weeks. Now I can't sleep at night wondering who else they're hurting."

Tessa sat down in the client chair across from the desk, tapping manicured nails on the armrest. "So, are you going to call him back today?"

Emily stared at the phone. She had promised Alan she'd call him to discuss a strategy for moving forward. Instead, she had spent the morning poring over her bank account. "Yeah," she answered. "I need a little more time, but... yeah."

"You want me to do anything?" Tessa asked.

"Maybe just give me a few minutes alone," Emily said. "I'm going to look over the finances one more time. Then I'll call him."

Tessa nodded, sensing Emily's need for space. On her way out, she paused at the door. "Remember: Sometimes it's not about whether we can beat them or not. Sometimes it's about whether we have the guts to try."

After Tessa left, Emily sat motionless, replaying her friend's words in her head. **It's about whether we have the guts to try.** If she didn't try, could she live with herself? Yet if she did and lost, would she curse herself for not knowing her limitations?

Rubbing her eyes, she decided to give herself at least one more day before deciding. She began glancing through the preliminary research Tessa had gathered - newspaper clippings from Ghana, local online articles in Spanish from clinics in Peru, references to a certain drug that had gone through suspiciously hasty clinical trials. The victims' names were swirling around in her mind. She could almost see the heartbreak in their families' faces. Several short paragraphs described children who had died from complications. The pharmaceutical giant had offered meager settlements or no explanation at all. One mother had written a letter - translated roughly into English - begging for clarity about her child's final days.

The idea of turning her back on these people felt like a betrayal of everything she believed in. She pictured the conference rooms in Hastings & Cole where such matters had often been "strategized" away. Once upon a time, that firm's brilliance had dazzled her. Now it repulsed her, though she still had complicated feelings about Mark Hastings - her former colleague, possibly her friend at one point. He was rumored to be on the legal team for GenTech, or at least circling the possibility. She knew he was an excellent lawyer, a formidable adversary if it came to that.

With a deep breath, Emily cleared her desk of the bank statements and spread out Tessa's research in front of her, determined to at least review it all carefully. Maybe the facts themselves would guide her next steps.

By noon, Emily had consumed two cups of coffee and scrawled countless notes across several legal pads. Her tension had not subsided; in fact, reading about the extent of GenTech's potential wrongdoing only heightened her sense of grim responsibility. She felt drawn to stand up and pace, so she did, walking the small length of her office floor as if that might disperse the restlessness in her limbs.

She was in mid-pace when the phone rang. She lunged for it, heart pounding slightly faster for fear it might be yet another bill collector. "Emily Blackwood's office," she answered in the most professional tone she could muster.

A sigh of relief escaped Emily's lips. "Hey, Tessa. You didn't have to call. You could've just come in."

"I'm actually downstairs," Tessa said, "running an errand. I just wanted to see if you were okay. You've been locked in the office for hours."

Emily managed a faint smile. "I'm good. Just finishing up some reading. Did you need anything?"

"Actually," Tessa said, her voice dropping slightly, "there's a man at the front desk. Didn't catch his name, but he's asking to see you. He doesn't look like a prospective client. More like some kind of corporate type. Suit and tie, an attitude to match."

Emily's stomach turned. "You think it's Mark Hastings?"

"I'm not sure. I've only seen Mark once or twice. This guy's older, looks more… polished. Or maybe 'hardened' is the word."

"All right," Emily said, swallowing the dryness in her throat. "Send him up if you think he's legit."

"Will do," Tessa replied and clicked off.

Emily hurriedly tried to organize the papers scattered across her desk, pushing aside references to lethal drug trials. If the visitor was from GenTech, showing all her cards in plain sight wouldn't be wise. She shoved the manila folder into the top drawer. Her heart hammered. Could GenTech already know she was considering representing a whistleblower?

A few minutes passed before she heard footsteps in the hallway. The door was ajar just enough for her to see a tall, silver-haired man in an impeccably tailored suit.

He carried a slim briefcase. When he stepped into the office, his presence seemed to fill the small space.

"Ms. Blackwood," he said, offering a hand in what felt like a perfunctory courtesy. "My name is Gerald Lawson."

Emily shook his hand. His grip was firm but not crushing. "I'm sorry, I didn't catch - what firm are you with?"

"I'm general counsel at GenTech," he said, eyes steady on hers. "My CEO asked me to have a conversation with you, in confidence, before any… formalities become necessary."

It took all Emily's composure not to let surprise register on her face. Already, she imagined that word "formalities" might include cease-and-desist letters, motions to silence her potential client, or threatened countersuits. She gestured for him to sit, and he lowered himself into the visitor's chair with an air of entitlement. She took her seat across the desk, forcing herself to look calm.

"You're here without an appointment," she said, carefully. "I'm happy to hear whatever you have to say, but I do have other commitments."

He glanced at his watch. "This won't take long."

"All right," Emily said. Her mouth felt dry again, so she sipped her lukewarm coffee - then wished she hadn't, as it tasted stale and bitter.

"Ms. Blackwood," Lawson began, "I understand you're considering representing a former employee of GenTech, Alan Priest, in what you believe to be a whistleblower case."

Emily said nothing, but the fact he already knew Alan's name confirmed her suspicion: GenTech was moving fast. Alan's story about being watched and blacklisted suddenly carried a more ominous weight.

Lawson cleared his throat. "We have reason to believe Mr. Priest has misrepresented certain internal documents and has, in fact, engaged in unauthorized distribution of confidential company materials. This is a serious breach of contract and possibly a violation of federal law. It would be in everyone's best interest if you advised Mr. Priest to withdraw any claims he might be making."

Emily's professional instincts kicked in. "Mr. Lawson, I can't speak about any client's decisions, nor can I confirm or deny who I represent. But I will note that if someone has evidence of wrongdoing, it's not in my nature to tell them to bury it."

The corners of Lawson's mouth tightened. "GenTech is not in the habit of burying anything, Ms. Blackwood. We have robust compliance procedures. If Mr. Priest believes he has evidence of misconduct, there are internal channels he could have used. Instead, he's chosen to leak documents in a way that suggests espionage or sabotage. I merely came here out of respect, to give you a chance to disengage from this… misguided enterprise."

"Respect," Emily repeated. She suppressed a sarcastic laugh. "And if I don't 'disengage'?"

He gave her a paternal smile, as though she were a misguided child. "Then I suspect your small practice could find itself overwhelmed by legal challenges. Not only from GenTech, but from third-party lawsuits that might arise once the details become public. I'm trying to save you the trouble. There is a place for talented attorneys in corporate law, Ms. Blackwood. You already know that."

The insult was palpable. Emily's neck prickled with indignation. "I appreciate the heads-up," she said in a measured tone. "But if I were you, I'd be more concerned about what your company has - or hasn't - done, rather than about my small practice."

Lawson inhaled slowly, drumming his fingertips on the arm of the chair. "Your reputation in the legal community is bright, Ms. Blackwood. You're respected, at least by some of my colleagues. Frankly, we don't want to see you ruin a promising career chasing conspiracies that do not exist."

Emily felt a swell of anger. "Thank you for the unsolicited career advice. Now, if there's nothing else…?"

He stood, smoothing his suit jacket. "I'll leave you my card. If at any point you wish to discuss this matter more privately, or if you'd like to explore opportunities for an amicable resolution, don't hesitate to call."

She accepted the card but didn't look at it, placing it face down on her desk. "I'll keep that in mind."

Without another word, Lawson nodded curtly and walked out, leaving behind the faint scent of expensive cologne and the acrid feeling of intimidation. Emily blew out a breath she hadn't realized she'd been holding. Her heart thumped in her chest, and her thoughts ran circles: GenTech had come to her. They were already trying to shut her down. That could only mean Alan's evidence had serious teeth.

When the door closed behind him, she snatched up the phone, intending to call Tessa. Instead, Tessa burst in moments later, out of breath. "I just saw him leave," Tessa said. "I tried to find out who he was, but he wouldn't talk to me. So I cornered the guy in the elevator and saw his ID card. Gerald Lawson, right?"

"Yup," Emily said, exhaling. "GenTech's top legal dog. He basically threatened me - told me I'm making a big mistake. If I proceed, they'll bury us in legal motions."

"That means we're onto something real," Tessa said, excitement and anxiety warring in her expression. "No big company lawyer visits a random attorney just to be friendly."

Emily rubbed her temples. "I know. It's terrifying. But it also confirms Alan's story. If they're resorting to intimidation at this stage, they must be worried."

"What are you going to do?" Tessa asked.

Emily swallowed. "I need to talk to Alan. See how he wants to move forward. But, Tessa... this just became very real. They're playing hardball."

Tessa nodded. "I'm with you, come what may."

Emily felt her eyes sting with sudden, grateful tears that she blinked away before they could fall. "Thank you," she whispered.

It was almost two in the afternoon when Emily finally called Alan Priest. He answered on the second ring, sounding breathless. "Ms. Blackwood?"

"Yes, it's me," she said gently. "I just had a visit from GenTech's counsel. They know you've talked to someone, presumably me. They threatened me in no uncertain terms."

Alan let out a trembling sigh. "I was afraid of that. I'm sorry you got dragged in. They've been calling me nonstop, sending emails offering hush money. But it's all hush money in disguise, you know? 'Generous severance package' if I sign an NDA. The usual tactics."

Emily pressed the phone closer to her ear. "Alan, I need to ask you something crucial: Are you ready to escalate this? It might mean going to court. It might mean depositions, public scrutiny, and a fight that could drag on for months - or longer. It won't be pleasant, and it won't be cheap. Are you prepared for that?"

A moment's silence. "I've thought about it every waking hour since I brought you those files," Alan said. "Look, I'm scared. I'm not going to pretend I'm some hero. But I can't walk away. Knowing what I know - I can't just live with myself if I let them keep doing what they're doing."

Emily felt a stirring of respect. He was a meek man outwardly, but something inside him refused to break. "All right. If we go forward, I'll need you to be ready to sign an official retainer agreement. We'll have to map out a strategy. Part of me is terrified, Alan. We're a small firm. We don't have the resources, the staff, the investigators - "

"I can pay you a retainer," Alan interjected, voice almost quivering with desperation. "It's not much, but I have some savings. And if it goes well, there may be a whistleblower reward - right? Doesn't the government have programs for that?"

Emily knew the theory: certain suits, like False Claims Act cases, could yield monetary awards for whistleblowers if the government was involved. But that was uncertain. "Potentially, yes," she allowed. "But we can't bank on that. This might be an uphill battle. Still, if you're truly resolved, I'll stand with you."

Alan's exhale sounded like a mixture of relief and fear. "Thank you. You have no idea how much this means. I'll scrape together whatever money I can. God, I just… I have to see this through."

"All right," Emily said softly. "Let's do it."

Emily spent the rest of the afternoon drafting a retainer agreement. As she typed the official language, she realized she was crossing a threshold in her career: She was about to take on GenTech as an adversary. Gone were the days of big-firm insulation, where a partner's name on a letterhead could intimidate the other side. Now it was just Emily Blackwood, attorney-at-law, and

Tessa Moretti, paralegal. They were heading into battle against a powerhouse with endless resources.

Despite her trepidation, something within her sparked to life. That sense of purpose that had led her to law school, that had once fueled her idealism as a young associate, roared back. This was the reason she had left Hastings & Cole: to do something that mattered, to uphold the law as a force for justice rather than a shield for corporations.

Once she finished writing the retainer, she emailed it to Alan with a polite request to review and sign. The moment she hit "send," a wave of exhaustion hit her. She had been riding a roller coaster of stress all day. Even her second coffee had done little to keep her nerves steady.

She mustered her last reserves of energy to lock up the office. On her way out, she passed Tessa's tiny cubicle in the shared workspace area - a corner of the office partitioned off by cheap plastic dividers. Tessa was furiously typing, her brow knitted in concentration.

"Research?" Emily guessed.

Tessa glanced up. "Yeah. I dug into some of the references that came up in the GenTech documents Alan gave us. Trying to see if there's a pattern - like if the same executives' names keep showing up or if the same subsidiary is used repeatedly."

"How's it looking so far?"

Tessa swiveled her chair to face Emily. "Promising. There are these email headers from a Dr. Howell at GenTech, referencing shipments to a research facility in Ghana. Then there are separate references to a shell company in the Caymans. It looks like some money might have been funneled to local clinics for 'special projects.' Nothing conclusive yet, but it's definitely fishy."

Emily suppressed a shudder. "All right. Don't burn yourself out. This is going to be a long haul."

Tessa gave a determined nod. "I'll head out soon. But I think I can at least map these data points. Maybe show you a flowchart in the morning."

"Sure," Emily said, reaching out to give Tessa's shoulder a reassuring squeeze. "Don't stay too late."

The Ghosts' Trial – Volume One

That evening, Emily returned to her studio apartment, a cramped space in a building that looked more drab each day. She microwaved a leftover dinner, then curled up on her worn-out couch to watch the local news. Her mind drifted in and out of the broadcast. Even the stories about a city corruption scandal and a high-profile real estate lawsuit failed to hold her attention. She was too consumed with her own legal drama.

She checked her phone obsessively, half expecting an email from Alan or a notification that GenTech had filed an injunction or some other bombshell. But aside from a promotional text message from her phone carrier, nothing came. The quiet was almost unnerving.

At around eight-thirty, the phone vibrated. She grabbed it: an email from Alan Priest. She opened it. It simply said:

I signed the retainer. Thank you for believing in me. I'll wire the deposit tomorrow. Let's talk next steps soon. I'll do whatever it takes.

Emily stared at the message, letting it sink in. Her firm - her tiny, precarious firm - was now officially taking on one of the biggest pharmaceutical companies in the world. Her heart fluttered in her chest, a complex dance of fear and excitement.

She typed a quick reply, thanking him and suggesting a phone call the following morning to strategize. After hitting send, she lay back on the couch, phone in hand, trying to quell the adrenaline surging through her system.

"Here we go," she murmured to herself, eyes drifting to the ceiling. "I hope I'm ready."

Emily arrived at her office at seven, far earlier than usual. She'd slept fitfully but woke up with a sense of grim determination. The day's first order of business was a phone conference with Alan to plan an initial approach. She also wanted to consult an old contact from her Hastings & Cole days - an accountant turned forensic expert who might help trace the shell companies Tessa had uncovered.

Stepping into the office, she could smell a faint stale odor from the carpet. She filed away a mental note to call the landlord about a possible cleaning. One more expense she couldn't afford yet. First, she switched on her computer, set out her notepad, and reviewed her bullet points:

1. **Legal Strategy**: Potential claims - whistleblower protections, wrongful termination, or even a civil suit alleging fraud.

2. **Document Organization**: Tessa's research needed to be systematically logged. They'd likely need an e-discovery platform soon.

3. **Media Strategy**: Should they go public if GenTech ramped up intimidation?

She had just begun crafting an outline of tasks when the phone rang. She grabbed it, only to find a frantic voice on the other end.

"Emily? This is Alan," the voice stammered. "They - someone just tried to break into my apartment last night. I'm scared. I don't know if it's them. Maybe I'm jumping to conclusions, but - "

Her heart dropped. "Oh my God. Slow down. Are you hurt?"

"No, I'm okay. I wasn't home when it happened. My neighbor said someone jimmied the lock on my door. Nothing's stolen, but the place is trashed, like they were searching for something."

Emily clenched her fist. "Your documents - do you have them safe?"

"I made copies. The originals are in a safe-deposit box. The rest is digitized, so even if they took my laptop, I have backups. But - God, Ms. Blackwood, I'm terrified."

She inhaled sharply. This was the real consequence of tangling with corporate muscle. "All right, Alan. First, call the police. File a report. Don't mention GenTech by name unless you have proof it was them. Just explain that you suspect a break-in. Second, we need to meet as soon as possible. Somewhere public. You can come to my office, or we can meet at a coffee shop."

"Your office," Alan managed, still sounding rattled. "I'll come there. Give me an hour."

They hung up, and Emily sat quietly in the hush of her small office. Her reflection in the blank computer screen looked unnervingly tense. She pictured Alan's fear, Mark Hastings' potential involvement from the shadows, and Gerald Lawson's smug face from the day before. Anxiety warred with righteous anger inside her.

She heard Tessa's footsteps in the hallway and stood to greet her. The moment Tessa walked in, Emily recounted Alan's frantic call. Tessa's expression darkened.

"This is all moving faster than I expected," Tessa said. "I'll get some coffee going and then see if I can find a local security consultant or someone who can advise him on protecting himself. Maybe we can even recommend a P.O. box or short-term relocation if he's truly in danger."

Emily nodded gratefully. "Yes, let's do that. We should also keep logs of every incident. If this turns into a case of witness intimidation, we'll need the evidence."

The weight of the situation pressed down on her again, but she took a deep breath and forced herself to remain steady. She realized Tessa was watching her with concern. "I'm okay," Emily assured her. "Just... a lot on my mind."

Tessa placed a hand gently on Emily's forearm. "We've got this. One step at a time."

Alan arrived forty-five minutes later, looking pale and shaky. He wore the same rumpled jacket from the day before, suggesting he might have spent the night somewhere else - maybe in his car, or a motel. He clutched a satchel that appeared stuffed with papers. Emily quickly ushered him into the office, where Tessa waited with coffee and a fruit muffin she'd picked up from a nearby bakery.

"Thank you," Alan mumbled, sinking into the visitor's chair. His eyes darted from Tessa to Emily, then back again, as if he were afraid of who else might be in the room. "I called the cops, like you said. They asked if I had any suspects. I told them I had no idea. Gave them a statement. I just… I don't feel safe. My landlord said it might be weeks before they fix the lock."

Emily's protective instincts flared. "You need to find a safer place to stay. At least until we figure this out."

Alan nodded weakly. "I have a friend across town who said I can crash on his couch. But I don't want to put him at risk."

Tessa jumped in. "We're working on some options, maybe a professional who can advise on securing your place or personal safety. In the meantime, do what you can to protect yourself. Keep your phone on, be mindful of your surroundings."

"Right," Alan said, staring at the floor.

Emily didn't want to crush him with an avalanche of legal talk, but they needed a plan. She pulled up her rolling chair to sit closer. "Alan, I appreciate that you signed the retainer agreement. Let's talk about the next steps. If we're going to file a lawsuit, we need solid grounds. We also have to be strategic about timing. If GenTech suspects we're about to blow this wide open, they may try to preempt us with legal measures - injunctions, restraining orders against you, who knows what else."

Alan swallowed. "What do you recommend?"

Emily took a deep breath. "Usually, in a whistleblower case, we gather as much evidence as possible before filing. We also consider whether to involve regulatory authorities, like the FDA or the Department of Justice, depending on the nature of the wrongdoing. Since your evidence pertains to clinical trials, which are under FDA oversight, we might have a federal angle."

Tessa chimed in. "We also have a question of whether these trials were funded with any federal money - grants or Medicare research funds. If so, that opens the door for a potential False Claims Act case, which includes whistleblower protections and possible monetary damages."

Alan's eyes flicked up with a glimmer of hope. "I didn't see any direct mention of federal grants in the documents, but it's possible. GenTech has so many subsidiaries and partnerships. They could be receiving funding indirectly."

Emily nodded. "We'll dig into that. Next step is to compile all the documents in a secure database. We'll need to index them so we can show a court - or a government agency - the chain of evidence. We'll do everything by the book so GenTech can't claim any mishandling or tampering."

A faint flush spread across Alan's cheeks. "I can't believe I'm doing this. Just last year, I was so proud to be working at GenTech - thought they were innovators, you know? Cutting-edge research, saving lives with new medicines. But then I found out about these trials. People died, Ms. Blackwood, and they acted like it was a rounding error in a spreadsheet."

Emily felt a surge of empathy. "We'll do our best to ensure those people get justice."

Tessa reached over to pat Alan's hand. "You made the right choice coming here."

Despite his fear, Alan managed a small, grateful smile. "What... what do you need from me right now?"

"First, get yourself somewhere safe," Emily said firmly. "I'm not exaggerating the danger. If your apartment was already compromised, these people are not messing around. Then, email Tessa any additional documents or leads you have. Keep your phone on. We'll maintain regular contact."

He nodded vigorously. "Okay. I'll do that."

Once Alan left, Tessa and Emily paused to absorb the gravity of the situation. Tessa pulled up a stool beside Emily's desk, setting down her notepad brimming with scribbles. "This is serious," she said. "If they broke into his apartment, they'll probably come after us, too."

Emily nodded. "I'll talk to building management about increasing our office security. We can't afford private guards, but maybe better locks, some cameras in the hallway."

"Also, I looked up a local detective agency. They do background checks, skip traces, stuff like that," Tessa offered. "I'm not sure we can afford them yet, but it might be helpful down the line."

Emily rubbed her forehead. The financial strain she had woken up to just the day before had not magically disappeared. If anything, it had multiplied. "Let's keep that in mind. First, though, I want to confirm the scope of Alan's claims. We need to decide on the best legal avenue before spending more money than we have."

Tessa placed a hand on Emily's shoulder. "We'll figure it out. One step at a time, right?"

A flicker of gratitude passed through Emily. "Right. One step at a time."

Emily and Tessa sat on the floor of the office, surrounded by printouts, clippings, and the digital backups Tessa had started to compile. They had discovered references to multiple clinical trial sites in various African and South American countries, each linked through obscure billing codes. The deeper they looked, the clearer it became that GenTech had systematically tested a developmental drug in impoverished areas, seemingly concealing lethal side effects.

The Ghosts' Trial – Volume One

At times, the emotional weight felt overwhelming. Tessa read out loud from a local Peruvian news piece: a father described how his previously healthy teenage son fell gravely ill after being recruited for "free medical testing." Two days later, the boy was dead. The father claimed no one from GenTech or the local clinic would speak to him. He never received an autopsy report.

Emily's voice cracked. "This is beyond negligence. It sounds like criminal recklessness."

Tessa's face was grim. "And they thought they could hush it up because these people are poor and far away from U.S. courts."

"That's exactly it," Emily murmured, feeling outrage simmer. "It's vile. They're counting on geography and economic disparity to hide their tracks."

Another silence settled in, broken only by the rustling of papers. Emily thought of Mark Hastings - her old colleague. She had admired him once for his legal acumen. Was he fully aware of these atrocities if he was indeed working with GenTech now? She dreaded the possibility of coming face-to-face with him in court. She dreaded even more the idea that he might be just another cog in a machine that exploited vulnerable lives.

Tessa broke the silence: "We have enough to build a compelling narrative, but not all the puzzle pieces. We don't know the exact chain of command within GenTech that authorized these trials."

Emily nodded. "We'll need depositions, internal memos. That's something we can only get through formal discovery once we file a complaint. But if we file too soon, we risk them burying us in motions or spoliating evidence."

Tessa took a breath. "We need a plan. A timeline. Let's bullet-point it."

They spent the next hour drafting a rough approach:

1. **Secure Alan's Safety**: Provide him with resources, encourage him to keep digital and physical copies locked away.

2. **Document Review**: Categorize, label, and cross-reference each item from Alan's trove.

3. **Preliminary Government Notification**: Potentially alert the FDA's Office of Criminal

Investigations or the Department of Justice, but only after finalizing the complaint so GenTech can't get ahead of them.

4. **Draft the Complaint**: Outline the legal grounds - whistleblower protections, wrongful termination, perhaps a class action if other victims come forward.

5. **Media Strategy**: Weigh the risks and benefits of a press conference or a leak to a reputable journalist.

They pinned the list to a whiteboard Tessa had managed to scrounge from an old supply closet. Emily stared at it, the markers and bullet points feeling like the blueprint to either her greatest triumph or her professional downfall.

"We can do this," Tessa said quietly, reading Emily's expression.

Emily forced a smile. "Yeah. We can try."

Shadows stretched across the office as the day wore on, and Emily's stomach rumbled. They'd both skipped lunch, sustained only by coffee and leftover muffins.

Tessa insisted she make a quick run to the corner deli. "You need to eat," she scolded gently, "before you collapse."

While Tessa was out, Emily flipped through her phone contacts, finding the number of a forensic accountant she had known at Hastings & Cole - a man named Joseph "Joe" Dagwood. Back then, Joe had specialized in tracing hidden assets for corporate clients. If anyone could unravel the shell company labyrinth, it was him.

Her finger hovered over the call button. She hadn't spoken to Joe since she left the firm under tense circumstances. Would he even be willing to help? Still, she had to try. If Joe was on board, he'd be a powerful ally in building a financial trail that proved GenTech's wrongdoing.

Steeling her nerves, she pressed the call icon. It rang three times before a familiar, gruff voice answered. "Dagwood here."

"Joe, hey. It's Emily Blackwood."

A pause. She pictured him frowning in confusion. "Emily. That's a blast from the past. How are you?"

"Complicated," she admitted. "I've set up my own shop, and I'm dealing with a case that might require your expertise - tracing corporate funds, shell companies, that kind of thing."

He let out a low whistle. "Sounds interesting. But you know I'm still at Hastings & Cole, right? Or at least affiliated with them."

Emily's stomach tightened. "You are? I heard a rumor you'd gone independent."

"I consult, but yeah, most of my contracts still come from them," Joe replied carefully. "Is this something they'd want me working on?"

"No," Emily said bluntly. "Actually, it might be in direct conflict with them. I'm representing a whistleblower against one of their potential clients."

Silence. Then a soft chuckle. "Ah, so you've turned rebel. Good for you."

Emily exhaled. "I guess so. Look, Joe, I know this is awkward. But if you're doing some side projects, I'd love to hire you for a discreet job. I can't pay you a big-firm rate, but I can do something. And if the case succeeds, you'd be compensated well."

Joe hesitated. "I won't lie, Emily, it's risky. Hastings & Cole doesn't like it when their associates - past or present - buck the system. But I've always liked you. And I'm not exactly a fan of certain corporate cases they handle. I'm… open to hearing more."

Relief swept through her. "That's all I ask. Let me send you a summary. We can talk next week if you want to see the data for yourself."

"All right," he said, his voice turning serious. "But let's keep it on the down-low. I don't want word getting back to Mark Hastings or the other partners. If I get a whiff that they're upset, I might have to bail."

"I understand," Emily said. "Thank you, Joe."

They hung up, and Emily allowed herself a tiny, hopeful smile. Maybe, just maybe, this was the start of assembling a team that could tackle GenTech's monstrous legal might.

Tessa returned a short while later with sandwiches and bottled water. They ate on the floor again - paper wrappers spread out as makeshift plates, the whiteboard looming in front of them like a silent witness to their plans.

"Did I miss anything?" Tessa asked, between bites.

Emily told her about the call with Joe Dagwood.

"That's huge," Tessa said, brightening. "We could really use someone who knows how to follow the money. That might give us the smoking gun if GenTech tried to hide transactions."

Emily nodded. "He's cautious, though. We have to be discreet. The second Hastings & Cole finds out, they'll try to spook him into cutting ties with us."

Tessa leaned back against the wall. "We'll manage. The important thing is, we're moving forward."

Dusk turned to night as they worked, and eventually Tessa insisted they both get some proper rest. Emily locked up the office feeling slightly more confident than she had in the morning. Yet, as she drove her aging sedan back to her apartment, she felt the old doubts creeping in. Could she really do this? Did she have enough skill, enough stamina, enough financial backing? Gerald Lawson's ominous warning echoed in her mind.

After parking on the street, she walked up the cracked concrete steps of her building. An autumn chill nipped at her cheeks. She glanced around, half-expecting some shadowy figure to be lurking by the entrance. Paranoia, maybe, but in the wake of Alan's break-in, she didn't want to take any chances.

Once inside her apartment, she double-locked the door. For a moment, she considered setting up an extra deadbolt, or even a small security camera. The tension of the day weighed on her like lead, pressing her shoulders down. Letting out a shaky breath, she flicked on the lamp beside her couch, the warm yellow glow comforting but also strangely solitary.

She set her purse on the kitchen counter, rummaging for her phone. Her mind spun with arguments and counterarguments for a lawsuit she hadn't yet officially filed. **In Doubt**. That phrase flitted through her consciousness, the perfect summary of her entire day. She was in doubt about her ability to take on GenTech, about her practice's survival, about how deep this corporate conspiracy ran.

Yet beneath the doubt was a spark of conviction - like a pilot light in an old stove, burning patiently, waiting for fuel to ignite into a full blaze. If she didn't stand up for

The Ghosts' Trial – Volume One

Alan, if she didn't try to expose GenTech's wrongdoing, then what was the point of all her ideals?

She sank onto her couch, rubbed her tired eyes, and thought about Tessa's unwavering encouragement. Tessa believed in her. Alan Priest believed in her enough to risk his safety and livelihood. If they believed in her, maybe she could believe in herself.

She fell asleep on the couch, fully clothed, phone still clutched in her hand. Her dreams swirled with images of courtrooms, men in suits with blurred faces, and a swirl of foreign news headlines she couldn't read. Even in slumber, the weight of the case pressed on her, reminding her that tomorrow, she would have to keep fighting - because GenTech's victims had no one else.

When she woke shortly before dawn, her neck stiff and her phone battery nearly dead, Emily realized that doubt might always shadow her. But the only way forward was through it - one step at a time, fueled by the faint but resolute flame of hope that maybe, just maybe, she could make a difference.

Chapter 9:
The Confidential Meeting

Emily Blackwood sat in her cramped office late Tuesday afternoon, the sun's amber rays slicing through the dusty blinds. It had been barely two months since she had left Hastings & Cole - one of the most illustrious law firms in the city - and the contrast between her old swanky eleventh-floor corner suite and her current humble workspace was becoming painfully obvious by the day. Yet every time she questioned her choice, a voice in her head reminded her of the reasons she had left. She wanted her freedom to fight the cases she believed in. She wanted the chance to wrestle her own demons without towing a corporate line. And most of all, she wanted to help the whistleblower who had stepped into her office trembling with secrets that could topple a pharmaceutical giant.

Alan Priest was the reason she had pushed herself into this lonely corner. He had arrived in a state of agitation, gripping a set of documents that seemed to burn right through their manila folder. Those documents told tales of questionable - and often lethal - drug trials run by a global behemoth called GenTech. In the past few weeks, she had skimmed over dozens of damning emails, internal memos, and coded references that hinted at a conspiracy so large, it was difficult to believe. But now, as she sat at her desk, scrawling notes in the margin of a motion for discovery she planned to file, Emily's belief in their authenticity grew sharper by the hour.

Her office phone buzzed, snapping her out of her thoughts. Tessa Moretti, her sharp-witted paralegal, crackled through on the line.

"Alan is on one of those burners again," Tessa said. "He called from another new number. Sounded like he was whispering."

Emily frowned. "Did he say anything about why?"

"He wants to meet tonight - somewhere public, but quiet enough that no one will overhear. Something about confirming that you've got enough evidence to pin GenTech down. He's worried, Em. More than usual."

Emily leaned back in her chair and felt the worn pleather squeak in protest. After the last close call -

Alan nearly bolting because he was convinced someone was following him - she had told him to keep his head low and avoid contact with suspicious strangers. But apparently, that wasn't enough to calm his nerves.

"All right," Emily said softly. "Tell him to meet me at Lorena's Café in the West End. Seven o'clock. I'll get there early, find a corner booth. Let's keep it quiet."

"Got it," Tessa replied. "He also kept saying we have no idea what GenTech's security team is really capable of."

A chill ran down Emily's spine. That was no surprise: just days before, she had spotted a black SUV tailing her for three consecutive blocks before taking a hard right. She couldn't prove it was connected to GenTech, but her intuition told her otherwise. "Thanks, Tess," she said. "Let's hope we can keep him calm enough so we can finally get a coherent statement from him."

Tessa paused. "You're sure you want to do this tonight? You haven't finished prepping for that hearing next week."

"I don't have a choice," Emily murmured, ending the call.

She reached for her purse, stuffed her notepad and digital recorder inside, and clicked off the lamp on her desk. The overhead fluorescent hummed, bathing the cramped space in cold light. She decided she'd review the rest of her notes for the meeting from home or from the café. If Alan was finally ready to reveal everything in a systematic way - concrete details about the African and South American clinical trials - then Emily needed to hear him out before he lost his nerve again.

By the time Emily arrived at Lorena's Café, night had thrown a velvet curtain across the city's skyline. The café was a small, unassuming place that offered an eclectic menu of Middle Eastern and South American dishes, along with a corner reading nook that rarely saw traffic after the dinner rush. She had chosen it because it was lively enough to deter suspicious onlookers from prying too closely, but calm enough that she and Alan could speak without shouting.

Emily settled into a booth near the back, eyes sweeping across the small crowd for any sign of unusual interest. A group of college students huddled over a laptop in one corner, a young couple in the middle debated the menu, and a man in a beanie hunched over a steaming cup of coffee near the entrance. No one looked particularly menacing. Still, Emily was acutely aware that anyone could be an observer. After a moment's hesitation, she ordered a mint tea - no coffee for her tonight. If Alan's testimony was half as damning as she suspected, she would need her nerves steady.

Seven o'clock came and went. Emily checked her phone again. Tessa had forwarded Alan's cryptic text: On my way. Not safe to talk by phone. Will come in from the side entrance. Wait for me.

At 7:11, she finally saw him: short, wiry, and carrying a subdued energy that made him blend easily into a crowd. He wore a faded gray hoodie and jeans that looked a size too big, probably deliberately. The overshadowing hood concealed his face in half-darkness. He slipped through the side door, scanned the room, and raised his chin in quick recognition when he spotted Emily.

She waved him over, swallowing the knot of unease forming in her throat. "Alan," she greeted quietly as he slid into the booth across from her. She noticed his eyes flicker to every corner of the café.

"Emily," he said, voice raspy. There was a hollow quality in his tone, the harried desperation of a man who hadn't slept soundly in weeks. His trembling hand rested on the table, and she saw faint ink stains on his knuckles - likely from scribbling notes or trying to rearrange evidence on the run.

"Are you okay?" she asked, leaning in so he could hear her hushed tone. "You look exhausted."

He managed a bitter smile. "I'm alive. That's a start."

Emily placed a comforting hand on top of his own. "Tell me what's going on."

He licked his lips, glancing around. "I… I got word that GenTech is taking more extreme measures now. Their internal security, the same group that told me to keep quiet after I discovered how many people died in those so-called 'trials,' is apparently monitoring me 24/7. I'm pretty sure they traced my phone again, so I changed it. But it's not just me they're after - they know you've got my documents. They know you filed that complaint."

Emily's pulse quickened. "I had to file the complaint, Alan. If we're going to blow the whistle on GenTech's lethal experiments, we need to go public."

Martyn Bellamy

He gave a reluctant nod. "That's why I requested this meeting. I - I'm starting to think people have had 'accidents' before. People who tried to come forward about the side effects. People who lost family members in those trials in Africa. People who were once on GenTech's payroll, but tried to do the right thing."

Emily tried to keep her voice level, though her stomach churned. "Accidents? Are you sure these weren't legitimate - "

He shook his head emphatically. "I'm not sure of anything. But I overheard something in a meeting I wasn't supposed to attend."

"Go on," Emily urged, forcing her mind to remain calm. She eased back and reached for her bag, making sure her digital recorder was ready.

Alan's gaze darted to the man in the beanie near the front of the café. Lowering his voice to a near-whisper, he leaned in. "I was finishing up some maintenance on a server for GenTech's internal communications - this was a few months before I resigned. I overheard an internal security agent bragging about how 'accidents' tend to happen when any breach gets too close to going public. Then, in one of those emails we found -

remember, the chain that references 'project hush'? - there's talk of damage control. If you connect the dots, well…"

He let the words trail off, eyes filled with a haunted look. Emily recalled reading those lines, a sanitized corporate expression about 'damage control protocol' - an odd phrase that seemed to pop up whenever incriminating data threatened to see the light of day.

"I'm listening," she said softly, flicking on the digital recorder in her bag without making it obvious.

Alan sighed, shoulders trembling. "The official story is always that these folks died in random accidents - car crashes, overdoses, house fires, you name it. But I don't think all of them were coincidences. There's a pattern, if you look close. It's not just the death itself, but the timing. And the hush that follows."

Emily's throat felt dry. "So this 'internal security' group… they could be contractors. Private investigators. Even ex-military. The name on the emails is often redacted. We suspect they're behind intimidation and sabotage. But you're saying they might also orchestrate actual killings?"

He nodded slowly. "I hate to jump to such a - "

He stopped. The server had arrived to take their order. Emily flashed a polite smile and asked for a refill of her tea. Alan waved the server away, tension bristling in his posture. Once the server retreated, he continued, "I hate to jump to such a horrifying conclusion, but yes. I don't want to be the next person who has an 'accident.' That's why I ran to you."

Emily swallowed. "You did the right thing. But you need to lay low. We'll figure out how to protect you."

Alan's mouth trembled. "You're the first person who believed me. At Hastings & Cole, when I tried to approach Mark Hastings - remember that guy, the one you used to work with? - he brushed me off. He said I needed to speak to the legal compliance department. But the compliance officers were the same ones threatening me."

A wave of complicated emotions flared in Emily's chest. She still couldn't believe the friend she had once trusted, Mark Hastings, was now stepping into the ring as GenTech's counsel. He had already issued a warning that she was "in over her head," but she refused to back down.

Alan's eyes darted toward the front entrance again. "I'm sorry to drag you into this, Emily. I really am."

"This is my job," she said gently. "And you're not dragging me anywhere. I chose to take this on."

He sank back, relief and fear mixing on his face. "I need to confirm some key facts with you tonight, especially about the existence of those trials in Africa. You mentioned you had a paralegal who was going through local African news outlets. Tessa, right?"

Emily nodded. "She's uncovered multiple stories - articles from small publications that never made it to mainstream media. Several families lost loved ones during GenTech's so-called 'fast-track drug trials.' The patterns are consistent: GenTech offered free medical care to impoverished communities, promised they were testing 'vitamins' or 'basic remedies.' Then, months later, some participants died of complications never disclosed publicly."

Alan's jaw flexed, and for the first time Emily saw tears brimming in his eyes. "I knew it. I mean, I saw emails that pointed to that, but I always hoped I was reading them wrong. A big chunk of the hush money was funneled into these side accounts. You remember that ledger I included in the documents I gave you?"

"Yes," Emily said, "the one with the offshore shell company."

"That shell company was used to pay out certain families for 'confidential settlements.' They never traced it back to GenTech because it was all done under shell corporations, multiple layers deep. But everything ends up at GenTech's main office. These so-called philanthropic programs in Africa and South America were effectively test labs."

Emily felt anger roll through her. She had spent weeks building up the courage to confront GenTech in court, but every time she had read more about those unsanctioned trials, she felt physically ill. "We're going to expose them," she said. "But I need your help in confirming the data. We have enough circumstantial evidence for a scandal, but for a legal victory, we have to be airtight."

Alan nodded, rubbing his temples. "That's why I risked coming here tonight. I can help you tie the ledger to real names - emails, dates, the exact chain of command. But you have to promise to protect me if I do. I can't show up in court in broad daylight, or I'm a dead man."

Emily's heart pounded. "There are witness protection measures. They're not perfect, but for whistleblowers, it's sometimes an option. However, we need to get the Department of Justice or at least the authorities involved if it's that serious. Are you willing to give a statement to them?"

He swallowed hard, face pale. "Yes. If that's the only way. But you can't let them bury my testimony or cut deals behind the scenes. I'm worried that GenTech has enough pull to mitigate the damage if they strike an agreement with the feds."

Her gaze flicked to the café entrance again, just to ensure no one was lingering too close. "Understood. We'll coordinate carefully, piece by piece. For now, let's focus on what's crucial. If we can prove the Africa and South America trials resulted in an undisclosed number of deaths - and that GenTech deliberately covered up the side effects - then we have a case. Once we file for formal discovery, they'll have to produce documents, and we can cross-reference the data."

Alan exhaled, a heavy sound that was half relief, half dread. "All right," he whispered. "But you need to know something else."

He hesitated. Emily waited, her pulse thrumming.

"There was a meeting in South America - near the Colombian border - where top GenTech executives gathered to witness a demonstration of the drug's effects on a test population. This was well before the final approval process was even started. The emails I salvaged mention it only in passing - like a bullet point about a 'field review.' But it was basically a hush-hush operation to see how well the drug suppressed certain illnesses in real conditions. And I think it killed at least a dozen people."

Emily's stomach lurched. "This is the first time I'm hearing about a demonstration in the field."

He nodded. "I hadn't told you because I only just remembered the conversation. A manager in the internal security team joked about the 'South America show' - how it made certain executives more confident they'd pass FDA approval if they kept the details under wraps."

"Do you have anything in writing?" she asked carefully, aware that this single piece of information could blow the case wide open.

"Only references to the trip. I can cross-match them with flight records if we can get them in discovery. Some are probably shredded by now, but large corporations always keep backups in the cloud, ironically enough."

"Then that's our angle," Emily said. "We'll request flight logs, expense reports - anything we can tie to that trip. If we can prove GenTech used an unapproved, hazardous drug on unsuspecting individuals, that's a direct violation of so many laws I can't even count them all."

Alan's eyes were red-rimmed, but a flicker of something close to hope gleamed there. "So, you see how they'll do anything to keep that from surfacing?"

"I do," Emily replied, unable to mask the gravity in her voice. "Look, I know you're scared. But we can't stop now. We can't let them keep getting away with this."

He pressed his lips together. "I know. I'm trying to keep it together. It's just... I've heard rumors about some poor souls who died under questionable circumstances after crossing GenTech. No official link, but it's suspicious."

She brushed her hair behind her ear, uneasy. "Tessa and I have already spotted a couple suspicious black SUVs around my neighborhood. I'm not sure if it's the same group or if it's a coincidence, but either way, we have to stay vigilant."

Alan gulped. "How can I help you do that? I'm just one person with some stolen files."

"You're more than that," she said firmly. "You're the key witness. The courts typically look kindly on whistleblowers if they can show real evidence. You could be the wedge that cracks GenTech's entire foundation. But that's only if you stay alive - and if we can keep you from vanishing."

He lowered his head, a trembling smile twisting his lips. "Staying alive sounds like a plan."

Emily flipped to a fresh page in her notepad. "Let's do this systematically. First, I'll outline the major points we need to confirm for the case. Then we'll figure out what you can personally attest to, and what we can support with documents. Once that's done, we'll plan how to protect you and your testimony. Deal?"

He nodded, glancing once more around the café before settling in. "Deal."

For the next half hour, Emily systematically walked Alan through each piece of evidence. She had compiled a preliminary docket of GenTech's internal emails, spreadsheet fragments, and notes on the African and South American clinical trials. With every question, Alan flipped through mental files, verifying details, clarifying incomplete references. Occasionally he would scribble something on a small notepad of his own - potential file names or servers where the data might still reside in GenTech's systems.

"Let's talk about the off-shore shell company," Emily said, tapping her pen on the notepad. "We have partial traces of money flowing through a bank in the Cayman Islands. That same account was used to settle with families in Cameroon and Kenya, from what Tessa found."

Alan leaned in. "Yes, that's correct. The main contact for those transactions is listed as Haviland Resources, Inc. That's the shell corporation GenTech used, but it doesn't show up anywhere on their official ledger. You'll need subpoena power to get the banking records."

"We've started that process," Emily replied. "Our complaint specifically requests financial records tied to any philanthropic medical outreach. They'll probably try to bury it in red tape, or claim it's proprietary, but we'll keep pressing."

Alan cleared his throat. "I can confirm that Haviland was definitely paying hush money. I coded a few of the authentication routines for wire transfers, ironically. I remember the transactions had codewords like 'Remedy Program' or 'Special Medical Scholarship.' And in internal emails, some managers called them 'sympathy payments.' But they were anything but."

Emily's pen scratched across the page. "Understood. Next: the emails referencing drug side effects. You highlighted a memo that specifically said the mortality rate among test subjects was at least five times the threshold deemed acceptable by regulators."

Alan nodded vigorously. "Yes. The email chain included a Senior VP named Elizabeth Cho. She forwarded these mortality rates to a small group. I remember lines like, 'We cannot allow these figures to surface without immediate spin or a protective narrative.' The phrase that made me do a double-take was 'protective narrative.' It implied they were planning a PR campaign to undermine or discredit any negative publicity."

Emily remembered reading that email. At first glance, it had sounded like corporate jargon for standard crisis management. But the more she dove into GenTech's material, the more it reeked of a coordinated cover-up. "We'll definitely introduce that email chain as Exhibit A," Emily said. "Do you have the original attachments?"

"Some," Alan admitted. "Though, to be honest, I might have missed a few. When I copied these files, I was rushed. I grabbed what I could before they realized I was in the system."

A spike of anxiety shot through Emily. "Let's hope we have enough to paint the big picture. Next question…" She scanned the notepad. "Regarding the actual drug - codenamed X-Thrive, right?"

"That's right," said Alan, almost reflexively lowering his voice. "It's supposedly an antiretroviral with extended immunomodulatory properties. But from what I saw, it was never stable enough in trials to go to market safely. There were anomalies in the results - brain swelling, organ failure, the works."

Emily exhaled slowly, her stomach roiling. "And they wanted to keep pushing it, presumably because the potential market was enormous - "

"Billions of dollars," Alan interjected. "If X-Thrive worked as advertised, it would dominate the global market for advanced immunotherapies. So they fast-tracked everything, cutting corners. South America was a big piece of that, too. Fewer regulatory hurdles, less press coverage."

She jotted down a note to cross-reference the mention of X-Thrive in the official complaint. The more Alan spoke, the more she understood the chilling logic behind GenTech's decisions: a potential goldmine at the expense of impoverished test subjects who would never have the resources to fight back.

As the half hour slipped into forty minutes, Emily noticed Alan's tension building again. His eyes kept darting to the corners of the café, and every time the door squeaked open, he flinched.

"Alan," she said gently, "you're safe here."

He snorted, trembling a bit. "I don't believe in 'safe' anymore. You shouldn't either."

Emily's chest tightened. "You said earlier you were afraid of 'accidents.' Did you get more direct threats?"

He hesitated, then nodded slowly. "A few days ago, I found a note taped to my windshield. It said, 'Stay silent or pay the price.' No signature, of course. Then I noticed my apartment door looked like it had been tampered with. Nothing was stolen, but I found footprints on the carpet that weren't mine."

Emily felt fury boil inside her. This was intimidation, plain and simple. "Have you told the police?"

Alan grimaced. "I tried. I filed a complaint. They took my statement, gave me a card for a detective. But the detective said unless there's camera footage or eyewitnesses, it's a he-said-she-said scenario. They can't do much for me."

She made a mental note to contact that detective herself. "Well, I'll see what I can do to get you some additional protections. It's not easy, but maybe we can ask the court for a protective order once the case is in full swing, especially if you'll be a key witness."

Alan's gaze flickered with gratitude. "That would help." Then his eyes narrowed. "I still think you should be careful. Mark Hastings might be someone you once trusted, but if he's representing GenTech, I doubt he'd cross the line into something… lethal. But the higher-ups he works for? That's a different story."

Emily forced a tight smile. "Mark gave me a friendly warning a week ago, basically telling me to back off. He said this lawsuit would destroy my practice and put me in an impossible financial hole. That's the only reason I'm still in that cheap, run-down office."

"You and me both," Alan muttered. "Living on the run. But we can't do this alone. You said Tessa was also helping you do background research?"

Emily nodded. "She's been incredible - digging up news clippings, contacting families overseas who are willing to talk. We'll be extremely cautious so none of them get spooked."

Alan's face tightened. "Or get targeted."

"Yes," Emily said somberly. "Or that."

They talked for another ten minutes, with Alan providing more specifics: file paths for certain documents he believed still existed on GenTech's server, the possible involvement of a European lab that might have collaborated with GenTech, and details about a hush fund that dwarfed the African payouts.

At one point, Emily saw a figure step out of the restroom hallway - someone tall and broad, dressed in a dark coat. He lingered near the café's back wall, not far from their booth, flipping through a newspaper. Emily's heart drummed harder, and she subtly nudged Alan.

"Do you know him?" she whispered.

Alan glanced briefly, then shook his head. "No."

The figure eventually drifted back toward the front exit, leaving behind only a faint sense of unease. Emily tried to push her paranoia down. It could be a harmless bystander, but she couldn't help recalling Alan's stories of infiltration, private investigators, and worse.

"Maybe we should finish up soon," she said under her breath. "We've got everything I need for tonight. We can always schedule a more secure meeting with Tessa or do it in a lawyer's meeting room."

Alan exhaled. "I agree. Let's just finalize one more thing: Are you sure your complaint requests the right categories of evidence? I think we need anything from that X-Thrive study, plus all the follow-up internal memos."

"Yes," Emily replied. "We're zeroing in on all emails, memos, or internal presentations referencing any immunotherapy trials. That'll force them either to lie to the court or produce the real documents - assuming they haven't been destroyed."

Alan nodded again. The mention of "destroyed documents" twisted both their expressions into grim masks of frustration. Corporations as large as GenTech had a million ways to shred, hide, or disclaim data.

They agreed to part ways, stepping outside into the cool night air. Emily glanced up at the neon sign for Lorena's Café, then back down the deserted sidewalk. The man in the beanie was gone, as was the tall figure in the coat. A few passing cars whooshed by, their headlights briefly illuminating the cracked pavement.

Alan hunched his shoulders inside his hoodie. "Thanks," he whispered. "I feel… a bit better now that you have the details. Just promise you'll watch your back."

"I will," Emily said, hooking her purse more securely over her shoulder. "And you?"

He tried to offer a reassuring smile but failed. "I'm heading to a safe spot - an extended-stay motel across town. I'll keep changing the place every few days. If you need me, use that encrypted messaging app we set up."

She gave a short nod. "Right. Do you need any help paying for your room?"

He shook his head, cheeks flushing. "I - no, I'll manage for now. I don't want to burden you any more than I already have."

"You're not a burden," she said firmly. "You're the reason this case exists."

Alan swallowed. "Let's just hope we can blow the lid off GenTech before they get to us. Because I can't shake the feeling they're one step ahead."

He glanced past Emily's shoulder, as though expecting an assailant to leap from the shadows. Sensing his growing paranoia, she touched his arm gently. "We'll win," she promised. "They've gotten used to scaring people into silence. We're not going silent."

They parted without another word, Alan disappearing into the night's shadows. Emily stood there a moment, forcing her mind to calm. She looked left and right, then moved to retrieve her car from a side street behind the café.

A single flickering streetlamp cast an anemic circle of light. The alley was littered with damp cardboard boxes and broken glass. Emily spotted her battered sedan parked against a graffiti-stained wall. Her chest felt tight as she approached it, ears straining for any sign of footsteps.

A cat screeched in the distance. She nearly jumped, shaking her head to rid herself of the jitters. *You're overreacting*, she told herself. *This is just an alley. Not everyone in a dark coat is a GenTech thug.*

Still, her adrenaline spiked as she reached her car door, keys clenched like a weapon in her fist. With a quick glance over her shoulder, she unlocked the driver's door and slid in, checking the backseat before she pulled the door shut. The quiet enclosed her.

The Ghosts' Trial – Volume One

She let out a shaking breath. "Damn," she muttered under her breath. "This is real."

She started the car, the engine coughing twice before it turned over. Just as she maneuvered out of the alley, she saw headlights flare in her rearview mirror. Another car had pulled in at the other end of the alley, engine idling. Emily's pulse thundered. *Coincidence or not?* she wondered, wiping clammy palms on her skirt.

For a moment, the other car sat perfectly still. Then it reversed out of the alley and disappeared into the night. Emily gripped the steering wheel so tightly her knuckles shone white.

She eased onto the main street, scanning the mirror to see if anyone was following. No sign of a tail. She reminded herself that not every suspicious movement was tied to GenTech. She had to maintain her composure if she was going to survive this battle.

Emily reached her small apartment a half hour later, pulling into a space next to a rusted dumpster. The building was an older four-story walk-up, with a broken buzzer and water stains crawling up the stucco walls. She locked the car and hurried up the concrete steps, keeping an ear out for any sign of pursuit.

Safe inside her apartment, she double-locked the door and slid the chain into place. It wasn't much, but at least it gave her a sense of control. She turned on the lamp, tossed her purse on the coffee table, and shed her jacket. Despite the overhead fan humming softly, the place felt stiflingly warm.

She pulled out her phone and noticed a missed call from Tessa. Quickly, she dialed back. Tessa picked up on the second ring.

"Everything okay?" Tessa asked, a note of worry in her voice.

Emily sank onto her threadbare couch. "Yeah, I'm fine. Just got home. The meeting with Alan... it was intense."

"Did you get what you needed?"

Emily let out a long breath. "Yes, and then some. He's confirmed a lot of details - specific references to hush money, a bigger death toll in Africa than we realized, plus a new lead on a demonstration in South America."

"Whoa," Tessa said, and Emily could envision her friend pushing aside a stack of files on her own living-room desk. "That's huge. If we can prove that demonstration happened, we can show GenTech knew the full risks from the start."

"That's the idea," Emily replied, reaching for her notepad. "Alan also hinted strongly that GenTech's security might have orchestrated so-called accidents to silence potential whistleblowers. That's... more terrifying than I want to admit."

Tessa's voice dropped. "Emily, you know we can't just treat this like any normal case. If they're that ruthless -"

"I know," Emily cut in. "But we're in now. I can't turn back. The lawsuit is filed; we're about to open discovery. Either we see this through, or we let them keep burying bodies."

A pause crackled on the line. "So what's next?"

Emily leaned back, trying to calm her racing mind. "We finalize the written discovery requests tomorrow. I want to reference every angle Alan gave us - especially the mention of that field review. Then we'll keep building our motion to compel once they stonewall."

"That's going to be a lot of hours, Em," Tessa said. "And we're basically doing this on a shoestring budget.

You sure we shouldn't think about bringing in a partner firm?"

Emily mulled that over. An alliance with another firm could give them resources, but it might also tie them into a messy arrangement or entangle them with people who had their own agendas. "Let's give it some more thought," she said carefully. "For now, keep it in-house. The fewer people who know everything, the safer for Alan."

A soft beep told her that her phone was running low on battery. "Tessa, I'll check in tomorrow morning. Be sure to keep an eye on your surroundings. If you notice anything suspicious, call me right away."

"I will," Tessa promised. "You too, Emily. Don't be a hero if it's not safe."

Emily chuckled grimly. "I'll try."

They said their goodnights, and Emily ended the call. She stared at the phone's dark screen for a moment, the hush of her apartment pressing in around her.

Though her body was worn, Emily doubted she'd sleep soundly. The adrenaline of the clandestine meeting buzzed under her skin, but exhaustion ultimately forced her to attempt some rest. She changed into a worn T-shirt and lounge pants, set the phone to charge, and then collapsed onto her bed.

The nightmares began almost immediately. She dreamt of a courtroom where the lights flickered ominously, GenTech lawyers towering at the prosecution's table (which made little sense, as she was the plaintiff's counsel), while Mark Hastings wore a judge's robe. He banged the gavel, and emails spilled out of the file, morphing into photos of suffering families in Africa. Then the families turned into ghosts, pointing accusing fingers at Emily, silently demanding justice.

She woke in a cold sweat, the ghostly images seared into her mind. A quick glance at the bedside clock told her it was just past 3:00 a.m. *Five hours until we start drafting discovery,* she thought wearily. She rolled over, but the restlessness wouldn't leave.

Am I really prepared to fight a billion-dollar company alone?

It was a question that lingered every day. Ever since she left Hastings & Cole, her finances had become precarious. This lawsuit against GenTech was the first big case that might bring both truth and the funds she desperately needed - *if* they won. If they lost, or if GenTech's intimidation drove Alan away, she might be bankrupt by the end of the year.

And that was the lesser concern compared to the terrifying possibility of "accidents." That word haunted her. *Accidents.* She tried to recall every time she'd seen a suspicious SUV or an unknown face lingering near her office building. Had one of those watchers been prepared to do more than watch?

Her mind rolled through the horrifying speculation until she forced herself to focus on the bigger picture: People had died. Real people in Africa and South America, whose families had no voice. Alan's documents showed that. *They deserve justice,* she thought fiercely. *I can't let them down.*

In the dim glow of the streetlight seeping through her curtains, Emily found a hint of resolve. She tugged the blanket around her, mentally rehearsing how she would craft tomorrow's discovery requests, how she would anticipate GenTech's motion to dismiss, how she would keep Alan safe.

Eventually, fitful sleep crept over her.

The Ghosts' Trial – Volume One

When her alarm blared at 8:00 a.m., Emily woke with a dull ache behind her eyes. She dragged herself to the kitchen, started coffee brewing, and forced down some toast and jam. Outside her window, the city was already bustling - delivery trucks rattling down the street, passersby hurrying with coffee cups, an ambulance siren wailing in the distance.

She peered out at the road, eyes scanning for anything suspicious. Her car was still parked at the curb, unmolested. No black SUVs in sight. Yet the feeling of being watched never fully faded. *Paranoia or caution?* she wondered. Perhaps a bit of both.

By 9:00 a.m., she was at her office, flipping on the fluorescent lights that buzzed overhead. Tessa was already there, waiting with a laptop open and a swirl of notes spread across the desk. The smell of stale coffee mingled with the faint odor of cheap carpet cleaner. This was her new world - barely large enough for two desks and a battered filing cabinet, but it was hers.

"You look like you barely slept," Tessa observed, pushing her reading glasses up the bridge of her nose.

"Perceptive." Emily dropped her purse and pulled her hair into a loose ponytail. "I had nightmares all night. But let's not dwell on that. We've got a plan for today."

Tessa gave a firm nod. "Right. Number one: finalize the request for production of documents. Number two: incorporate the references to that demonstration in South America. Number three: start preparing Alan's affidavit to accompany the complaint, in case we need to show the judge probable cause for deeper discovery."

Emily flipped open her notepad. "Perfect. Let's add a confidentiality measure, too. If the judge sees that Alan's testimony is at risk, maybe we can at least get an order that prevents GenTech from outing him."

Tessa typed quickly, her fingers flying over the keys. "Yes, that's wise. I'll draft a preliminary motion for a protective order. We can't rely on it alone, but it's a start."

Emily nodded, trying to bury the lingering dread with busywork. For the next two hours, they fell into their usual routine, pouring over the language of each request. Emily insisted on being meticulous: If they left any loophole, GenTech's lawyers would exploit it.

Around eleven, Tessa rose to grab fresh coffee from the tiny break room. Emily took the chance to stretch. She massaged the back of her neck, letting her mind drift to the meeting with Alan.

The sheer scale of the alleged wrongdoing made her breath catch. The company had done more than just test an unapproved drug - they had orchestrated a scheme to avoid accountability, funnel money into shell accounts, and silence would-be whistleblowers. And in the background loomed the specter of "accidents."

She recalled Alan's trembling voice, the guilt etched into his face. He had worked for GenTech, never realizing the full extent of their operations until he stumbled over that server. A part of her worried: *What if Alan is next on their list?*

Tessa returned with two cups of coffee, interrupting the dark train of thought. "Want sugar?" she asked.

"Yeah, thanks," Emily replied, forcing a smile. "We've got a lot to do."

As Emily reached for her mug, the phone buzzed. She snatched it up, half expecting it to be Mark calling with more threats. "Emily Blackwood," she said.

A raspy voice on the other line replied, "Emily, it's me."

"Alan?" she asked sharply, exchanging a glance with Tessa. "Everything all right?"

Alan coughed, voice tense. "I - I just had to let you know. I got a tip from someone inside the company. They know you and I met last night. They said GenTech's top brass is furious. I don't know how they found out so quickly."

Emily felt her heart slam into her ribcage. "Are you sure?"

"Yes," Alan hissed. "And there's more. Someone's been sniffing around the motel I was staying at. I had to move again."

She gripped the phone. "Where are you now?"

"Doesn't matter," he whispered. "I'm safe for the moment, but I wanted to warn you. They might try to file a motion against you, or maybe something else. Just - just be careful."

Emily swallowed. "All right. Thanks for letting me know."

He hung up abruptly, leaving Emily holding a dial tone. She slowly replaced the phone in its cradle, her pulse racing.

Tessa frowned. "He sounded spooked."

Emily filled her in, and Tessa pursed her lips thoughtfully. "They must have a mole somewhere. Or maybe they followed him. I thought we were careful."

"So did I," Emily murmured. "But it looks like GenTech's net is tighter than we realized."

Despite the new burst of anxiety, they spent the rest of the day finalizing the discovery requests. By the late afternoon, Emily had signed off on a neat stack of documents that Tessa would file electronically with the court the following morning. On the surface, it was a standard set of demands: produce all internal communications regarding X-Thrive's safety trials, all financial records relating to philanthropic medical outreach, all documents referencing the potential lethal side effects of the new drug.

The difference was that Emily and Tessa now knew exactly where to look. Each request included subtle references designed to corner GenTech into acknowledging the existence of the hush money, the African testing sites, and that fateful demonstration in South America. It was a gamble; if GenTech balked or stonewalled, Emily would use that as ammunition to argue they were hiding incriminating evidence.

By the time they locked up the office, dusk was settling over the city once more. Emily felt the burn in her eyes from staring at a computer screen for hours, and the tension from the previous night still coiled in her neck.

"Be safe going home, Tessa," she said, flipping off the main lights. "Call me if you see anything - anything at all - that doesn't feel right."

Tessa nodded. "You too. I'll get these documents filed first thing tomorrow. Try to actually sleep tonight, okay?"

Emily mustered a wan smile. "I'll do my best."

Returning to her apartment, Emily couldn't shake the sense of vulnerability. She double-checked the locks, then settled onto her couch with a homemade sandwich. Her mind was too tired to cook, and the day's events left her with jumbled thoughts. Alan was on the run,

GenTech was on high alert, and she was about to wage legal war against a multi-billion-dollar juggernaut.

She thought of her old life at Hastings & Cole - polished floors, designer suits, lunch meetings at exclusive restaurants. Sure, the hours were brutal, but it was stable. She had an impressive salary, a comfortable lifestyle, and the sort of prestige that turned heads in any legal circle. Walking away from that had been the boldest - and perhaps the best - thing she'd ever done. Yet the cost was mounting.

Another night passed in fitful rest. Emily dreamt of a labyrinthine building with endless corridors, each door labeled with a GenTech logo. In the dream, she'd open a door only to find it was bricked up. She'd open another, see Tessa's face, call out, but Tessa vanished behind swirling papers. Then she'd open a third door and spot Alan screaming silently as security men in black suits closed in.

She jerked awake at dawn, heart pounding, the echo of silent screams reverberating in her head.

Yet with dawn came routine. Emily forced herself up, brewed a strong cup of coffee, then made her way to the office. Tessa was already filing the requests electronically, each line item typed with the precision of a paralegal who knew how to box in even the slipperiest corporate defendants.

"You ready?" Tessa asked, giving Emily a quick glance over her shoulder as she clicked the final "submit" button.

"As ready as I'll ever be," Emily sighed. "I'm heading out to see a judge this afternoon to request that protective order for Alan."

Tessa nodded. "Need me to come?"

"I got this," Emily said, mustering confidence. "You just keep an eye on the phone and email. We might hear from Mark Hastings or the GenTech legal team. I'm sure they won't wait long to respond to these discovery demands."

Sure enough, less than an hour later, the phone rang. Tessa answered and pressed the receiver to her chest, eyes flicking to Emily. "It's Mark," she mouthed.

Emily took a measured breath. "Put him through," she said.

Tessa's face was grim as she handed over the phone. Emily grabbed it, already bracing herself.

"Hello, Mark," she said, straining to keep her voice neutral.

"Emily," Mark replied, his tone clipped, professional. "I just saw the discovery requests you filed. Ambitious."

She forced a smile that he couldn't see. "We're just doing our job, Mark. GenTech's alleged wrongdoing is massive. You shouldn't be surprised that we're seeking broad discovery."

A pause. "We'll be objecting to virtually every request on grounds of confidentiality and relevance," Mark said matter-of-factly. "If you think a fishing expedition is going to force GenTech's hand, you're mistaken. This case is on thin ice, Emily."

She bristled. "We have strong evidence, Mark. You know it. And if you bury or destroy documents, it'll look even worse in front of a judge."

She could hear him exhale sharply. "I'm not calling to threaten you; this is just a heads-up. We're filing a motion to dismiss within the week. Don't be surprised if the judge is sympathetic to us, especially when they see how unsubstantial your claims are."

For a moment, Emily's anger flared. "You know these claims aren't unsubstantial," she said. "People died. This isn't some nuisance lawsuit."

She expected him to shoot back a corporate line, but instead there was a brief silence. Then Mark's voice came again, subdued. "I'm doing my job, Emily. Same as you. Just watch yourself."

He hung up before she could reply. The conversation left a film of anxiety on her skin. She stared at the silent receiver for a moment, placing it gently on the cradle.

Tessa raised her brows. "What did he say?"

"Exactly what I expected. That they'll try to dismiss our suit. And he told me to watch myself - again."

"Another one of those warnings?" Tessa said softly.

Emily shrugged, feigning nonchalance. "Let them bring it on. We'll fight."

But inside, fear churned. She couldn't escape the sense that each new step in the lawsuit brought her closer to a dangerous line - one that GenTech's security might be all too willing to cross.

That evening, as Emily locked up, she realized that she had not heard from Alan all day. Usually, after such a tense meeting, he would text or call to confirm he had made it to his next safe spot. This time, there was nothing. Part of her wanted to call him, but she worried about drawing attention to his phone.

She tossed her jacket over her arm and stepped out into the chilly night air. The street outside was quiet, illuminated by the orange glow of streetlamps. A stray piece of newspaper tumbled across the sidewalk, and in the distance, a siren wailed.

We have to keep going. That single, stubborn thought pushed aside her exhaustion. GenTech might have an army of corporate lawyers, unlimited funds, and a shadowy security team, but Emily had something they lacked - a witness with a conscience, a paralegal who believed in justice, and her own unwavering dedication to the truth.

As she made her way to her car, the events of the past twenty-four hours looped through her mind: the clandestine meeting with Alan, the secrets of Africa and

South America, the talk of so-called accidents. With each repetition, her resolve only hardened. She might be a small-town solo practitioner now, but she had once been a top corporate associate. She understood the game. She knew how to take depositions, draft motions, and corner adversaries in ways they wouldn't expect.

Standing beneath the streetlamp, she paused to look up at the sky. The moon was hidden behind a swirl of clouds, leaving the world in a hazy half-light. *I'm not alone*, she reminded herself. *Alan, Tessa, the families overseas - they're counting on me.*

She inhaled the brisk air, slid into her car, and steered away from the curb. If GenTech's internal security truly had blood on their hands, if they had orchestrated lethal "accidents," then fear was their weapon. They wanted to terrorize the whistleblowers, keep them running, break them down until they abandoned hope.

Not this time, Emily vowed silently. *Not this lawyer.*

She cast one last glance at the rearview mirror, checking for any tail. The road behind was empty. Whether it remained empty was anyone's guess. But for now, she would cling to the momentary peace, stoking her determination to see this through.

The Ghosts' Trial – Volume One

Tomorrow, the real legal battle would intensify. But tonight, at least, she had made progress. She had gleaned crucial details that would strengthen her case. She had assured Alan of her support - though she worried about his safety, she now had enough from him to pursue GenTech with unrelenting force.

Yes, the real war was just beginning. And somewhere in that looming darkness, Emily could almost sense the presence of those who wished she would fail. But she drove forward into the night, unbroken, a single vow echoing in her mind: **No more silence.**

Martyn Bellamy

Chapter 10: Legal Quagmire

Emily Blackwood stared at the stack of documents in front of her, a knot of tension pulling tighter with each page she flipped. It was approaching nine o'clock at night, and a single fluorescent lamp cast a narrow beam of light across her modest office. She and Tessa Moretti had abandoned the usual routine of tidying up by seven; the potential lawsuit now consumed every spare minute of their waking hours. In truth, Emily had never been this tired, or this uncertain. The question that circled her mind over and over again was whether she could handle something of this magnitude - international pharmaceutical litigation, whistleblower revelations, and an opponent with seemingly bottomless resources.

Alan Priest's files were splayed across her desk: internal emails, partial clinical trial notes, ominous references to anonymous shell companies, and suggestions of under-the-table payments to officials in multiple countries. Tessa's delicate, looping handwriting decorated the margins of many pages: small notes, red-ink question marks, or the occasional exclamation of alarm.

In the preceding weeks, Emily had left the swanky corridors of Hastings & Cole and ventured out on her own, renting this modest third-floor suite above a bakery that smelled like sugar and coffee every morning. She had dreamed of independence, of serving clients she truly believed in. But she never could have guessed that her first major case would involve a whistleblower claiming that a giant pharmaceutical corporation - GenTech - had been running illicit and potentially fatal drug trials in Africa and South America.

Now, all the doubts from the past few days gnawed at her in earnest. Taking this on by herself would be the biggest risk of her career. Her financials were already precarious; she had sunk her savings into this fledgling practice. If GenTech decided to play hardball - and there was no "if" about it - they could bury her in motions, depositions, and enough legal fees to crater her entire operation. It was not only her practice at stake; it was Tessa's job, Alan's safety, and the lives of numerous unnamed individuals who might have been harmed by GenTech's experimental drug.

She sighed heavily, catching a glimpse of her reflection in the window. She looked older, with faint dark circles under her eyes. Sleep had been elusive lately, as every path forward branched into a tangle of new complications. Taking a final sip of lukewarm coffee, Emily planted her palms on the desk.

"Tessa?" she called out, her voice rough from fatigue.

A moment later, Tessa appeared in the doorway. She wore jeans, a snug cardigan, and that unwaveringly determined expression Emily had come to rely on. "Still at it?" Tessa asked quietly.

"Still at it," Emily confirmed. She tapped a finger on the biggest stack of paper. "I've spent the last hour reviewing potential civil causes of action under both federal and state law, but half of this would also require us to coordinate with foreign courts. And that's not even counting the compliance issues with local regulations in sub-Saharan Africa and parts of South America. It's a labyrinth."

Tessa nodded, lips pursed. "I spoke to Alan again today. He's…spooked. He mentioned seeing someone following him outside his motel last night."

Emily's heart tightened at that. She recalled the anxious look in Alan's eyes during their clandestine meeting just a few days ago. He had practically trembled when he handed her a flash drive containing further evidence of internal GenTech memos. "Did he say anything else?"

"Only that the tension is getting to him. He's worried about stepping inside a courtroom. He wants to remain anonymous if possible, or at least under some kind of whistleblower protection, but we both know how tricky that can be. The minute we file, GenTech's attorneys will comb through the docket and link every piece of evidence to him."

Emily nodded. Whistleblower laws existed for a reason, but they could only do so much - especially if GenTech had a security apparatus determined to root out leaks. "Thanks, Tessa. Could you do me a favor and see if the Pro Bono Legal Advocacy Consortium might have any experts in international pharmaceutical litigation?"

"I can do that first thing in the morning," Tessa said, "though we might be cutting it close with the timelines you proposed."

Emily exhaled a weary chuckle. "I know. But we need to see if we can bring in someone with experience in cross-border suits. Otherwise, we're flying blind."

Tessa offered a reassuring half-smile. "You're not flying blind, Em. You've got me - and Alan - and a lot of grit."

Emily's chest fluttered with gratitude. "Thanks. Sometimes grit doesn't feel like enough, though."

They exchanged looks, both acknowledging the sheer enormity of what lay before them. Then Tessa withdrew back to her makeshift desk in the reception area, leaving Emily alone with her thoughts and the hushed swirl of the overhead fan.

Two hours later, Emily had barely moved from her seat. Her eyes scanned the language of international treaties, the Foreign Corrupt Practices Act, precedents for wrongful death suits involving overseas victims, and a host of federal regulations that governed pharmaceutical trials. She jotted down potential angles: negligence, breach of fiduciary duty, product liability, fraudulent misrepresentation, even RICO if there was a pattern of racketeering. But each angle led to more questions: Where would they sue? Could these foreign plaintiffs be brought under a single class action in a U.S. court? Did they have standing? Were there statute-of-limitations issues?

The legal complexities were the sort she used to gloss over in law school - when the professor mentioned multi-jurisdictional litigation, the entire class would groan. Yet now it was her reality. She momentarily wished she were back at Hastings & Cole, where a department of paralegals and junior associates could be tasked with dissecting these tangles.

A wave of longing washed over her. She thought of her old colleague, Mark Hastings, who had come to warn her off the case. Even though Mark was now on the opposing side, she remembered the times they had worked late nights together, analyzing reams of data for big corporate clients. They used to split the workload, which felt more bearable than facing it alone. Now, as she rubbed her temples, she realized with a pang of regret that even if she could call Mark for help, he would be ethically and professionally obligated to stand firm with GenTech. And she doubted they would simply hand over any admissions of wrongdoing - even if he were personally inclined to do the right thing.

At a quarter past midnight, Emily set aside the papers and stood. Her spine popped from the hours of sitting still. Tessa had fallen asleep at her desk, chin on her folded arms, hair askew. Emily carefully draped a light sweater over her friend's shoulders. She inhaled to speak - maybe to suggest they both go home - but Tessa stirred and sat upright, blinking in confusion.

"Did I - did I drift off?" Tessa mumbled, rubbing her eyes.

"You did," Emily said gently. "It's late. We should get some sleep. You can take a cab home. I'll lock up."

Tessa frowned. "What time is it?"

"A little after midnight."

Tessa shook her head vehemently. "You need rest too, Emily. When do you plan to actually, you know, sleep in a bed?"

Emily shrugged, a smile tugging at her lips. "I'll leave soon. I promise."

"Alright," Tessa said, heaving her bag onto her shoulder. "But I'll hold you to it. No all-nighters. If we burn out, GenTech wins."

That comment sent a fresh jolt of resolve through Emily's tired limbs. "True enough," she admitted. "I'll give myself another half-hour, then I'm out."

They bid each other goodnight, and Emily listened for Tessa's footsteps on the creaky stairs. Alone again, she gazed at the city lights outside the window. A pang of both fear and excitement swept over her. This was the biggest challenge she had ever faced, and there was still a flicker of possibility that she could do real good here. Yet, the weight of the responsibility was immense. So many unknown variables loomed.

Emily quietly gathered the most sensitive documents, locked them in a file cabinet, and decided to call it a night.

Bright morning light streamed through the window when Emily returned to her office the next day. True to her word, she had dragged herself home before one, managing a meager five hours of restless sleep. She was re-caffeinated now, a fresh cappuccino in hand from the bakery downstairs.

Tessa was already at work. She'd pinned her hair up in a neat bun and wore a crisp white blouse. "Good morning," she greeted Emily, sounding far more energetic than Emily felt. "I started calling a few nonprofit legal groups to see if there are attorneys who specialize in cross-border suits involving pharmaceuticals."

Emily arched her brow. "Any luck?"

"They all say the same thing: They're at capacity. You wouldn't believe the backlog of cases they handle. Environmental lawsuits, immigration issues, you name it." Tessa's eyes flickered with frustration. "I'm still following up with a couple more. One group said they might put me in touch with a volunteer group of ex-prosecutors who occasionally consult on big cases like this. But it's not guaranteed."

"Keep trying," Emily murmured, sipping her cappuccino. "I have a feeling we might end up forging a patchwork team of specialists. If that's what it takes, so be it."

Tessa opened her mouth to say something but paused as Emily's phone rang. Emily lifted the receiver. "Emily Blackwood."

"Emily," a familiar voice said, low and cautious. It was Alan. "I - uh - I need to talk to you. In person."

The Ghosts' Trial – Volume One

"Is everything alright? Are you safe?"

A short, humorless laugh crackled through the line. "Safe? Hardly. I think I'm being tailed. I tried switching motels last night, but a black sedan followed me for about six blocks. Then, when I left to grab dinner, I saw the same parking loted across the street."

Emily's pulse quickened. "Alan, you need to be careful. We can work with law enforcement if it gets more serious, maybe arrange some temporary protective measures."

"Law enforcement can be compromised," Alan replied tersely. "I'm not saying all of them, but I have no idea who might be on GenTech's payroll. They've got massive financial reach."

Emily's gaze flicked to Tessa, who was watching her intently. "Alright," she said, keeping her voice calm. "Come by the office in a couple of hours if you can manage it. We'll find a safe place to talk. And we'll figure this out together."

"Okay," Alan said, exhaling shakily. "I'll see you then. Please - just be careful."

The line went dead. Emily hung up the phone, turning to Tessa. "Alan is convinced he's being followed. I don't blame him. We need to stay on guard, Tessa. Especially once we file anything in court, it's going to get more intense."

Tessa nodded, her expression grim. "I'll finalize a list of possible pro bono or low-cost security consultants. Maybe we can get someone with experience in corporate intimidation tactics. We're in over our heads if GenTech decides to go full tilt."

Emily rubbed her temple. "We'll do our best. The sooner we have at least a skeleton crew of external experts, the less alone we'll be."

Mid-morning found Emily on the phone with an old acquaintance: Dr. Robert Madigan, a professor of biomedical ethics at a nearby university. She recalled crossing paths with him briefly during a pro bono case at Hastings & Cole. His interest was purely academic at the time, but he had lamented the ways big corporations sometimes manipulated trial data. If anyone might guide her through the labyrinth of medical oversight and international clinical protocols, it was Dr. Madigan.

He picked up on the third ring. "Professor Madigan speaking."

"Robert, this is Emily Blackwood. I'm not sure if you remember me - from Hastings & Cole, about two years ago?"

He took a moment. "Emily. Yes, I remember. You assisted on that health-insurance lawsuit. How are you?"

She explained her new situation in a brisk but polite tone, culminating in the main thrust: "I have a potential lawsuit against GenTech. Their whistleblower claims the company conducted lethal drug trials in Africa and South America. I know you've researched some of these issues academically. Is there any chance you'd be available to consult? Even on a limited basis? I'd need your expertise to interpret certain medical documents and trial protocols."

A stunned silence lingered. Then he replied, "That…that's quite the case to tackle from a small practice, Emily. GenTech's a behemoth. They have extensive government contracts, from what I recall."

"Yes," Emily said quietly. "I'm aware."

Madigan sighed. "I could potentially look at a few documents and offer an informal opinion. I can't promise more than that, at least not right away. The university has strict guidelines on outside consulting. But if there's something truly egregious in those trial results - something that suggests a systemic cover-up - I'd feel obligated to help, at least in an unofficial capacity."

Relief trickled through Emily. "That would be incredible, Robert. Even a few hours of your time could guide me in the right direction."

"Send me what you've got - carefully, of course. Email it to my secure academic address. And Emily…be cautious. If GenTech is as ruthless as rumor says, you and your whistleblower could be in danger."

Emily thanked him profusely and ended the call. That was one piece of the puzzle: a credible medical ethics expert who could at least lay out the real-world impact of these trials. It might help in court to have someone explain how properly run clinical trials are supposed to look versus what GenTech allegedly did.

She relayed the update to Tessa, who looked pleased for the first time all morning. "It's not quite the cavalry arriving," Tessa said, "but it's a start."

Emily couldn't help but grin. "Precisely."

Shortly after noon, Alan Priest slipped into the office, wearing dark sunglasses and a beanie pulled low. He glanced over his shoulder three times before shutting the door behind him. Sweat had gathered on his forehead, and he looked more like a fugitive than a pharmaceutical employee.

"Emily," he greeted, offering a tense nod to Tessa. "Thank you for letting me come by."

He settled into the chair across from Emily's desk, removing his sunglasses and exhaling shakily. "I'm sorry if I sound paranoid. You must think I'm losing my mind."

Emily's gaze softened. "I don't think that at all. I believe you."

He nodded. "Good. Because I'm telling you, someone's following me." He placed a folder on the desk. "I managed to copy more data from the company server before I left. I don't have it all - anytime I tried to download entire directories, the system flagged it. But these partial files may paint enough of a picture. Emails from top executives, internal memos from legal about how to 'handle' trial participants who complained of side effects, that kind of thing."

Emily felt her heartbeat quicken as she opened the folder. Pages of emails, typed transcripts, timestamps, and references to meeting notes were inside. "This is...very specific," she said quietly, scanning the first few lines. "Multiple references to hush money for families in Ghana, a few mentions of forging local IRB approvals in Peru..."

Alan's cheeks reddened. "I told you. It's real. I was just a low-level project manager, but I saw enough to realize something was off. When I started asking too many questions, a senior director threatened me. So I took what I could and ran."

Tessa chimed in, her voice calm but laced with concern. "Alan, with these new documents, we might be able to build a stronger case. But it also raises the stakes for GenTech. If they know you have this, they won't hesitate to discredit you or worse."

He swallowed hard. "I was afraid you'd say that. Do we…do we have any sort of protection or safe house arrangement? I'm worried about my physical safety."

Emily tapped her pen against the desk. "I've been exploring some channels. If you're truly in immediate danger, we could approach the authorities for whistleblower protection. But that also means revealing more about your identity and these documents earlier than we might like."

Alan shook his head. "I don't trust them. At least not the local authorities."

Emily understood the hesitation. Corruption could seep into the system at many levels, especially when a corporation as large as GenTech was at stake. "We'll find a solution," she said at last. "In the meantime, do you have a safe place to stay - a friend or relative out of town?"

He cast his gaze downward. "I'm keeping to motels, paying cash. I have a cousin in another state, but that's the first place anyone would look if they started pulling my background."

"Alright," Emily said, measuring her words. "We'll figure out a strategy that keeps you off the radar. For now, give me a day or two to review this new data. We'll coordinate a more secure approach for your lodging. And Alan, please - keep a low profile."

He offered a shaky nod, then rose to leave. "I appreciate everything. I'll be in touch by burner phone."

Emily stood as well, placing a reassuring hand on his shoulder. "We'll get through this," she said, though the certainty in her voice felt forced.

Once he left, Tessa turned to Emily. "He's right to be scared, you know."

Emily sank back into her chair, the tension pounding at her temples again. "I know. And now that we have more evidence, we can't unsee it. It's definitely enough for a lawsuit. But it's also enough to make us prime targets."

Tessa's gaze flickered. "That's why we need more help. Maybe a high-powered partner or co-counsel - someone with the resources to stand up to GenTech."

Emily frowned. She remembered how she had sworn never to go crawling back to a giant law firm. But Tessa had a point. There was an entire war chest of money on the other side, and they had only begun to guess at the power GenTech could wield.

"I hate the thought of signing on with another big firm," Emily admitted, "but if it's the only way to protect Alan and keep this case alive, I might not have a choice."

That afternoon, Emily shut herself inside her office with the new documents. She pored over them, cross-referencing them with the earlier revelations Alan had shared. The story they told was more damning than she had imagined. Emails showed senior executives discussing "unflattering side effects" in a cavalier manner, with lines like, *"Be sure to keep local officials happy - use discretionary funds if necessary."*

One chunk of text referenced a potential outbreak of serious neurological complications in test subjects, quickly followed by instructions to *limit reporting to local institutions only*. The subtext was chillingly clear: GenTech not only hid negative results; they actively manipulated regulatory systems in multiple countries to skirt accountability.

Emily's chest tightened as she recognized how enormous this could become. If they pushed forward, they could uncover widespread wrongdoing that might implicate not just GenTech but also local government officials in Africa and South America who had accepted bribes. This was international corruption - a spiderweb of complicity.

She was fully immersed in the files when Tessa knocked softly, cracking the door open. "Hey," Tessa said. "I've been trying to reach a contact at a well-known civil rights firm. They have some background in class actions against major corporations - though not specifically pharmaceutical. They said they might be willing to hear our pitch in a few days."

Emily pressed the back of her hand to her forehead. "A pitch, huh? Like we're selling something."

Tessa shrugged. "That's how these big firms work. They need to see how winnable it is and what the potential fees could be. Even if you want them to help pro bono, they'll assess the case's strategic value. They also want to know if there's a media angle. Unfortunately, that's just the reality."

Emily allowed a tired smile. "You're not wrong. Let's set it up, if they'll hear us out."

"And Emily…" Tessa paused. "I know how you feel about big firms, especially after what happened at Hastings & Cole. But maybe we can find a smaller firm with a strong track record in medical malpractice or consumer-rights litigation. Doesn't have to be a mega-firm."

Emily nodded thoughtfully. "That's a good point. A specialized boutique might offer enough muscle without all the baggage."

Tessa's phone buzzed in her hand, and she glanced down. "Oh - Mark Hastings just called."

Emily's gut twisted at the mention of her former colleague. "What did he want?"

"He asked to speak with you. I said you were in a meeting. He wouldn't say what it was about, but he sounded…urgent."

Emily's mind raced. Mark had already warned her off GenTech once. If he was calling again, it might be to renew that warning - or to step it up a notch. She hesitated. "Let me see if I can guess. It's probably an attempt to scare me or offer a settlement to hush up Alan's claims. He's playing the corporate side now."

Tessa looked uncertain. "You don't want to call him back?"

"I will - after I have time to think. Right now, we need to keep momentum. If he has something to say, I'm sure I'll hear it soon enough."

By late afternoon, the weight of the case was pressing on Emily with a suffocating force. She took a short walk down the block to clear her head, stopping by a local coffee shop she used to frequent. The weather was mild, a gentle breeze fluttering the leaves in the street's sparse trees. But Emily could barely appreciate the pleasant day.

She sat at an outdoor table, coffee in hand, letting the city's ambient chatter wash over her. For a moment, she tried to recall the idealistic excitement she felt when she first opened her own practice. She'd envisioned a small but dedicated firm, taking on cases that truly mattered to ordinary people. Now, it felt like she'd jumped straight into a corporate David-and-Goliath saga, only this Goliath had armies of lawyers and billions in resources.

Her phone buzzed, startling her from her reverie. The caller ID flashed: *Mark Hastings*. She hesitated - again.

Then, gathering her composure, she pressed the accept button.

"Emily," Mark's voice greeted her. He spoke tersely. "I tried calling your office."

"Yes, I got the message."

He sighed. "Look, I'll make this quick. You know what I represent - who I represent. I'm calling to give you a friendly piece of advice: Don't escalate this. You can't imagine the blowback. Not for you, not for your paralegal, not for…others involved."

A burst of anger flared in Emily's chest. "Are you threatening me, Mark?"

A brief pause. "No, of course not. I'm cautioning you. You're in a precarious situation, and we both know how these big corporate cases can go. The second they realize you're serious, they'll go for the kill. This isn't a petty slip-and-fall lawsuit. You know that."

Emily set her jaw. "I do know that. And I also know what's in the documents. You should be aware, Mark - Alan Priest has more evidence than you might think. GenTech could be facing major fallout if this sees the inside of a courtroom."

He exhaled again, this time with a tint of frustration. "I can't discuss specifics, obviously. But you should ask yourself if you really want to go down this road. GenTech doesn't settle easily, and they certainly won't pay a dime until they exhaust every possible advantage. That includes your personal weaknesses, Emily. You're not at Hastings & Cole anymore. You don't have the same firewall or resources. I'm trying to help you see reason."

She swallowed a retort, momentarily blindsided by the swirl of conflicted emotions. Mark used to be a friend, once. Now his voice was laced with corporate condescension she found infuriating. "Thank you for your…concern. But I'm not backing down."

A muffled sound came across the line, perhaps a frustrated shuffle of papers. "Then I can only hope you know what you're doing."

The line disconnected. Emily let out a shaky breath, her coffee untouched on the table. She felt a mixture of rage and anxiety coiling within her. Mark's words confirmed her worst fears: GenTech would stop at nothing.

That evening, Tessa stayed late again, helping Emily plan next steps. They took over the small conference table in the corner of Emily's office - really just a round table that could seat four comfortably, but it was all they had. The overhead light buzzed faintly.

Emily laid out an impromptu plan:

1. **Retain Expert Help** – They needed Dr. Madigan or someone with a similar background to interpret the medical documents, providing a credible argument that GenTech's trials were unethical and potentially criminal.

2. **Coordinate With an NGO or Boutique Firm** – She couldn't go it alone. She had started reaching out to potential partners and nonprofits.

3. **Preserve Alan's Safety** – They needed a strategy to keep him under the radar or secure. Without him, their case was severely weakened.

4. **Gather Additional Plaintiffs** – If they could locate families who had lost loved ones in these drug trials, it would strengthen the case

immeasurably - turning it from a single whistleblower suit into a broader claim.

Tessa tapped her pen on the table. "For number four, that means we need to look overseas - Ethiopia, Ghana, maybe Kenya for the African trials, and Peru or Brazil for South America. We can't just fly over there. We'd need contacts on the ground, translators, interpreters for depositions."

"That's another reason to partner with someone bigger," Emily admitted. "A firm with the capital to handle international travel or at least coordinate with local counsel."

They worked until hunger drove them downstairs to the bakery. They grabbed sandwiches and came back up to the office, chewing with mechanical efficiency as they kept brainstorming.

At one point, Tessa looked at Emily with an almost maternal concern. "I worry about you. If you try to handle everything on your own, you'll break. Mark's warning is ominous. I don't want them to come after you personally - and that includes your finances, your reputation, everything. They can dig up any skeletons in your closet and fling them at you."

Emily's shoulders tensed. "I'm aware. But if I walk away, what does that say about me as an attorney? And what happens to Alan - and the victims who died or were maimed by these experimental drugs?"

Tessa nodded slowly. "I know. I'm with you. Just…be careful."

They spent another hour drafting a preliminary complaint, or at least an outline of one, referencing statutory violations. Emily tried to incorporate language about ignoring regulatory protocols, bribery, and falsification of safety data. Tessa typed frantically, occasionally muttering to herself as she cross-referenced legal citations.

Outside, the city grew dark. Streetlights flickered on, shining in the window. The day had slipped into night without either of them noticing. When Tessa finally paused, massaging her stiff neck, she gazed at Emily. "So…file soon?"

Emily chewed her lip. "I want to. But we might need to hold off just a bit longer until we've secured some backup. Filing would trigger a legal storm. If we do it alone, we'll be buried under motions to dismiss. And that's only the beginning."

Tessa pushed back from the table. "Yeah, if we file prematurely, they'll come after us for every procedural misstep, tearing at the complaint's technicalities. Let's see what the civil rights firm says, or if Dr. Madigan can line up some fellow experts."

They packed up for the night, both drained yet committed. Tessa gave Emily a hug - unusual for their typical professional boundaries, but it felt warranted given the stress.

"Thanks for sticking with me," Emily murmured.

Tessa's eyes shone with determination. "I wouldn't be anywhere else."

The following day, Emily woke with a pit in her stomach. Her sleep had been fitful, populated by nightmares of black sedans and ominous legal documents with her name spelled incorrectly - some strange anxiety-laced dream. She tried to shake off the dread as she got dressed, choosing a sharp navy blazer to project an image of confidence she didn't entirely feel.

The Ghosts' Trial – Volume One

At the office, Tessa was already on the phone with a contact from the civil rights firm. She motioned for Emily to pick up on the extension in her office.

"Right, it's definitely a complex case," a measured female voice was saying. "If Ms. Blackwood can provide a summary of the claims - scope, timeframe, what kind of whistleblower evidence you have - we can do a preliminary assessment. But I'll be upfront: We get about a hundred requests for co-counsel a month, and we can only take on a fraction of them."

Emily cleared her throat. "I understand, Ms. Lam. My paralegal can send you an overview of the documented side effects and the countries involved. We also have internal emails suggesting knowledge of fatal outcomes. We believe there could be a strong product liability element, as well as potential criminal implications."

Ms. Lam paused. "Criminal? That's tricky. Usually the government prosecutes criminal matters, while we'd be handling a civil action. Unless you have the Department of Justice on board, which is an entirely different process."

Emily pressed her lips together. "We're aware. But given the magnitude of the alleged wrongdoing - bribery, concealment of fatalities - it might catch the DOJ's interest. Or at least a U.S. Attorney's office. But first, we need to secure representation to strengthen the civil side."

"Alright," Ms. Lam replied. "Send what you can. If it looks feasible, we'll arrange a call to discuss co-counsel. Understand that if we come aboard, we'll need the lead plaintiff to sign a representation agreement with us as well. And the whistleblower, of course. We have to see if that arrangement is workable from an ethical standpoint."

After they ended the call, Tessa slumped in her chair. "More hoops."

Emily forced a wan smile. "That's how the big leagues operate. Everything is a risk assessment for them."

She tried not to dwell on how Ms. Lam seemed far from convinced. But at least it wasn't a firm no.

Afternoon bled into evening, and Emily found herself alone again in her office, reviewing Dr. Madigan's initial feedback via email. He had scanned a handful of the trial documents, noting glaring irregularities in the study design. He also flagged the suspicious timing of patient deaths and how the trial staff in Africa had reported them as "unrelated" to the drug with minimal supporting evidence.

Tessa was right, Emily thought grimly. *We're in deep. But we're onto something real.*

A knock sounded on her door - Tessa poking her head in. "I grabbed some takeout. You need a break?"

"Actually, that sounds great."

They relocated to the conference table, flipping open boxes of noodles and stir-fried vegetables. Emily realized she'd barely eaten all day. After a few bites of food, Tessa asked, "What's your gut feeling about Mark?"

Emily paused, chopsticks hovering over her container. "Honestly, I think he's torn. Part of him might still respect me as a lawyer, maybe even a friend. But he's also under pressure at Hastings & Cole to shut me down. He's a rising star there. This is exactly the kind of cutthroat environment that leads to big promotions.

He's probably anxious to prove himself by destroying my case, or at least scaring me off."

Tessa sipped her water. "Do you think we could leverage your history with him somehow? Maybe get him to slip up? Reveal something he shouldn't?"

Emily shook her head firmly. "I won't manipulate him. Not only is that unethical, but it's also dangerous. If we're going to do this, we have to build our case on legitimate evidence, not on some emotional leverage I might have over Mark."

Tessa nodded, though a flicker of disappointment crossed her features. "Fair point."

They continued eating in silence until Tessa placed her container aside. "So, do we approach Mark about a settlement if we can't get a bigger firm to back us? Or do we risk it all in court?"

Emily chewed slowly, letting the question sink in. "If I chase a settlement before we even file, GenTech will sense weakness. They might offer something paltry just to muzzle Alan, but it won't address the real harm done to people overseas. This case deserves to see the light of day - if not for me, then for the families who lost loved ones."

A hint of admiration lit Tessa's eyes. "You really mean that, don't you?"

Emily nodded. "I do. I left Hastings & Cole to stand up for people who can't fight for themselves. If I cave at the first sign of trouble, I might as well have stayed in my old office, collecting a comfortable paycheck and ignoring my conscience."

Tessa reached over and gave Emily's hand a squeeze. "Then that's our path. We stand and fight. But we'll be smart about it. We won't rush blindly into a lawsuit. We'll shore up our allies and prepare for the worst."

Night fell heavily. Emily insisted Tessa go home - no arguments this time - and found herself alone once again, the hush of the empty building settling over her. She opened the window a crack, inhaling the faint scent of the bakery's lingering sweetness. Outside, a few passing cars rumbled by, but otherwise, the street was quiet.

Emily studied the partial draft of their complaint. The bullet points of wrongdoing, the references to Alan's whistleblower documents, the tortured legal theories bridging foreign victims to a U.S. courtroom - it was ambitious, to say the least. She pictured a judge's skeptical gaze, a stack of GenTech's motions to dismiss, and Mark Hastings delivering a poised argument about how her claims were legally insufficient or out of jurisdiction. The thought was enough to stir a tumult of anxiety.

Yet, beneath the anxiety simmered a flicker of righteous anger. The data points spelled out tragedy on a grand scale - people dying or sustaining permanent harm due to a drug that should have never passed early safety testing. If the documents were to be believed, GenTech's top brass knew the dangers and hid them. The stark, bottom-line corporate mentality revealed in those internal memos made Emily's stomach churn. *We can't let them get away with it,* she told herself.

Her phone chirped, and she glanced at the screen. A text from an unknown number: *I'm safe for now. Will share more if I learn anything. AP.*

Alan. Emily typed back quickly: *Keep your head down. We're working on a plan.*

She set her phone aside, trying not to dwell on the risks to Alan's life. In an ideal world, she could have marched him to the FBI, or demanded federal whistleblower protections. But in the real world, GenTech likely had the resources to muddy the waters before law enforcement even decided if an investigation was warranted.

The only way forward was to file this lawsuit in such a robust, airtight manner that it couldn't be dismissed or hidden from public scrutiny. That alone would give them some measure of protection, shining a bright light on GenTech's actions. *Light is the best disinfectant,* she recalled reading once. But stepping into that light meant an escalation of the conflict - one that could cost Emily everything.

She closed her eyes, leaned back in her chair, and let her mind drift to the future. She imagined a trial, the courtroom packed with reporters, the families from Africa and South America telling their heartbreaking stories. She imagined Mark Hastings across the aisle, wearing his trademark stoic expression as he tore into every piece of evidence she presented. She pictured the judge's gavel coming down and the possibility of a verdict that could shake GenTech to its core.

That was the vision that kept her going - the idea that justice might be served if she held her ground.

Finally, weariness overcame her, and she decided to call it a night. Gathering the sensitive documents into a secure lockbox, she grabbed her coat and headed for the door. But before she flicked off the lights, she lingered by the window, scanning the street below. A sleek black sedan crawled around the corner and paused momentarily near the entrance. Emily's heart leapt into her throat.

She stood motionless, half-concealed by the window's frame. Through the dim glow of streetlights, she couldn't see who was behind the wheel, but the silhouette suggested a single driver. For a heartbeat or two, the sedan idled. Then, almost as if it sensed her watching, it crept forward and vanished into the night.

She shuddered, stepping away from the glass. *It might be nothing,* she told herself. *Just a random driver.* But doubt curled in her gut. GenTech had the resources to put eyes on her - and Alan. That was no secret.

The Ghosts' Trial – Volume One

With a steeling breath, Emily switched off the office lights, locked the door behind her, and made her way down the stairs, scanning for any sign of the sedan. The street was empty. Yet her anxiety buzzed like a live wire as she headed for her car, keys clutched in a white-knuckled grip.

The next morning, Emily awoke to a flurry of emails. Tessa had forwarded multiple messages from potential allies. Most were rejections: *Our docket is full. We do not have capacity for international litigation. We can't offer assistance at this time.* But one email looked promising - a local boutique firm that had once won a high-profile case against a medical device manufacturer.

The senior partner, a woman named Cassandra Li, wrote: *I'm intrigued by your claims against GenTech. Let's set up a meeting to discuss potential co-counsel. Please forward any non-confidential materials.*

Emily's nerves fluttered with cautious optimism. She immediately responded, suggesting a meeting date. Then she texted Tessa: *We might have a lifeline. Let's gather the best summary of the case.*

Around midday, Tessa burst into Emily's office, brimming with excitement. "We just got a call from Cassandra Li's assistant. They're interested in having us come by this week to talk it over. I'm sending them a bare-bones overview of the evidence, minus the sensitive whistleblower docs."

Emily nodded. "That's perfect. We don't want to expose Alan or any specific references to the lethal trials just yet, not without a protective order or an agreement in place."

Tessa frowned slightly. "Do you think Ms. Li might push for a quick settlement? I mean, that's often how these boutique firms operate - they'll find a vantage point, threaten trial, and see if GenTech coughs up a big settlement."

Emily sighed. "That's a possibility, yes. But that's also how we force GenTech to the table. A settlement that properly compensates victims while forcing some accountability can be better than a protracted courtroom battle. I still want the truth out, though - so we'd have to carefully structure any deal."

Tessa arched an eyebrow. "Well, I guess we'll see how open Ms. Li is to moral crusades."

"Let's just hope it's not purely about money," Emily said softly.

They spent the rest of the afternoon preparing a polished case overview for Ms. Li's firm, including references to potential statutes and the broad allegations of wrongdoing, carefully omitting anything that would identify Alan or tip off GenTech prematurely. Emily felt a surge of renewed energy - this was actual progress, a step beyond drowning in the complexity of the claims alone.

Late that evening, they found themselves once more seated around the conference table, but this time with an air of wary hope. A sense of direction was emerging. They had a potential partner in Cassandra Li's firm, a near-commitment from Dr. Madigan to offer expertise, and Alan's trove of documents that could anchor the lawsuit.

"Next steps?" Tessa asked.

Emily glanced at her notes. "1) Finalize our meeting with Ms. Li and her associates. 2) Keep Alan updated and find a safer arrangement for him. 3) Prepare the complaint to file - once we secure co-counsel, we'll want to move quickly, so GenTech doesn't have time to destroy or alter key evidence."

A faint smile tugged at Tessa's lips. "That sounds like a real plan. We're not just flailing in the dark anymore."

Emily let herself smile back, albeit faintly. "I won't lie - this is still a mountainous challenge. Even if Ms. Li's firm joins us, we're looking at years of litigation and massive expenses. But at least we won't be alone."

Tessa checked her phone. "Alan texted me. He says he's lying low, but he's worried about draining his savings on motel bills. We should address that soon."

Emily took a deep breath. "We will. If Ms. Li's firm invests in this case, maybe they can help coordinate a more secure lodging situation for him, or at least help us with some protective arrangements."

They lapsed into silence, each pondering the precarious balance they were trying to maintain: saving Alan from potential retaliation, building a bulletproof lawsuit, and preserving their own mental and emotional reserves.

When Tessa finally left for the night, Emily lingered, letting her eyes roam the pinned-up documents, the sticky notes peppering her wall, and the scrawled whiteboard that attempted to diagram GenTech's global web of corporate entities. *A quagmire,* she thought, recalling the label she had mentally assigned to this ordeal. Indeed, it was a morass of legal complexities, ethical conundrums, and real-world danger.

She let the word echo in her mind: *Quagmire.* But even in a quagmire, there were steps one could take, one at a time, to wade through the muck. If she stayed organized, if she formed the right alliances, if she could maintain her courage - maybe, just maybe, she could drag GenTech into the light of accountability.

Emily shut off the lights and quietly left the office, stepping into the cool night air. A part of her still flinched at the possibility of a black sedan lurking around the corner. But her determination burned brighter than her fear. This wasn't just about taking on a corporate juggernaut; it was about proving to herself - and to the shadowy forces that thrived on intimidation - that the pursuit of justice was a force more powerful than any hush money or legal threat.

Tomorrow, there would be more phone calls, more negotiations, and an important meeting with Cassandra Li's team. The legal quagmire was vast, but Emily felt more certain than ever that she was doing the right thing. Clutching her keys, she walked briskly toward her car, eyes scanning the quiet street.

She was no longer an attorney in doubt - she was an attorney on the cusp of war, a war she fully intended to win.

Chapter 11:
Threatening Shadows

Emily Blackwood's morning routine began with a dull headache that stubbornly refused to recede. She had slept fitfully, plagued by half-remembered nightmares in which her phone rang incessantly, each call heralding a disembodied voice issuing cryptic threats. More troubling was the sensation - nearly impossible to shake off - that someone was watching from the shadows. She had never been this paranoid before. After all, in her years at Hastings & Cole, she had worked on big cases against formidable opponents. But none carried quite this aura of lurking danger.

The moment she opened her eyes, she knew something was off. It was just a vague feeling at first - an awareness of the hush that seemed to blanket her modest apartment. Outside, the early morning light filtered through blinds she had meticulously closed the night before. Checking her phone, she found a string of missed calls - three, all from unknown numbers. Her heartbeat spiked. Could GenTech have escalated its tactics so quickly?

She stepped carefully out of bed, toeing aside a stack of legal briefs. Much of the previous night had passed in a haze of study, poring over the complexities of an international lawsuit that might snag her if she pressed forward against GenTech. Her ankles ached from tension she couldn't quite place; she decided it was the strain of knowing she was becoming a target.

When she set the coffee brewing, she squinted at her phone's too-bright screen again. The missed calls had come after midnight - one at 12:47 a.m., another around 1:15, and the last at 2:02, all while she was too exhausted to rouse. Beneath them glowed a text from Tessa:

We have another lead from Alan. He's more nervous than ever. Call me ASAP.

She sighed and massaged her temples, remembering Alan Priest's gaunt face. His revelations about GenTech's darkest secrets - the lethal trials in Africa and South America, the emails hinting at covered-up deaths - weighed on her. He was the whistleblower who could break the entire case wide open, but only if he survived. And if GenTech had any say, he wouldn't.

The Ghosts' Trial – Volume One

The coffee maker spat out a weak stream of brew. She had a fleeting thought to call the unknown number back, but decided it would be pointless. The caller would likely have blocked or abandoned that line. But the calls, after midnight, were too pointed to be random. She forced down a slice of toast while re-checking the bolts on her door, then turned to the blinds. Outside, the street lay quiet: parked cars, tidy sidewalks, a handful of neighbors leaving for work. Nothing suspicious - at least not in daylight.

She dressed with the careful confidence that had been second nature at Hastings & Cole: a crisp blouse, tailored jacket, modest heels. Even if her new life meant a far more humble practice, she refused to relinquish the self-assured poise of a successful attorney. Gathering her satchel of case notes, she opened her front door, heart pounding faintly, half expecting something - or someone - lurking at the threshold.

She hadn't ventured more than ten yards when she spotted a black sedan parked across the street. Tinted windows hid its interior. At this early hour, any occupant might be easily visible behind the windshield, but the windows stayed rolled up. She paused, trying not to stare too obviously, then resumed her walk. Maybe it was nothing. Then again, maybe it wasn't.

Her neighbor, Rosa - an affable nurse - was locking up her own car. Emily offered a tight smile and a wave. Having another person nearby was oddly reassuring.

"Mornin', Emily," Rosa said with a friendly grin. "Headed out early?"

"Busy day," Emily replied. Her gaze slid back to the sedan. "That black car over there - any idea who it belongs to?"

Rosa squinted. "Nope. Don't think it's from around here. Could be someone visiting or an Airbnb, I guess."

"That's what I figured. Thanks, Rosa. Have a good shift."

Still unsettled, Emily clutched her keys until they bit into her palm. Climbing into her own car, she risked a glance in the rearview mirror. The sedan remained stationary. No movement, no occupant stepping out. She reminded herself that it could be coincidence. Plenty of visitors roamed the neighborhood. Yet a flicker of fear lingered.

Pulling into traffic, she immediately called Tessa. The phone rang twice before her paralegal answered, sounding frazzled.

"Finally," Tessa breathed. "I've been worried. I almost drove over to your place."

"Sorry," Emily said. "I didn't see your text until a few minutes ago. What's going on with Alan?"

"He's spooked. He left me a voicemail around midnight, swearing someone was taking pictures of his car near the motel. He's terrified they traced him."

Emily swallowed. "They probably did. I got some late-night calls from unknown numbers, and there was a black sedan parked outside my place this morning."

Tessa's voice dropped. "You think it's GenTech?"

"I'm not ruling it out. We always knew intimidation was likely." Emily paused, checking the rearview mirror again. Nothing suspicious followed her - yet. "Let's do this. I'm on my way in. We'll regroup at the office and figure out a safe place for Alan."

Tessa exhaled in relief. "All right. Just - keep your eyes open."

Emily ended the call. She wanted to reassure Tessa that it would be fine, but deep down she knew they'd entered dangerous territory. If GenTech had stooped to midnight calls and possible surveillance, the real trouble was only beginning.

Her new office building, a squat and forgettable structure in an older part of town, showed no sign of watchers. She parked in the small lot, scanning for the black sedan. Not there. For a moment, she felt foolish for expecting to see it. But the sense of being observed clung to her.

The frosted glass door bore a plain sign: **Law Office of Emily Blackwood.** She let herself inside, flicked on the meager overhead light, and found Tessa behind a desk piled high with manila folders and post-it notes. Tessa was a force of organized energy - loyal, sharp, and unfailingly supportive.

"You look like you didn't sleep," Tessa greeted, pushing aside her coffee.

"Yeah, well, the phone calls didn't help," Emily said, setting her bag down. "Tell me about Alan."

Tessa flipped through her notepad. "He called in a whisper, said he saw a suspicious man snapping pictures by his room. Wants to leave. I offered reassurance, told him we'd find a temporary safe place. But if GenTech's on to him, that's not enough."

Emily nodded. "We might have to expedite filing our complaint. The longer we wait, the more time they have to intimidate him - or us."

"You think we can push up the timeline?" Tessa asked hopefully.

Emily sighed. "I'd like a few more days to ensure the complaint is solid. But we might not have that luxury. Also, we need to move Alan somewhere else, away from that motel."

"I could look into witness protection," Tessa ventured, then grimaced. They both knew that route required formal involvement by law enforcement - and typically a criminal investigation. This was a civil case, albeit with potential criminal ramifications if regulators ever took notice. "What if we just find him a new place to stay, under the radar?"

"That's probably the best immediate solution," Emily said. "I know someone who has a small cottage outside the city - someone with no ties to the big law firms. She might let him stay for a while."

Tessa brightened. "That's perfect. Meanwhile, we should sweep our office phones, our computers - everything. GenTech might already have us bugged."

Emily pinched the bridge of her nose. "Agreed. We'll need an IT specialist, though, and that won't be cheap."

Tessa's nod was resolute. "We can't skimp on safety."

"Right." Emily took a breath. "Let me email Harriet, the cottage owner. See if she can offer us a favor. Then we'll handle the IT side."

Over the next hour, Emily composed a careful email to Harriet, keeping details vague. She described needing a discreet, temporary hideaway for a "client" in danger. Harriet was the type to jump at a chance to help, though Emily worried she might be on a business trip. Still, it was worth trying.

She attempted to work on other cases - small claims, contract disputes, the sorts of bread-and-butter matters that kept her modest practice afloat. But her concentration kept fracturing. The black sedan. The midnight calls. Alan's desperate fear. It was as though a cloud of dread hung in the office.

Finally, Tessa knocked on the door. "I called Alan's motel. They said he checked out early, didn't leave a forwarding address."

Emily's stomach flipped. "Maybe he left before dawn to shake any tails."

"Could be," Tessa said grimly. "Or he's running scared with no real plan."

"We'll find him," Emily said, though she felt less sure than she sounded.

Shortly after, Harriet's reply buzzed into Emily's inbox:

Emily, of course you can use the cottage! Let me know the details. I'll send the address and digital lock code. It's remote, no neighbors to bother him. Just promise you'll keep the place tidy!

Relief poured through Emily. She thanked Harriet immediately and waited anxiously for the lock code and address. Tessa gave her a small smile.

"That's one crisis handled," Tessa said. "Now if Alan would just check in."

They kept glancing at their phones, hoping for a call. Mid-morning slipped into noon, and Tessa convinced Emily to step out for a quick lunch. The fresh air might clear their heads, she insisted. Outside, the sun shone bright and hot, as if oblivious to their troubles. They set off on foot to a sandwich shop a couple of blocks away, but Emily's eyes flicked nervously from car to car. Any one of them might be the watchers.

The sandwich shop was half-full. They slipped into a line, placed their orders, and grabbed a small plastic table number. Emily's appetite was minimal, but she forced herself to eat. She could sense Tessa's worried gaze.

"Are you going to talk to Mark Hastings?" Tessa asked quietly, fiddling with a straw. "He's the lead on GenTech's side, right?"

Emily stiffened. "He's with the firm that's circling GenTech, yes. But I doubt he'll want to help me."

Tessa shrugged. "Maybe not. But if Mark has any moral compass left, maybe he'll tip you off if GenTech tries something extreme."

Emily picked at her sandwich, remembering how Mark had sounded on the phone. He'd warned her off the case, claiming it was too big for her. Yet beneath the professional bravado, there'd been a flicker of genuine concern. "It's risky," she said. "He's bound to confidentiality agreements, and we're about to be adversaries if we sue."

"I know. Just keep it in mind," Tessa said, her voice soft. "I hate seeing you so isolated."

Emily managed a wan smile. She did feel alone. The resources of a large firm were gone, replaced by her new shoestring practice. Mark and she had once shared friendly banter over late-night briefs and coffee. That camaraderie was gone, replaced by caution and suspicion.

She was about to stand when her phone buzzed. Harriet's name flashed on the screen. Emily answered on the second ring.

"Harriet, hey. Thanks for getting back."

"No problem," Harriet said warmly. "I have an electronic lock code for the cottage. How soon do you need it?"

"Immediately," Emily replied. "We're dealing with some safety concerns."

Harriet didn't pry, which Emily appreciated. She gave Harriet her email, and Harriet promised to send the code and directions right away.

By the time they returned to the office, Tessa had a fresh set of color-coded notes pinned on her board about GenTech's possible shell corporations. Emily sank into her chair, re-checking her phone for missed calls. Nothing - until, abruptly, it chimed.

Harriet's email:
Address: 5608 Pine Hollow Lane. Code: 7764
There was a kindly note about how to run the small generator if needed, plus instructions on where to find extra blankets.

"Perfect," Emily murmured. "Now if Alan would just call."

He did, close to sunset. Tessa answered her phone, switching to speaker so Emily could listen.

"Tess?" Alan's voice was shaky, hushed. "I can't stay out here. I saw a black SUV follow me for miles."

"Where are you now?" Emily asked.

Alan paused. "A bus station in the suburbs. Don't want to name it in case they're listening. But I need somewhere safe - fast."

"We have a place," Tessa said, describing Harriet's rural cottage. "We'll get you there, but we have to be careful. We'll pick you up and drive part of the way, then switch cars."

"I'll do whatever you say," Alan breathed. "I just can't keep looking over my shoulder."

They arranged to meet at a diner in the suburbs, well lit and typically crowded. Tessa scribbled notes, Emily gave instructions, and the call ended abruptly.

"Let's do this," Tessa said. "We need to be discreet."

They left the office by the back alley, worried that watchers might lurk on the main street. Tessa's car was parked in a small lot a block away. Once on the road, they kept checking the mirrors. No sign of the black sedan. Still, Emily's nerves refused to settle.

The diner was a squat building with neon signage that flickered erratically. Half a dozen cars were in the lot. They pulled up, scanning for any suspicious vehicles. Nothing stood out. Inside, a waitress waved them toward a half-empty row of booths.

"See a guy in a blue jacket come through?" Emily asked quietly.

The waitress nodded, pointing to the far corner. They found Alan huddled over a cup of coffee, face drawn. Relief flitted across his features when he saw them.

"Thank you," he said, voice trembling, as Emily and Tessa slid into the booth opposite him. "I left the motel this morning. Caught a bus, but saw that SUV everywhere I went."

Emily gently reached across the table. "We have a safe spot for you. A friend's cottage. No neighbors, no prying eyes."

Alan exhaled raggedly. "I'll go anywhere. I just don't want to get killed."

Tessa swallowed. "We won't let that happen. But once you're there, you need to stay under the radar - no credit cards, no calls except on a burner phone."

Alan nodded. "Anything you say. Did you file the complaint yet?"

"Not yet," Emily said, hating the stress in his eyes. "But soon. Once it's filed, GenTech will be in the spotlight. They can't just vanish you."

"I hope you're right," Alan said. "They have eyes everywhere."

The waitress interrupted to ask if they wanted to order. Tessa asked for coffees all around, though no one seemed interested in food. When the waitress left, Emily laid out the plan: she and Tessa would drive Alan out of the city, then switch to a rental car Tessa had procured under a corporate name. That was safer than letting him stay in the open. They'd meet again, in secret, once Emily was ready to file the complaint.

Alan listened, nodding rapidly. "I'll do exactly what you say."

A few minutes later, they left enough cash on the table for the coffees and stepped out into the parking lot. The air felt cool against Emily's skin, as if the temperature had dropped with the sun. She scanned for watchers. Nothing obvious. Tessa led them to her car, and Alan climbed into the backseat, curling in on himself as though trying to disappear.

They set off, merging onto a highway that cut through the outer suburbs. Emily's eyes flicked constantly to the rearview mirror. She took note of headlights, but none trailed them consistently.

After half an hour, Tessa took an exit leading to a dimly lit gas station. A beat-up sedan - a rental arranged under Tessa's name - was parked near the side. Emily's pulse hammered as they stepped out into the night air. They transferred Alan's duffel bag from Tessa's trunk to the rental. Alan trembled slightly, as though braced for someone to leap from the shadows.

Emily handed him a folded piece of paper. "That's Harriet's address and the digital code. Once you're there, keep the lights low. Don't go into town unless absolutely necessary. We'll contact you soon."

"Got it." Alan clutched the paper and exhaled. "Thank you. I mean it."

Tessa pressed a cheap flip phone into his hand. "Burner phone. We'll call you. Don't use anything else."

The Ghosts' Trial – Volume One

He nodded and climbed into the rental. They stood there watching as he pulled away, his taillights swallowed by the empty road. It was a tense, silent moment, each of them wondering if they had done enough to protect him.

A chill ran up Emily's spine as she stared after the vanished car. "Let's hope we gave him a head start."

Tessa touched her shoulder. "We did our best. Let's get back."

They drove in the opposite direction. Emily's phone vibrated in her lap. Another unknown number. She swallowed, hesitating.

"You going to answer?" Tessa asked.

Emily pressed the screen. "Hello?"

Silence at first - then a faint hiss of static, followed by a click.

Tessa blew out a breath. "They want you to know they're still watching."

Emily's voice shook. "Yes. They do."

She set the phone down, skin crawling with the sense of eyes fixed on her, even out here on a quiet stretch of highway. For the first time, she grasped how lethal GenTech's game might become. She knew, in that instant, there was no turning back. She had chosen to fight them. Now she would have to see it through, no matter what shadows lurked on the horizon.

By the time they neared the city limits again, the weight of the day pressed heavily on Emily's mind. They returned to the office to pick up her car, using the back alley entrance once more. She had no desire to risk anyone spotting them from the street. The black sedan was nowhere in sight - perhaps a hopeful sign, though it did little to soothe her nerves.

"Let's keep each other updated tonight," Tessa said, as Emily slipped out of the passenger seat. "Text me if anything strange happens. If that sedan shows up outside your place again, call me right away."

Emily managed a weary nod. "Thanks. I appreciate everything you're doing."

"That's what I'm here for," Tessa replied, though worry creased her features. "This is bigger than us, Emily. Don't forget that. We need to file soon."

Emily's heart twisted. She nodded, pressing Tessa's hand briefly before sliding her keys into her own car's ignition. Tessa drove off into the night, headlights disappearing around the corner. Emily waited a moment, checking her phone. No new calls. She glanced around at the empty alleyway, shadows stretching along the ground. A flickering streetlamp offered a weak glow.

"Okay," she whispered to herself, "time to go home."

She forced her mind to stay alert. She locked the office door, verifying it twice. Then she walked briskly to her car, scanning every corner for watchers. The city nights no longer felt neutral and indifferent. Now each shape could hide an observer, each parked car might be a roving threat. She couldn't wait to get off the dark streets.

Starting her engine, she pulled out with a squeal of tires she hadn't intended. Fear spiked her adrenaline. She forced herself to slow down, merging onto the familiar thoroughfare that led back to her neighborhood. She studied every vehicle around her, suspecting each of them. No one followed her directly, but the tension refused to fade.

She reached her apartment building just past nine. The black sedan was gone. She parked in her usual spot and hurried inside, feeling foolishly like a terrified child afraid of the dark. Yet she couldn't stop checking over her shoulder until the door to her apartment clicked shut.

She dead-bolted it, then slid the chain lock into place. Only when she was safely inside did she allow herself a moment to breathe. But comfort was fleeting. She set her satchel down and noticed the blinking light on her answering machine. Yes, she still had a landline, though it rarely rang. Another relic from the days she had parted ways with Hastings & Cole, wanting a separate, private line.

Her chest tightened as she pressed the button. A mechanical voice announced: "You have one new message."

Silence at first. Then a faint, rhythmic sound - breathing? Static? Then the call ended. Emily's pulse drummed in her ears. No name, no voice, just another hint that someone, somewhere, wanted her to know they could reach her anytime, on any phone.

She pressed her back against the wall, heart pounding, and debated calling the police. But she had no license plate number, no direct threat, nothing to show them except silent calls. She suspected the police would take a statement, promise to "keep an eye out," and that would be the end of it. GenTech wasn't a small-time operation. If they truly had an intelligence network of sorts, local cops wouldn't do much good. Federal authorities might. Yet she had no direct link to criminal wrongdoing, aside from the whistleblower's claims, at least not enough to open a formal investigation. And if she jumped straight to the feds, GenTech might retaliate in ways she couldn't predict.

She opted for the next best thing: She grabbed her phone and typed a text to Tessa:

Another silent call on my landline. I'm okay but it's creepy. I'll keep you updated.

Tessa's reply came a minute later:

Lock up tight. Text me if anything else happens. We'll meet early tomorrow.

Emily sank onto the couch, letting the tension roll off in waves. The day's events had her exhausted. She flicked off the main lights, opting for the soft glow of a single lamp, hoping to create less of a visible target from outside. Then she turned on her laptop, scanning the headlines for anything about GenTech. It was a major pharmaceutical giant, so there were always press releases about new drug trials, expansions, and philanthropic endeavors. Nothing about whistleblowers or lawsuits, of course.

After a few aimless minutes, she closed the laptop. Her mind kept drifting to Alan, alone in that rental car, heading toward Harriet's remote cottage. She pictured him navigating unlit roads, jumping at every stray headlight. She wished there was some immediate way to give him safety, but all she could offer was secrecy. A lesser lawyer might have turned him away. But Emily felt compelled to help him - she couldn't let a corporation bury their dark truths.

Clutching her phone, she curled under a throw blanket, trying to stave off the sense of being watched. She dozed occasionally, jolting awake at each sound from the street. By midnight, she hadn't heard more from Alan. She assumed he'd arrived safely and was lying low as instructed. Meanwhile, she fielded another unknown call on her cell - nothing but muffled static before clicking off. One came in on the landline at around 1 a.m., prompting her to unplug it altogether. Enough was enough.

In the hollow quiet of her apartment, she whispered to herself, "We'll file soon. We'll put them under scrutiny. Then they can't just scare us into silence."

But even as she spoke the words, she wondered if GenTech had ways to make trouble, lawsuit or not. She recalled the stories Tessa had found, the hush-money deals, the "accidental" deaths or disappearances. Now she has become part of that story.

Eventually, after countless restless twists beneath her blanket, she fell into a shallow sleep just before dawn. Her dreams once again filled with ringing phones and the silhouette of someone outside her window, waiting.

In the gray light of early morning, she woke with a jolt, her neck sore from dozing on the couch. A faint beep reminded her that she'd unplugged the landline. Checking her cell phone, she found two more unknown missed calls. She set the phone down, refusing to let the fear paralyze her any further.

A quick shower did little to soothe her exhaustion. She dressed, willing herself to look professional rather than petrified. Over cheap coffee she typed a bullet-point list on her laptop:

1. **Call Harriet** – Confirm Alan arrived safely.

2. **Contact IT Specialist** – Garrett to do an office sweep.

3. **Revise complaint** – Aim to file within 48 hours.

4. **Set up safety check** – Evaluate home security measures.

5. **Document** – Keep a record of all harassing calls or suspicious activity.

She wrote it out, because having a plan felt marginally better than being overwhelmed. Then she grabbed her coat and left, determined to keep moving.

Her neighborhood looked almost serene in the morning light. No black sedan in sight. Maybe her watchers had retreated for now. She breathed a shaky sigh of relief as she drove off, but the sense of paranoia refused to fade.

At the office, Tessa was already present, bleary-eyed yet alert as she organized files on her desk. She greeted Emily with a sympathetic nod.

"You look like I feel," Tessa said, stifling a yawn. "Any more calls?"

"Two, both unknown," Emily replied, flicking her gaze around. "We need that IT sweep, pronto."

"I got Garrett's confirmation," Tessa said. "He'll be here this afternoon. He said he can check the office lines, the computers. He also recommended a basic bug sweep for the offices, in case anyone planted something."

Emily's stomach churned. The idea that her own office might be bugged was terrifying - but better to know than to keep wondering. "Let's do it," she said. "And Harriet?"

Tessa brightened. "She emailed just now. Alan texted her from the burner phone, said he arrived safely. He's spooked but okay."

Relief unfurled in Emily's chest. "Good. That's one less crisis. Now we just have to make sure we draft this complaint perfectly."

Tessa nodded. "I'll gather our evidence - Alan's emails, the snippet from African media about the unreported deaths, the corporate filings. We want to show a pattern of wrongdoing."

Emily opened her laptop, posture stiffening with renewed resolve. "Yes. Let's build an airtight case. Enough that GenTech won't dare come after us physically. Or at least they'll think twice about it."

The day passed in a flurry of preparations. Emily and Tessa refined the complaint, meticulously weaving the evidence into a coherent legal narrative. If they aimed too high with claims they couldn't prove, GenTech's lawyers would hammer them. If they aimed too low, it wouldn't capture the severity of GenTech's alleged crimes. Striking the right balance meant hours of tense back-and-forth.

By mid-afternoon, Garrett arrived. He was a tall, lean man with a wiry beard, lugging a rolling suitcase full of gadgets. After a quick handshake, he quietly sealed off the conference room and began scanning everything: phones, computers, walls, even overhead light fixtures. Emily felt both embarrassed and grateful to see him handle it so systematically.

A short while later, Tessa found Emily in her office, laptop open, text swirling across the screen.

"How does it look?" Tessa asked, nodding to the complaint draft.

"Nearly there," Emily said. "I'm polishing the sections on international jurisdiction. That's tricky, since the trials occurred overseas. But we have to show that GenTech's corporate base is here, that decisions were made here."

Tessa perched on the edge of Emily's desk. "I wonder if Mark Hastings has caught wind yet that we're serious."

Emily's mouth set into a thin line. "He'll know soon. Maybe he'll try to warn us off again."

"If he does, we'll know we're onto something," Tessa said wryly.

Garrett emerged at around four, wiping sweat from his brow. "Good news, I don't see any direct wiretaps or covert devices in your walls or phones. But your Wi-Fi network is vulnerable. Your router is older, and your firewall's minimal."

Emily exchanged a look with Tessa. "So someone could intercept our online communications?"

"Potentially, yes," Garrett replied. "I can install better encryption today, but you'll want to replace that router altogether. Also, I found some suspicious pings to your main office computer. Hard to say if it's an outside hack attempt, but it's concerning."

Emily nodded slowly, trying to keep her composure. "Thanks, Garrett. Do what you can - upgrade the security. I'll reimburse you for any new hardware."

He gave her a half-smile. "I know money's tight, but trust me, you need this. If a big corporation wants in, they'll find a way. Let's not make it easy for them."

It took another couple hours for Garrett to upgrade everything, culminating in a new router, reconfigured settings, and encrypted backups of their case files. Emily felt a fraction safer, though she knew it was a game of cat and mouse. GenTech likely had resources that dwarfed any precaution she could afford.

When Garrett finally packed up, Tessa walked him out. Emily saved the newly bolstered complaint to multiple locations - USB, encrypted drives, even a password-locked cloud account. If GenTech trashed her office tomorrow, the evidence would live on. She refused to let them bury the truth.

Evening settled in, and the weight of fear had not lifted, but Emily felt a surge of grim determination. She was ready to finalize the complaint, maybe in the next day or so. Every hour they delayed, Alan's safety teetered on a razor's edge.

As Tessa tidied her desk, Emily stepped into the waiting room, scanning the dark windows. The street outside was empty. She peered toward the curb. Her heart lurched - was that a black sedan again, gliding past? She caught only a fleeting glimpse. Too far away to confirm, but she stiffened reflexively.

Tessa came up behind her, peering over her shoulder. "See something?"

"Not sure," Emily murmured, stepping away from the window. "Could be them, could be nothing."

"We should lock up," Tessa said quietly. "Call it a night. No reason to linger."

Emily nodded. She closed the blinds. They double-checked the locks on every door. The building was old and hardly fortified, but it was better than nothing. In the hallway, they paused.

"Going to be all right driving home?" Tessa asked.

Emily forced a small smile. "I have to be. What about you?"

Tessa shrugged, eyes glimmering with a trace of nerves. "I'll be fine. Just text me when you get home safely."

They parted ways, stepping out into the night. Emily gripped her car keys tightly, scanning every passing vehicle as she walked to the lot. No black sedan in sight. She felt a twinge of relief.

But as she pulled onto the main road, her phone rang - unknown number. Heart pounding, she ignored it. Let it ring. A minute later, it rang again. She forced her eyes to stay on the road, refusing to answer. Finally, the ringing stopped.

At a red light, she risked a glance around. Normal traffic, normal pedestrians. Yet the sense of being stalked pressed down on her. She told herself she'd made the right choice. This had to be done, or else GenTech would keep exploiting vulnerable populations without consequence.

Back in her apartment, she triple-locked the door and plugged in her landline again, half expecting it to ring immediately. Nothing. The silence was worse in some ways. She set aside her phone, changed into comfortable clothes, and tried to read a novel. Her eyes slid off the page, unable to hold focus. All she saw in her mind's eye were tinted windows and silent phone calls.

A pang of guilt nudged her about not calling Mark. If anyone had insight into GenTech's next moves, it might be him. But crossing that line could endanger her case, or tip her hand. She decided it was too risky. If Mark had something to say, he'd call her. Or he'd remain her adversary, dutifully carrying out the firm's will.

Finally, she forced herself to check her voicemail. She found only a single message, left around six p.m., from her mother: a quick, casual greeting about family matters. Emily felt a wave of homesickness. Her mother didn't know the situation she was in, and Emily had no intention of sharing details that might cause more worry.

She typed a brief text to Tessa: **Home safe, no sightings. Let's finalize the complaint tomorrow.**

Then she collapsed onto her couch again, exhaustion seeping through her bones.

Amid that exhaustion, she realized something had shifted in her. The fear was still there - visceral, undeniable. But beneath it burned a defiance she hadn't felt before. She had walked away from Hastings & Cole precisely because she wanted to do the right thing, to stand up for those who had no voice against powerful interests. Now she was living that choice in the most perilous way.

As she drifted into uneasy slumber, her last conscious thought was of Alan, alone in Harriet's secluded cottage. She prayed he was safe, prayed they hadn't been followed. Prayed that the phone calls and suspicious cars were only intimidation, not a prelude to violence.

The shadows were indeed threatening. But with each breath, Emily steeled herself to face them. Tomorrow, she vowed, she would push the case forward another crucial step. The next day, she would take another step. And if GenTech wanted a fight, she would give them one - no matter how dark the road ahead.

Chapter 12:
Looking Back to Africa

Tessa Moretti had always been the kind of paralegal who delighted in obscure research - if there was a rock to be lifted, she would pry it up and examine the wriggling secrets underneath. But on this brisk Tuesday morning, the nature of her work felt different. There was something both exciting and unnerving in the task Emily Blackwood had given her: Find concrete evidence - anything that might tie GenTech's shadowy past to the allegations of illicit drug trials abroad.

Ever since the unsettling developments of the previous week - suspicious calls at the office, strange cars idling outside the building, and the relentless sense of being watched - Emily and Tessa both knew that the time for half-measures had passed. GenTech was more dangerous than either of them had first assumed.

By the time Tessa settled into her cubicle, coffee mug in hand, she had already mentally prepared a plan of action. She would systematically comb through African news outlets, especially smaller, local newspapers that might have reported inexplicable deaths or secretive clinical trials. Just days ago she had discovered that a handful of references to suspicious "medical outreach programs" pointed to GenTech's name in a backhanded sort of way, usually buried in disclaimers or overshadowed by philanthropic spin. That had been enough to fan her curiosity, but not enough to mount a lawsuit. Now, she intended to go deeper.

Before diving in, Tessa paused at the hallway to Emily's small corner office. Through the slightly open door, she could see Emily hunched over her desk, rifling through a stack of manila folders. The overhead light highlighted the tension that had formed on Emily's brow. Just a few short months ago, Emily had been a top-tier associate at Hastings & Cole, the swankiest law firm in town, a place known for representing the biggest corporate heavyweights - like GenTech. But Emily had left that gilded cage for reasons both financial and moral, hoping to champion the everyday person rather than protect corporate bottom lines.

She'd found a kindred spirit in Tessa, who was similarly disillusioned by the large-firm environment. Now they were both perched in a modest office suite that smelled faintly of fresh paint and coffee, launching

The Ghosts' Trial – Volume One

a David-versus-Goliath lawsuit on behalf of Alan Priest - the whistleblower whose documents hinted at something far more sinister than just corporate corner-cutting. The hush-ups, the threats, the suspicious black SUVs lurking around corners... all of it suggested GenTech had significant secrets to hide. And Tessa was about to uncover some of those secrets - or die trying, she thought with a humorless chuckle.

She returned to her desk and opened her laptop. A half-dozen browser tabs were already open, each showcasing a different African news site or aggregator. Tessa started by filtering for keywords: "GenTech," "drug trial," "fatal side effects," "unexplained deaths," "health outreach," and even "chemical testing." Because many of the outlets didn't publish in English, she used an online translation tool - a clumsy approach, but enough to glean the general meaning of suspicious headlines. Occasionally, the translation software spat out something unintelligible or comedic, but Tessa's intuitive leaps helped her sift through the nonsense.

It didn't take long before she stumbled upon a small Liberian newspaper article from a year ago, archived behind a minimal paywall. The snippet teased a story about a "pharmaceutical giant from North America" conducting an experimental vaccine trial in remote communities. Strange illnesses had broken out soon after, affecting mostly children and the elderly - though the article's final lines cryptically hinted at "unresponsive officials" and "medical records withheld." No direct mention of GenTech. But the timeframe matched Alan Priest's internal documents, which described testing a new antibiotic under clandestine conditions. Tessa's pulse quickened.

She noted the article's reference number in her growing digital notebook and delved deeper, her morning coffee forgotten. Each new discovery seemed to confirm a pattern: local African journalists occasionally reported controversies around "foreign medical research programs." Then, after a few short weeks or months, the stories vanished or morphed into fluffy coverage praising the philanthropic efforts of a "major multinational sponsor." What frightened Tessa the most was how the pattern repeated in region after region - Kenya, Uganda, Nigeria, Tanzania. The shift always happened too quickly to be a coincidence.

The Ghosts' Trial – Volume One

By late morning, Tessa had assembled a collage of short articles, half-complete news briefs, and social media posts from local activists, each describing oddly similar incidents: abrupt spikes in illnesses during "clinical research," families mourning loved ones while claiming they'd been coerced into signing suspicious consent forms, and allegations that "big men" in the local government had accepted bribes to stay quiet. Though GenTech's name rarely appeared explicitly, Tessa recognized enough overlap with Alan Priest's timeline and corporate jargon to suspect the pharmaceutical titan's hidden hand.

Still, suspicion was not proof. Tessa knew Emily would demand sources, testimonies, affidavits - anything that could be used in a court of law to fortify their whistleblower's claims. As she scrolled, Tessa found a reference to a Zimbabwean journalist, a woman named Ines Dube, who had once run an exposé on corporate medical testing. Her piece, originally titled "The Ghost Trials," had since been scrubbed from the major archives, but vestiges remained on smaller aggregator sites. That name alone was interesting enough for Tessa to bookmark.

"Looks like you're onto something."

Tessa jumped at the sudden voice. She glanced up to see Emily standing beside her desk, arms folded, wearing the faint ghost of a grin. Emily's tired eyes held a spark - perhaps the same flicker of determination that had led her to walk away from Hastings & Cole in the first place.

"Jesus, Em, you scared me," Tessa said, pressing a hand to her chest. "I was so deep in this that I didn't hear you come out."

"Sorry," Emily replied, though she didn't sound too remorseful. "I just wanted to know how it's going. You look like you've discovered a gold mine."

Tessa pushed her laptop in Emily's direction. "I can't say it's a mine yet, but… let's just say we're seeing a pattern in local African news outlets. Disturbing stuff. And in some cases, it's vanished from official records. The further I dig, the more convinced I am that something was systematically covered up."

Emily leaned down, scanning the headlines and the short summaries Tessa had compiled. "Exactly the kind of hush-ups Alan Priest was talking about."

"Yeah," Tessa said softly. "At first, it's always portrayed as charitable medical work. Free vaccinations, free consultations - stuff you'd see from philanthropic arms of big corporations. Then, a sudden wave of strange complications. People fall sick in droves, and within a month, the journalists reporting it either recant or their stories vanish. Some of them claim the official data was locked away or mysteriously changed."

Emily exhaled. "Makes you wonder what Mark Hastings - my old colleague - and his team at Hastings & Cole know. Or if they're conveniently turning a blind eye."

"You think Mark's actively covering it up?"

"He's a competent lawyer, but I'm not sure how deeply he's been read into the secrets. Hastings & Cole is a fortress of compartments; they only tell you exactly what you need to defend the client."

Tessa nodded. "Well, from what I can piece together, these local African papers might help us prove that GenTech engaged in illegal, unethical drug testing without proper oversight. That's what we need - concrete instances that tie GenTech to actual harm."

Emily smiled grimly. "Brilliant. Keep digging, Tessa. Keep everything organized. We'll need to present it in a way that's ironclad if we ever get to the discovery phase of this lawsuit."

By early afternoon, Tessa had consolidated enough leads to feel the first stirrings of genuine optimism. Yes, it was horrifying - people had died, families destroyed. But from a legal standpoint, the evidence might become the building blocks of a strong case. If they could corroborate local allegations with the records from Alan Priest's flash drive - once fully deciphered - GenTech's facade of legitimacy might crack wide open.

Her phone buzzed, the screen lighting up with a name she recognized: **Alan Priest**. She nodded at Emily, who was on a call in her office, then answered quietly.

"Tessa," she said in a low voice.

"Tessa, it's me," Alan whispered. His tone was fraught. "Is Emily there? I need to talk - something's happened."

"She's on another call," Tessa said. "Are you safe?"

A long silence followed, marked only by Alan's ragged breathing. "I... I think so, for the moment. But I caught someone following me this morning. A man in a black car. He parked outside my cottage, watched me for a long time. When I tried to approach, he sped off."

Tessa's stomach turned. "Stay inside if you can. Emily will want to relocate you. We suspected GenTech had private investigators or security contractors on your tail. We can get you somewhere safer."

Alan let out a trembling sigh. "Tessa, they're covering more tracks than you realize. I'm finding more references to hush-money payoffs in accounting records. Internal emails between executives referencing bribes to local health officials in... well, in Africa. It's... bigger than I thought."

She lowered her voice further. "I've been digging, too. I found news stories about unexplained fatalities. All of them eventually retracted or buried. We're trying to connect the dots. Don't panic, okay? We're building a real case. Emily will call you in a few minutes."

Alan ended the call abruptly, leaving Tessa clutching the phone in a swirl of worry. She immediately typed a quick summary of Alan's new information into her notes. With each new detail, the scope of GenTech's wrongdoing seemed to widen.

Emily ended her own phone call a few minutes later and strode out, an intent expression replacing the exhaustion on her face. "Was that Alan?" she asked.

Tessa nodded. "He's terrified, Em. Says he was followed this morning. He's also uncovering more about bribery to local health authorities in Africa."

Emily set her hands on her hips. "I was just speaking to a colleague who might arrange safe housing for Alan under a pseudonym. We'll need to act fast. The more he digs, the bigger the target on his back."

"Agreed," Tessa said, pulling up the consolidated notes on her screen. "And look: I've got multiple stories about the same pattern. People in villages near test sites started getting sick. Some died. Journalists tried to blow the whistle, but then the stories disappeared."

Emily peered over Tessa's shoulder. "Give me the short version: how many separate incidents did you confirm?"

"So far, I have references to at least five. Liberia, Kenya, Uganda, Nigeria, and Zimbabwe. Might be more if I dig deeper. The earliest I can find is from about eight years ago. That lines up with the older corporate emails we saw - some that Alan said were from the start of GenTech's expansion strategy in emerging markets."

Emily pressed her lips together in anger. "My God... This might go back nearly a decade. Do we have any names, any local attorneys or NGOs we can reach out to for statements?"

"A few. I'm drafting emails to them, though it's a long shot. Some are out of date, and the rest might be too afraid to talk. But it's worth a try."

Emily patted Tessa's shoulder. "Good. Keep going. We're not only building our complaint but also protecting Alan's credibility. If GenTech tries to smear him as just a disgruntled ex-employee, we'll counter with verifiable facts."

Around two o'clock, Tessa finally came across the elusive article by Zimbabwean journalist Ines Dube - well, the scraps of it that remained online. The aggregator site summarized her original piece, "The Ghost Trials," which claimed a multinational pharma outfit had been secretly testing an experimental antiviral drug in rural areas. Scores of locals fell ill, and some died, though local clinics insisted it was a seasonal flu outbreak. Ines, however, had apparently interviewed families who described men in "white coats with foreign accents" distributing pills and promising miraculous results.

Tessa's heart skipped a beat when she reached the aggregator's footnote: "Multiple references to drug shipments labeled 'Phase 3 Horizon' with code-names referencing North American corporate sponsors. Attempts to confirm with local government officials were rebuffed. Ms. Dube's article has since been removed from major publications due to legal pressure."

GenTech's name was never explicitly stated, but Tessa recognized a phrase from Alan's files: **Phase 3: Horizon** - the same code name Alan had described as a hush-hush trial for a new antiviral in Zimbabwe. This was a smoking gun, or at least a curling wisp of smoke.

"Tessa, you look like you just saw a ghost," Emily said, returning from her phone call with Alan.

"I might have, in a sense. I've got something big, Em," Tessa replied, beckoning Emily closer. "Journalist named Ines Dube. Wrote an exposé on a so-called 'Ghost Trials' fiasco. The entire piece was yanked. Legal pressure. Possibly from GenTech. She wrote about Phase 3 drug shipments, foreign doctors, families falling ill."

Emily's eyes widened. "Phase 3: Horizon. It's in the documents from Alan."

"Exactly. The timelines match. If we can track down Ms. Dube, we could potentially get on-the-ground testimony. Even if she won't talk publicly, maybe she'd give us a deposition under oath."

Emily gently massaged her temples. "That's going to be complicated. She might be living in fear after whatever legal threat got her work censored. But it's worth a shot. Anything that corroborates Alan's evidence is priceless."

Tessa nodded. "I'll see if I can trace her personal blog, social media, anything. If she's not easy to find, maybe we can locate family members or coworkers."

Later in the afternoon, Emily convened a quick strategy meeting in her office with Tessa. She was perched on the corner of her desk, trying to look calm, though

Tessa noticed how her foot tapped nervously against the leg of the table.

"Here's the situation," Emily began. "Alan is too exposed where he's staying. I've arranged for him to move to a friend's vacant cottage about two hours from here, under the name James Daly. There's a decent chance GenTech's private eyes might still find him, but it'll buy us time."

Tessa nodded. "Good idea. We can't have him kidnapped - or worse - before we build our legal case."

Emily forced a half-smile. "Right. Meanwhile, I want you to keep working on these African sources. If you uncover actual contact info for any journalist or local lawyer who might confirm GenTech's involvement, that's gold."

"I'll focus on that. Also, I think we need to reference these African outlets in the initial complaint. If we can show a pattern, it lends credibility. It's not just Alan's word."

"I agree. But we should be cautious about naming them specifically until we have more proof. If we just fling unverified accusations into the complaint, GenTech's legal team will shred us."

Tessa grimaced. "Which probably means Mark Hastings. God, I remember how he dissected every piece of an opposing counsel's argument back in the day. He can be brutal."

Emily exhaled slowly. "Yes, Mark can be formidable. But he's never faced me on the other side of the courtroom before. If he tries anything unethical, I'll make sure it backfires."

By late evening, Tessa decided to do a final sweep of mainstream African English-language outlets, hoping to see if any mention of a GenTech lawsuit had surfaced. She typed "GenTech lawsuit Africa" into the search bar, expecting little. Instead, she stumbled upon a short, fresh piece from a Nigerian outlet referencing "legal concerns" around a U.S.-based pharmaceutical company. The article was cagey, perhaps worried about defamation laws. It mentioned only that "anonymous sources suggest renewed legal action abroad regarding questionable clinical practices."

Heart pounding, Tessa read on. It wasn't definitive, but the timing aligned suspiciously with Emily's ongoing discussions about whether or not to file a formal complaint soon. Could GenTech have begun pressuring African outlets proactively, anticipating the suit?

Deciding to read deeper, Tessa navigated to the site's editorial page. Sure enough, there was an editorial from two months prior, condemning "pharmaceutical colonialism." The language was scathing, accusing unnamed foreign companies of treating African lives as expendable test subjects. The editorial ended on a rallying cry for local governments to stand up against corporate exploitation. Nowhere was GenTech explicitly named, but the editorial did mention the same regulatory dance Tessa had seen in Alan's emails - where the local health authorities were pressured to sign documents waiving liabilities in exchange for "research grants."

If Tessa had harbored any lingering doubt about GenTech's wrongdoing, it melted away. It felt like standing at the edge of a vast labyrinth, each corridor leading to more dark corners.

Around nine p.m., Tessa was still clicking through her aggregator sites, eyes bleary from the backlit screen. Emily emerged from her office, coat draped over her arm. The small overhead lights in the corridor gave her a lean, tired silhouette.

"Tessa, you're still here?" Emily asked softly. "You should go home and rest."

"I will," Tessa said. "I just want to finish compiling these last bits. You never know when these sites might take the articles down or get pressured to do so."

Emily set her coat on the back of Tessa's chair and peered at the screen. "You worry they might disappear by morning?"

"You bet. We're up against a corporation that can and will pay people off to bury the truth. If some local editor is threatened or bribed, these stories might vanish."

Emily nodded, her jaw set. "Then do a full offline backup. Screenshot everything, download the PDFs, preserve the web pages. We need a record."

"That's exactly what I'm doing," Tessa said, gesturing to the folders on her desktop. "Tomorrow morning, I'll cross-reference them with Alan's latest accounting details. Then we'll start drafting a framework to incorporate them into the complaint."

Martyn Bellamy

Emily placed a hand on Tessa's shoulder. "Thank you. This is invaluable. You know... on days like this, I realize how right I was to leave Hastings & Cole. Sure, the money was good, but the cost to my conscience was too high."

Tessa gave her a tired smile. "I guess we're the little guys now. But we're on the right side of history - assuming GenTech doesn't squash us like bugs."

Emily sighed. "They'll try. We just have to gather enough proof that they can't silence everyone. And after seeing what you've uncovered today, Tessa, I believe we have more than a fighting chance."

After Emily left, Tessa continued working. Yet her mind itched with a sliver of doubt. What if GenTech had deeper resources than they could comprehend? It was one thing to gather articles from local outlets; it was another to convert them into a bulletproof legal strategy. Mark Hastings and the army of lawyers at Hastings & Cole would dissect every piece of evidence, looking for any sign of exaggeration or hearsay.

Already Tessa could imagine the cross-examinations: "Ms. Moretti, can you confirm the authenticity of this Zimbabwean journalist's claims?" "Are you sure these articles aren't sensationalism?" She closed her eyes, wishing she could jump forward in time, past all the depositions, motions, and pretrial battles.

But if that day ever came - if they stood in a courtroom, facing down GenTech's suits - she wanted the truth to shine like a beacon. She wanted to see justice done for the victims in Africa, for every family member who didn't have a voice. That, she reminded herself, was what the law was supposed to be about.

Near midnight, Tessa made one last phone call, to a small East African NGO's helpline number. She expected voicemail. To her surprise, a man with a deep, lilting accent answered. His name was Joseph, and he spoke in quietly measured words. He'd once assisted families in rural Kenya who suffered losses during a "suspicious medical program." The NGO had documented the plight of dozens of individuals who reported severe reactions and at least two deaths.

Tessa's pulse soared. "That's... that's exactly what I need. Are you aware of which company sponsored the trials?"

Joseph paused, and Tessa thought she heard quiet voices in the background. "We tried to find out. The group that arrived wore unbranded lab coats. We only learned later, through local healthcare workers, that the funders were from a large American pharmaceutical. Rumor pointed to GenTech, but it was never confirmed. I gather you have more details?"

She carefully explained that she worked with a small law practice in the U.S., building a case that might involve GenTech's alleged wrongdoing. Without going too deep - she didn't want to scare him off or compromise his safety - she said she'd share documentation if it could help.

Joseph grew quiet. "We lost one of our staff investigators a few months back. Hit-and-run, they said. But he'd been receiving threats for months. I can't prove it was related, but… it felt tied to the work we were doing. I'm telling you this so you understand the danger."

Tessa felt her throat tighten. "I'm so sorry. We… we do know how serious it is. Trust me, we have security concerns of our own. But we can't give up. These families deserve justice."

Joseph gave a soft hum of agreement. "I'll see what old files we have. Send me your contact info, and I'll do what I can."

They exchanged email addresses. After the call ended, Tessa leaned back in her chair, adrenaline coursing through her veins. It was one of the most crucial leads yet - someone on the ground, with direct involvement, and documents that might actually tie GenTech to the tragedies. If Joseph could confirm a link, it would be a game-changer.

Tessa glanced at the clock. Nearly half past midnight. Her body insisted she go home, but her mind raced with possibilities. She reached for her phone again, starting a text to Emily:

Emily, I just spoke with a contact at a Kenyan NGO who might have actual docu -

She stopped mid-sentence as she caught movement in the reflection of her screen. The shape of a figure outside their office window. Heart hammering, Tessa jerked her head around. Through the blinds, she could make out the silhouette of a man standing on the sidewalk across the street, partially lit by a dim streetlamp. He was staring straight at the building.

Martyn Bellamy

Her breath caught. Her first thought: maybe it's a random pedestrian. But something about his stillness, the tilt of his head, made her uneasy. He just stood there, as though waiting, or perhaps trying to see if anyone was still inside the office. Tessa's car was parked on the curb below, the only one left on the block.

Anxiety gnawed at her. Had GenTech's watchers tracked her here? She'd been paranoid ever since the suspicious calls began. Emily had even joked that they were living in a spy thriller. Yet right now, it didn't feel remotely amusing. Carefully, Tessa reached for the light switch on the adjacent wall and flicked it off, plunging the office into shadows. She ducked behind her desk.

She dared a peek through the blinds. The man was gone. Or, at least, he had moved out of view. A jolt of terror shot through her as she considered the possibility that he might be heading into the building.

Her phone buzzed in her hand. Startled, she nearly dropped it. The screen showed a text from Emily: *Leaving for home. Don't stay too late. Lock up.*

Tessa typed back with trembling fingers: *Saw a suspicious figure outside. Heading home now.* She logged off, hurriedly stacking up her printouts, and stuffed them into a locked file cabinet - just in case. Then she grabbed her coat, shut off the overhead lights, and headed for the door.

Her footsteps echoed in the stairwell. She repeated a mantra in her mind: *Stay calm. Just get to your car.* The night air felt icy against her cheeks as she stepped onto the sidewalk. She scanned both ends of the block - no sign of anyone.

With a half-run, half-speed-walk, Tessa made it to her car. She fumbled with her keys. Her heart pounded until she slid into the driver's seat and locked the doors. As she pulled away, headlights behind her flickered on. She couldn't see the vehicle's make or color, but it followed her for two intersections before eventually turning off onto another street - maybe nothing, maybe someone heading home.

By the time she reached her apartment, Tessa's mind reeled with scenarios. She realized the crucial significance of the leads she'd gathered. *They're watching us,* she thought, slamming her car door shut. *They know we're onto something.*

Despite the fear, Tessa's determination only grew. As soon as she was inside her apartment, she rushed to her home office. She cross-checked every African news article, editorial, and reference with the corresponding sections in Alan's documents. Then she saved it all to an encrypted external hard drive.

Her mind replayed Joseph's story of a staff investigator lost to a "hit-and-run." She recalled Alan's trembling voice on the phone. She remembered how Emily had talked about Mark Hastings possibly being kept in the dark by Hastings & Cole. And she thought of that figure outside the office window - silent, ominous.

Yet something else flickered inside her, stronger than fear: *anger*. Anger that innocent people - people halfway across the world - had been made disposable in the pursuit of corporate profit. Anger that this shadowy figure might try to scare them off. Anger that lives had been quietly snuffed out and neatly swept under the rug with bribes and spin.

That fury fueled her. She spent the next two hours writing a comprehensive memo that Emily could review in the morning. She itemized each piece of evidence related to African hush-ups. She flagged the Zimbabwe case as the most promising lead, due to the direct mention of "Phase 3: Horizon," and she highlighted the possibility of contacting Ms. Dube or the Kenyan NGO to secure official statements.

When she finally set aside her laptop, the digital clock on her desk glowed 2:25 a.m. Tessa rubbed her eyes, exhaustion washing over her. Tomorrow would be another long day of forging ahead, but at least she had a plan. If GenTech thought intimidation would make them back down, they were in for a surprise.

At precisely 7:30 a.m., Tessa trudged into the office, fueled by two cups of coffee and a near-sleepless night. Emily was already there, dressed in a sharp navy suit, hair pulled into a tight bun.

"Any sign of trouble on your way in?" Emily asked, concern creasing her features.

Tessa shook her head. "Not this morning. But last night, I saw someone outside the building. Or at least, I think I did. He disappeared. Might have just been my imagination."

Emily frowned. "Let's not assume it was harmless. Going forward, we'll need to vary our schedules, be mindful of suspicious vehicles. I'm also installing a better security system here."

"Agreed." Tessa set her bag down and opened her laptop. "I compiled everything last night. You're going to be shocked by how many local African sources point to exactly the same wrongdoing Alan described. GenTech might have a decade-long record of hush-ups."

Emily exhaled slowly. "If that's true, it's bigger than I imagined. This isn't just one or two unethical trials - this is a systemic operation. We need to confirm it."

Tessa nodded. "We do. I'm going to start by trying to contact that Zimbabwean journalist. Then see if Joseph from the Kenyan NGO can give us scanned documents."

"Good. Meanwhile, I'm talking to a potential expert witness - a professor of international health law who might confirm the legal ramifications of running unapproved trials. If we can link it all together, we have the makings of a bombshell complaint."

They exchanged determined looks. Despite the swirling dangers, something electric hung between them - a sense of collective purpose. For Emily, it was the righteous fight she'd always dreamed of waging. For Tessa, it was the kind of research puzzle that turned her fear into resolve.

Over the course of the next few hours, Tessa meticulously charted timelines. On one axis, she listed the African nations where suspicious trials seemed to have taken place. On another, she listed the approximate dates gleaned from local news snippets. Then she overlaid references from Alan Priest's whistleblower documents, matching coded project names (like "Horizon," "FrontLine," "SoteriaRx") to each timeframe.

The overlap was too consistent to be coincidence:

- **Project Horizon**: Zimbabwe, ongoing between seven and eight years ago.

- **FrontLine**: Kenya, five years ago, plus potential expansions to Uganda.

- **SoteriaRx**: Nigeria, 18 months ago, focusing on a new vaccine.

Martyn Bellamy

Every project had a trail of local complaints - unexplained illnesses, sudden retractions of investigative articles, alleged bribes to health officials. Tessa's heart pounded in her chest as each new piece of evidence fell into place.

By midday, she had consolidated the entire puzzle into a coherent timeline. Emily reviewed it, eyes scanning the spreadsheet with mounting disbelief.

"This is horrifying," Emily whispered. "And it's exactly what we need to show a pattern of deliberate cover-ups. If we can just get statements from a handful of local witnesses - journalists, families, NGOs - GenTech won't be able to pretend it's all rumor."

Tessa gulped. "They'll fight us tooth and nail, though. We're basically claiming they committed mass negligence, possibly manslaughter. That's not just a civil lawsuit; that could lead to criminal inquiries."

Emily nodded. "Which is why they'll do anything to keep this under wraps. Let's get the ball rolling on protective measures for Alan. Then we start drafting the complaint, piece by piece."

Just as they were about to break for lunch, Emily's phone vibrated. She glanced at the screen and frowned. "It's Mark Hastings," she said, giving Tessa a meaningful look. "I'd better take this in private."

Tessa watched Emily stride into her office and close the door. The next fifteen minutes passed in tense silence. From beyond the glass pane, Tessa could see Emily's animated gestures - a furrowed brow, the occasional frustrated shake of her head. Finally, Emily emerged, looking grim.

"What is it?" Tessa asked.

"He's warning me off the case," Emily said flatly. "He says GenTech is prepared to file a motion to dismiss on any complaint we bring, claiming it's frivolous and that we lack jurisdiction. He also let slip that GenTech's top brass knows we've been digging into their African operations."

Tessa's stomach sank. "So they're basically telling us: 'Stay in your lane, or we'll flatten you.'"

"More or less," Emily said. She tossed her phone onto her desk. "I told Mark we're proceeding anyway. He insists I'm out of my depth, that I don't have the resources to handle an international pharmaceutical lawsuit."

Tessa bristled. "He always was condescending. But we do have resources, Em - namely, the truth."

Emily's eyes flashed with defiance. "Exactly."

The conversation with Mark only reinforced what Tessa and Emily already knew: GenTech was vast, well-funded, and would do anything to preserve its reputation. But Tessa felt a surge of conviction. If they were being threatened, it meant their research was close to the mark - close enough to scare GenTech.

She went back to her laptop, opening a fresh document. The heading read **"Evidence Summary: Africa."** Beneath it, in bullet points, she laid out the key facts, each carefully cited to a news snippet or testimonial. Then she started drafting a short script for potential phone calls with African journalists, braced for the possibility that many would be too scared to speak.

Each typed word felt like laying a brick in a fortress. Soon, they'd have a structure so sturdy that GenTech's endless resources couldn't topple it. In the back of her mind, Tessa remembered that figure outside the office last night, the half-glimpsed man in the streetlight glow. She remembered Joseph's warning about his coworker's "accident." She remembered the hush in Alan Priest's voice when he talked about being tailed by a black car.

And she refused to be intimidated.

By the time the day wound down, Tessa had compiled enough material to fill a binder - digitally speaking - on GenTech's alleged misdeeds in Africa. She'd even begun a separate folder labeled "South America," suspecting the pattern might extend there, too. Emily ordered takeout, and the two women ate in the office's small reception area, the pungent aroma of Thai noodles mingling with the crisp smell of new carpet.

Tessa recounted her conversation with Joseph from the Kenyan NGO. "He sounded nervous but willing to help. We might get scanned copies of death certificates, testimonies, maybe even medical logs. That alone could make for a devastating exhibit in court."

Emily nodded, chopsticks in hand. "We'll have to ensure those people's identities are protected. If GenTech is as ruthless as we think, they might retaliate against witnesses."

"It's insane, isn't it? We're basically dealing with a corporation that treats entire populations as test subjects."

Emily looked away, her expression haunted. "It's monstrous. I remember hearing rumors about 'risky expansions' back at Hastings & Cole, but I never dug deeper. I was too busy chasing partner track. Makes me sick to think about it now."

Tessa placed a comforting hand on Emily's arm. "You're here now. You're doing the right thing."

Emily gave a tight smile, then rose to her feet. "Let's call it a night soon. We'll finalize a plan tomorrow - start drafting the complaint, prep Alan's relocation, and keep building our network of potential witnesses."

Tessa nodded. "Sure. I'll just wrap up a final email to Joseph, letting him know we can handle any documents he sends securely. Then I'm out."

When Tessa finally did leave the office, she was relieved to see no mysterious silhouettes lurking in the shadows. The city lights flickered over her car's windshield as she navigated the streets. Yet her mind roamed across oceans, picturing the dusty roads of small African villages where GenTech's so-called "medical outreach" might have inflicted untold harm.

In her imagination, she saw mothers mourning children who never should have died, reporters threatened into silence, entire communities with no recourse. The thought fueled her sense of mission. She wasn't a hero - just a paralegal with a knack for research - but in some ways, that was enough. Because knowledge could be weaponized against even the mightiest corporate juggernaut.

As Tessa drove home, she couldn't help but think about all the new evidence waiting in her phone, her laptop, her encrypted drives. She wondered how Mark Hastings would respond when this data inevitably found its way into court motions and depositions. She wondered if GenTech's executives realized just how close the net was drawing.

Then she shook her head. Tomorrow was another day, and they would keep piling up the truth until it was too colossal to hide. GenTech could watch them, threaten them, smear them - but they couldn't bury the proof of their own misdeeds forever.

Martyn Bellamy

Chapter 13:
Whistleblower's Fear

Emily Blackwood's fingers paused over the laptop's keyboard. She was alone in her small law office, the late afternoon sun sending amber streaks across the chipped parquet floor. Despite the warmth of the day, a chill rippled through her body. A small, blinking cursor on her screen seemed to taunt her, as if daring her to move forward with the damning disclosures about GenTech she'd been assembling all week.

It was still early in the saga of her new solo practice, but already Emily found herself in the eye of a storm: an unfolding high-stakes lawsuit pitting her - and the whistleblower she had come to trust - against one of the most powerful pharmaceutical giants in the country. The last few months had tested her in ways she never anticipated when she left Hastings & Cole, a top-tier corporate firm, in pursuit of genuine justice. Now, the precarious position of her star witness, Alan Priest, threatened not only her case's viability but also his very life.

She saved her notes and glanced at her watch. 5:47 p.m. Alan was already late. Her mind flashed to the conversation they'd had two days prior, when he'd insisted on an "urgent" meeting at an undisclosed location - a dingy parking lot downtown. Alarmingly, he wouldn't say why he refused to come to her office. He had simply said, "They might be watching." She had spoken to Tessa Moretti, her paralegal and trusted friend, about it; Tessa had insisted that Alan might be paranoid, but in light of recent events - anonymous phone calls, suspicious cars idling by the curb, Mark Hastings's cryptic warnings - Emily could not dismiss Alan's concerns.

She was about to stand up and pace when the office door handle rattled. In an instant, her tension skyrocketed. The door swung open, and Tessa stepped inside, breathing heavily, her eyes wide with urgency.

"I just saw Alan getting out of a cab," Tessa reported, brushing aside a dark strand of hair that had fallen loose from her bun. "He's... He looks really nervous. He's glancing over his shoulder like he's expecting someone to leap out from behind a column."

The Ghosts' Trial – Volume One

Emily exhaled the breath she hadn't realized she was holding. "At least he made it. Let's give him a moment to gather himself."

Tessa nodded and disappeared back into the hallway. Emily closed the laptop, tidied the stack of GenTech papers on her desk - printouts of corporate emails, partial lab reports from the drug trials in Africa and South America, half-complete sets of data that suggested horrifying cover-ups - and tried to quell the swirl of dread building in her stomach.

Just a minute later, Alan Priest appeared in the threshold of her office. He wore a hooded sweatshirt that had definitely seen better days and an ill-fitting cap that shadowed most of his face. Pale, with a light sheen of sweat across his forehead, he shuffled inside. Even from behind her desk, Emily could sense that he was trembling.

"Alan," she said gently, standing up. "It's okay, come in. Sit."

He glanced over his shoulder, as if verifying that no one else was behind him, then shut the door firmly. The metallic click reverberated in the quiet space.

Wordlessly, he took a seat in front of her desk. She watched as he swallowed, still trembling.

Tessa stepped in after him, leaning against the closed door. She gave Emily a look that said, *He's in bad shape.*

Emily approached softly, arms at her sides, projecting an air of calm. "You're safe here," she said, though she wasn't entirely sure that was true. But the first rule she had learned about dealing with a skittish source was to offer a sense of security. "Take a moment, breathe."

For a long few seconds, Alan stared at his hands, which he'd folded in his lap as if to keep them from shaking. Then, he began in a hushed, desperate voice, "I don't think I can do this anymore."

A thousand thoughts flashed in Emily's mind. *Oh no. Not this.*

He raised his eyes and they shone with panic. "I've been followed," he said. "Last night. And the night before that. There was a black sedan - no plates - prowling around my apartment building. I left for the store around eight, and it was right there at the end of the block. When I came back, it was gone. But this morning... I found a note taped to my door. It said, 'Don't be a hero.' That's all. No name, no address. But I - " His voice caught as he tried to hold it together. "It's definitely them, Emily."

Emily felt her stomach twist. "Sit tight. Tessa, lock the door, would you?" She hated feeling paranoid in her own space, but safety was paramount. Tessa nodded and flipped the deadbolt.

"Tessa," Emily said, "why don't you get Alan some water?"

Alan nodded gratefully. "Yes, please."

While Tessa disappeared into the small kitchenette, Emily moved to the chair next to him. She wanted to be at eye level, not imposing behind a desk. "Alan," she said gently, "I'm sorry. No one should have to live in fear for doing the right thing. Is there something more you haven't told me yet?"

He pressed a hand to his forehead. "I... I think so." A tear of frustration escaped him. "They might have blackmailed me. Or they're *trying* to. My personal email was hacked. I got an email from some random address that said they had access to a bunch of private files from my past. I don't know how they got it, but it's the kind of stuff that could ruin me if it's made public. Messages with my ex-wife about finances, medical records..." His eyes darted anxiously around the room. "They threatened to leak it to reporters and to your opposition if I don't recant my statements. Or if I keep... keep working with you."

The anger hit Emily like a punch to the gut. GenTech's intimidation tactics were no surprise - she had seen powerful corporate clients resort to dirty tricks back when she worked at Hastings & Cole - but the raw fear on Alan's face made it impossible to remain detached. These were real people with real lives at stake.

"That's disgusting," she said under her breath. "I'm sorry. And no matter what, I promise you this: I will do everything in my power to protect you. We're going to figure out how to keep your identity under wraps as much as possible, at least until we can get an injunction or push for protective measures in court. We'll do depositions quietly. I can file motions to conceal your name from public records, or at least heavily redact them. There are ways, Alan."

He gave a short, bitter laugh. "I appreciate the vow. But you can't exactly stop them from tailing me or from blackmailing me, can you?"

Tessa returned with a glass of water. She crouched beside him as if to keep him calm, pressing the cup into his hand. "It's going to be okay," she said gently. "We have ways to fight back."

"How?" he demanded, voice cracking. "I've seen these guys operate from the inside. GenTech invests millions every year in hush money and specialized security forces. Their executives have ties to law enforcement, corporate espionage companies, and who knows who else. They'll do anything to protect themselves."

Alan's words fell heavily in the silent office. Emily felt a wave of déjà vu from her old corporate days, the ones she'd fled in hopes of becoming the kind of lawyer who *really* cared. Working for Hastings & Cole, she'd sometimes glimpsed the underhanded tactics used to keep big clients happy - but she'd never stood on the *opposite* side of that table. Now it was her turn to be the underdog, defending the whistleblower who threatened to expose a major pharmaceutical scandal. She was up against the kind of power she once served.

"Alan," she said slowly, "before you decide whether to walk away, I need you to remember why we're here in the first place. Those documents you brought to me?" She gestured at the manila folders stacked on her desk. "Emails, lab results, corporate directives - those are the backbone of our lawsuit. These trials in Africa and South America... People died. People who never should have been test subjects in the first place. You're the only direct witness we have who can connect all the dots."

He closed his eyes, exhaling shakily. "I know. I know that. Believe me, I lose sleep over it every single night. If there's even a chance we can stop them from doing it again - God, I *want* to help." Then he opened his eyes, letting them fix on Emily. "But... I'm scared. I don't know how to keep living under this threat. I want to vanish, maybe leave the state. But I can't afford that. And even if I could, they'd find me."

Emily felt the deep ache of empathy. "Let me put this plainly: if you walk away now, if you retract everything you've said, they'll still treat you as a liability. And we'll have no recourse to protect you. They're not going to suddenly forget that you once blew the whistle.

Their entire system runs on intimidation. If you disappear, you'll do so without the legal or public spotlight that can keep you safe. The truth - and a strong legal case - are your best defenses."

Alan's eyes flickered from despair to something akin to hope. Tessa added, "Emily's right. The more public we make this, the less likely they'll act rashly against you. They hate attention. And if they do try anything else? We'll document every threat, every suspicious move, and present it to the judge in your protective order hearing. There are lines even GenTech can't cross in broad daylight."

He nursed the glass of water, still trembling. "So, what... what do you want from me?"

"I want you to be strong," Emily said. "To stand by the testimony you gave me so far. I want you to trust me when I say we'll do everything humanly possible to keep your identity protected in the short term, and to push for a sealed deposition. Once we get the court on our side, we'll file protective orders. We'll force them to see you not just as a target but as a recognized, protected witness. You'll be safer under that shield than wandering alone."

Alan stared into his glass, the watery reflection of fluorescent lights shimmering. Finally, he exhaled heavily. "All right. All right, I - I won't back out. But I can't do this alone. I need you to tell me the next steps."

Relief fluttered in Emily's chest. "That's all I needed to hear."

Tessa touched Alan's shoulder reassuringly. "We'll start by documenting every incident you've told us about. The tailing, the black sedan, the note on your door. We'll keep a log. Even the blackmail threat, if you're comfortable disclosing it. We need a paper trail."

"I - I can show you the emails I've gotten," Alan said, voice quieter now. "I forwarded some to a secure account."

"Great," Emily replied. "We'll gather that as evidence of intimidation. Then I'll file a motion in court first thing tomorrow requesting a hearing to place you under a protective order as a confidential whistleblower. It's not a guarantee the judge will grant it, but we have strong grounds. We can show that you're already facing retaliation."

A flicker of possibility settled into Alan's eyes. "That's something... But do you think the judge will buy it? I mean, GenTech is powerful. Maybe they'll convince the judge that I'm making all this up."

Emily managed a reassuring smile. "Don't forget, I'm from a prestigious background, too. I know how to handle defense counsel, and I know how to compile the right arguments. I won't let them steamroll us. And Tessa is unstoppable once she sets her mind to something."

Tessa gave him a small, confident grin. "I'll be your personal research bloodhound. If there's a legal angle or a precedent we can use, I'll find it."

Alan swallowed hard and nodded. Emily reached for the pen and notepad on her desk. "All right. Let's lay out the immediate steps we need to take, and then we'll talk strategy for the long run."

For the next hour, the three of them constructed a plan:

1. **Documented Incidents**
   Alan recounted every suspicious event, including dates, times, and locations, while Emily jotted them down carefully. Tessa added

questions when needed: "What time did you first see the black sedan? Did you manage to get a partial plate? Did it follow you from your building, or was it parked waiting for you?"

2. **Digital Trail**

   Alan agreed to forward all threatening emails to a newly created secure address that Emily had set up specifically for whistleblower communications. She had learned from prior experience that funneling sensitive data through a single channel made it easier to track and present to the court in organized form.

3. **Legal Filings**

   Emily would draft the protective order request. Given the seriousness of the intimidation and the public interest nature of the case - the alleged wrongdoing involved fatalities in foreign clinical trials - she was confident the judge would at least schedule an urgent hearing.

4. **Personal Security Measures**

   Though Alan was reluctant at first, Tessa insisted on some basic steps for him: changing his routine commute, parking in different spots, possibly staying with a friend or relative for a few days. They also discussed installing a simple front-door camera. Alan was unconvinced it would deter anyone, but Emily emphasized the importance of capturing any evidence of trespassing or leaving menacing notes.

Throughout the conversation, Alan's anxiety gradually subsided. Having a concrete plan seemed to ground him. He offered more details about the internal workings of GenTech's compliance department - details that would be invaluable later in discovery. By the time the clock on the wall read 7:15 p.m., a semblance of calm had settled over the office.

Yet Emily sensed that for all the solace they had tried to give him, Alan was still a man on the brink. She gently asked if he was okay to return home alone. He hesitated, then agreed. "I need to show them I'm not cowering," he said. "But I'll stay alert. And I'll call you if anything happens."

As he rose to leave, Tessa retrieved a long tan coat from the coat rack. "Here," she said, handing it to him. "It's mine, but it's unisex enough. Wear it out. If anyone's watching for a guy in a hoodie, they might not spot you."

He took it gratefully, pulling it on and giving them both a small, nervous smile. "Thank you, Tessa. Thank you, Emily."

She walked him to the door, opening it just a crack to survey the dim corridor. The old building's overhead lighting flickered ominously. Emily felt a pang of protective instinct. *He's risking everything to expose the truth.*

She ushered him into the hallway, whispering, "Call me as soon as you're safe at home."

He nodded and hurried toward the elevator. Tessa locked up behind him, and the echo of metal sliding into place reverberated in the hush.

For a moment, Emily leaned against the door, exhaling. "This is bigger than anything I've tackled," she murmured. "But we can't let GenTech scare us off."

Tessa stepped closer and rested a hand gently on Emily's shoulder. "You're not alone in this. I'm with you every step."

Emily gave a tight, grateful nod. "We have to prepare for a fight."

By the time Tessa and Emily settled back in the office, the sun had vanished behind the cityscape, and warm lamplight cast their shadows on the wall. The hush of the corridors outside was broken only by the occasional hum of a vacuum cleaner - someone cleaning another suite in the building. The faint smell of disinfectant wafted through the hallway.

Emily opened her laptop once more. "Let's get started on the protective order motion. The sooner we file it, the better. If we can get it in front of a judge tomorrow afternoon, we might have a hearing in a few days."

Tessa pulled up a battered rolling chair beside Emily's desk. "I'll gather relevant precedents. There's bound to be a big set of case law around whistleblower protection. We'll want to highlight the ones involving corporate intimidation and the near-certain risk to personal safety."

Emily nodded and began dictating the skeleton of the motion, her nimble fingers flying across the keyboard. "I'll craft a statement explaining that without confidentiality, Alan's well-being is in jeopardy, which also jeopardizes the integrity of the evidence. Let's see... *The whistleblower, an individual who shall hereafter be referred to as John Doe,* - yes, we'll have to assign an alias in the public filing - *has been subjected to threats and harassment from unknown but presumably connected persons...."*

She typed ferociously, only pausing to ask Tessa for relevant legal citations. Every so often, Tessa would read out a phrase from a case. "Here's something: *Wright v. Independent Medical Labs, 2002,* the whistleblower's motion for protective order was granted after demonstrating credible threats..."

"Perfect. That's similar to what we're dealing with," Emily said, weaving it into the text. They continued like this for the better part of an hour, forging a persuasive argument that might sway the court.

Eventually, Tessa let out a yawn. "Man, the day's been a roller coaster."

Emily stretched, leaning back in her chair. "You're not kidding. I keep thinking about Mark Hastings, my old colleague. He called me last week, telling me I was out of my league. I wonder what he'd say if he knew we had a real whistleblower and not just circumstantial data."

Tessa shrugged. "He might already suspect. After all, GenTech's lawyers must realize something new spurred you to file that complaint with so much detail. I'm sure they're digging just as hard to find out who's fueling our case."

"And that's what scares me. If they piece it together that Alan is the source, they'll tighten the vise around him."

They exchanged a troubled look. Tessa rested her elbows on her knees. "But we can't hide him forever. If he's going to testify, it'll be public eventually, unless the judge grants a fully sealed proceeding, which is rare. We just have to do our best to buy time until we have enough momentum that GenTech can't crush us in the dark."

"I know," Emily said softly. "I'm worried, though. About Alan. About how far they'll go." She paused, chewing her lip. "In my old firm, I saw million-dollar deals struck in small conference rooms, deals that left communities bankrupt and powerless. GenTech has infinitely more resources. They'll hire investigators to harass him, or worse."

Tessa turned her eyes to the sliver of moon through the window. "Alan's right: they have specialized corporate security teams. We can't underestimate them."

Emily looked down at the final paragraphs of the motion. "Then we'll have to out-strategize them," she said, voice steady. "I want to call the courthouse first thing in the morning and get this on the docket. We might have to fight tooth and nail to get the hearing expedited, but we can't wait. *No one* is intimidating my client into silence."

A silent moment passed before Tessa quietly added, "Ever regret leaving Hastings & Cole, Em? Maybe life would be easier if we just didn't know."

Emily let out a soft laugh, tinged with bitterness. "Sometimes. But then I remember why I left. I was done being the person who helped bury the truth. I want to stand for something real."

They looked at each other in that half-lit space, the weight of the entire lawsuit pressing on them. "Then we keep going," Tessa said.

"Absolutely," Emily replied.

They sealed that unspoken pact with a resolute nod.

An hour later, Tessa left for the night, promising to show up bright and early. Emily closed her office door behind her paralegal and trudged back to her desk, shoulders stiff from tension. The building was eerily quiet. Now and then, the air conditioner kicked on, its hollow rumble echoing in the corridor.

She skimmed the newly written motion, eyeing the details. It looked good - solid, persuasive. She had included everything: the intimidation, the suspicious vehicle, the blackmail attempt. If any judge had a heart, they would be compelled to act.

Her phone buzzed. She picked it up, relief coloring her face when she saw Alan's number. "Hello?"

His voice was hushed. "I'm home. No sign of a black sedan. But that doesn't mean anything. I just… needed to let you know I'm all right."

She breathed easier, hearing that he'd arrived safely. "I'm glad you are. Alan, try to get some rest. We'll file that motion in the morning. I'll keep you updated every step."

"Okay. Thanks, Emily," he said, exhaustion dripping from every syllable. "And… thanks for not letting me give up."

"Of course," she said. "Talk soon."

She ended the call and stared out the narrow window behind her desk. The city lights twinkled below. She couldn't help but think of all the unsuspecting people going about their lives, blissfully unaware of the corporate corruption swirling in the heart of the city - unaware that in those same shining buildings, powerful players signed off on lethal human trials in places too remote for American headlines. Now, that darkness had spilled over, chasing a single man determined to set things right.

Yet, in that moment, Emily felt resolute. Alan had given her the impetus she needed to lock horns with GenTech. She only hoped that the scales of justice would tip in favor of truth before intimidation or violence choked it out. Clutching the motion in her hand, she switched off the office lights, preparing to walk into whatever storm awaited her.

Emily woke before dawn, her nerves already buzzing. After a quick shower and a mug of coffee, she whisked herself to the courthouse, a stately sandstone building with Corinthian columns that always made her think of old-world institutions. She'd rarely had reason to come here alone, especially not as lead counsel on such a weighty lawsuit.

By 8:30 a.m., she stood at the filing counter, politely smiling at the weary court clerk. "I'd like to file this motion, please," she said, sliding the protective order request through the gap in the Plexiglas. She kept her voice calm, though her heart pounded with urgency. "I'd also like to request an expedited hearing."

The clerk, a middle-aged woman with curly hair and horn-rimmed glasses, scanned the top page. Her expression betrayed no emotion. "All right. Let me see if the docket has any openings." She reached for her computer, typing with quick efficiency. "Any chance you have an emergency or urgent affidavit? Usually we see these protective order motions in certain circumstances - domestic disputes, child protective cases."

"Yes, it's a whistleblower intimidation case," Emily explained in hushed but insistent tones. "The respondent is a multinational pharmaceutical company. There have been credible threats."

The clerk glanced up. "A big lawsuit?"

"Yes." Emily offered a tight smile. "A lawsuit of significant public interest. We're seeking immediate protection."

The clerk weighed the motion in her hands, as if measuring the heft. "The earliest I can slot you in is probably next week - "

"Please," Emily interrupted, stepping closer, "this is extremely urgent. The harassment has already begun. My client's safety is at real risk."

A thoughtful frown creased the clerk's brow. She tapped at the computer again. "All right, Ms. Blackwood, let me see if I can shuffle the schedule. Judge Walden might consider it if you can provide an affidavit from your client detailing the intimidation."

"I can do that," Emily said at once. "We have a signed statement."

The Ghosts' Trial – Volume One

"Great. I can place you in a preliminary hearing docket for two days from now. It's not guaranteed, though. The judge has to accept the request."

"That's fine," Emily said. "We'll take it."

The clerk stamped the motion with an official seal, scanning it into the system. "You'll receive a time and courtroom assignment by email if the judge decides to hear it. Keep your phone on you."

Emily thanked her profusely and stepped away, adrenaline pumping. *Two days.* She would have to ensure that Alan was safe until then.

On her walk back to the car - a battered used sedan that still bore the faint whiff of stale coffee - her phone rang. She was surprised to see the caller ID read *Mark Hastings*. The name alone jolted her. Mark had been her friend, once upon a time, back at Hastings & Cole. Since Emily's departure, their friendly rapport had disintegrated into a tense rivalry. She hadn't forgotten his cryptic calls warning her off the GenTech case.

Emily steadied herself before answering. "Hello?"

"I assume you're filing a new motion this morning," Mark's voice came through, crisp and professional.

Her heart skipped. *Had he already heard?* "Is that so?" she said, trying to stay neutral.

A small pause crackled on the line. "Don't bother playing coy, Emily. We both know you're making a move to protect your star witness. My firm has a vested interest in all developments regarding GenTech."

Heat prickled behind Emily's eyes. *He's not even being subtle.* "Well, I see news travels fast," she said. "Anything else you'd like to know, Mark?"

She heard him exhale. "You need to understand something. GenTech is not a typical adversary. They will use every resource at their disposal. Just… think carefully if you want to double down on this protective order. It might escalate matters."

"That's exactly why I need it. They've already started threatening the man who's blowing the whistle on them."

Silence. Then Mark's tone dropped, quieter, more personal. "Emily, I've known you a long time. I know you have good intentions. But sometimes you should *stop* before you find yourself in over your head. You can still settle. They might even be open to a quiet arrangement... out of court."

Emily clenched her jaw. "You really think we can just hush up the fact that people died as a result of a drug trial? That their families never got justice? You were once better than that, Mark."

A sharp intake of breath told her she'd touched a nerve. "I'm doing my job," he said curtly. "I'm representing my client. You know what that means."

"Then let me do *my* job."

He paused again, perhaps searching for the right words. "Fine," he said at last, voice controlled. "Just know GenTech will respond to any motion with their own. They're not going to let you set a narrative that they intimidate employees."

"They *do* intimidate employees, Mark. You know it as well as I do. But let's see what the court says. Good day."

She ended the call, heart racing. His thinly veiled warning only fortified her resolve. If Mark and the defense attorneys were spooked enough to call her on a morning when she was filing a motion, that meant they feared the public exposure a protective order might bring. *Good,* she thought. *Let them worry.*

Back in her office, Emily spent the rest of the day in a swirl of activity. Tessa was already there, diligently typing away. She had been compiling detailed timelines correlating every suspicious event around Alan with the major steps in the lawsuit. Patterns emerged, like clockwork: the day after Emily had filed her complaint, that was when suspicious phone calls to Alan began. The day after a local newspaper had run a small piece about a "potential whistleblower lawsuit," Alan's car was broken into. Every incident practically screamed corporate intimidation campaign.

Emily heard Tessa let out a low whistle. "Look at this," Tessa said, spinning her monitor around so Emily could see. "One of Alan's emails specifically references a gentleman named Kenneth Vale, who apparently heads the GenTech 'Security and Compliance' team. Alan's note says he overheard Vale instruct staffers to 'keep an eye on the problem employees.' We've got a name."

Emily's eyes scanned the text. "This is good. If we can tie Kenneth Vale to these intimidation tactics, maybe the court will order the company to produce internal logs or memos that mention him. We can see if he allocated funds for personal investigators or hush money."

Tessa nodded, her expression grimly satisfied. "Which will help prove this intimidation is top-down, not just random rogue agents."

They traded a fierce, determined look. The more proof they gathered, the harder it would be for GenTech to brush the intimidation off as baseless.

Alan's protective order hearing was scheduled for two days from now - pending Judge Walden's final approval. Tessa and Emily had decided to host a thorough debriefing with Alan so they could get his sworn affidavit ready and lock down all the supporting details. Emily also wanted to make sure he wasn't second-guessing his decision to stay on board.

By lunchtime, she'd arranged for him to come in the back way - a service entrance typically used for deliveries. She reasoned it might draw less attention if someone was indeed staking out the building.

She was on edge the entire morning, waiting. Finally, at 1:00 p.m., Tessa opened the door to find Alan in the narrow corridor, looking as though he'd aged ten years overnight. He offered a shaky smile. "No trouble on the way here," he said by way of greeting.

"Good," Emily said, leading him inside quickly. "Let's talk in the conference room."

She guided him into a small rectangular space that served as both conference room and makeshift library, stacked high with law books and binders. There, Tessa already had an affidavit template printed out. Snacks and bottled water waited on the table - a small courtesy that Emily hoped would ease Alan's tension.

He sank into one of the seats. Emily sat across from him, while Tessa perched on the corner of the table, pen in hand, ready to note any key points. The midday sun streamed through the blinds, casting slatted shadows that seemed to slice the table in stripes of light and dark.

Emily began, "All right, Alan. We're going to formalize your affidavit for the protective order hearing. We need to describe the threats in detail. The judge needs to grasp just how real and frightening this is."

The Ghosts' Trial – Volume One

He nodded, swallowing. "Where do I start?"

"From the beginning," Tessa said kindly. "We want each incident in chronological order. Then we'll attach your emails and statements as exhibits."

Alan ran a hand over his close-cropped hair. "All right. It started the day after I told you about the drug trial emails."

He went on to describe the phone calls - anonymous, always from blocked numbers, with menacing silence or a single phrase like "You don't want to do this." Emily asked clarifying questions: Did he remember exact times? Did the caller mention his name? The more details, the better for their motion.

Then he explained, voice trembling, how three days later he noticed the black sedan outside his apartment. He documented license plate partials, times he came and went, how it disappeared if he tried to snap a photo. Next, he recounted discovering the note taped to his door. *Don't be a hero.*

Emily let him speak uninterrupted, carefully writing down the key points. When he got to the blackmail email - where the sender threatened to leak old personal information - Emily's blood boiled. Alan described how the email included partial screenshots of medical bills from his mother's bout with cancer years ago, sensitive documents that no one should have. It hammered home the lengths to which GenTech or its associates would go.

"You're doing the right thing," Tessa reassured him, finishing up her notes. "It's horrifying that they invaded your privacy like that, but if we can demonstrate all these connections, the judge will be compelled to protect you."

Alan nodded, eyes glistening. "I'll sign whatever you need."

Emily slid the affidavit across the table, lines of black text waiting for his signature. "Check everything carefully. Let us know if we missed a detail or if something is inaccurate. Once you're satisfied, sign and date."

He spent several minutes reading every line. The hush of the office was tense, broken only by the ticking clock. Eventually, Alan sighed and scribbled his signature, sliding the pages back to Emily. She placed them in a folder, stamped them with the official notary seal she'd acquired from her earlier days of corporate law.

"There," she said softly. "That's it. Now we have a sworn statement. I'll attach all the exhibits and get them to the judge as soon as the hearing's confirmed."

Alan leaned back in his seat, as though physically spent. For a moment, none of them spoke. Then Tessa asked, "Have you noticed anything else unusual? Especially since last night?"

He shook his head. "No calls, no emails today. Which somehow scares me more. Like they're planning something bigger."

Emily set a comforting hand on his arm. "Remember the plan we discussed: vary your routine, keep a log of everything. And call the police if you see that sedan again. Even if they just take a report, it's documentation."

He nodded shakily. "Right. I'll do that."

Tessa escorted him out the back entrance. Emily lingered in the conference room, organizing the newly minted affidavit. When she glanced out the side window, she spotted Alan leaving through the alley.

Her heart clenched when she realized how carefully he studied his surroundings, head swiveling as he walked. Gone was the mild-mannered scientist who'd first stepped into her office; in his place was a man who felt hunted, never fully relaxed.

Quietly, Emily promised herself she would not let that fear become his permanent reality. *We will see this through. We will make them pay for what they've done.*

Tessa had just returned from walking Alan out when a booming knock sounded at the office door. Emily startled - no one was scheduled to visit. She and Tessa exchanged uneasy glances. Slowly, Tessa unlatched the door, the memory of Alan's paranoia fresh in their minds.

A uniformed courier stood there, sporting a company ball cap. He held a large envelope. "Delivery for Ms. Blackwood."

Emily stepped forward, heart hammering. She didn't recall ordering anything. "That's me," she said, half expecting a subpoena or some ominous letter from GenTech's legal team.

The courier asked for her signature on a digital pad. She scrawled her name, and he handed over the envelope before turning to depart without another word. Tessa shut the door and locked it.

They stared at the unmarked envelope. "No return address," Tessa said, brow furrowed. "Could be from them."

Emily set it on her desk, exhaling. "Let's open it carefully."

Inside was a single sheet of paper - a typed letter with one line:

"We know you filed a motion. You're playing with fire."

No signature, no letterhead. Emily felt a chill. "They're not even pretending to be subtle anymore."

Tessa scowled, pulling out her phone. "We have to add this to the harassment log. Let the court see how brazen this is."

Emily swallowed. "Absolutely." She forced herself to keep calm. If GenTech's foot soldiers thought intimidation alone would knock her off balance, they had another think coming. "Scan this. Then bag it up as evidence. Let's keep the original safe."

Her paralegal nodded, methodically going through the routine they had established for preserving suspicious communications.

Emily struggled to keep her composure. If *she*, the attorney, was now being threatened so openly, then how much danger did that put Alan in? It reaffirmed the necessity of that protective order - and her need to see it through.

Evening arrived again, and Tessa left for home, her arms clutching a stack of documents to review. Emily remained behind, compelled to finish drafting arguments in case the judge demanded more detail. She could hear her own breath in the silent room, the fluorescent lights overhead casting a stark glow. Shadows from the hallway made the office feel narrower than usual.

As she typed, her mind wandered to the final months she'd spent at Hastings & Cole. She remembered the late nights spent crafting bulletproof arguments for big corporate clients. She recalled hushed conversations in glass-walled conference rooms where decisions were made to bury certain bits of evidence or bury certain lawsuits altogether. That had been the final straw - the moral dissonance that forced her to walk away. Now, ironically, she was up against the very kind of machine she once served.

Her phone vibrated, shaking her from the memory. Another unknown number. She hesitated, then answered, hoping it wasn't another threat.

It turned out to be *Prisha Shah,* the investigative journalist who'd shown an interest in the GenTech story. They'd met briefly earlier in this case - a quiet coffee shop meeting where Prisha had gleaned enough to run a small piece about "possible corruption in drug trials."

"Emily," Prisha said in a low voice, "I heard rumors you're filing a protective order for a whistleblower. Off the record - should I be watching for a story?"

Emily's gut told her to keep Alan's identity hidden. But shining a public spotlight on the intimidation might also deter GenTech's more dangerous tactics. She thought for a moment, then responded carefully, "I can't confirm any whistleblower's name. But yes, we're taking steps to protect someone who's come forward with incriminating information about GenTech's drug trials."

Prisha's tone grew serious. "Word in the journalist circles is that GenTech's top brass are scrambling. They're preparing a media blitz if anything about these foreign trial deaths goes mainstream."

Emily's breath caught. "So they know it's getting bigger."

"Absolutely. And for what it's worth, I have a contact in a region of West Africa where GenTech ran a suspicious trial a few years back. I'm following up. I'll share anything I find that might help your case."

A rush of gratitude warmed Emily. "That would be incredible. Thank you. And be careful yourself - these people aren't shy about intimidation."

Prisha gave a short, knowing laugh. "I've had my share of threats over less. But this - this is major. I can't look away. Stay safe, Emily."

They ended the call. Emily let the phone slip from her fingers onto the desk, her heart pounding with fresh resolve. Journalists might bring the scorching light of public scrutiny. That was exactly the kind of thing that could turn the tide against a massive corporate entity.

In that moment, she realized that perhaps the greatest shield for Alan - and for her - was not to hide in the shadows but to bring everything into the open. Because once the public took notice, GenTech's risk in harming them increased tenfold.

Still, caution was vital. There was a delicate balance between exposing wrongdoing and revealing so much that Alan's life became even more endangered. She stood up to stretch, battling the moral labyrinth that had become her daily life: *Expose them or remain discreet?*

A dozen steps back and forth, pacing the floor, calmed her nerves enough to return to the glowing screen. She made a silent vow: once that protective order was in place, once the judge recognized the seriousness of these threats, she'd push for further measures. She'd bring in the press if needed. No half-measures.

It was well past 9:00 p.m. when Emily decided to call Alan for a final check-in. She worried that a new wave of intimidation might strike once GenTech realized they'd been formally reported for whistleblower harassment.

She dialed his number. Three rings. Four. Her anxiety mounted. Five…

Finally, he picked up. "Hello?" His voice was timid, as though muffled.

"Alan, it's me - Emily. I just wanted to see how you're holding up."

He let out a breath. "I'm all right. At least no new threats today. But every time I look out the window, I swear I see headlights parked across the street."

Her heart clenched. "I'm so sorry. Just two more days, hopefully, until we can get into that hearing. Hang tight. Log every detail, like we said."

"I am," he assured her. "I even tried calling local precinct to see if they'd patrol the area more often. I don't know if it'll help."

"It's worth a shot," Emily said softly. "Alan, for what it's worth, you're doing the right thing. I know it doesn't feel like it right now, but… the people who died in those trials, the families who never saw justice - this is for them, too."

The Ghosts' Trial – Volume One

He was silent for a moment. Then, voice trembling, he asked, "Emily, do you really think we can win against them? Honestly?"

She inhaled slowly. "We can at least bring the truth to light. In my book, that's already a victory. But yes, I believe if we keep pressing, if we find the right evidence and don't back down, we can hold them accountable in court. They've gotten away with too much for too long."

A quiet exhalation on his end, as though he was fighting back tears. "All right," he whispered. "I'll stay strong. I promise."

"Thank you," Emily said, voice full of empathy. "Get some rest if you can."

She ended the call, drained but resolute. Outside, a streetlamp flickered in the deserted block, and she thought about how precarious life felt for all of them. But her determination surged: if the intimidation was ramping up, it meant GenTech was feeling cornered. And cornered animals tended to lash out.

It was after midnight when Emily finally switched off her computer, leaving the protective order motion in polished form. She gathered her things - jacket, purse, a stack of notes - and walked out into the corridor. The overhead lights buzzed with a faint electric hum.

Her footsteps echoed on the vinyl tiles as she headed toward the elevator. She tried not to recall the creeping paranoia that now defined her days and nights. Checking her phone one last time, she noticed a single text from Tessa: *Don't stay too late. Be safe.*

If only it were that simple, she thought, summoning a half-smile. She typed back, *Leaving now. Locking up. Thanks for everything. See you tomorrow.*

The elevator doors creaked open. She stepped inside, pressing the ground floor button. The ride was rickety, reminding her of the building's modest status - far from the glass palaces of her old firm.

Exiting onto the street, she clutched her purse and scanned the block. No black sedans in sight, but that didn't mean someone wasn't lurking. She could almost feel eyes on her. She forced herself to walk calmly to her sedan, which was parked under a dim streetlamp that only half worked.

Once safely in the car, she locked the doors and turned the ignition. The engine rattled to life. She let out a shaky breath. *You're fine,* she told herself. *And you're doing the right thing.*

Yet, as she pulled away from the curb, a dull anxiety settled in her chest. In the rearview mirror, the reflection of the street stretched behind her, empty yet menacing. The day's events looped in her mind: the letter from the courier, Mark's call, the affidavit Alan signed. And overshadowing everything was the knowledge that a powerful corporation was determined to silence them.

Let them try, she told herself fiercely. *We won't give up. Not when we're this close to justice.*

She was certain that this chapter of her winding journey would mark the turning point. Alan Priest hadn't run, despite every reason to do so. He had chosen to stand with her, to shine a light on GenTech's lethal secrets.

And Emily, for her part, would stand with him. Even if it meant drawing threats like a magnet. Even if it meant unraveling her own sense of security. Because in a world where corporations played God with vulnerable lives far away, a single whistleblower's courage to speak up could be the one spark that ignited a blaze of accountability.

As she drove off into the night, she braced herself for the battles to come, determined that neither fear nor threats would derail their fight for truth.

Chapter 14: Mark's Warning

Emily Blackwood lowered herself into the creaky wooden chair behind her desk, heart pounding as she mentally replayed the whirlwind of events from the past few days. The cramped confines of her new office offered no sanctuary from the swirling tension that had become her new normal. The overhead fluorescent light blinked ominously, momentarily casting flickers of uneven brightness against the off-white walls. She had moved into this tiny space not long ago, leaving behind the lavish corridors of Hastings & Cole. Here, the outdated furniture, the flickering lights, and the persistent smell of dust served as daily reminders that she was no longer under the protective umbrella of one of the country's most elite law firms. Instead, she was on her own: financially strapped, brimming with moral outrage, and fully committed to unearthing the truth about GenTech's lethal drug trials.

The muffled hum of the traffic outside rose and fell in waves through the large, cracked window behind her. She exhaled slowly, trying to curb the persistent sense of being watched - an unsettled feeling that had crept into every aspect of her life of late. After Alan Priest, the GenTech whistleblower, revealed emails and documents implicating the pharmaceutical giant in the deaths of African and South American test subjects, Emily knew she was treading dangerous waters. Anonymous phone calls, suspicious cars parked near her building, even a few nights of hearing footsteps outside her apartment had left her on high alert. Any illusions she had about playing the role of a small-town attorney handling benign business deals had evaporated. GenTech's reach, she feared, was disturbingly wide.

On the desk lay a slim folder stuffed with photocopies of incriminating emails Alan had handed over just days earlier. She had been poring over them for hours, searching for the best legal angle to file a complaint that would stick. It was still early in the process. She was aware that a lawsuit of this magnitude - accusing a powerhouse pharmaceutical conglomerate of corporate negligence, cover-ups, and possibly manslaughter - would require robust evidence and, ideally, the resources of a far larger firm than her fledgling practice. Yet backing down wasn't an option; the moral weight was too heavy, and the cost of inaction too high. People had died, hidden in plain sight by corporate spin and nondisclosure agreements, and Emily refused to let GenTech bury that truth.

Her paralegal, Tessa Moretti, stepped into the office, her short dark hair framing a concerned expression. Tessa carried a small stack of documents in one hand, a half-eaten energy bar in the other. Even Tessa, usually quick with an encouraging quip, appeared more serious these days. The lines of worry around her eyes had deepened since they'd taken on Alan Priest's case.

"Emily," Tessa said softly, "you need a break. You've been at it since dawn."

Emily rubbed her temples, trying to dispel the fatigue that threatened to overwhelm her. "I'm fine. Really. I just need to figure out how best to structure this complaint. We're pointing some strong accusations at GenTech, and they're going to come back swinging."

Tessa placed the stack of documents on the edge of the desk. "I just organized the new records Alan sent over. He says he's working on tracing funds from a shell company tied to GenTech's hush-money deals. He's terrified. Thinks they're on to him. He's not sure if he should keep digging or lie low for a while."

Emily swallowed a knot of worry. "We're his attorneys, in a sense. We have to protect him. But I can't deny - if GenTech suspects him of leaking documents, he's in real danger."

Tessa nodded, her voice dropping. "And so are we."

They exchanged a tense look. Emily knew Tessa was right. She'd already experienced the hush of footsteps outside her apartment door. Whether it was intimidation or something more ominous, she had no idea. But it was clear that her old life of polished suits and lofty corporate deals had been replaced by a new reality in which intimidation and potential violence lurked around every corner.

The phone on her desk rang, jolting her from her grim thoughts. The landline had barely rung in the past few weeks - most prospective clients reached out via her cell phone or email - so this call at such an odd hour drew her immediate attention. Tessa arched an eyebrow curiously.

Emily picked up the handset. "Emily Blackwood speaking."

The Ghosts' Trial – Volume One

A brief pause crackled over the line. Then a low male voice responded. "Emily… it's Mark Hastings."

She felt her throat tighten. Mark Hastings. The name alone packed an emotional punch. He had once been her colleague and, on occasion, friend at Hastings & Cole. They'd grabbed late-night coffees during marathon discovery sessions, even shared a few jokes about senior partners. But now he'd emerged as GenTech's counsel, or at least part of the high-powered legal team circling the pharmaceutical giant's wagons. He was also a rising star in the same firm she had left behind - a swanky BigLaw attorney with bottomless resources.

"Mark," she managed. "To what do I owe the pleasure?"

Tessa picked up on Emily's subtly sharpened tone and hovered near the door, as if standing guard. Emily would have asked her to stay, but Tessa seemed to know that no request was needed.

On the other end, Mark released a faint sigh. "I'm calling as a courtesy. Consider it a friendly warning."

Emily bristled. "A warning?"

Martyn Bellamy

"You're getting in over your head." His words were clipped. "There's no easy way to say this. You know how serious these allegations are. We have reason to believe you're preparing a lawsuit against GenTech - "

"That's correct," she interjected, not bothering to deny it. "We have a whistleblower. We have documents. This isn't idle speculation."

Mark's voice quieted, almost as though he was trying to maintain composure. "Emily, you left Hastings & Cole to start a small practice. This case could destroy you. GenTech is a multibillion-dollar corporation. You can't possibly believe you'll walk away from this unscathed."

Emily felt the hair at the back of her neck rise. She forced a level tone. "I'm prepared to see this through. People died because of GenTech's negligence. I know what the documents say."

"And I know the capabilities of my firm," Mark countered. "I also know the lengths GenTech is willing to go. Do you remember the Donovan case? You saw how we undermined that class-action lawsuit with discovery motions, strategic delays, and… other tactics."

She remembered all too well. The Donovan case had been a consumer protection lawsuit - meritorious in many ways - yet Hastings & Cole had shredded it through deft legal maneuvering. She had been part of the team, though she'd felt increasingly uncomfortable the deeper she got. That memory was one of many that prompted her departure, along with a creeping sense that she was only fueling injustice from the inside.

She fought not to let her voice shake. "You're forgetting something, Mark. I'm not at Hastings & Cole anymore. I don't have to toe the line or compromise my conscience."

A heavy sigh crackled through the line. "You're also without backup," he said bluntly. "I'm being straight with you here: you won't find it easy to get expert witnesses. GenTech can scare them off or offer hush money. The moment you file, they'll bury you in procedural motions, depositions, counterclaims. They're ready to drag this on for years. Don't do it to yourself. Don't do it to your client."

Emily clenched her jaw. "We both know you're not calling out of pure benevolence. GenTech is worried.

Are you scared we might actually have enough to bring them down?"

Mark's voice wavered. "I called because I remember how you used to talk about justice, about wanting to make a difference. Maybe I believed in that too - once. But the world isn't that simple. Big corporations have money, influence. They can make you wish you'd never set foot in a courtroom."

"I'm not naive," she said evenly. "You can tell GenTech they'd do well to start preparing their defense."

A pause hung between them, thick with tension and unspoken history.

"You think you're the crusader in this story, Emily," Mark said at last, "but it's not going to end like some triumphant Hollywood script. I'm giving you an out. Drop this, move on, and maybe someday you can pick a less dangerous fight."

She recognized the subtle shift in his tone - resignation, maybe even regret. She closed her eyes, recalling the nights in the Hastings & Cole library when Mark had confided his frustration about serving corporate

The Ghosts' Trial – Volume One

Goliaths. It stung to see him now as an opponent, but the path he'd chosen was set.

"I'm not backing down," she said, her voice resolute. "Thanks for your concern, but I can handle this."

He let out a breath. "Then you should know: if you continue, you're on your own. And GenTech plays rough. I don't want to see you get hurt."

The line went dead. Emily slowly lowered the phone back onto its cradle. She felt oddly hollow. Anxiety warred with a flare of pride in her chest. This was confirmation: Mark - or rather, the entire legal muscle behind GenTech - was taking her seriously. But that also meant GenTech recognized her potential threat and was moving to snuff her out early.

Tessa stepped forward. "That didn't sound good."

Emily forced a crooked smile. "Mark's trying to scare me off. He basically said the same line we used to feed plaintiffs at the old firm: you'll be buried, it's too big, you can't handle it."

"Are we letting that spook us?"

"No." She set her jaw. "They're worried, Tessa. Mark wouldn't have called if they weren't. But we need to be even more careful - this is getting real. I want to comb through our building's security system, if we even have one. And we should advise Alan to stay somewhere safe. A hotel under a different name, maybe."

Tessa nodded. "I'll call Alan right away. See if we can move him to that extended-stay place a few blocks out. We'll try to keep a low profile until we can file. And I'll keep researching the references to that shell company in Africa." She paused. "Are you sure you're okay?"

Emily pressed her fingertips to her temple. "I'm... not sure. But letting GenTech bully us isn't an option."

Tessa smiled, a glint of steely determination in her eyes. "You're right. Let's beat them at their own game."

An hour later, Tessa had stepped out to gather more documents from the local records office, leaving Emily alone with the echo of Mark's voice still bouncing around in her mind. She found her thoughts slipping back to the day she'd first met him. She had been a fresh associate at Hastings & Cole, full of enthusiasm about using the law as a tool for fairness. Mark, only slightly her senior, had been assigned to show her around the labyrinth of offices and introduce her to the partners. He'd joked that new associates at Hastings & Cole were like seeds in a greenhouse - watered and tended until they either thrived or shriveled under the pressure.

For a while, it seemed that they both thrived. Mark's mind was razor-sharp - one partner had called him a "walking legal encyclopedia" - and Emily possessed a knack for dissecting ethical pitfalls in ways that brought nuance to the firm's arguments. They had worked late nights on high-stakes cases, tossing ideas back and forth, occasionally losing track of time until a cleaning crew reminded them to go home. But gradually, Emily had noticed how their perspectives diverged. Mark's ambition outpaced his conscience, at least in her eyes, whereas she found it increasingly difficult to justify the firm's tactics. She had tried to talk to him about it, but he always brushed it off as "the nature of the business."

It was painful to realize how deeply he'd assimilated the Hastings & Cole ethos. In contrast, Emily had found her moral lines cracking under the constant assault of questionable defense strategies for corporate clients. It was that gnawing sense of complicity that finally pushed her to leave. Mark, meanwhile, soared to new heights within the firm, apparently unconcerned or - worse - actively complicit in the tough defense strategies that protected corporations like GenTech from accountability.

Now, after that phone call, she understood that Mark hadn't lost his capacity for empathy entirely. He'd sounded almost regretful. But she also recognized that he was in too deep. He wanted her to quit, not out of genuine altruism, but because her fight posed a threat to his client - and to him. If she had walked away from the whistleblower's case, Mark's life would remain simple. With no determined opposing counsel, he could continue up the corporate ladder without needing to face the moral quagmire that this lawsuit would bring. It was easier for him if Emily never forced him to question his own conscience.

She set those thoughts aside. Dwelling on Mark's motivations would only cloud her strategy. She and Tessa had a formidable task ahead: building a case that proved GenTech's wrongdoing in a way that could stand up to the harshest scrutiny. The press might latch onto sensational bits if they filed a complaint with partial evidence, but that could backfire if GenTech dismantled their claims. They needed to be thorough, unwavering, and prepared.

Emily rose from her desk and walked to the window, the city's late-morning light streaming across her face. In the reflection of the glass, she glimpsed her own features - a slightly pale complexion, dark hair pulled into a hasty bun, eyes ringed by the shadows of sleepless nights. She didn't look like the polished, confident attorney who had once given presentations at corporate board meetings; she looked like a woman on the edge of exhaustion, fueled purely by a sense of righteous indignation. And she realized she was okay with that. If this was what it took to expose a pharmaceutical giant's dangerous misconduct, so be it.

By noon, Emily's phone buzzed again. Half expecting Mark's voice, she hesitated before answering. To her relief, it was Tessa.

"Hey," Tessa said. "I'm at the county records office, checking into some building ownership records. Turns out the property used for GenTech's stateside clinical testing used to be under a different subsidiary name. That might help confirm a pattern of shell entities."

Emily felt a flicker of excitement. "That's exactly what we need. We can show a deliberate attempt to hide these trials behind multiple corporations. A judge might see that as indicative of intent to deceive."

"That's what I'm thinking. One snag: a lot of the documents here are incomplete or too old to be digitized. They've got stacks of manila folders in a back room. I'll see how much I can copy, but it's going to take a while."

"Do what you can," Emily said, an edge of caution in her voice. "And watch your back, Tessa. We don't know who else might be poking around there."

Tessa sighed. "I will. I'll check in later."

When Emily ended the call, she felt a fresh wave of determination mixed with anxiety. She was unbelievably lucky to have Tessa's support. If Tessa had found a more stable job, she would be working normal hours at a standard wage, not rummaging through dusty archives for a whistleblower case that could land them both in hot water. The fact that Tessa chose to remain said everything about her loyalty and sense of justice.

Half an hour later, Emily tried to return to drafting the complaint, but Mark's phone call kept echoing in her head. In the corporate world, a "friendly warning" was never just friendly. It was strategic. Hastings & Cole, through Mark, wanted to sow seeds of doubt in her mind so that she'd hesitate, second-guess herself, maybe even abandon the fight. But the more she thought about it, the more resolute she became. If Mark was giving warnings now, what would happen when the real litigation started? She needed to steel herself.

The rest of the afternoon crawled by in a haze of legal research and quiet paranoia. Emily skimmed through old case precedents involving whistleblower suits against major corporations, making copious notes about potential pitfalls and success strategies. She was forming the skeleton of her complaint - allegations of fraud, negligence, wrongful death, possibly even RICO violations if they could prove a pattern of racketeering in covering up fatal trials.

Yet every time she heard a noise in the hallway, she tensed. The overhead light flickered incessantly, adding to the sense of impending danger. By three o'clock, she had drunk more coffee than she cared to admit, her nerves raw.

A sudden knock at the door made her jump. She clutched the edge of her desk, her pulse racing. "Who is it?"

"It's me," came a muffled voice. Alan Priest. The whistleblower.

She hurried over to unlock the door. Alan stood there, flannel jacket wrinkled, hair disheveled, and eyes bloodshot. He looked as though he hadn't slept in days. Clutched under one arm was a battered briefcase. He slipped inside, glancing anxiously over his shoulder before she closed and locked the door behind him.

"Alan, what are you doing here?" she asked softly. "We talked about you laying low."

He swallowed hard, the fear in his eyes palpable. "I - I had to come. I've got something else you need to see." He set his briefcase on the small coffee table near the corner of the office. "They're not just burying adverse events. They're outright lying to regulators - creating entire fictitious patient profiles. This is bigger than I thought."

He flipped open the briefcase and pulled out a thick folder, edges tattered. Documents spilled out, revealing spreadsheets, internal memos, and correspondence that seemed to depict the manipulation of trial data. Emily's breath caught in her throat. If these documents were authentic, they proved not only negligence but deliberate deceit. She carefully flipped through the pages, her stomach twisting with each new revelation.

"Dear God," she muttered. "They systematically replaced real patient data with sanitized versions to make the drug appear safe. This is monstrous."

Alan nodded vehemently. "It started small, a handful of questionable edits here and there. Then it snowballed. I was part of the data management team - just an entry-level contractor at first. When I realized what was happening, I tried to talk to my supervisors. They threatened me, told me I'd lose my job if I didn't shut up. Eventually, I discovered that not only were they forging data, but people on the ground in South America were dying, and GenTech was blaming it on local conditions, malnourishment, or concurrent illnesses. The families got hush money. It's... it's horrific."

Emily felt a surge of anger, her hands shaking as she arranged the documents. "These are crucial. We'll keep them safe, Alan, but you shouldn't have risked coming here in person."

He cast a haunted glance at the closed door. "I didn't know where else to go. My apartment is definitely being watched. I swear I've seen the same silver sedan idling outside my building every night. Then it shows up at the grocery store when I'm there. I can't do anything without feeling eyes on me."

Her heart twisted in sympathy. Alan was risking everything: his career, his personal safety, his peace of mind. "We'll figure out a safe place for you," she said gently. "Tessa's looking into extended-stay hotels. Somewhere nobody would think to look. We'll get you there tonight."

He nodded, relief flickering in his eyes. Then, almost as if an afterthought, he added, "Have you heard from the other side?"

The Ghosts' Trial – Volume One

She swallowed. "Yes, actually. Mark Hastings called this morning. He tried to dissuade me from moving forward."

Alan grimaced. "That means they know how close you are to filing. It also means they're prepared to strike back."

Emily gently placed the new documents in the folder, then slid them into a locked file cabinet near her desk. "I'd imagine so. But we can't let that stop us, Alan. The truth is more important."

He stared at her a long moment, his voice trembling slightly. "You don't regret taking this on, do you? Sometimes I wonder if I should have stayed quiet. Maybe no one would have believed me anyway."

Placing a reassuring hand on his shoulder, Emily shook her head. "Don't think that way. If you'd stayed silent, GenTech would continue their lethal trials with impunity. You did the right thing, even if it's terrifying. We'll see it through - together."

A tear glistened in the corner of his eye, and he quickly brushed it away. "Thank you," he whispered.

Shortly after Alan left, Emily double-checked the locks on the office door and closed the blinds. A swirl of unease settled in her chest. Mark's call, Alan's fear, the ominous new documents - everything pointed to a confrontation that was no longer just theoretical. She had to assume that as soon as she filed the complaint, GenTech would unleash a legal and possibly extralegal blitz to bury her.

She found herself pacing the floor, considering strategies. Perhaps she needed an ally with more resources. Another firm might be hesitant to join, though, especially if they feared going up against a behemoth like Hastings & Cole. Even so, she decided to put out a few quiet feelers to attorneys she trusted - if there were any left who hadn't fully succumbed to BigLaw cynicism.

Around six in the evening, as she was gathering her coat and keys to leave, the phone rang again. Emily's throat clenched. She debated letting it go to voicemail, but something compelled her to pick up.

"Emily Blackwood," she said curtly.

A low, male voice that wasn't Mark's responded. "Ms. Blackwood. This is Elliot Bronson, counsel for GenTech. I'm sure you recognize the name."

She did. Bronson was known for his cutthroat approach to litigation, rumored to have orchestrated some of the most brutal depositions in the profession. His involvement meant GenTech was dispatching its top enforcers.

"I do," she replied calmly, forcing her voice to remain steady.

"I'm calling to schedule a meeting," Bronson said. "We'd prefer to have a civil conversation before you decide to file anything that might be misinformed or defamatory. We believe open dialogue can clear up misunderstandings."

Emily's grip on the phone tightened. She recognized the tactic immediately: lure her into a "meeting" that would be part intimidation, part fishing expedition. Bronson would test how far along she was, see if they could kill her momentum with a direct confrontation.

"I'm quite busy," she said neutrally. "I don't see the need for an informal meeting at this stage."

Bronson chuckled. "Ms. Blackwood, if you pursue these allegations publicly, you'll be stepping on some very big toes. My advice is to meet with me and perhaps avoid a costly legal spectacle. GenTech has no desire to tarnish your budding practice - this entire matter might be resolved quietly."

Her stomach turned. "I'm not open to hush money or quiet deals if that's what you're implying, Mr. Bronson."

He hesitated for a beat. "We're discussing a potential misunderstanding," he said, carefully enunciating each word. "But if you insist on refusing our professional courtesy, then so be it. We'll see you in court."

The line clicked off. Emily slowly set the phone down, her heart hammering in her ears. Bronson was more direct than Mark - a bulldozer, unconcerned with subtlety. His words confirmed that GenTech wanted to bend or break her before she ever set foot in a courtroom.

Night fell, and the city's lights twinkled through the windows. Emily remained in her office, waiting for Tessa to return from the records office. She spent the time organizing the newly acquired documents, double-checking references, scanning pages for digital backups. She didn't trust that physical copies alone would remain safe if someone decided to break in.

At last, Tessa arrived, her arms laden with yet more folders and a face etched in fatigue. She dropped the folders on a side table and sank into the chair across from Emily.

"I need about ten showers," Tessa groaned. "That records office is a relic from the 1970s."

Emily offered a sympathetic smile. "Anything interesting?"

Tessa yawned, then tapped one of the top folders. "This one shows the official transfer of property from a defunct entity called 'Harrisvale Laboratories' to GenTech's subsidiary. I found references to overseas wire transfers, suspicious addresses that lead nowhere. It's more evidence of deliberate obfuscation. They're definitely trying to cover their tracks."

Emily nodded. "Excellent work. Alan came by earlier. He had even more proof - doctored data and evidence of forging patient records."

Tessa's eyebrows shot up. "That's a gold mine if we can authenticate it. Did he say where he got it?"

"More or less. He used to do data entry, so he had direct access to the back-end systems. He's terrified. I told him to find a safer place for the night. We need to keep him from harm."

Tessa nodded gravely. "We should hurry up and file. The longer we wait, the more time GenTech has to anticipate our moves."

Emily let out a breath. "I know. But Bronson just called. He wants a meeting. Mark already tried to warn me off. We're definitely on their radar now."

"You want to meet them?"

Emily shook her head. "It's a trap. They'll use the meeting to gauge our case, maybe try to intimidate me in person. If they were offering some major settlement, they'd use more discreet channels."

Tessa smirked. "They're panicking."

"Seems like it."

The two women exchanged a determined glance. As they began to clean up the office for the night, Emily felt a strange surge of exhilaration. Yes, the stakes were high, and yes, they were effectively alone in this. But they were making progress, collecting enough evidence to back GenTech into a corner. She only prayed that they could keep themselves - and Alan - safe long enough to see it through.

The next morning, Emily found herself balancing her phone between her shoulder and ear as she typed on her laptop. She was speaking to an old acquaintance, a mid-level partner at a smaller but reputable firm in the city. His name was Andrew Liu, someone she remembered as principled enough to consider taking on a David-versus-Goliath case. Yet his tone on the other end of the line was hesitant.

"That's a big lawsuit, Emily," Andrew said, his words punctuated by the occasional static crackle. "And let's face it, you're up against Hastings & Cole. They have an entire department for complex litigation. They'll drown you in paper."

Emily resisted the urge to let frustration seep into her voice. "I know. That's why I need support. Listen, I'm not asking for a full partnership. Even a co-counsel arrangement would be helpful. We can share the workload - your firm's resources, my whistleblower's documents."

Andrew paused. "I'll have to run it by the other partners. We don't have the budget to handle something that could spiral into a multi-year battle, especially if the other side files a flood of motions."

Emily typed a few more notes into her complaint template, carefully drafting allegations regarding falsified data. "I understand. Just… keep an open mind, okay? I don't want to see a legitimate case against a major corporation get squashed because we lacked manpower."

"Of course," Andrew replied, though Emily could hear the doubt in his voice. "I'll get back to you soon."

She thanked him and ended the call, feeling a pang of disappointment. The large-scale suits she had been part of at Hastings & Cole had taught her how crucial it was to have a team of attorneys. Filing briefs, responding to motions, traveling for depositions, combing through thousands of documents - doing it all with just Tessa's help would be Herculean. But she couldn't afford to be picky. Andrew's firm might be her best bet for some measure of backup.

The Ghosts' Trial – Volume One

Late in the afternoon, as the sun dipped behind the row of skyscrapers visible from Emily's office window, the door swung open, and Tessa poked her head in, looking tense.

"Emily, you have a… visitor," she said, carefully measuring her tone.

"Who?" Emily asked warily.

In answer, Mark Hastings stepped into view, looking every bit the polished corporate lawyer. He wore a charcoal suit that draped flawlessly over his athletic frame, and he held a slim leather briefcase in one hand. His tie was a subdued shade of blue, and a hint of aftershave drifted through the office. The biggest difference from the Mark she remembered was the tightness in his jaw and the hardened glint in his eyes, as though he'd been forced into a role he found both familiar and distasteful.

Emily stood. "This is unexpected."

Tessa folded her arms, clearly reluctant to leave them alone, but Mark offered her a polite nod. "I was hoping we could speak privately, Tessa," he said, not unkindly.

Martyn Bellamy

Tessa's gaze flicked to Emily, who gave a subtle nod. "It's fine," Emily murmured. "Could you, uh, see if the mail came in? I'm expecting a few items from the courthouse."

Once Tessa stepped out, the door clicked shut, and Mark let out a breath. "Emily, I won't take much of your time."

She motioned for him to sit, though he remained standing. The tension in the room felt like static electricity just before a storm.

Mark set his briefcase on the small table near the door. "First off, I'm not here in an official capacity, though if you want to interpret everything I say as part of a negotiation, that's your call."

She folded her arms, leaning against the edge of her desk. "Cut to the chase, Mark."

He pursed his lips. "GenTech's lead counsel is planning to file a motion to disqualify you - claiming that your time at Hastings & Cole might have given you access to privileged information about the firm's defense strategies. They'll argue that it's unethical for you to sue a client your old firm might represent."

A surge of anger coiled in her gut. "That's ridiculous. I never worked on any GenTech cases when I was there."

"Doesn't matter," Mark said. "They'll try to make the argument that, by virtue of being at Hastings & Cole, you have an insider's perspective on the firm's approach and that it's unfair to GenTech."

She let out a short laugh of disbelief. "So they want to cripple me before I can even file the complaint?"

He nodded, eyes flicking around the small office, perhaps noting every sign of her modest resources. "They've done it before in other cases. Sometimes they succeed, sometimes not. But it could tie you up in a side battle for months."

Rubbing her temples, Emily struggled to keep her frustration in check. "You're here to deliver that threat in person?"

Mark shifted on his feet. "I'm here because, despite everything, I respect your integrity. I thought it might be better for you to hear it now rather than be blindsided in open court."

"So considerate," she said, bitterness creeping into her tone. "Is that all?"

Martyn Bellamy

He took a moment to answer. "No. If you withdraw now - if you step away from any intention of filing a lawsuit - then Bronson won't pursue the motion. They'll let it go."

She felt her jaw tighten. "That's blackmail."

A flicker of something crossed his face - regret, shame, maybe. Then he steadied his expression. "Call it what you will. It's a straightforward option. You wouldn't be risking your license or your financial stability. You can move on to other cases, ones that won't endanger you."

Emily stared at him, her eyes narrowing. "Mark, you know as well as I do that these allegations are real. The documents I've seen - "

He raised a hand to cut her off. "I don't want to hear specifics. That's not my role here."

She refused to be silenced. "People died. GenTech concealed fatal side effects in Africa and South America. I've got proof that entire data sets were forged. Are you okay defending that?"

His expression tightened, and he shifted his gaze to the floor. "It's not about being okay with it. It's about my job. The system is adversarial, remember? You once believed in it. You said the truth would come out in the end if both sides fought hard enough."

She bristled at the memory of her own naive words. "That was before I realized how heavily the deck is stacked. If I fight for the truth, I stand to lose everything. If you fight for a lie, you get a promotion and a corner office."

"That's not fair," Mark murmured, but his eyes flickered with guilt. "Maybe... maybe I'm too far down this path to turn back, Emily."

She exhaled. "It doesn't have to be that way, but it's your choice. And I've made mine: I'm not dropping this case. Not for you, not for GenTech. Not for anyone."

Mark studied her face for a long moment, and she remembered a time when she found comfort in his company. Now, all she saw was a man clinging to the safety of a powerful firm, even if it meant bending his moral compass.

He finally nodded. "Then be prepared. GenTech will come at you from every angle. Your finances, your reputation, your personal relationships - they'll all be targets."

Emily steadied her voice. "Let them come."

A heavy silence pressed between them. At last, Mark reached for his briefcase, snapping it shut with decisive finality. Without a word, he walked to the door. Just before he left, he paused, his back to her.

"I warned you," he said softly. "Don't say I never tried."

The door clicked shut behind him. Emily stood there, staring at the empty space he had occupied, her hands balled into fists. Waves of anger, fear, and sadness rippled through her. Mark's parting words sounded eerily like an ultimatum: step aside or be destroyed.

She walked to the window, looking out at the hustle of the street below as twilight began to paint the sky in muted pinks and purples. Instead of fear, she found a steely resolve forging itself in her chest. Mark's warning had the opposite effect of what he likely intended: it strengthened her conviction. If GenTech was so desperate that they'd mobilize Mark to personally deliver threats, she had to be on the right track.

The Ghosts' Trial – Volume One

But as she turned away from the window, she caught her own reflection once more. The line between right and wrong felt crystal clear, but the line between success and catastrophic failure was razor-thin. She only hoped she and Tessa could stay one step ahead of a corporation with deep pockets and a legion of attorneys.

In the days that followed, Emily found renewed energy - and no small measure of defiance - driving her work. She pored over legal precedent, carefully structuring every paragraph of her complaint to withstand scrutiny. Tessa continued her deep dive into public records, occasionally updating Emily with each new piece of evidence that confirmed GenTech's deceit. The sense of looming danger never left, but it felt more like a dark thundercloud overhead than an immediate bolt of lightning. If GenTech was going to strike, perhaps they were waiting for a high-profile moment, or maybe they were busy preparing a more cunning sabotage.

One morning, Tessa stepped into Emily's office, waving a printout. "Got a notification on the docket system. Looks like Hastings & Cole is representing GenTech in a separate matter, but it's suspiciously similar - there's some reference to drug trials in an undisclosed foreign location."

Emily cocked an eyebrow. "Could be relevant. That might confirm a pattern of hush-hush lawsuits."

They spent the better part of the morning analyzing the newly discovered docket entry, searching for clues that might bolster their argument of systemic wrongdoing. With each new bit of evidence, Emily's sense of purpose grew. Mark's phone call and subsequent visit had left no doubt: they were in for a fierce battle. She could almost picture him in a sleek conference room, advising GenTech executives on how best to neutralize her lawsuit.

The memory of his final words still stung: *"Don't say I never tried."* Once upon a time, Mark might have advocated for justice alongside her. Now, they stood on opposite sides of a gaping moral chasm.

By the following week, Emily had finished drafting a robust version of the complaint. Spanning nearly seventy pages, it laid out a painstaking account of GenTech's alleged malfeasance, replete with references to forged data sets, hush money payments, and whistleblower accounts. Though the final product likely needed polishing and cross-referencing, Emily felt a deep sense of accomplishment. This document was their opening salvo - an official statement to the world that GenTech wouldn't get away with sacrificing vulnerable communities for profit.

Tessa leaned over Emily's shoulder as they reviewed the final paragraphs. "I think the timeline is solid. We show how the trials in Africa were set up under a shell corporation, how the data was channeled to GenTech stateside, and how negative outcomes were systematically scrubbed. Then we link it to the South American trials with similar methods."

Emily nodded, her eyes scanning each sentence carefully. "I want to make sure we're not overstating anything. GenTech's first move will be to file a motion to dismiss, claiming we have no factual basis. We have to prove we do."

They spent hours footnoting each assertion, cross-referencing each fact with the attached exhibits. By the time they reached the last page, the sunlight pouring through the window had shifted from morning brightness to the warm gold of late afternoon.

Emily leaned back in her chair, rubbing her tired eyes. "All right, that's a draft. We'll need a final read tomorrow before filing. I want Andrew Liu to look at it, too, if he'll agree."

Tessa turned to face her. "Are you going to let Mark know we're filing, or do we just let him find out when it hits the docket?"

"Part of me wants to call him," Emily admitted, "but honestly, it's probably best to let them find out officially. They're going to come after us no matter what. Might as well keep the element of surprise, if we have any left."

Tessa's lips curved into a determined smile. "Agreed."

That evening, Emily lingered in the office long after Tessa left, double-checking the locks and gazing out at the quiet street below. A flicker of movement caught her eye - a figure leaning against a lamppost, partially hidden in shadow. She watched for a few moments, her pulse quickening. The figure didn't move, and she couldn't see a face. Could it be a random passerby, or someone surveilling her? After several tense minutes, a bus rumbled up, and the figure climbed on, disappearing into the glow of the interior lights. Emily let out a trembling breath.

She turned from the window and focused on the thick file cabinet where Alan's documents were locked away. She had scanned digital copies onto an external hard drive that she kept hidden off-site, but the physical copies were irreplaceable. With each step deeper into this legal battle, she felt as though invisible watchers were converging, waiting for the right moment to pounce.

Yet the adversity also propelled her forward. Mark's warning call had amplified her resolve more than any pep talk ever could. In a twisted way, she felt grateful. She knew now that her old colleague had severed any last illusions she might have held about their friendship. The rivalry, simmering for months, was now laid bare. Her path was chosen, and she intended to walk it no matter how treacherous it became.

She closed her eyes for a moment, remembering the conversation Mark and she had once shared over late-night coffee, in which she insisted that the law could be a force for good. She had said that if you believed in justice, you had to fight for it. Mark had responded that the law was a business, not a religion. They had laughed it off then, not realizing how prophetic that exchange would become.

Now, as she stood in her modest office, with a nearly finished complaint that would take on a corporate Goliath, she felt a profound sense of purpose. She wasn't sure how it would all end - whether she'd lose her license, go bankrupt, or even face threats to her life. But she did know she was on the side of truth.

When she finally turned out the lights and stepped into the hallway, she remembered Mark's words again: *"Don't say I never tried."* He might have tried to warn her, but she wouldn't be intimidated. Whether that made her a hero or a fool, she couldn't say. What she did know was that a door had closed on their relationship. From here on out, they were adversaries in the purest legal sense of the word. The fight was truly on, and in this high-stakes case was only the beginning.

Chapter 15: A Leap of Faith

Emily Blackwood had not slept more than two or three hours each night for nearly a week. If her creased pillow and the half-eaten takeout on the counter were not enough proof, the purplish smudges beneath her eyes certainly were. Ever since the moment she told Alan Priest she would help him blow the whistle on GenTech, the pharmaceutical behemoth that once seemed untouchable, Emily felt as if she were tiptoeing across a minefield in the dead of night.

Tonight was no different. She sat at a small dining table jammed against the wall of her cramped one-bedroom apartment, reading through an ever-growing pile of case law on the federal rules for whistleblower protection suits. In a week, she had devoured more statutes and civil procedure manuals than she had in a year at Hastings & Cole, her old law firm. There was a difference between parsing these volumes under the security net of a powerful employer and devouring them under the solitary glow of a single desk lamp, knowing her personal resources were on the line. Each page contained a labyrinth of legal nuance she had to master if she hoped to draft a bulletproof complaint.

As the clock neared midnight, she leaned back in her chair and exhaled slowly. Her eyes burned. Her laptop hummed with the heat of an overworked fan. On the screen was a half-completed draft of the lawsuit that she planned to file in federal court the following morning - a daring move that would mark her official transformation from a struggling solo practitioner into GenTech's sworn legal adversary. The final push she needed was half adrenaline, half reckless courage.

A ping from her phone startled her. She blinked to refocus and grabbed it. A text from Tessa Moretti, her paralegal, glowed on the screen.

Tessa (11:58 PM): Still awake? Don't forget you have to sign & file tomorrow. I'll meet you at the courthouse at 9. Get some rest. We can do this.

Emily typed back a brief thumbs-up emoji and forced a tight smile. Tessa had been her rock these last few weeks, diving headlong into each new research lead, rummaging through obscure news archives, and tracking down possible witnesses from Africa and South America. Even so, Emily had sensed Tessa's underlying fear. If this case crashed and burned under a hailstorm of GenTech's retaliation, Tessa could lose her livelihood and reputation too.

Hastily, Emily minimized her phone screen and scrolled through the complaint she was drafting. It was a patchwork of allegations, each meticulously backed by statute and citation to prior whistleblower cases. The central premise: GenTech had knowingly concealed lethal side effects discovered during its clinical trials in developing countries, forging test results to secure approval for a blockbuster medication. Alan Priest's documents - unearthed emails, internal memos, and non-disclosure agreements - painted a damning portrait of a company willing to risk human lives for massive profit.

All Emily had to do was take that portrait and put it on display for the world to see.

At 1:00 AM, she finally powered down her laptop. Her back felt like a twisted ball of rope, and her eyes threatened to slam shut from exhaustion. Shuffling to the couch, she realized she couldn't bring herself to get into bed. Her mind was still ablaze with possibilities: tactics GenTech might use to counter her claims, the personal attacks they might launch, the possibility that Mark Hastings - her old friend turned adversary - would be assigned to destroy her in court.

She let out a near-silent laugh of disbelief. Less than a year ago, Mark had been her respected colleague, sometimes her confidant, occasionally something more. Now, the promise of facing him down in a federal courtroom at the biggest moment of her career filled her with dread. It felt like only yesterday that they had parted ways on tense but civil terms, his ominous remark echoing in her memory: *You're over your head, Emily. This is bigger than you can handle.*

Despite her exhaustion, Emily's heart pounded whenever she thought about that conversation. She could not quite place the exact emotion behind Mark's warning: pity, anger, or maybe even concern. But it was too late to unravel it now. Tomorrow, she would file the complaint. The turning back point had already passed.

With that last thought, she forced her weary limbs toward the bedroom, determined to catch at least a few hours of rest.

Emily awoke to her phone's alarm at 6:30 AM, the neon digits in the dimly lit room punctuating how little she had slept. She stumbled through a quick shower, pinned her hair into a modest bun, and forced down half a cup of coffee. Outside, gray clouds threatened a storm, matching her unsettled nerves.

Her reflection in the bathroom mirror made her pause. She wore a wrinkled navy blazer that had seen better days and an ironed white blouse she hoped would convey a sense of determined professionalism. She gave herself a quick pep talk under her breath: "You're doing this because it's right. You're protecting the helpless. You can't let GenTech intimidate you."

The words rang hollow, but she repeated them anyway. If she couldn't talk herself into confidence, how could she hope to project it in court?

Her coffee thermos in hand, she hurried out the door. The damp morning air enveloped her as she jogged to her car, scanning her surroundings out of long-growing paranoia. She had received more than one strange call lately, and more than once she had glimpsed a dark sedan parked idly near her apartment at odd hours. Today, at least, the curb was empty. The world felt desolate as early commuters began to trickle onto the streets.

She drove carefully, rehearsing mental arguments to bolster her official complaint. The legal standard for whistleblower suits gave her some hope: if Alan Priest's documents could establish wrongdoing on GenTech's part, she had every right to proceed. But she also knew that the burden of proof would be monumental once GenTech mobilized its top-tier defense. She had no illusions that the small window of calm she felt in the morning's half-light would last for long.

When she finally parked by the county courthouse, Tessa was already waiting by the front steps. The rain had begun to fall, and Tessa stood huddled beneath a small black umbrella. Her bright eyes and quick smile offered a semblance of reassurance.

"Morning, boss," Tessa said, stepping closer. "You holding up?"

"Barely," Emily admitted, taking shelter under the umbrella with her. "But I'm ready."

Tessa nodded, rummaging in her tote bag for the final copies of the complaint. "Here," she said, handing Emily the crisp documents. "Fresh from the printer, all properly collated. You just need to sign."

Emily flipped through the pages. There it was in black and white: *United States District Court* heading the top of the page, followed by the official title of her lawsuit. Her name, on behalf of whistleblower Alan Priest, versus the corporate monolith GenTech Pharmaceuticals.

"We can do a quick review in the hallway," Tessa continued, swallowing. "But we need to make sure they file it before noon if we want to catch the judicial docket before the weekend."

Emily, staring at the pages, inhaled deeply. This was it. The moment that would set the wheels in motion. There was no going back. With a surge of resolve, she straightened her shoulders. "Let's do it."

A low buzz filled the courthouse halls, a blend of clacking heels and murmured voices echoing in the marble-floored corridors. The place had always fascinated Emily. Even back at Hastings & Cole, she felt a strange comfort in these halls. Here was where justice was pursued - sometimes twisted, often delayed, but always sought after.

Tessa guided her toward a wooden bench near the clerk's office where they could finalize everything.

Emily set her bag down and pulled out a sleek black pen. A memory surfaced of how she used to sign off on meticulously prepared documents at her old firm - a paralegal or junior associate would stand by, flipping each page to the right place, eager to expedite the process. Now it was just Tessa, effectively her entire staff, handing her one more chance to back out or forge ahead.

Emily scribbled her signature on multiple lines, her name appearing beneath every paragraph detailing the allegations, citing every relevant code. Each stroke felt like a small explosion in her chest, a mixture of excitement and dread.

When she finished, she capped her pen. "All right," she said, handing the complaint back to Tessa. "It's done."

Tessa let out a shaky breath. "We're truly doing this."

"We are."

They exchanged a look of mutual resolve, though Emily noted a flicker of fear in Tessa's eyes. Before she could offer any reassurance, a voice startled them from behind.

"Well, well. Filing day, I presume?"

Emily spun around, and her stomach clenched. Mark Hastings stood just a few feet away, clad in a perfectly tailored charcoal suit, the distinctive hush of expensive Italian loafers on the marble floor. He had changed little since she last saw him. Sharp cheekbones, an aristocratic bearing - if not for the tension in the air, she might have let her eyes linger a moment longer on the trace of sympathy in his expression.

"Mark," she said, forcing a neutral tone.

He nodded, shifting his briefcase from one hand to the other. "I thought I'd see you here, given the rumor mill. Word on the street is you're about to file quite a bombshell."

"Funny how the rumor mill works," Tessa muttered, setting her jaw.

Mark's gaze flicked to Tessa before returning to Emily. "Look, I'm only here for an unrelated motion hearing. But I have to ask…are you absolutely sure about this?" He glanced toward the sheaf of papers in Tessa's grasp. "I meant it when I said you might be over your head."

A flicker of anger ignited in Emily. "I appreciate your concern - if that's what it is. But yes, I'm sure. If you're so worried, Mark, maybe you should question what kind of firm you work for or what kind of client you're defending."

He took a step closer, lowering his voice. "You have no idea how many resources GenTech has. Their reach is -" He paused, evidently searching for the right word. "Extensive."

Emily tensed at the reminder of the phone calls, the suspicious cars, Alan's fear. But she refused to back down. "Then they can meet me in court."

For a moment, Mark's eyes held a flicker of something she could not name - regret, worry, or maybe disapproval. Then he adjusted his tie. "All right," he said. "I won't try to stop you. Just…be careful, Emily."

She felt an odd pang. *Be careful.* The words resonated differently coming from him. She cleared her throat. "Thanks for the warning," she managed.

Mark shifted his gaze to Tessa, nodded politely, then turned and strode away. His footsteps reverberated until the corridor swallowed him up.

"That was…awkward," Tessa said quietly, looking after him.

The Ghosts' Trial – Volume One

"Awkward doesn't begin to cover it," Emily murmured. Her heart pounded. She felt an unsteady mix of anger and nostalgia. When she had first joined Hastings & Cole, Mark was the senior associate who took her under his wing. She never expected that they would one day stand on opposite sides of a moral chasm.

Tessa pulled her back to the moment by tapping the sheaf of papers. "Are we ready?"

Emily nodded firmly. "Let's get this on record."

The filing process itself was deceptively simple. Inside the clerk's office, a low partition separated the public from a row of desks. A clerk looked over the complaint, stamped it, and assigned a case number. A few keystrokes, an official seal, and suddenly it was real. Emily watched each step with a knot in her stomach. She had spent years preparing documents for major corporate lawsuits, but never had her personal sense of justice and professional future hinged so precariously on a single filing.

With a final flourish of the clerk's stamp, the deed was done.

"All set," the clerk said, sliding the file back across the counter.

Emily's pulse hammered. "That's it?"

"Yes, Ms. Blackwood. You'll receive an electronic notice soon. You may also check the docket online for the judge assignment."

Tessa squeezed Emily's arm. Without a word, they turned and walked out of the office, hearts pounding like marathon runners crossing a finish line.

They stepped into the corridor, where the hush of a hundred hushed conversations felt amplified. Emily closed her eyes for a moment, listening to the rumble of footsteps. She clutched the file to her chest as if it were a shield against whatever might come next.

"You did it," Tessa said softly. "We did it."

Emily exhaled, mustering a small smile. "Now the real battle begins."

They left the courthouse as the drizzle turned into a steady downpour. Tessa walked Emily to her car, umbrella struggling against the wind. Once they reached the curb, Emily hopped inside quickly. Tessa leaned in through the open window, her hair damp with errant raindrops.

"Are you heading to the office?" Tessa asked.

Emily nodded. "Yeah. I want to double-check Alan's deposition outline, make some calls to potential co-counsel. We're going to need more help."

Tessa pursed her lips. "We can't really afford to split the potential contingency fee with too many partners, right?"

"True," Emily conceded. "But this is bigger than us. This lawsuit could easily escalate to class-action territory if more witnesses or victims come forward. We'll drown in discovery if we try to do it all alone."

"All right," Tessa said, resigned. "I'll join you there in an hour. I need to pick up a few things from the post office first."

Emily thanked her, and Tessa shut the car door. The sudden quiet inside the vehicle felt claustrophobic. The only sound was the patter of heavy rain on the roof. Emily's hand trembled on the steering wheel. She reminded herself that nerves were normal, but a small

Martyn Bellamy

voice in her head whispered that the repercussions might be more severe than a few sleepless nights.

She turned the key, half expecting the engine not to start - her paranoid mind conjuring images of saboteurs messing with her car again. But the engine roared to life. She pulled away from the courthouse, merging into the busy downtown traffic. A short time later, she found herself parked outside the modest two-story building that housed her fledgling practice.

Rain plastered her blazer as she ran to the entrance. Her name, *Emily Blackwood, Attorney at Law*, was printed in gold lettering on the glass door. She had paid for that sign with the last of her meager savings, hoping it would exude the legitimacy she needed to attract clients. Stepping inside, she flicked on the lights. The overhead fluorescent hum greeted her with a sterile monotony.

She tossed her wet blazer over a coat rack in the tiny reception area and sank into the single office chair behind the front desk. Weary, she reached for a notepad and scribbled down a to-do list:

- **Confirm complaint docket & judge assignment**

- **Call Alan to update him**
- **Reach out to pro bono or co-counsel**
- **Check security measures**

The last item made her pause. She had been brushing off Alan's fear for too long, telling him it would be fine, that intimidation was just a scare tactic. But the suspicious calls, the tampering with her car - those were no illusions. As soon as GenTech's lawyers realized she had actually filed, their next move could be swift and ruthless.

Swallowing hard, she glanced at her watch. Barely 10:30 AM. The day had only just begun, yet she felt as though she had run a marathon.

A wave of exhaustion overcame her. She closed her eyes, indulging in a moment of stillness. Then the phone rang, jarring her upright. Snatching the receiver, she answered with as professional a tone as she could muster.

"Emily Blackwood's office."

There was a moment of silence on the line, accompanied by faint static. Her grip tightened.

Martyn Bellamy

"Hello?" she repeated.

Another beat of silence. Then the line clicked dead.

She set the phone down, heart pounding. *Great,* she thought. *We're not even an hour into the official lawsuit, and the calls have started.*

She looked at her list again. "Check security measures," she said aloud, her voice echoing in the tiny office. "Yes. That definitely goes up the priority list."

By noon, Tessa had arrived, shaking off her umbrella and handing Emily a sandwich. Emily realized she had forgotten to eat breakfast. Her stomach rumbled, so she accepted the sandwich gratefully.

"Any new developments?" Tessa asked, dropping a stack of mail on the front desk.

"Nothing from the clerk's office yet," Emily said between bites. "But I got another creepy phone call."

Tessa's eyes widened. "Anyone say anything?"

"No, just static. Then they hung up."

"Well, maybe it's not them," Tessa said, though the tremor in her voice suggested otherwise.

"Maybe." Emily sighed, too weary to argue. "Let's keep an eye on everything. Start calling some of those attorneys I flagged for possible co-counsel. Maybe a local firm with experience in major product liability suits."

Tessa nodded, setting down her umbrella. "I'll get on that. Also, I left a message for Alan. I told him we officially filed. He didn't pick up, but I'm sure he'll call back once he sees my message."

"Good," Emily said. For all the trouble swirling in her mind, Alan's wellbeing was at the top. He was the one risking his life to expose GenTech's wrongdoing. She needed to ensure he did not vanish into the cracks, the way so many whistleblowers did when the pressure became too intense.

As Tessa moved to the back office to start her calls, Emily pulled out her laptop. She logged into the federal court's electronic filing system. Within minutes, she found her complaint listed, along with a note about which judge had been assigned.

"Judge Marianne Garfield," Emily murmured. She paused to recall if she knew anything about Garfield's reputation. She vaguely remembered that Garfield was known for strict courtroom decorum and for an unflinching approach to corporate malfeasance cases. Could be good, or it could be tricky, depending on how Garfield interpreted the evidence. Still, it was a relief not to be assigned to a judge famous for corporate-friendly rulings.

Satisfied, she typed up a short note to Alan, letting him know who the judge was, and summarizing the next steps. She included a reassurance that they could request additional protective measures if GenTech escalated any harassment tactics.

Then she paused to look at her phone. She debated calling Mark, or perhaps texting him, but that was nonsense. *What would I say?* she thought. *Hey Mark, just letting you know I can't be intimidated, but also, thanks for caring if you do.* No. That door was closed. She was on a new path, and Mark was on his.

Around 2:00 PM, Emily and Tessa were hunched over a conference table in the corner, discussing the depositions they might need to schedule, when the phone rang again. Tessa glanced at the caller ID.

"It's Alan."

Emily picked up the call, pressing the speakerphone button at Tessa's nod.

"Alan? You're on speaker with Tessa and me," Emily said.

Alan's voice came through ragged and breathless. "You filed?"

"We did," Emily replied, her heart tightening at his tone. "It's official as of this morning. How are you holding up?"

A shaky exhale filled the line. "They - someone - was following me again. A black SUV. I swear it's the same one I saw last week. They were parked near my apartment this morning."

Tessa shot Emily a concerned look.

"Alan, I want you to remain calm," Emily said, trying to steady her own racing heart. "Now that the complaint is filed, we have additional legal recourse if GenTech or anyone affiliated with them tries to harass you. But we need to be systematic. Document everything."

"I don't know if the police will help," he said with a bitter laugh. "I have no proof, just this dread - like I'm being watched."

Emily leaned forward. "We'll see about hiring a private security contractor, at least temporarily. I know it's an expense, but we might manage something short-term."

Tessa scribbled a note, *Check costs & references for security firms.*

"Please do," Alan said weakly. "I'm not trying to be paranoid, but I...I don't want to end up a cautionary tale. I can't do this alone."

"You're not alone," Emily said firmly. "You have us. And we're not backing down."

He fell silent for a moment, except for his ragged breathing. Then: "I'm meeting someone tonight - an old contact from GenTech R&D. He says he has more documents to back up my claims. I haven't told him about you yet. Should I?"

Emily hesitated. "That's your call, Alan. But if this contact is legit, we might want to bring him onboard as another witness. Still, do it carefully. No matter what, keep us informed."

"Okay," he said quietly. "I'll call you after I meet him."

"Stay safe," Emily said.

After the line went dead, Tessa let out a long breath. "This is getting real."

Emily nodded. "It was always real. Now it's just inescapable."

Night fell quickly. By 7:30 PM, heavy clouds blotted out any moonlight, and the persistent drizzle rendered the streetlamps hazy. Emily was still at her desk, scanning every major case involving whistleblower protections, trying to identify any parallel in which the defendant was as powerful as GenTech. The phone was silent for once, but that silence was almost more unsettling than the calls.

Around 8:00 PM, Tessa's voice jolted Emily from a bleary haze. "I'm going to call it a night," she said, sounding hesitant. "Are you sure you don't want me to stay?"

Emily shook her head. "Go home, Tess. I'll wrap up here. You've done enough for one day."

"Lock the doors," Tessa said pointedly. "And be careful when you leave."

Emily offered a small, reassuring smile she did not quite feel. After Tessa left, the office felt emptier than ever. The fluorescent lighting bounced off the walls, revealing every scuff and imperfection in the small space. She turned it off and flicked on a modest desk lamp instead, creating a more comfortable ambience.

She worked for another hour, forcing herself to focus on the legal intricacies of the case. Just as she was about to power down her laptop, the phone rang again. Cold adrenaline spiked in her veins. For a moment, she debated letting it go to voicemail, but her sense of duty compelled her to pick it up.

"Hello?"

A muffled voice whispered her name - "Emily Blackwood?" - followed by quick, shallow breaths.

She recognized Alan's voice immediately. "Alan, what's wrong?"

A rustle, then a bang like a door slamming. "I - I think someone followed me," he gasped. "I was supposed to meet that contact, but I saw an SUV in the alley behind the building. It was just sitting there, engine running, lights off."

"Where are you now?" she demanded, heart hammering.

"I hid in a doorway," he said, voice trembling. "I've been creeping along a side street. I can't go back to my car - it's parked right where that SUV is. I'm alone, and I'm afraid - "

"Alan, calm down," Emily interrupted. "Listen carefully. You need to get somewhere safe and public immediately. A convenience store, a police station - anywhere with cameras and people around. Do you have cash or credit cards on you?"

"Y-yes, some."

"Then hail a cab or rideshare, get out of there, and check yourself into a hotel for the night. A place you haven't been before, so no one tracks you."

His breathing ragged, he said, "Okay. I'll try. But I left the documents in my car - "

"Forget the documents for now. *You* matter more. If you can safely retrieve them later, we'll do that. Just get yourself to safety."

A pause, then the static of him shifting the phone. "All right. I'll call you once I'm somewhere secure."

"Do that," Emily urged. "And Alan? You made the right choice by calling me."

He let out a trembling exhale. "I hope so."

Then the line clicked dead. Emily sagged back into her chair, sweat beading on her forehead. She glanced at the blank office walls, an unsettling thought gnawing at her: *If they're going after Alan this aggressively, what's to stop them from targeting me or Tessa next?*

She slammed her laptop shut. She couldn't do more legal research tonight. Right now, the priority was ensuring the safety of the client who had just risked his life. She grabbed her bag, double-checked the front door lock, and stepped outside.

The parking lot behind her office was dimly lit by a single flickering lamp. Emily clutched her keys between her fingers, scanning the corners for any sign of movement. A light breeze carried the scent of wet asphalt. She inhaled sharply, listening for footsteps. The only sound was the distant rush of tires on the main road.

She hurried to her car, almost laughing at how she must look - like some paranoid detective from a late-night drama. But events of the past weeks justified her anxiety. She slid into the driver's seat, locked the doors, and started the engine with trembling hands.

As she backed out, she checked her rearview mirror constantly. No suspicious SUV. No headlights creeping closer. After pulling onto the main thoroughfare, she felt a slight relief in the presence of other cars. It was a shared vulnerability, a sense that she was at least in public view.

She dialed Tessa's number over the hands-free system. Tessa answered groggily on the third ring.

"Hey, Tessa," Emily said, trying not to sound as rattled as she felt. "Just an update. Alan called. He was being followed again."

"Oh my God," Tessa breathed. "Is he okay?"

"He's rattled, but physically fine. I told him to hide somewhere safe for the night. He'll check in again."

Tessa was silent for a moment. "Em, this is getting dangerous."

"I know. But we can't back down. If we do - "

"I'm not suggesting we do," Tessa cut in. "I'm just worried."

"So am I," Emily admitted softly. "Listen, I just wanted to keep you in the loop. I'm heading home to see if I can coordinate some security for Alan tomorrow. If we can't do that, maybe we'll approach the court for a protective order or something."

"Right," Tessa said. "Call me if you need anything."

Emily ended the call and focused on driving. Thunder rumbled overhead, and the city lights gleamed off the wet streets. Once she reached her apartment building, she quickly parked, hurried upstairs, and locked herself inside. The quiet was overwhelming. Every shift of the old pipes and creak of the floorboards set her nerves on edge.

She spent the next half-hour calling a handful of private security firms. Most demanded exorbitant fees. Some politely declined, explaining they only took on large corporate contracts. A sense of desperation filled her. If she, a trained attorney, had such trouble securing help for a whistleblower at immediate risk, how many others had simply fallen through the cracks?

Finally, she found a smaller outfit that offered short-term protective services. Their rates were steep, but not entirely out of reach if Emily was frugal. She arranged for two guards to shadow Alan discreetly for the next few days. It was the best she could do on short notice.

Exhausted, she sank onto her couch, phone clutched in her hand, waiting for Alan's call. The digital clock on her microwave blinked 9:45 PM. Rain still pattered against her windows, a soothing yet ominous lullaby.

At around 10:15 PM, Emily's phone buzzed. She answered it instantly, bracing for Alan's trembling voice, but instead heard an unexpected caller.

"Emily," the deep voice said. "It's Mark."

Her pulse quickened. "Mark? Why are you calling me? Did you get wind that we filed the complaint?"

He hesitated. "Yes, I heard from the office. But that's not the reason for this call. I…I wanted to see if you were all right."

She rolled her eyes, though part of her felt a tremor of warmth. "I'm fine, thanks. Why wouldn't I be?"

"Because you just declared war on one of the largest corporations in the state, maybe the country," Mark said, an edge of frustration creeping into his tone. "You do realize their board of directors will do anything to protect their share price, right?"

"I'm well aware of the stakes," Emily snapped. She half expected him to lecture her, to fling more warnings and condescending remarks.

But he only sighed. "Emily, you're not at Hastings & Cole anymore. You don't have the safety net of 500 lawyers behind you. You're alone."

"Not entirely. I have Tessa. And I have a moral duty to Alan Priest, and to those whose families have been harmed by GenTech's negligence."

A strained silence crackled over the line. After a moment, Mark spoke softly, almost tenderly. "Listen, just…don't let your sense of justice blind you to the reality of these people's power. I - "

She cut him off, anger flaring. "I can't have this conversation with you, Mark. You represent them. Or your firm does. I can't trust you."

He hesitated, as though stung. "I'm not asking for your trust. I just don't want - "

When he didn't finish, she prodded, "Don't want what?"

A sigh. "Never mind. Good luck, Emily."

The line went dead. She stared at her phone, feeling conflicting emotions swirl. It was as though Mark wanted to warn her, even protect her, but was bound by professional loyalty to his firm and to GenTech. She tossed her phone onto the coffee table, her mind churning. *He's too late,* she thought. *There's no turning back now.*

Time dragged on. By 11:00 PM, her phone had still not rung with any update from Alan. She paced her apartment, flipping channels on mute, scanning a local news feed for any mention of a whistleblower or a skirmish near the biotech corridor. Nothing. She found herself wishing Mark had said more, or that Tessa was around to calm her frayed nerves.

Finally, at 11:28 PM, the phone rang. She snatched it up.

"Alan?" she whispered, breath hitching.

"Yeah, it's me," he said, sounding subdued but calmer. "I made it to a motel off the interstate. I don't think they followed me here."

Relief swept over Emily. "Oh, thank God. Are you sure you're safe for the night?"

"I think so. But I'm still rattled." His voice quivered. "I never expected it to get this intense."

Emily bit her lip. "I spoke with a small private security firm. They can station two guards near your apartment or even escort you around if needed. It's not cheap, but it might keep you safe until I can file for some form of protective order."

Alan hesitated. "I don't want you draining your resources. I know your practice is small."

"Don't worry about that. We'll figure out the finances. For now, I'd prefer you keep your location to yourself. Tomorrow morning, Tessa or I will coordinate a schedule with the security guys."

A soft sniffle, followed by a determined tone. "All right. I'll meet them. Just…thank you, Emily."

She closed her eyes, exhaustion washing over her. "We're in this together, Alan. After all, you're the one who provided the documents that can bring GenTech to justice. You're the bravest person I know."

He let out a shaky laugh. "Brave or stupid. Time will tell."

"Maybe both," she said softly. "Get some rest if you can."

They hung up, and Emily stared at her reflection in the dark TV screen. She wondered if her own bravery might one day be labeled as stupidity, too. But that was a thought for another time.

Tonight, she had done all she could. She had filed the complaint, set a security plan in motion, and reassured her terrified client. She was stepping onto the battlefield with no illusions about how steep the odds were. In her heart, though, she felt that flicker of conviction that had originally led her to quit Hastings & Cole. If she turned a blind eye to injustice now, what was the point of being a lawyer at all?

Martyn Bellamy

Shortly after midnight, Emily forced herself to lie in bed, though rest eluded her for nearly an hour. When sleep finally arrived, she dreamed of long court corridors where the lights flickered and hallways twisted in endless loops, each door labeled with variations of *GenTech v. Blackwood*. She ran from corridor to corridor, hearing Mark's voice echo warnings in the distance, but never seeing him. Shadows crept at the edges of her vision, and the filing stamp from the clerk's office pounded like a gavel.

She woke with a start, heart thudding, uncertain of the time. Bleary-eyed, she groped for her phone on the nightstand. 5:12 AM. Outside, the rain had finally stopped, leaving the streets glistening under the early morning light. Emily sat up, her mind already racing with the tasks of the day.

Today, she was a new person: the attorney of record in a high-stakes lawsuit against GenTech. No illusions. No turning back. Just a leap of faith.

If only faith alone could guarantee victory, she thought as she stood and moved toward the shower, a sense of cautious determination trailing her every step.

The Ghosts' Trial – Volume One

Emily reached her office earlier than usual, the sunrise casting an orange sheen on the building's glass doors. She stood outside for a moment, sipping a rushed coffee and surveying the intersection. No suspicious SUVs, no lurking strangers - at least not at first glance.

She unlocked the door and stepped in. The stale smell of old carpeting and last night's stress greeted her. While everything looked ordinary, she felt a sea change roiling beneath the surface. Filing that complaint had thrust her into a new realm, one where every conversation, every phone call, might hold a hidden threat.

She found a message on her office phone, time-stamped a few minutes earlier:

"This is Mark Hastings. Emily, I - well, I'd like to talk to you in person. You can call me back at the office or my cell."

Her finger hovered over the *delete* button. A conversation with Mark could mean gleaning valuable information about GenTech's strategy, or it could be a self-serving attempt by Mark to dissuade her from going further. She decided to hold off responding, at least until she could gauge Alan's situation and consult with Tessa.

Moments later, Tessa arrived, hair pulled back in a neat ponytail, eyes thick with worry. She carried two tall coffees.

"Morning," she said, handing one coffee to Emily. "Any more ominous calls?"

"Not yet. But Mark left a voicemail. I think he wants to meet."

Tessa raised an eyebrow. "That's suspicious. I'm not sure it's wise to talk with him without counsel present, especially given we're now officially on opposite sides."

Emily nodded. "I know. Still, I can't shake the feeling he's trying to tell me something. He's dropped enough warnings. Could be a trap, or it could be a genuine tip."

Tessa frowned but said nothing. Instead, she turned to more pressing matters. "We should coordinate with the security firm for Alan. Also, I made a list of potential experts we might hire to testify about the drug trials in Africa and South America. Many require a retainer, though, so we need to decide who's essential."

The Ghosts' Trial – Volume One

Emily let out a quiet groan. "We're hemorrhaging money we don't have. But we need a strong case." She glanced at her reflection in the window, noticing how fatigue dulled her features. "Let's do it. One step at a time."

They spent the next few hours orchestrating phone calls. Emily negotiated a short-term contract with the security firm for Alan, while Tessa fired off emails to possible expert witnesses - public health specialists, medical ethicists, epidemiologists who had studied the side effects of advanced drug trials on vulnerable populations.

By late morning, the office buzzed with a sense of purpose. A legal battle had begun, and they were forging alliances, building defenses, gathering arms for the fight.

During a brief lull, Tessa poked her head into Emily's office. "Judge Garfield's clerk just posted your hearing date for the initial motions. It's in two weeks."

Emily nodded slowly. "That's not much time to gather enough evidence to survive any motion to dismiss. I'm sure GenTech's lawyers are already drafting."

"They will come hard and fast," Tessa agreed. "We need to be ready."

Emily tapped her pen nervously on a stack of papers. "I'll start drafting the arguments in opposition, focusing on the standard for whistleblower suits and the strength of Alan's evidence."

"And Mark," Tessa said, "he's probably going to be the one who shows up in court, right?"

Emily ran a hand through her hair. "Likely. Hastings & Cole might send more senior partners, but Mark is the rising star. They might use him as their frontman to rattle me."

Tessa snorted. "Like a psychological weapon."

"Exactly," Emily murmured, though she felt a pang of something else - regret, sadness, nostalgia. She swallowed that feeling down. This was war, and she had chosen her side.

By the time the day wound down, they had made considerable progress. Alan's security was arranged. Expert consultations were scheduled. A few attorneys they reached out to expressed mild interest in co-counseling, but none had committed yet. A major class-action suit was a daunting proposition, especially against a titan like GenTech.

Still, as Emily compiled notes for the next day, she felt a spark of cautious optimism. Against all odds, the pieces were coming together.

Tessa stood by the door, about to leave for the night. "You okay if I head out now?" she asked. "I'm meeting a friend for dinner."

Emily nodded. "Go, you've more than earned it. I'll lock up."

Tessa paused, her gaze softening. "Em, for what it's worth - I'm proud of you. What you did by filing that complaint today was huge. Scary, but huge."

A small smile formed on Emily's lips. "Thank you, Tessa. I appreciate you sticking with me. It means everything."

Tessa nodded and left. The warm glow of camaraderie lingered in the empty office for a moment before the hum of the fluorescent lights reclaimed the silence.

At her desk, Emily pushed aside the swirl of dread to focus on the sense of purpose that had brought her here.

Martyn Bellamy

One leap of faith had landed her in the crosshairs of a powerful corporation, but she believed - truly believed - that what she was doing might save lives and expose wrongdoing on a massive scale.

She gently rested her hand on the corner of the new case file. *Emily Blackwood vs. GenTech Pharmaceuticals* had officially begun. And that was enough for one day.

Find out what happens with Emily's lawsuit in Volume Two of this exciting trilogy.....

Printed in Great Britain
by Amazon